The Roald Dahl Omnibus

BOOKS BY ROALD DAHL

THE
ROALD
DAHL
OMNIBUS

BARNES
&NOBLE
BOOKS
NEW YORK

This collection contains stories from SWITCH
BITCH, SOMEONE LIKE YOU, and KISS KISS.

This edition published by Barnes & Noble, Inc.,
by arrangement with Alfred A. Knopf, Inc.

1993 Barnes & Noble Books

ISBN 0-88029-123-0

Printed and bound in the United States of America
M 20 19 18 17 16

Acknowledgements

The following stories originally appeared in The New Yorker: THE CHAMPION OF THE WORLD, DIP IN THE POOL, EDWARD THE CONQUEROR, THE LANDLADY, SKIN, TASTE, THE WAY UP TO HEAVEN.

The following stories originally appeared in Playboy: BITCH, GENESIS AND CATASTROPHE (*under the title* A FINE SON), THE GREAT SWITCHEROO, THE LAST ACT.

Contents

From *Someone Like You*

From *Kiss Kiss*

From *Switch Bitch*

The Roald Dahl Omnibus

TASTE

THERE were six of us to dinner that night at Mike Scho-field's house in London: Mike and his wife and daughter, my wife and I, and a man called Richard Pratt.

Richard Pratt was a famous gourmet. He was president of a small society known as the Epicures, and each month he circulated privately to its members a pamphlet on food and wines. He organized dinners where sumptuous dishes and rare wines were served. He refused to smoke for fear of harming his palate, and when discussing a wine, he had a curious, rather droll habit of referring to it as though it were a living being. "A prudent wine," he would say, "rather diffident and evasive, but quite prudent." Or, "a good-humored wine, benevolent and cheerful—slightly obscene, perhaps, but nonetheless good-humored."

I had been to dinner at Mike's twice before when Rich-ard Pratt was there, and on each occasion Mike and his wife had gone out of their way to produce a special meal for the famous gourmet. And this one, clearly, was to be no exception. The moment we entered the dining room, I could see that the table was laid for a feast. The tall candles, the yellow roses, the quantity of shining silver, the three wineglasses to each person, and above all, the faint scent of roasting meat from the kitchen brought the first warm oozings of saliva to my mouth.

As we sat down, I remembered that on both Richard Pratt's previous visits Mike had played a little betting game with him over the claret, challenging him to name its breed and its vintage. Pratt had replied that that should not be too difficult provided it was one of the great years. Mike had then bet him a case of the wine in question that he could not do it. Pratt had accepted, and had won both times. Tonight I felt sure that the little game would be played over again, for Mike was quite willing to lose the bet in order to prove that his wine was good enough to be recognized, and Pratt, for his part, seemed to take a grave, restrained pleasure in displaying his knowledge.

The meal began with a plate of whitebait, fried very crisp in butter, and to go with it there was a Moselle. Mike got up and poured the wine himself, and when he sat down again, I could see that he was watching Richard Pratt. He had set the bottle in front of me so that I could read the label. It said, "Geierslay Ohligsberg, 1945." He leaned over and whispered to me that Geierslay was a tiny village in the Moselle, almost unknown outside Germany. He said that this wine we were drinking was something unusual, that the output of the vineyard was so small that it was almost impossible for a stranger to get any of it. He had visited Geierslay personally the previous summer in order to obtain the few dozen bottles that they had finally allowed him to have.

"I doubt anyone else in the country has any of it at the moment," he said. I saw him glance again at Richard Pratt. "Great thing about Moselle," he continued, raising his voice, "it's the perfect wine to serve before a claret. A lot of people serve a Rhine wine instead, but that's because they don't know any better. A Rhine wine will kill a delicate claret, you know that? It's barbaric to serve a Rhine before a claret. But a Moselle—ah!—a Moselle is exactly right."

Mike Schofield was an amiable, middle-aged man. But he was a stock-broker. To be precise, he was a jobber in the stock market, and like a number of his kind, he seemed to be somewhat embarrassed, almost ashamed to find that he had made so much money with so slight a talent. In his heart he knew that he was not really much more than a bookmaker—an unctuous, infinitely respectable, secretly unscrupulous bookmaker—and he knew that his friends knew it, too. So he was seeking now to become a man of culture, to cultivate a literary and aesthetic taste, to collect paintings, music, books, and all the rest of it. His little sermon about Rhine wine and Moselle was a part of this thing, this culture that he sought.

"A charming little wine, don't you think?" he said. He was still watching Richard Pratt. I could see him give a rapid furtive glance down the table each time he dropped his head to take a mouthful of whitebait. I could almost *feel* him waiting for the moment when Pratt would take his first sip, and look up from his glass with a smile of pleasure, of astonishment, perhaps even of wonder, and then there would be a discussion and Mike would tell him about the village of Geierslay.

But Richard Pratt did not taste his wine. He was completely engrossed in conversation with Mike's eighteen-year-old daughter, Louise. He was half turned toward her, smiling at her, telling her, so far as I could gather, some story about a chef in a Paris restaurant. As he spoke, he leaned closer and closer to her, seeming in his eagerness almost to impinge upon her, and the poor girl leaned as far as she could away from him, nodding politely, rather desperately, and looking not at his face but at the topmost button of his dinner jacket.

We finished our fish, and the maid came around removing the plates. When she came to Pratt, she saw that he had not yet touched his food, so she hesitated, and Pratt noticed her. He waved her away, broke off his conversation, and quickly began to eat, popping the little crisp brown fish quickly into his mouth with rapid jabbing movements of his fork. Then, when he had finished, he reached for his glass, and in two short swallows he tipped the wine down his throat and turned immediately to resume his conversation with Louise Schofield.

Mike saw it all. I was conscious of him sitting there, very still, containing himself, looking at his guest. His round jovial face seemed to loosen slightly and to sag, but he contained himself and was still and said nothing.

Soon the maid came forward with the second course. This was a large roast of beef. She placed it on the table in front of Mike who stood up and carved it, cutting the slices very thin, laying them gently on the plates for the maid to take around. When he had served everyone, including himself, he put down the carving knife and leaned forward with both hands on the edge of the table.

"Now," he said, speaking to all of us but looking at Richard Pratt. "Now for the claret. I must go and fetch the claret, if you'll excuse me."

"You go and fetch it, Mike?" I said. "Where is it?"

"In my study, with the cork out—breathing."

"Why the study?"

"Acquiring room temperature, of course. It's been there twenty-four hours."

"But why the study?"

"It's the best place in the house. Richard helped me choose it last time he was here."

At the sound of his name, Pratt looked around.

"That's right, isn't it?" Mike said.

"Yes," Pratt answered, nodding gravely. "That's right."

"On top of the green filing cabinet in my study," Mike said. "That's the place we chose. A good draft-free spot in a room with an even temperature. Excuse me now, will you, while I fetch it."

The thought of another wine to play with had restored his humor, and he hurried out the door, to return a minute later more slowly, walking softly, holding in both hands a wine basket in which a dark bottle lay. The label was out of sight, facing downward. "Now!" he cried as he came toward the table. "What about this one, Richard? You'll never name this one!"

Richard Pratt turned slowly and looked up at Mike;

then his eyes travelled down to the bottle nestling in its small wicker basket, and he raised his eyebrows, a slight, supercilious arching of the brows, and with it a pushing outward of the wet lower lip, suddenly imperious and ugly.

"You'll never get it," Mike said. "Not in a hundred years."

"A claret?" Richard Pratt asked, condescending.

"Of course."

"I assume, then, that it's from one of the smaller vineyards?"

"Maybe it is, Richard. And then again, maybe it isn't."

"But it's a good year? One of the great years?"

"Yes, I guarantee that."

"Then it shouldn't be too difficult," Richard Pratt said, drawling his words, looking exceedingly bored. Except that, to me, there was something strange about his drawling and his boredom: between the eyes a shadow of something evil, and in his bearing an intentness that gave me a faint sense of uneasiness as I watched him.

"This one is really rather difficult," Mike said, "I won't force you to bet on this one."

"Indeed. And why not?" Again the slow arching of the brows, the cool, intent look.

"Because it's difficult."

"That's not very complimentary to me, you know."

"My dear man," Mike said, "I'll bet you with pleasure, if that's what you wish."

"It shouldn't be too hard to name it."

"You mean you want to bet?"

"I'm perfectly willing to bet," Richard Pratt said.

"All right, then, we'll have the usual. A case of the wine itself."

"You don't think I'll be able to name it, do you?"

"As a matter of fact, and with all due respect, I don't," Mike said. He was making some effort to remain polite, but Pratt was not bothering overmuch to conceal his contempt for the whole proceeding. And yet, curiously, his next question seemed to betray a certain interest.

"You like to increase the bet?"

"No, Richard. A case is plenty."

"Would you like to bet fifty cases?"

"That would be silly."

Mike stood very still behind his chair at the head of the table, carefully holding the bottle in its ridiculous wicker basket. There was a trace of whiteness around his nostrils now, and his mouth was shut very tight.

Pratt was lolling back in his chair, looking up at him, the eyebrows raised, the eyes half closed, a little smile touching the corners of his lips. And again I saw, or thought I saw, something distinctly disturbing about the man's face, that shadow of intentness between the eyes, and in the eyes themselves, right in their centers where it was black, a small slow spark of shrewdness, hiding.

"So you don't want to increase the bet?"

"As far as I'm concerned, old man, I don't give a damn," Mike said. "I'll bet you anything you like."

The three women and I sat quietly, watching the two men. Mike's wife was becoming annoyed; her mouth had gone sour and I felt that at any moment she was going to interrupt. Our roast beef lay before us on our plates, slowly steaming.

"So you'll bet me anything I like?"

"That's what I told you. I'll bet you anything you damn well please, if you want to make an issue out of it."

"Even ten thousand pounds?"

"Certainly I will, if that's the way you want it." Mike was more confident now. He knew quite well that he could call any sum Pratt cared to mention.

"So you say I can name the bet?" Pratt asked again.

" That's what I said."

There was a pause while Pratt looked slowly around the table, first at me, then at the three women, each in turn. He appeared to be reminding us that we were witness to the offer.

"Mike!" Mrs. Schofield said. "Mike, why don't we stop this nonsense and eat our food. It's getting cold."

"But it isn't nonsense," Pratt told her evenly. "We're making a little bet."

I noticed the maid standing in the background holding a dish of vegetables, wondering whether to come forward with them or not.

"All right, then," Pratt said. "I'll tell you what I want you to bet."

"Come on, then," Mike said, rather reckless. "I don't give a damn what it is—you're on."

Pratt nodded, and again the little smile moved the corners of his lips, and then, quite slowly, looking at Mike all the time, he said, "I want you to bet me the hand of your daughter in marriage."

Louise Schofield gave a jump. "Hey!" she cried. "No! That's not funny! Look here, Daddy, that's not funny at all."

"No, dear," her mother said. "They're only joking."

"I'm not joking," Richard Pratt said.

"It's ridiculous," Mike said. He was off balance again now.

"You said you'd bet anything I liked."

"I meant money."

"You didn't *say* money."

"That's what I meant."

"Then it's a pity you didn't say it. But anyway, if you wish to go back on your offer, that's quite all right with me."

"It's not a question of going back on my offer, old man. It's a no-bet anyway, because you can't match the stake. You yourself don't happen to have a daughter to put up against mine in case you lose. And if you had, I wouldn't want to marry her."

"I'm glad of that, dear," his wife said.

"I'll put up anything you like," Pratt announced. "My house, for example. How about my house?"

"Which one?" Mike asked, joking now.

"The country one."

"Why not the other one as well?"

"All right then, if you wish it. Both my houses."

At that point I saw Mike pause. He took a step forward and placed the bottle in its basket gently down on the table. He moved the saltcellar to one side, then the pepper, and then he picked up his knife, studied the blade thoughtfully for a moment, and put it down again. His daughter, too, had seen him pause.

"Now, Daddy!" she cried. "Don't be *absurd!* It's *too* silly for words. I refuse to be betted on like this."

"Quite right, dear," her mother said. "Stop it at once, Mike, and sit down and eat your food."

Mike ignored her. He looked over at his daughter and he smiled, a slow, fatherly, protective smile. But in his eyes, suddenly, there glimmered a little triumph. "You know," he said, smiling as he spoke. "You know, Louise, we ought to think about this a bit."

"Now, stop it, Daddy! I refuse even to listen to you! Why, I've never heard anything so ridiculous in my life!"

"No, seriously, my dear. Just wait a moment and hear what I have to say."

"But I don't *want* to hear it."

"Louise! Please! It's like this. Richard, here, has offered us a serious bet. He is the one who wants to make it, not me. And if he loses, he will have to hand over a considerable amount of property. Now, wait a minute, my dear, don't interrupt. The point is this. *He cannot possibly win.*"

"He seems to think he can."

"Now listen to me, because I know what I'm talking about. The expert, when tasting a claret—so long as it is not one of the famous great wines like Lafite or Latour—can only get a certain way toward naming the vineyard. He can, of course, tell you the Bordeaux district from which the wine comes, whether it is from St. Emilion, Pomerol, Graves, or Médoc. But then each district has several communes, little counties, and each county has many, many small vineyards. It is impossible for a man to differentiate between them all by taste and smell alone. I don't mind telling you that this one I've got here is a wine from a small vineyard that is surrounded by many other small vineyards, and he'll never get it. It's impossible."

"You can't be sure of that," his daughter said.

"I'm telling you I can. Though I say it myself, I understand quite a bit about this wine business, you know. And anyway, heavens alive, girl, I'm your father and you don't think I'd let you in for—for something you didn't want, do you? I'm trying to make you some money."

"Mike!" his wife said sharply. "Stop it now, Mike, please!"

Again he ignored her. "If you will take this bet," he said to his daughter, "in ten minutes you will be the owner of two large houses."

"But I don't want two large houses, Daddy."

"Then sell them. Sell them back to him on the spot. I'll arrange all that for you. And then, just think of it, my dear, you'll be rich! You'll be independent for the rest of your life!"

"Oh, Daddy, I don't like it. I think it's silly."

"So do I," the mother said. She jerked her head briskly up and down as she spoke, like a hen. "You ought to be ashamed of yourself, Michael, ever suggesting such a thing! Your own daughter, too!"

Mike didn't even look at her. "Take it!" he said eagerly, staring hard at the girl. "Take it, quick! I'll guarantee you won't lose."

"But I don't like it, Daddy."

"Come on, girl. Take it!"

Mike was pushing her hard. He was leaning toward her, fixing her with two hard bright eyes, and it was not easy for the daughter to resist him.

"But what if I lose?"

"I keep telling you, you can't lose. I'll guarantee it."

"Oh, Daddy, must I?"

"I'm making you a fortune. So come on now. What do you say, Louise? All right?"

For the last time, she hesitated. Then she gave a helpless little shrug of the shoulders and said, "Oh, all right, then. Just so long as you swear there's no danger of losing."

"Good!" Mike cried. "That's fine! Then it's a bet!"

"Yes," Richard Pratt said, looking at the girl. "It's a bet."

Immediately, Mike picked up the wine, tipped the first thimbleful into his own glass, then skipped excitedly around the table filling up the others. Now everyone was watching Richard Pratt, watching his face as he reached slowly for his glass with his right hand and lifted it to his nose. The man was about fifty years old and he did not have a pleasant face. Somehow, it was all mouth—mouth and lips—the full, wet lips of the professional gourmet, the lower lip hanging downward in the center, a pendulous, permanently open taster's lip, shaped open to receive the rim of a glass or a morsel of food. Like a keyhole, I thought, watching it; his mouth is like a large wet keyhole.

Slowly he lifted the glass to his nose. The point of the nose entered the glass and moved over the surface of the wine, delicately sniffing. He swirled the wine gently around in the glass to receive the bouquet. His concentration was intense. He had closed his eyes, and now the whole top half of his body, the head and neck and chest, seemed to become a kind of huge sensitive smelling-machine, receiving, filtering, analyzing the message from the sniffing nose.

Mike, I noticed, was lounging in his chair, apparently unconcerned, but he was watching every move. Mrs. Schofield, the wife, sat prim and upright at the other end of the table, looking straight ahead, her face tight with disapproval. The daughter, Louise, had shifted her chair away a little, and sidewise, facing the gourmet, and she, like her father, was watching closely.

For at least a minute, the smelling process continued; then, without opening his eyes or moving his head, Pratt lowered the glass to his mouth and tipped in almost half the contents. He paused, his mouth full of wine, getting the first taste; then he permitted some of it to trickle down his throat and I saw his Adam's apple move as it passed by. But most of it he retained in his mouth. And now, without swallowing again, he drew in through his lips a thin breath of air which mingled with the fumes of the wine in the mouth and passed on down into his lungs. He held the breath, blew it out through his nose, and finally began to roll the wine around under the tongue, and chewed it, actually chewed it with his teeth as though it were bread.

It was a solemn, impressive performance, and I must say he did it well.

"Um," he said, putting down the glass, running a pink tongue over his lips. "Um—yes. A very interesting little wine—gentle and gracious, almost feminine in the after-taste."

There was an excess of saliva in his mouth, and as he spoke he spat an occasional bright speck of it onto the table.

"Now we can start to eliminate," he said. "You will pardon me for doing this carefully, but there is much at stake. Normally I would perhaps take a bit of a chance, leaping forward quickly and landing right in the middle of the vineyard of my choice. But this time—I must move cautiously this time, must I not?" He looked up at Mike and he smiled, a thick-lipped, wet-lipped smile. Mike did not smile back.

"First, then, which district in Bordeaux does this wine come from? That is not too difficult to guess. It is far too light in the body to be from either St. Emilion or Graves. It is obviously a Médoc. There's no doubt about *that*.

"Now—from which commune in Médoc does it come? That also, by elimination, should not be too difficult to decide. Margaux? No. It cannot be Margaux. It has not the violent bouquet of a Margaux. Pauillac? It cannot be Pauillac, either. It is too tender, too gentle and wistful for a Pauillac. The wine of Pauillac has a character that is almost imperious in its taste. And also, to me, a Pauillac contains just a little pith, a curious, dusty, pithy flavor that the grape acquires from the soil of the district. No, no. This—this is a very gentle wine, demure and bashful in the first taste, emerging shyly but quite graciously in the second. A little arch, perhaps, in the second taste, and a little naughty also, teasing the tongue with a trace, just a trace, of tannin. Then, in the aftertaste, delightful—consoling and feminine, with a certain blithely generous quality that one associates only with the wines of the commune of St. Julien. Unmistakably this is a St. Julien."

He leaned back in his chair, held his hands up level with his chest, and placed the fingertips carefully together. He was becoming ridiculously pompous, but I thought that some of it was deliberate, simply to mock his host. I found myself waiting rather tensely for him to go on. The girl Louise was lighting a cigarette. Pratt heard the match strike and he turned on her, flaring suddenly with real anger. "Please!" he said. "Please don't do that! It's a disgusting habit, to smoke at table!"

She looked up at him, still holding the burning match in one hand, the big slow eyes settling on his face, resting there a moment, moving away again, slow and contemptuous. She bent her head and blew out the match, but continued to hold the unlighted cigarette in her fingers.

"I'm sorry, my dear," Pratt said, "but I simply cannot have smoking at table."

She didn't look at him again.

"Now, let me see—where were we?" he said. "Ah, yes. This wine is from Bordeaux, from the commune of St. Julien, in the district of Médoc. So far, so good. But now

we come to the more difficult part—the name of the vineyard itself. For in St. Julien there are many vineyards,
and as our host so rightly remarked earlier on, there is
often not much difference between the wine of one and
the wine of another. But we shall see."

He paused again, closing his eyes. "I am trying to
establish the 'growth,'" he said. "If I can do that, it will
be half the battle. Now, let me see. This wine is obviously not from a first-growth vineyard—nor even a
second. It is not a great wine. The quality, the—the—what
do you call it?—the radiance, the power, is lacking. But
a third growth—that it could be. And yet I doubt it. We
know it is a good year—our host has said so—and this is
probably flattering it a little bit. I must be careful. I must
be very careful here."

He picked up his glass and took another small sip.

"Yes," he said, sucking his lips, "I was right. It is a
fourth growth. Now I am sure of it. A fourth growth
from a very good year—from a great year, in fact. And
that's what made it taste for a moment like a third—or
even a second-growth wine. Good! That's better! Now
we are closing in! What are the fourth-growth vineyards
in the commune of St. Julien?"

Again he paused, took up his glass, and held the rim
against that sagging, pendulous lower lip of his. Then I
saw the tongue shoot out, pink and narrow, the tip of it
dipping into the wine, withdrawing swiftly again—a repulsive sight. When he lowered the glass, his eyes remained closed, the face concentrated, only the lips mov-

ing, sliding over each other like two pieces of wet, spongy rubber.

"There it is again!" he cried. "Tannin in the middle taste, and the quick astringent squeeze upon the tongue. Yes, yes, of course! Now I have it! This wine comes from one of those small vineyards around Beychevelle. I remember now. The Beychevelle district, and the river and the little harbor that has silted up so the wine ships can no longer use it. Beychevelle . . . could it actually be a Beychevelle itself? No, I don't think so. Not quite. But it is somewhere very close. Château Talbot? Could it be Talbot? Yes, it could. Wait one moment."

He sipped the wine again, and out of the side of my eye I noticed Mike Schofield and how he was leaning farther and farther forward over the table, his mouth slightly open, his small eyes fixed upon Richard Pratt.

"No. I was wrong. It was not a Talbot. A Talbot comes forward to you just a little quicker than this one; the fruit is nearer to the surface. If it is a '34, which I believe it is, then it couldn't be Talbot. Well, well. Let me think. It is not a Beychevelle and it is not a Talbot, and yet—yet it is so close to both of them, so close, that the vineyard must be almost in between. Now, which could that be?"

He hesitated, and we waited, watching his face. Everyone, even Mike's wife, was watching him now. I heard the maid put down the dish of vegetables on the sideboard behind me, gently, so as not to disturb the silence.

"Ah!" he cried. "I have it! Yes, I think I have it!"

For the last time, he sipped the wine. Then, still holding the glass up near his mouth, he turned to Mike and he smiled, a slow, silky smile, and he said, "You know what this is? This is the little Château Branaire-Ducru."

Mike sat tight, not moving.

"And the year, 1934."

We all looked at Mike, waiting for him to turn the bottle around in its basket and show the label.

"Is that your final answer?" Mike said.

"Yes, I think so."

"Well, is it or isn't it?"

"Yes, it is."

"What was the name again?"

"Château Branaire-Ducru. Pretty little vineyard. Lovely old château. Know it quite well. Can't think why I didn't recognize it at once."

"Come on, Daddy," the girl said. "Turn it round and let's have a peek. I want my two houses."

"Just a minute," Mike said. "Wait just a minute." He was sitting very quiet, bewildered-looking, and his face was becoming puffy and pale, as though all the force was draining slowly out of him.

"Michael!" his wife called sharply from the other end of the table. "What's the matter?"

"Keep out of this, Margaret, will you please."

Richard Pratt was looking at Mike, smiling with his mouth, his eyes small and bright. Mike was not looking at anyone.

"Daddy!" the daughter cried, agonized. "But, Daddy, you don't mean to say he's guessed it right!"

"Now, stop worrying, my dear," Mike said. "There's nothing to worry about."

I think it was more to get away from his family than anything else that Mike then turned to Richard Pratt and said, "I'll tell you what, Richard. I think you and I better slip off into the next room and have a little chat?"

"I don't want a little chat," Pratt said. "All I want is to see the label on that bottle." He knew he was a winner now; he had the bearing, the quiet arrogance of a winner, and I could see that he was prepared to become thoroughly nasty if there was any trouble. "What are you waiting for?" he said to Mike. "Go on and turn it round."

Then this happened: The maid, the tiny, erect figure of the maid in her white-and-black uniform, was standing beside Richard Pratt, holding something out in her hand. "I believe these are yours, sir," she said.

Pratt glanced around, saw the pair of thin horn-rimmed spectacles that she held out to him, and for a moment he hesitated. "Are they? Perhaps they are. I don't know."

"Yes sir, they're yours." The maid was an elderly woman—nearer seventy than sixty—a faithful family retainer of many years standing. She put the spectacles down on the table beside him.

Without thanking her, Pratt took them up and slipped them into his top pocket, behind the white handkerchief.

But the maid didn't go away. She remained standing beside and slightly behind Richard Pratt, and there was something so unusual in her manner and in the way she stood there, small, motionless, and erect, that I for one found myself watching her with a sudden apprehension. Her old gray face had a frosty, determined look, the lips were compressed, the little chin was out, and the hands were clasped together tight before her. The curious cap on her head and the flash of white down the front of her uniform made her seem like some tiny, ruffled, white-breasted bird.

"You left them in Mr. Scofield's study," she said. Her voice was unnaturally, deliberately polite. "On top of the green filing cabinet in his study, sir, when you happened to go in there by yourself before dinner."

It took a few moments for the full meaning of her words to penetrate, and in the silence that followed I became aware of Mike and how he was slowly drawing himself up in his chair, and the color coming to his face, and the eyes opening wide, and the curl of the mouth, and the dangerous little patch of whiteness beginning to spread around the area of the nostrils.

"Now, Michael!" his wife said. "Keep calm now, Michael, dear! Keep calm!"

LAMB TO THE SLAUGHTER

THE ROOM was warm and clean, the curtains drawn, the two table lamps alight—hers and the one by the empty chair opposite. On the sideboard behind her, two tall glasses, soda water, whiskey. Fresh ice cubes in the Thermos bucket.

Mary Maloney was waiting for her husband to come home from work.

Now and again she would glance up at the clock, but without anxiety, merely to please herself with the thought that each minute gone by made it nearer the time when he would come. There was a slow smiling air about her, and about everything she did. The drop of the head as she bent over her sewing was curiously tranquil. Her skin —for this was her sixth month with child—had acquired a wonderful translucent quality, the mouth was soft, and the eyes, with their new placid look, seemed larger, darker than before.

When the clock said ten minutes to five, she began to

listen, and a few moments later, punctually as always, she heard the tires on the gravel outside, and the car door slamming, the footsteps passing the window, the key turning in the lock. She laid aside her sewing, stood up, and went forward to kiss him as he came in.

"Hullo darling," she said.

"Hullo," he answered.

She took his coat and hung it in the closet. Then she walked over and made the drinks, a strongish one for him, a weak one for herself; and soon she was back again in her chair with the sewing, and he in the other, opposite, holding the tall glass with both his hands, rocking it so the ice cubes tinkled against the side.

For her, this was always a blissful time of day. She knew he didn't want to speak much until the first drink was finished, and she, on her side, was content to sit quietly, enjoying his company after the long hours alone in the house. She loved to luxuriate in the presence of this man, and to feel—almost as a sunbather feels the sun—that warm male glow that came out of him to her when they were alone together. She loved him for the way he sat loosely in a chair, for the way he came in a door, or moved slowly across the room with long strides. She loved the intent, far look in his eyes when they rested on her, the funny shape of the mouth, and especially the way he remained silent about his tiredness, sitting still with himself until the whiskey had taken some of it away.

"Tired darling?"

"Yes," he said. "I'm tired." And as he spoke, he did an

unusual thing. He lifted his glass and drained it in one swallow although there was still half of it, at least half of it left. She wasn't really watching him, but she knew what he had done because she heard the ice cubes falling back against the bottom of the empty glass when he lowered his arm. He paused a moment, leaning forward in the chair, then he got up and went slowly over to fetch himself another.

"I'll get it!" she cried, jumping up.

"Sit down," he said.

When he came back, she noticed that the new drink was dark amber with the quantity of whiskey in it.

"Darling, shall I get your slippers?"

"No."

She watched him as he began to sip the dark yellow drink, and she could see little oily swirls in the liquid because it was so strong.

"I think it's a shame," she said, "that when a policeman gets to be as senior as you, they keep him walking about on his feet all day long."

He didn't answer, so she bent her head again and went on with her sewing; but each time he lifted the drink to his lips, she heard the ice cubes clinking against the side of the glass.

"Darling," she said. "Would you like me to get you some cheese? I haven't made any supper because it's Thursday."

"No," he said.

"If you're too tired to eat out," she went on, "it's still

not too late. There's plenty of meat and stuff in the freezer, and you can have it right here and not even move out of the chair."

Her eyes waited on him for an answer, a smile, a little nod, but he made no sign.

"Anyway," she went on, "I'll get you some cheese and crackers first."

"I don't want it," he said.

She moved uneasily in her chair, the large eyes still watching his face. "But you *must* have supper. I can easily do it here. I'd like to do it. We can have lamb chops. Or pork. Anything you want. Everything's in the freezer."

"Forget it," he said.

"But darling, you *must* eat! I'll fix it anyway, and then you can have it or not, as you like."

She stood up and placed her sewing on the table by the lamp.

"Sit down," he said. "Just for a minute, sit down."

It wasn't till then that she began to get frightened.

"Go on," he said. "Sit down."

She lowered herself back slowly into the chair, watching him all the time with those large, bewildered eyes. He had finished the second drink and was staring down into the glass, frowning.

"Listen," he said. "I've got something to tell you."

"What is it, darling? What's the matter?"

He had now become absolutely motionless, and he kept his head down so that the light from the lamp beside him fell across the upper part of his face, leaving the chin and mouth in shadow. She noticed there was a little muscle moving near the corner of his left eye.

"This is going to be a bit of a shock to you, I'm afraid," he said. "But I've thought about it a good deal and I've decided the only thing to do is tell you right away. I hope you won't blame me too much."

And he told her. It didn't take long, four or five minutes at most, and she sat very still through it all, watching him with a kind of dazed horror as he went further and further away from her with each word.

"So there it is," he added. "And I know it's kind of a bad time to be telling you, but there simply wasn't any other way. Of course I'll give you money and see you're looked after. But there needn't really be any fuss. I hope not anyway. It wouldn't be very good for my job."

Her first instinct was not to believe any of it, to reject it all. It occurred to her that perhaps he hadn't even spoken, that she herself had imagined the whole thing. Maybe, if she went about her business and acted as though she hadn't been listening, then later, when she sort of woke up again, she might find none of it had ever happened.

"I'll get the supper," she managed to whisper, and this time he didn't stop her.

When she walked across the room she couldn't feel her feet touching the floor. She couldn't feel anything at all—except a slight nausea and a desire to vomit. Everything was automatic now—down the steps to the cellar, the light switch, the deep freeze, the hand inside the cabinet taking hold of the first object it met. She lifted it out, and looked at it. It was wrapped in paper, so she took off the paper and looked at it again.

A leg of lamb.

All right then, they would have lamb for supper. She carried it upstairs, holding the thin bone-end of it with both her hands, and as she went through the living-room, she saw him standing over by the window with his back to her, and she stopped.

"For God's sake," he said, hearing her, but not turning round. "Don't make supper for me. I'm going out."

At that point, Mary Maloney simply walked up behind him and without any pause she swung the big frozen leg of lamb high in the air and brought it down as hard as she could on the back of his head.

She might just as well have hit him with a steel club.

She stepped back a pace, waiting, and the funny thing was that he remained standing there for at least four or five seconds, gently swaying. Then he crashed to the carpet.

The violence of the crash, the noise, the small table overturning, helped bring her out of the shock. She came out slowly, feeling cold and surprised, and she stood for a while blinking at the body, still holding the ridiculous piece of meat tight with both hands.

All right, she told herself. So I've killed him.

It was extraordinary, now, how clear her mind became all of a sudden. She began thinking very fast. As the wife of a detective, she knew quite well what the penalty would be. That was fine. It made no difference to her.

In fact, it would be a relief. On the other hand, what about the child? What were the laws about murderers with unborn children? Did they kill them both—mother and child? Or did they wait until the tenth month? What did they do?

Mary Maloney didn't know. And she certainly wasn't prepared to take a chance.

She carried the meat into the kitchen, placed it in a pan, turned the oven on high, and shoved it inside. Then she washed her hands and ran upstairs to the bedroom. She sat down before the mirror, tidied her hair, touched up her lips and face. She tried a smile. It came out rather peculiar. She tried again.

"Hullo Sam," she said brightly, aloud.

The voice sounded peculiar too.

"I want some potatoes please, Sam. Yes, and I think a can of peas."

That was better. Both the smile and the voice were coming out better now. She rehearsed it several times more. Then she ran downstairs, took her coat, went out the back door, down the garden, into the street.

It wasn't six o'clock yet and the lights were still on in the grocery shop.

"Hullo Sam," she said brightly, smiling at the man behind the counter.

"Why, good evening, Mrs. Maloney. How're *you*?"

"I want some potatoes please, Sam. Yes, and I think a can of peas."

The man turned and reached up behind him on the shelf for the peas.

"Patrick's decided he's tired and doesn't want to eat out tonight," she told him. "We usually go out Thursdays, you know, and now he's caught me without any vegetables in the house."

"Then how about meat, Mrs. Maloney?"

"No, I've got meat, thanks. I got a nice leg of lamb from the freezer."

"Oh."

"I don't much like cooking it frozen, Sam, but I'm taking a chance on it this time. You think it'll be all right?"

"Personally," the grocer said, "I don't believe it makes any difference. You want these Idaho potatoes?"

"Oh yes, that'll be fine. Two of those."

"Anything else?" The grocer cocked his head on one side, looking at her pleasantly. "How about afterwards? What you going to give him for afterwards?"

"Well—what would you suggest, Sam?"

The man glanced around his shop. "How about a nice big slice of cheesecake? I know he likes that."

"Perfect," she said. "He loves it."

And when it was all wrapped and she had paid, she put on her brightest smile and said, "Thank you, Sam. Goodnight."

"Goodnight, Mrs. Maloney. And thank *you*."

And now, she told herself as she hurried back, all she was doing now, she was returning home to her husband and he was waiting for his supper; and she must cook it good, and make it as tasty as possible because the poor man was tired; and if, when she entered the house, she happened to find anything unusual, or tragic, or terrible, then naturally it would be a shock and she'd become frantic with grief and horror. Mind you, she wasn't *expecting* to find anything. She was just going home with the vegetables. Mrs. Patrick Maloney going home with the vegetables on Thursday evening to cook supper for her husband.

That's the way, she told herself. Do everything right and natural. Keep things absolutely natural and there'll be no need for any acting at all.

Therefore, when she entered the kitchen by the back door, she was humming a little tune to herself and smiling.

"Patrick!" she called. "How are you, darling?"

She put the parcel down on the table and went through into the living room; and when she saw him lying there on the floor with his legs doubled up and one arm twisted back underneath his body, it really was rather a shock. All the old love and longing for him welled up inside her, and she ran over to him, knelt down beside him, and began to cry her heart out. It was easy. No acting was necessary.

A few minutes later she got up and went to the phone. She knew the number of the police station, and when the man at the other end answered, she cried to him, "Quick! Come quick! Patrick's dead!"

"Who's speaking?"

"Mrs. Maloney. Mrs. Patrick Maloney."

"You mean Patrick Maloney's dead?"

"I think so," she sobbed. "He's lying on the floor and I think he's dead."

"Be right over," the man said.

The car came very quickly, and when she opened the front door, two policemen walked in. She knew them both—she knew nearly all the men at that precinct—and she fell right into Jack Noonan's arms, weeping hysterically. He put her gently into a chair, then went over to join the other one, who was called O'Malley, kneeling by the body.

"Is he dead?" she cried.

"I'm afraid he is. What happened?"

Briefly, she told her story about going out to the grocer and coming back to find him on the floor. While she was talking, crying and talking, Noonan discovered a small patch of congealed blood on the dead man's head. He showed it to O'Malley who got up at once and hurried to the phone.

Soon, other men began to come into the house. First a doctor, then two detectives, one of whom she knew by name. Later, a police photographer arrived and took pictures, and a man who knew about fingerprints. There was a great deal of whispering and muttering beside the corpse, and the detectives kept asking her a lot of questions. But they always treated her kindly. She told her story again, this time right from the beginning, when Patrick had come in, and she was sewing, and he was tired, so tired he hadn't wanted to go out for supper. She told how she'd put the meat in the oven—"it's there now, cooking"—and how she'd slipped out to the grocer for vegetables, and come back to find him lying on the floor.

"Which grocer?" one of the detectives asked.

She told him, and he turned and whispered something to the other detective who immediately went outside into the street.

In fifteen minutes he was back with a page of notes, and there was more whispering, and through her sobbing she heard a few of the whispered phrases—". . . acted quite normal . . . very cheerful . . . wanted to give him a good supper . . . peas . . . cheesecake . . . impossible that she . . ."

After a while, the photographer and the doctor departed and two other men came in and took the corpse away on a stretcher. Then the fingerprint man went away. The two detectives remained, and so did the two policemen. They were exceptionally nice to her, and Jack Noonan asked if she wouldn't rather go somewhere else, to her sister's house perhaps, or to his own wife who would take care of her and put her up for the night.

No, she said. She didn't feel she could move even a yard at the moment. Would they mind awfully if she stayed just where she was until she felt better. She didn't feel too good at the moment, she really didn't.

Then hadn't she better lie down on the bed? Jack Noonan asked.

No, she said. She'd like to stay right where she was, in this chair. A little later perhaps, when she felt better, she would move.

So they left her there while they went about their business, searching the house. Occasionally one of the detectives asked her another question. Sometimes Jack Noonan spoke at her gently as he passed by. Her husband, he told her, had been killed by a blow on the back of the head administered with a heavy blunt instrument, almost certainly a large piece of metal. They were looking for the weapon. The murderer may have taken it with him, but on the other hand he may've thrown it away or hidden it somewhere on the premises.

"It's the old story," he said. "Get the weapon, and you've got the man."

Later, one of the detectives came up and sat beside her. Did she know, he asked, of anything in the house that could've been used as the weapon? Would she mind having a look around to see if anything was missing—a very big spanner, for example, or a heavy metal vase.

They didn't have any heavy metal vases, she said.

"Or a big spanner?"

She didn't think they had a big spanner. But there might be some things like that in the garage.

The search went on. She knew that there were other policemen in the garden all around the house. She could hear their footsteps on the gravel outside, and sometimes she saw the flash of a torch through a chink in the curtains. It began to get late, nearly nine she noticed by the clock on the mantle. The four men searching the rooms seemed to be growing weary, a trifle exasperated.

"Jack," she said, the next time Sergeant Noonan went by. "Would you mind giving me a drink?"

"Sure I'll give you a drink. You mean this whiskey?"

"Yes please. But just a small one. It might make me feel better."

He handed her the glass.

"Why don't you have one yourself," she said. "You must be awfully tired. Please do. You've been very good to me."

"Well," he answered. "It's not strictly allowed, but I might take just a drop to keep me going."

One by one the others came in and were persuaded to take a little nip of whiskey. They stood around rather awkwardly with the drinks in their hands, uncomfortable in her presence, trying to say consoling things to her. Sergeant Noonan wandered into the kitchen, came out quickly and said, "Look, Mrs. Maloney. You know that oven of yours is still on, and the meat still inside."

"Oh *dear* me!" she cried. "So it is!"

"I better turn it off for you, hadn't I?"

"Will you do that, Jack. Thank you so much."

When the sergeant returned the second time, she looked at him with her large, dark, tearful eyes. "Jack Noonan," she said.

"Yes?"

"Would you do me a small favour—you and these others?"

"We can try, Mrs. Maloney."

"Well," she said. "Here you all are, and good friends of dear Patrick's too, and helping to catch the man who killed him. You must be terrible hungry by now because it's long past your suppertime, and I know Patrick would never forgive me, God bless his soul, if I allowed you to remain in his house without offering you decent hospitality. Why don't you eat up that lamb that's in the oven. It'll be cooked just right by now."

"Wouldn't dream of it," Sergeant Noonan said.

"Please," she begged. "Please eat it. Personally I couldn't touch a thing, certainly not what's been in the house when he was here. But it's all right for you. It'd be a favour to me if you'd eat it up. Then you can go on with your work again afterwards."

There was a good deal of hesitating among the four policemen, but they were clearly hungry, and in the end they were persuaded to go into the kitchen and help themselves. The woman stayed where she was, listening to them through the open door, and she could hear them speaking among themselves, their voices thick and sloppy because their mouths were full of meat.

"Have some more, Charlie?"

"No. Better not finish it."

"She *wants* us to finish it. She said so. Be doing her a favour."

"Okay then. Give me some more."

"That's the hell of a big club the guy must've used to hit poor Patrick," one of them was saying. "The doc says his skull was smashed all to pieces just like from a sledgehammer."

"That's why it ought to be easy to find."

"Exactly what I say."

"Whoever done it, they're not going to be carrying a thing like that around with them longer than they need."

One of them belched.

"Personally, I think it's right here on the premises."

"Probably right under our very noses. What you think, Jack?"

And in the other room, Mary Maloney began to giggle.

MAN FROM THE SOUTH

It was getting on toward six o'clock so I thought I'd buy myself a beer and go out and sit in a deck chair by the swimming pool and have a little evening sun.

I went to the bar and got the beer and carried it outside and wandered down the garden toward the pool.

It was a fine garden with lawns and beds of azaleas and tall coconut palms, and the wind was blowing strongly through the tops of the palm trees making the leaves hiss and crackle as though they were on fire. I could see the clusters of big brown nuts hanging down underneath the leaves.

There were plenty of deck chairs around the swimming pool and there were white tables and huge brightly colored umbrellas and sunburned men and women sitting around in bathing suits. In the pool itself there were three or four girls and about a dozen boys, all splashing about and making a lot of noise and throwing a large rubber ball at one another.

I stood watching them. The girls were English girls from the hotel. The boys I didn't know about, but they sounded American and I thought they were probably naval cadets who'd come ashore from the U.S. naval training vessel which had arrived in harbor that morning.

I went over and sat down under a yellow umbrella where there were four empty seats, and I poured my beer and settled back comfortably with a cigarette.

It was very pleasant sitting there in the sunshine with beer and cigarette. It was pleasant to sit and watch the bathers splashing about in the green water.

The American sailors were getting on nicely with the English girls. They'd reached the stage where they were diving under the water and tipping them up by their legs.

Just then I noticed a small, oldish man walking briskly around the edge of the pool. He was immaculately dressed in a white suit and he walked very quickly with little bouncing strides, pushing himself high up onto his toes with each step. He had on a large creamy Panama hat, and he came bouncing along the side of the pool, looking at the people and the chairs.

He stopped beside me and smiled, showing two rows of very small, uneven teeth, slightly tarnished. I smiled back.

"Excuse pleess, but may I sit here?"

"Certainly," I said. "Go ahead."

He bobbed around to the back of the chair and inspected it for safety, then he sat down and crossed his

legs. His white buckskin shoes had little holes punched
all over them for ventilation.

"A fine evening," he said. "They are all evenings fine
here in Jamaica." I couldn't tell if the accent were Italian
or Spanish, but I felt fairly sure he was some sort of a
South American. And old too, when you saw him close.
Probably around sixty-eight or seventy.

"Yes," I said. "It is wonderful here, isn't it."

"And who, might I ask, are all dese? Dese is no hotel
people." He was pointing at the bathers in the pool.

"I think they're American sailors," I told him. "They're
Americans who are learning to be sailors."

"Of course dey are Americans. Who else in de world
is going to make as much noise at dat? You are not American, no?"

"No," I said. "I am not."

Suddenly one of the American cadets was standing in
front of us. He was dripping wet from the pool and one
of the English girls was standing there with him.

"Are these chairs taken?" he said.

"No," I answered.

"Mind if I sit down?"

"Go ahead."

"Thanks," he said. He had a towel in his hand and
when he sat down he unrolled it and produced a pack of
cigarettes and a lighter. He offered the cigarettes to the
girl and she refused; then he offered them to me and I
took one. The little man said, "Tank you, no, but I tink
I have a cigar." He pulled out a crocodile case and got
himself a cigar, then he produced a knife which had a

small scissors in it and he snipped the end off the cigar.

"Here, let me give you a light." The American boy held up his lighter.

"Dat will not work in dis wind."

"Sure, it'll work. It always works."

The little man removed his unlighted cigar from his mouth, cocked his head on one side and looked at the boy.

"*All*-ways?" he said slowly.

"Sure, it never fails. Not with me anyway."

The little man's head was still cocked over on one side and he was still watching the boy. "Well, well. So you say dis famous lighter it never fails. Iss dat you say?"

"Sure," the boy said. "That's right." He was about nineteen or twenty with a long freckled face and a rather sharp birdlike nose. His chest was not very sunburned and there were freckles there too, and a few wisps of pale-reddish hair. He was holding the lighter in his right hand, ready to flip the wheel. "It never fails," he said, smiling now because he was purposely exaggerating his little boast. "I promise you it never fails."

"One momint, pleess." The hand that held the cigar came up high, palm outward, as though it were stopping traffic. "Now juss one momint." He had a curiously soft, toneless voice and he kept looking at the boy all the time.

"Shall we not perhaps make a little bet on dat?" He smiled at the boy. "Shall we not make a little bet on whether your lighter lights?"

"Sure, I'll bet," the boy said. "Why not?"

"You like to bet?"

"Sure, I'll always bet."

The man paused and examined his cigar, and I must say I didn't much like the way he was behaving. It seemed he was already trying to make something out of this, and to embarrass the boy, and at the same time I had the feeling he was relishing a private little secret all his own.

He looked up again at the boy and said slowly, "I like to bet, too. Why we don't have a good bet on dis ting? A good big bet."

"Now wait a minute," the boy said. "I can't do that. But I'll bet you a quarter. I'll even bet you a dollar, or whatever it is over here—some shillings, I guess."

The little man waved his hand again. "Listen to me. Now we have some fun. We make a bet. Den we go up to my room here in de hotel where iss no wind and I bet you you cannot light dis famous lighter of yours ten times running without missing once."

"I'll bet I can," the boy said.

"All right. Good. We make a bet, yes?"

"Sure. I'll bet you a buck."

"No, no. I make you very good bet. I am rich man and I am sporting man also. Listen to me. Outside de hotel iss my car. Iss very fine car. American car from your country. Cadillac—"

"Hey, now. Wait a minute." The boy leaned back in his deck chair and he laughed. "I can't put up that sort of property. This is crazy."

"Not crazy at all. You strike lighter successfully ten times running and Cadillac is yours. You like to have dis Cadillac, yes?"

"Sure, I'd like to have a Cadillac." The boy was still grinning.

"All right. Fine. We make a bet and I put up my Cadillac."

"And what do I put up?"

The little man carefully removed the red band from his still unlighted cigar. "I never ask you, my friend, to bet something you cannot afford. You understand?"

"Then what do I bet?"

"I make it very easy for you, yes?"

"Okay. You make it easy."

"Some small ting you can afford to give away, and if you did happen to lose it you would not feel too bad. Right?"

"Such as what?"

"Such as, perhaps, de little finger of your left hand."

"My *what!*" The boy stopped grinning.

"Yes. Why not? You win, you take de car. You looss, I take de finger."

"I don't get it. How d'you mean, you take the finger?"

"I chop it off."

"Jumping jeepers! That's a crazy bet. I think I'll just make it a dollar."

The little man leaned back, spread out his hands palms upward and gave a tiny contemptuous shrug of the shoulders. "Well, well, well," he said. "I do not understand. You say it lights but you will not bet. Den we forget it, yes?"

The boy sat quite still, staring at the bathers in the pool. Then he remembered suddenly he hadn't lighted his cigarette. He put it between his lips, cupped his hands around the lighter and flipped the wheel. The wick lighted and burned with a small, steady, yellow flame and the way he held his hands the wind didn't get to it at all.

"Could I have a light, too?" I said.

"Gee, I'm sorry. I forgot you didn't have one."

I held out my hand for the lighter, but he stood up and came over to do it for me.

"Thank you," I said, and he returned to his seat.

"You having a good time?" I asked.

"Fine," he answered. "It's pretty nice here."

There was a silence then, and I could see that the little man had succeeded in disturbing the boy with his absurd proposal. He was sitting there very still, and it was obvious that a small tension was beginning to build up inside him. Then he started shifting about in his seat, and rubbing his chest, and stroking the back of his neck, and finally he placed both hands on his knees and began tap-tapping with his fingers against the knee-caps. Soon he was tapping with one of his feet as well.

"Now just let me check up on this bet of yours," he said at last. "You say we go up to your room and if I make this lighter light ten times running I win a Cadillac. If it misses just once then I forfeit the little finger of my left hand. Is that right?"

"Certainly. Dat is de bet. But I tink you are afraid."

"What do we do if I lose? Do I have to hold my finger out while you chop it off?"

"Oh, no! Dat would be no good. And you might be

tempted to refuse to hold it out. What I should do I should tie one of your hands to de table before we started and I should stand dere with a knife ready to go *chop* de momint your lighter missed."

"What year is the Cadillac?" the boy asked.

"Excuse. I not understand."

"What year—how old is the Cadillac?"

"Ah! How old? Yes. It is last year. Quite new car. But I see you are not betting man. Americans never are."

The boy paused for just a moment and he glanced first at the English girl, then at me. "Yes," he said sharply. "I'll bet you."

"Good!" The little man clapped his hands together quietly, once. "Fine," he said. "We do it now. And you, sir," he turned to me, "you would perhaps be good enough to, what you call it, to—to referee." He had pale, almost colorless eyes with tiny bright black pupils.

"Well," I said. "I think it's a crazy bet. I don't think I like it very much."

"Nor do I," said the English girl. It was the first time she'd spoken. "I think it's a stupid, ridiculous bet."

"Are you serious about cutting off this boy's finger if he loses?" I said.

"Certainly I am. Also about giving him Cadillac if he win. Come now. We go to my room."

He stood up. "You like to put on some clothes first?" he said.

"No," the boy answered. "I'll come like this." Then he turned to me. "I'd consider it a favor if you'd come along and referee."

"All right," I said. "I'll come along, but I don't like the bet."

"You come too," he said to the girl. "You come and watch."

The little man led the way back through the garden to the hotel. He was animated now, and excited, and that seemed to make him bounce up higher than ever on his toes as he walked along.

"I live in annex," he said. "You like to see car first? Iss just here."

He took us to where we could see the front driveway of the hotel and he stopped and pointed to a sleek pale-green Cadillac parked close by.

"Dere she iss. De green one. You like?"

"Say, that's a nice car," the boy said.

"All right. Now we go up and see if you can win her."

We followed him into the annex and up one flight of stairs. He unlocked his door and we all trooped into what was a large pleasant double bedroom. There was a woman's dressing gown lying across the bottom of one of the beds.

"First," he said, "we 'ave a little Martini."

The drinks were on a small table in the far corner, all ready to be mixed, and there was a shaker and ice and plenty of glasses. He began to make the Martini, but meanwhile he'd rung the bell and now there was a knock on the door and a coloured maid came in.

"Ah!" he said, putting down the bottle of gin, taking a wallet from his pocket and pulling out a pound note.

"You will do something for me now, pleess." He gave the maid the pound.

"You keep dat," he said. "And now we are going to play a little game in here and I want you to go off and find for me two—no tree tings. I want some nails; I want a hammer, and I want a chopping knife, a butcher's chopping knife which you can borrow from de kitchen. You can get, yes?"

"A *chopping knife!*" The maid opened her eyes wide and clasped her hands in front of her. "You mean a *real* chopping knife?"

"Yes, yes, of course. Come on now, pleess. You can find dose tings surely for me."

"Yes, sir, I'll try, sir. Surely I'll try to get them." And she went.

The little man handed round the Martinis. We stood there and sipped them, the boy with the long freckled face and the pointed nose, bare-bodied except for a pair of faded brown bathing shorts; the English girl, a large-boned, fair-haired girl wearing a pale blue bathing suit, who watched the boy over the top of her glass all the time; the little man with the colourless eyes standing there in his immaculate white suit drinking his Martini and looking at the girl in her pale blue bathing dress. I didn't know what to make of it all. The man seemed serious about the bet and he seemed serious about the business of cutting off the finger. But hell, what if the boy lost? Then we'd have to rush him to the hospital in the Cadillac that he hadn't won. That would be a fine thing. Now wouldn't that be a really fine thing? It would be a damn silly unnecessary thing so far as I could see.

"Don't you think this is rather a silly bet?" I said.

"I think it's a fine bet," the boy answered. He had already downed one large Martini.

"I think it's a stupid, ridiculous bet," the girl said. "What'll happen if you lose?"

"It won't matter. Come to think of it, I can't remember ever in my life having had any use for the little finger on my left hand. Here he is." The boy took hold of the finger. "Here he is and he hasn't ever done a thing for me yet. So why shouldn't I bet him. I think it's a fine bet."

The little man smiled and picked up the shaker and refilled our glasses.

"Before we begin," he said, "I will present to de—to de referee de key of de car." He produced a car key from his pocket and gave it to me. "De papers," he said, "de owning papers and insurance are in de pocket of de car."

Then the colored maid came in again. In one hand she carried a small chopper, the kind used by butchers for chopping meat bones, and in the other a hammer and a bag of nails.

"Good! You get dem all. Tank you, tank you. Now you can go." He waited until the maid had closed the door, then he put the implements on one of the beds and said, "Now we prepare ourselves, yes?" And to the boy "Help me, pleess, with dis table. We carry it out a little."

It was the usual kind of hotel writing desk, just a plain rectangular table about four feet by three with a blotting pad, ink, pens and paper. They carried it out into the room away from the wall, and removed the writing things.

"And now," he said, "a chair." He picked up a chair and placed it beside the table. He was very brisk and very animated, like a person organizing games at a children's party. "And now de nails. I must put in de nails." He fetched the nails and he began to hammer them into the top of the table.

We stood there, the boy, the girl, and I, holding Martinis in our hands, watching the little man at work. We watched him hammer two nails into the table, about six inches apart. He didn't hammer them right home; he allowed a small part of each one to stick up. Then he tested them for firmness with his fingers.

Anyone would think the son of a bitch had done this before, I told myself. He never hesitates. Table, nails, hammer, kitchen chopper. He knows exactly what he needs and how to arrange it.

"And now," he said, "all we want is some string." He found some string. "All right, at last we are ready. Will you pleess to sit here at de table," he said to the boy.

The boy put his glass away and sat down.

"Now place de left hand between dese two nails. De nails are only so I can tie your hand in place. All right, good. Now I tie your hand secure to de table—so."

He wound the string around the boy's wrist, then several times around the wide part of the hand, then he fastened it tight to the nails. He made a good job of it and when he'd finished there wasn't any question about the boy being able to draw his hand away. But he could move his fingers.

"Now pleess, clench de fist, all except for de little finger. You must leave de little finger sticking out, lying on de table."

"*Ex*-cellent! *Ex*-cellent! Now we are ready. Wid your right hand you manipulate de lighter. But one momint, pleess."

He skipped over to the bed and picked up the chopper. He came back and stood beside the table with the chopper in his hand.

"We are all ready?" he said. "Mister referee, you must say to begin."

The English girl was standing there in her pale blue bathing costume right behind the boy's chair. She was just standing there, not saying anything. The boy was sitting quite still, holding the lighter in his right hand, looking at the chopper. The little man was looking at me.

"Are you ready?" I asked the boy.

"I'm ready."

"And you?" to the little man.

"Quite ready," he said and he lifted the chopper up in the air and held it there about two feet above the boy's finger, ready to chop. The boy watched it, but he didn't flinch and his mouth didn't move at all. He merely raised his eyebrows and frowned.

"All right," I said. "Go ahead."

The boy said, "Will you please count aloud the number of times I light it."

"Yes," I said. "I'll do that."

With his thumb he raised the top of the lighter, and again with the thumb he gave the wheel a sharp flick. The flint sparked and the wick caught fire and burned with a small yellow flame.

"One!" I called.

He didn't blow the flame out; he closed the top of the lighter on it and he waited for perhaps five seconds before opening it again.

He flicked the wheel very strongly and once more there was a small flame burning on the wick.

"Two!"

No one else said anything. The boy kept his eyes on the lighter. The little man held the chopper up in the air and he too was watching the lighter.

"Three!"

"Four!"

"Five!"

"Six!"

"Seven!" Obviously it was one of those lighters that worked. The flint gave a big spark and the wick was the right length. I watched the thumb snapping the top down onto the flame. Then a pause. Then the thumb raising the top once more. This was an all-thumb operation. The thumb did everything. I took a breath, ready to say eight. The thumb flicked the wheel. The flint sparked. The little flame appeared.

"Eight!" I said, and as I said it the door opened. We all turned and we saw a woman standing in the doorway, a small, black-haired woman, rather old, who stood there for about two seconds then rushed forward shouting, "Carlos! Carlos!" She grabbed his wrist, took the chopper from him, threw it on the bed, took hold of the little man by the lapels of his white suit and began shaking him very vigorously, talking to him fast and loud and fiercely all the time in some Spanish-sounding language. She shook him so fast you couldn't see him any more. He became a faint, misty, quickly moving outline, like the spokes of a turning wheel.

Then she slowed down and the little man came into view again and she hauled him across the room and pushed him backward onto one of the beds. He sat on the edge of it blinking his eyes and testing his head to see if it would still turn on his neck.

"I am so sorry," the woman said. "I am so terribly sorry that this should happen." She spoke almost perfect English.

"It is too bad," she went on. "I suppose it is really my fault. For ten minutes I leave him alone to go and have my hair washed and I come back and he is at it again." She looked sorry and deeply concerned.

The boy was untying his hand from the table. The English girl and I stood there and said nothing.

"He is a menace," the woman said. "Down where we live at home he has taken altogether forty-seven fingers from different people, and he has lost eleven cars. In the end they threatened to have him put away somewhere. That's why I brought him up here."

"We were only having a little bet," mumbled the little man from the bed.

"I suppose he bet you a car," the woman said.

"Yes," the boy answered. "A Cadillac."

"He has no car. It's mine. And that makes it worse," she said, "that he should bet you when he has nothing to bet with. I am ashamed and very sorry about it all." She seemed an awfully nice woman.

"Well," I said, "then here's the key of your car." I put it on the table.

"We were only having a little bet," mumbled the little man.

"He hasn't anything left to bet with," the woman said. "He hasn't a thing in the world. Not a thing. As a matter of fact I myself won it all from him a long while ago. It took time, a lot of time, and it was hard work, but I won it all in the end." She looked up at the boy and she smiled, a slow sad smile, and she came over and put out a hand to take the key from the table.

I can see it now, that hand of hers; it had only one finger on it, and a thumb.

54

THE SOLDIER

It was one of those nights that made him feel he knew what it was like to be a blind man: not the shadow of an image for his eyes to discern, not even the forms of the trees visible against the sky.

Out of the darkness he became aware of small rustling noises in the hedge, the breathing of a horse some distance away in the field, the soft thud of a hoof as it moved its foot; and once he heard the rush of a bird flying past him low overhead.

"Jock," he said, speaking loud. "We'll go home now." And he turned and began to walk back up the slope of the lane, the dog pulling ahead, showing the way in the dark.

It must be nearly midnight, he thought. That meant that soon it would be tomorrow. Tomorrow was worse than today. Tomorrow was the worst of all because it was going to become today—and today was now.

Today had not been very nice, especially that business with the splinter.

Stop it, he told himself. There isn't any sense thinking about it. It doesn't do anyone any good thinking about things like that. Think about something else for a change. You can kick out a dangerous thought, you know, if you put another in its place. Go right back as far as you can go. Let's have some memories of sweet days. The sea-side holidays in the summer, wet sand and red buckets and shrimping nets and the slippery seaweedy rocks and the small clear pools with sea anemones and snails and mussels and sometimes one grey translucent shrimp hovering deep down in the beautiful green water.

But how *could* that splinter have gotten into the sole of his foot without him feeling it.

It is not important. Do you remember hunting for cowries along the margin of the tide, each one so fine and perfect it became a precious jewel to be held in the hand all the way home; and the little orange coloured scallops, the pearly oyster shells, the tiny bits of emerald glass, a live hermit crab, a cockle, the spine of a skate, and once, but never to be forgotten, the dry seawashed jawbone of a human being with teeth in it, white and wonderful among the shells and pebbles. Oh mummy, look what I've found! Look, Mummy, look!

But to go back to the splinter. She had really been rather unpleasant about that.

"What do you mean, you didn't notice?" she had asked, scornful.

"I just didn't notice, that's all."

"I suppose you're going to tell me if I stick a pin into your foot you won't feel it?"

"I didn't say that."

And then she had jabbed him suddenly in the ankle with the pin she had been using to take out the splinter, and he hadn't been watching so he didn't know about it till she had cried out in a kind of horror. And when he had looked down, the pin was sticking into the flesh all by itself behind the ankle-bone, almost half of it buried.

"Take it out," he had said. "You can poison someone like that."

"You mean you can't *feel* it?"

"Take it out, will you?"

"You mean it doesn't *hurt*?"

"The pain is terrible. Take it out."

"What's the *matter* with you?"

"I said the pain is terrible. Didn't you hear me?"

Why did they *do* things like that to him?

When I was down beside the sea, a wooden spade they gave to me, to dig the sandy shore. My holes were empty as a cup, and every time the sea came up, till it could come no more.

A year ago the doctor had said, "Shut your eyes. Now tell me whether I'm pushing this toe up or down."

"Up," he had said.

"And now?"

"Down. No, up. I think it's up."

It was peculiar that a neuro-surgeon should want to play with his toes.

"Did I get them all right, doctor?"

"You did very well."

But that was a year ago. He had felt pretty good a year

ago. The sort of things that happened now never used to happen then. Take, for example, just one item—the bathroom tap.

Why was the hot tap in the bathroom on a different side this morning? That was a new one.

It is not of the least importance, you understand, but it would be interesting to know why.

Do you think she could have changed it over, taken a spanner and a pipe-wrench and sneaked in during the night and changed it over?

Do you? Well—if you really want to know—yes. The way she'd been acting lately, she'd be quite capable of doing that.

A strange and difficult woman, that's what she was. Mind you, she used not to be, but there's no doubt at all that right now she was as strange and difficult as they come. Especially at night.

Yes, at night. That was the worst time of all—the night.

Why, when he put out his right hand in bed at night, could his fingers not feel what they were touching? He had knocked over the lamp and she had woken up and then sat up suddenly while he was feeling for it on the floor in the dark.

"What are you doing now?"

"I knocked over the lamp. I'm sorry."

"Oh Christ," she had said. "Yesterday it was the glass of water. What's the *matter* with you?"

Once, the doctor had stroked the back of this hand with a feather, and he hadn't been able to feel that either. But he had felt it when the man scratched him with a pin.

"Shut your eyes. No—you mustn't look. Shut them tight. Now tell me if this is hot or cold."

"Hot."

"And this?"

"Cold."

"And this?"

"Cold. I mean hot. Yes, it's hot, isn't it?"

"That's right," the doctor had said. "You did very well."

But that was a year ago.

Why were the switches on the walls, just lately, always a few inches away from the well-remembered places when he felt for them in the dark?

Don't think about it, he told himself. The only thing is not to think about it.

And while we're on the subject, why did the walls of the living-room take on a slightly different shade of colour each day?

Green and blue-green and blue; and sometimes—sometimes slowly swimming like colours seen through the heat-haze of a brazier.

One by one, neatly, like index cards out of a machine, the little questions dropped.

Whose face appeared for one second at the window during dinner? Whose eyes?

"What are you staring at?"

"Nothing," he had answered. "But it would be nice if we could draw the curtains, don't you think?"

"Robert, what were you staring at?"

"Nothing."

"Why were you staring at the window like that?"

"It would be nice if we could draw the curtains, don't you think?" he had answered.

He was going past the place where he had heard the horse in the field and now he could hear it again: the breathing, the soft hoof thuds, and the crunch of grass-cropping that was like the noise of a man munching celery.

"Hello old horse," he said, calling loud into the darkness. "Hello old horse over there."

Suddenly he heard the footsteps behind him, slow, long-striding footsteps close behind, and he stopped. The footsteps stopped. He turned around, searching the darkness.

"Good evening," he said. "You here again?"

In the quiet that followed he could hear the wind moving the leaves in the hedge.

"Are you going my way?" he said.

Then he turned and walked on, the dog still pulling ahead, and the footsteps started after him again, but more softly now, as though the person were walking on toes.

He stopped and turned again.

"I can't see you," he said, "because it's so dark. Are you someone I know?"

Again the silence, and the cool summer wind on his cheeks, and the dog tugging on the leash to get home.

"All right," he called. "You don't have to answer if you don't want to. But remember I know you're there."

Someone trying to be clever.

Far away in the night, over to the west and very high,

he heard the faint hum of an airplane. He stopped again, head up, listening.

"Miles away," he said. "Won't come near here."

But why, when one of them flew over the house, did everything inside him come to a stop, and his talking and what he was doing, while he sat or stood in a sort of paralysis waiting for the whistle-shriek of the bomb. That one after dinner this evening.

"Why did you duck like that?" she had asked.

"Duck?"

"Why did you duck? What are you ducking for?"

"Duck?" he had said again. "I don't know what you mean."

"I'll say you don't," she had answered, staring at him hard with those hard, blue-white eyes, the lids dropping slightly, as always when there was contempt. The drop of her eyelids was something beautiful to him, the half-closed eyes and the way the lids dropped and the eyes became hooded when her contempt was extreme.

Yesterday, lying in bed in the early morning, when the noise of gunfire was just beginning far away down the valley, he had reached out with his left hand and touched her body for a little comfort.

"What on earth are you doing?"

"Nothing, dear."

"You woke me up."

"I'm sorry."

It would be a help if she would only let him lie closer to her in the early mornings when he began to hear the noise of gunfire.

He would soon be home now. Around the last bend of the lane he could see a light glowing pink through the curtain of the living-room window, and he hurried forward to the gate and through it and up the path to the front door, the dog still pulling ahead.

He stood on the porch, feeling around for the door-knob in the dark.

It was on the right when he went out. He distinctly remembered it being on the right-hand side when he shut the door half an hour ago and went out.

It couldn't be that she had changed *that* over too? Just to fox him? Taken a bag of tools and quickly changed it over to the other side while he was out walking the dog?

He moved his hand over to the left—and the moment the fingers touched the knob, something small but violent exploded inside his head and with it a surge of fury and outrage and fear. He opened the door, shut it quickly behind him and shouted, "Edna, are you there?"

There was no answer so he shouted again, and this time she heard him.

"What do you want now? You woke me up."

"Come down here a moment, will you. I want to talk to you."

"Oh for heaven's sake," she answered. "Be quiet and come on up."

"Come here!" he shouted. "Come here at once!"

"I'll be damned if I will. You come here."

The man paused, head back, looking up the stairs into the dark of the second floor. He could see where the stair-rail curved to the left and went on up out of sight in the black toward the landing and if you went straight on across the landing you came to the bedroom, and it would be black in there too.

"Edna!" he shouted. "Edna!"

"Oh go to hell."

He began to move slowly up the stairs, treading quietly, touching the stair-rail for guidance, up and around the left-hand curve into the dark above. At the top he took an extra step that wasn't there; but he was ready for it and there was no noise. He paused a while then, listening, and he wasn't sure, but he thought he could hear the guns starting up again far away down the valley, heavy stuff mostly, seventy-fives and maybe a couple of mortars somewhere in the background.

Across the landing now and through the open doorway —which was easy in the dark because he knew it so well —through onto the bedroom carpet that was thick and soft and pale grey although he could not feel or see it.

In the centre of the room he waited, listening for sounds. She had gone back to sleep and was breathing rather loud, making the slightest little whistle with the air between her teeth each time she exhaled. The curtain flapped gently against the open window, the alarm-clock tick-tick-ticked beside the bed.

Now that his eyes were becoming accustomed to the dark he could just make out the end of the bed, the white blanket tucked in under the mattress, the bulge of her feet under the bedclothes; and then, as though aware of the presence of the man in the room, the woman stirred. He heard her turn, and turn again. The sound of her breathing stopped. There was a succession of little move-ment-noises and once the bedsprings creaked, loud as a shout in the dark.

"Is that you, Robert?"

He made no move, no sound.

"Robert, are you there?"

The voice was strange and rather unpleasant to him.

"Robert!" She was wide awake now. "Where are you?"

Where had he heard that voice before? It had a quality of stridence, dissonance, like two single high notes struck together hard in discord. Also there was an inability to pronounce the R of Robert. Who was it that used to say Wobert to him?

"Wobert," she said again. "What are you doing?"

Was it that nurse in the hospital, the tall one with fair hair? No, it was further back. Such an awful voice as that he ought to be able to remember. Give him a little time and he would get the name.

At that moment he heard the snap of the switch of the bedside lamp and in the flood of light he saw the woman half-sitting up in bed, dressed in some sort of a pink nightdress. There was a surprised, wide-eyed expression on her face. Her cheeks and chin were oily with cold cream.

"You better put that thing down," she was saying, "before you cut yourself."

"Where's Edna?" He was staring at her hard.

The woman, half-sitting up in bed, watched him care-fully. He was standing at the foot of the bed, a huge, broad man, standing motionless, erect, with heels together, almost at attention, dressed in his dark-brown, woolly, heavy suit.

"Go on," she ordered. "Put it down."

"Where's Edna?"

"What's the matter with you, Wobert?"

"There's nothing the matter with me. I'm just asking you where's my wife."

The woman was easing herself up gradually into an erect sitting position and sliding her legs toward the edge of the bed. "Well," she said at length, the voice changing, the hard blue-white eyes secret and cunning, "if you really want to know, Edna's gone. She left just now while you were out."

"Where did she go?"

"She didn't say."

"And who are you?"

"I'm just a friend of hers."

"You don't have to shout at me," he said. "What's all the excitement?"

"I simply want you to know I'm not Edna."

The man considered this a moment, then he said, "How did you know my name?"

"Edna told me."

Again he paused, studying her closely, still slightly puzzled, but much calmer now, his eyes calm, perhaps even a little amused the way they looked at her.

"I think I prefer Edna."

In the silence that followed they neither of them moved. The woman was very tense, sitting up straight with her arms tense on either side of her and slightly bent at the elbows, the hands pressing palms downward on the mattress.

"I love Edna, you know. Did she ever tell you I love her?"

The woman didn't answer.

"I think she's a bitch. But it's a funny thing I love her just the same."

The woman was not looking at the man's face; she was watching his right hand.

"Awful cruel little bitch, Edna."

And a long silence now, the man standing erect, motionless, the woman sitting motionless in the bed, and it was so quiet suddenly that through the open window they could hear the water in the millstream going over the dam far down the valley on the next farm.

Then the man again, speaking calmly, slowly, quite impersonally:

"As a matter of fact, I don't think she even likes me any more."

The woman shifted closer to the edge of the bed. "Put that knife down," she said, "before you cut yourself."

"Don't shout, please. Can't you talk nicely." Now, suddenly, the man leaned forward, staring intently into the woman's face, and he raised his eyebrows. "That's strange," he said. "That's very strange."

He took a step forward, his knees touching the bed.

"You look a bit like Edna yourself."

"Edna's gone out. I told you that."

He continued to stare at her and the woman kept quite

still, the palms of her hands pressing deep into the mattress.

"Well," he said. "I wonder."

"I told you Edna's gone out. I'm a friend of hers. My name is Mary."

"My wife," the man said, "has a funny little brown mole just behind her left ear. You don't have that, do you?"

"I certainly don't."

"Turn your head and let me look."

"I told you I didn't have it."

"Just the same, I'd like to make sure."

The man came slowly around the end of the bed. "Stay where you are," he said. "Please don't move." And he came toward her slowly, watching her all the time, a little smile touching the corners of his mouth.

The woman waited until he was within reach, and then, with a quick right hand, so quick he never even saw it coming, she smacked him hard across the front of the face. And when he sat down on the bed and began to cry, she took the knife from his hand and went swiftly out the room, down the stairs to the hall, where the telephone was.

DIP IN THE POOL

On the morning of the third day, the sea calmed. Even the most delicate passengers—those who had not been seen around the ship since sailing time—emerged from their cabins and crept up onto the sun deck where the deck steward gave them chairs and tucked rugs around their legs and left them lying in rows, their faces upturned to the pale, almost heatless January sun.

It had been moderately rough the first two days, and this sudden calm and the sense of comfort that it brought created a more genial atmosphere over the whole ship. By the time evening came, the passengers, with twelve hours of good weather behind them, were beginning to feel confident, and at eight o'clock that night the main dining room was filled with people eating and drinking with the assured, complacent air of seasoned sailors.

The meal was not half over when the passengers became aware, by a slight friction between their bodies and the seats of their chairs, that the big ship had actually started rolling again. It was very gentle at first, just a slow, lazy leaning to one side, then to the other, but it was enough to cause a subtle, immediate change of mood over the whole room. A few of the passengers glanced up from their food, hesitating, waiting, almost listening for the next roll, smiling nervously, little secret glimmers of apprehension in their eyes. Some were completely unruffled, some were openly smug, a number of the smug ones making jokes about food and weather in order to torture the few who were beginning to suffer. The movement of the ship then became rapidly more and more violent, and only five or six minutes after the first roll had been noticed, she was swinging heavily from side to side, the passengers bracing themselves in their chairs, leaning against the pull as in a car cornering.

At last the really bad roll came, and Mr. William Botibol, sitting at the purser's table, saw his plate of poached turbot with hollandaise sauce sliding suddenly away from under his fork. There was a flutter of excitement, everybody reaching for plates and wineglasses. Mrs. Renshaw, seated at the purser's right, gave a little scream and clutched that gentleman's arm.

"Going to be a dirty night," the purser said, looking at Mrs. Renshaw. "I think it's blowing up for a very dirty night." There was just the faintest suggestion of relish in the way he said it.

A steward came hurrying up and sprinkled water on the tablecloth between the plates. The excitement subsided. Most of the passengers continued with their meal.

A small number, including Mrs. Renshaw, got carefully to their feet and threaded their ways with a kind of concealed haste between the tables and through the doorway.

"Well," the purser said, "there she goes." He glanced around with approval at the remainder of his flock who were sitting quiet, looking complacent, their faces reflecting openly that extraordinary pride that travellers seem to take in being recognized as "good sailors."

When the eating was finished and the coffee had been served, Mr. Botibol, who had been unusually grave and thoughtful since the rolling started, suddenly stood up and carried his cup of coffee around to Mrs. Renshaw's vacant place, next to the purser. He seated himself in her chair, then immediately leaned over and began to whisper urgently in the purser's ear. "Excuse me," he said, "but could you tell me something please?"

The purser, small and fat and red, bent forward to listen. "What's the trouble, Mr. Botibol?"

"What I want to know is this." The man's face was anxious and the purser was watching it. "What I want to know is will the captain already have made his estimate on the day's run—you know, for the auction pool? I mean before it began to get rough like this?"

The purser, who had prepared himself to receive a personal confidence, smiled and leaned back in his seat to relax his full belly. "I should say so—yes," he answered. He didn't bother to whisper his reply, although automatically he lowered his voice, as one does when answering a whisperer.

"About how long ago do you think he did it?"

"Some time this afternoon. He usually does it in the afternoon."

"About what time?"

"Oh, I don't know. Around four o'clock I should guess."

"Now tell me another thing. How does the captain decide which number it shall be? Does he take a lot of trouble over that?"

The purser looked at the anxious frowning face of Mr. Botibol and he smiled, knowing quite well what the man was driving at. "Well, you see, the captain has a little conference with the navigating officer, and they study the weather and a lot of other things, and then they make their estimate."

Mr. Botibol nodded, pondering this answer for a moment. Then he said, "Do you think the captain knew there was bad weather coming today?"

"I couldn't tell you," the purser replied. He was looking into the small black eyes of the other man, seeing the two single little sparks of excitement dancing in their centers. "I really couldn't tell you, Mr. Botibol. I wouldn't know."

"If this gets any worse it might be worth buying some of the low numbers. What do you think?" The whispering was more urgent, more anxious now.

"Perhaps it will," the purser said. "I doubt the old man allowed for a really rough night. It was pretty calm this afternoon when he made his estimate."

The others at the table had become silent and were trying to hear, watching the purser with that intent, half-cocked, listening look that you can see also at the race track when they are trying to overhear a trainer talking about his chance: the slightly open lips, the upstretched eyebrows, the head forward and cocked a little to one side—that desperately straining, half-hypnotized, listening look that comes to all of them when they are hearing something straight from the horse's mouth.

"Now suppose *you* were allowed to buy a number, which one would *you* choose today?" Mr. Botibol whispered.

"I don't know what the range is yet," the purser patiently answered. "They don't announce the range till the auction starts after dinner. And I'm really not very good at it anyway. I'm only the purser, you know."

At that point Mr. Botibol stood up. "Excuse me, all," he said, and he walked carefully away over the swaying floor between the other tables, and twice he had to catch hold of the back of a chair to steady himself against the ship's roll.

"The sun deck, please," he said to the elevator man.

The wind caught him full in the face as he stepped out onto the open deck. He staggered and grabbed hold of the rail and held on tight with both hands, and he stood there looking out over the darkening sea where the great waves were welling up high and white horses were riding against the wind with plumes of spray behind them as they went.

"Pretty bad out there, wasn't it, sir?" the elevator man said on the way down.

Mr. Botibol was combing his hair back into place with

a small red comb. "Do you think we've slackened speed at all on account of the weather?" he asked.

"Oh my word yes, sir. We slacked off considerable since this started. You got to slacken off speed in weather like this or you'll be throwing the passengers all over the ship."

Down in the smoking room people were already gathering for the auction. They were grouping themselves politely around the various tables, the men a little stiff in their dinner jackets, a little pink and overshaved and stiff beside their cool, white-armed women. Mr. Botibol took a chair close to the auctioneer's table. He crossed his legs, folded his arms, and settled himself in his seat with the rather desperate air of a man who has made a tremendous decision and refuses to be frightened.

The pool, he was telling himself, would probably be around seven thousand dollars. That was almost exactly what it had been the last two days with the numbers selling for between three and four hundred apiece. Being a British ship they did it in pounds, but he liked to do his thinking in his own currency. Seven thousand dollars was plenty of money. My goodness yes! And what he would do he would get them to pay him in hundred-dollar bills and he would take it ashore in the inside pocket of his jacket. No problem there. And right away, yes right away, he would buy a Lincoln convertible. He would pick it up on the way from the ship and drive it home just for the pleasure of seeing Ethel's face when she came out the front door and looked at it. Wouldn't that be something, to see Ethel's face when he glided up to the door in a brand-new pale-green Lincoln convertible! Hello Ethel honey, he would say, speaking very casual. I just thought I'd get you a little present. I saw it in the window as I went by, so I thought of you and how you were always wanting one. You like it, honey? he would say. You like the colour? And then he would watch her face.

The auctioneer was standing up behind his table now. "Ladies and gentlemen!" he shouted. "The captain has estimated the day's run, ending midday tomorrow, at five hundred and fifteen miles. As usual we will take the ten numbers on either side of it to make up the range. That makes it five hundred and five to five hundred and twenty-five. And of course for those who think the true figure will be still farther away, there'll be 'low field' and 'high field' sold separately as well. Now, we'll draw the first number out of the hat . . . here we are . . . five hundred and twelve?"

The room became quiet. The people sat still in their chairs, all eyes watching the auctioneer. There was a certain tension in the air, and as the bids got higher, the tension grew. This wasn't a game or a joke; you could be sure of that by the way one man would look across at another who had raised his bid—smiling perhaps, but only the lips smiling, the eyes bright and absolutely cold.

Number five hundred and twelve was knocked down for one hundred and ten pounds. The next three or four numbers fetched roughly the same amount.

The ship was rolling heavily, and each time she went over, the wooden panelling on the walls creaked as if it were going to split. The passengers held on to the arms of their chairs, concentrating upon the auction.

"Low field!" the auctioneer called out. "The next number is low field."

Mr. Botibol sat up very straight and tense. He would wait, he had decided, until the others had finished bidding, then he would jump in and make the last bid. He had figured that there must be at least five hundred dollars in his account at the bank at home, probably nearer six. That was about two hundred pounds—over two hundred. This ticket wouldn't fetch more than that.

"As you all know," the auctioneer was saying, "low field covers every number *below* the smallest number in the range, in this case every number below five hundred and five. So, if you think this ship is going to cover less than five hundred and five miles in the twenty-four hours ending at noon tomorrow, you better get in and buy this number. So what am I bid?"

It went clear up to one hundred and thirty pounds. Others besides Mr. Botibol seemed to have noticed that the weather was rough. One hundred and forty . . . fifty . . . There it stopped. The auctioneer raised his hammer.

"Going at one hundred and fifty . . ."

"Sixty!" Mr. Botibol called, and every face in the room turned and looked at him.

"Seventy!"

"Eighty!" Mr. Botibol called.

"Ninety!"

"Two hundred!" Mr. Botibol called. He wasn't stopping now—not for anyone.

There was a pause.

"Any advance on two hundred pounds?"

Sit still, he told himself. Sit absolutely still and don't look up. It's unlucky to look up. Hold your breath. No one's going to bid you up so long as you hold your breath.

"Going for two hundred pounds . . ." The auctioneer had a pink bald head and there were little beads of sweat sparkling on top of it. "Going . . ." Mr. Botibol held his breath. "Going . . . Gone!" The man banged the hammer on the table. Mr. Botibol wrote out a check and handed it to the auctioneer's assistant, then he settled back in his chair to wait for the finish. He did not want to go to bed before he knew how much there was in the pool.

They added it up after the last number had been sold and it came to twenty-one hundred-odd pounds. That was around six thousand dollars. Ninety per cent to go to the winner, ten per cent to seamen's charities. Ninety per cent of six thousand was five thousand four hundred. Well—that was enough. He could buy the Lincoln convertible and there would be something left over, too. With this gratifying thought he went off, happy and excited, to his cabin.

When Mr. Botibol awoke the next morning he lay quite still for several minutes with his eyes shut, listening for the sound of the gale, waiting for the roll of the ship. There was no sound of any gale and the ship was not rolling. He jumped up and peered out of the porthole. The sea—Oh Jesus God—was smooth as glass, the great ship was moving through it fast, obviously making up for time lost during the night. Mr. Botibol turned away and sat slowly down on the edge of his bunk. A fine electricity of fear was beginning to prickle under the skin of his stomach. He hadn't a hope now. One of the higher numbers was certain to win it after this.

"Oh my God," he said aloud. "What shall I do?"

What, for example, would Ethel say? It was simply not possible to tell her that he had spent almost all of their two years' savings on a ticket in the ship's pool. Nor was it possible to keep the matter secret. To do that he would have to tell her to stop drawing checks. And what about the monthly installments on the television set and the Encyclopaedia Britannica? Already he could see the anger and contempt in the woman's eyes, the blue becoming gray and the eyes themselves narrowing as they always did when there was anger in them.

"Oh my God. What *shall* I do?"

There was no point in pretending that he had the slightest chance now—not unless the goddam ship started to go backward. They'd have to put her in reverse and go full speed astern and keep right on going if he was to have any chance of winning it now. Well, maybe he should ask the captain to do just that. Offer him ten per cent of the profits. Offer him more if he wanted it. Mr. Botibol started to giggle. Then very suddenly he stopped, his eyes and mouth both opening wide in a kind of shocked surprise. For it was at this moment that the idea came. It hit him hard and quick, and he jumped up from his bed, terribly excited, ran over to the porthole and looked out again. Well, he thought, why not? Why ever not? The sea was calm and he wouldn't have any trouble keeping afloat until they picked him up. He had a vague feeling that someone had done this thing before, but that didn't prevent him from doing it again. The ship would have to stop and lower a boat, and the boat would have to go back maybe half a mile to get him, and then it would have to return to the ship and be hoisted back on board. It would take at least an hour, the whole thing. An hour was about thirty miles. It would knock thirty miles off the day's run. That would do it. "Low field" would be sure to win it then. Just so long as he made certain someone saw him falling over; but that would be simple to arrange. And he'd better wear light clothes, something easy to swim in. Sports clothes, that was it. He would dress as though he were going up to play some deck tennis—just a shirt and a pair of shorts and tennis shoes. And leave his watch behind. What was the time? Nine-fifteen. The sooner the better, then. Do it now and get it over with. Have to do it soon, because the time limit was midday.

Mr. Botibol was both frightened and excited when he stepped out onto the sundeck in his sports clothes. His small body was wide at the hips, tapering upward to extremely narrow sloping shoulders, so that it resembled, in shape at any rate, a bollard. His white skinny legs were covered with black hairs, and he came cautiously out on deck, treading softly in his tennis shoes. Nervously he looked around him. There was only one other person in sight, an elderly woman with very thick ankles and immense buttocks who was leaning over the rail staring at the sea. She was wearing a coat of Persian lamb and the collar was turned up so Mr. Botibol couldn't see her face.

He stood still, examining her carefully from a distance. Yes, he told himself, she would probably do. She would probably give the alarm just as quickly as anyone else. But wait one minute, take your time, William Botibol, take your time. Remember what you told yourself a few minutes ago in the cabin when you were changing? You remember that?

The thought of leaping off a ship into the ocean a thousand miles from the nearest land had made Mr. Botibol—a cautious man at the best of times—unusually advertent. He was by no means satisfied yet that this woman he saw before him was *absolutely certain* to give the alarm when he made his jump. In his opinion there were two possible reasons why she might fail him. Firstly, she might be deaf and blind. It was not very probable, but on the other hand it *might* be so, and why take a chance? All he had to do was check it by talking to her for a moment beforehand. Secondly—and this will demonstrate how suspicious the mind of a man can become when it is working through self-preservation and fear—secondly, it had occurred to him that the woman might herself be the owner of one of the high numbers in the pool and as such would have a sound financial reason for not wishing to stop the ship. Mr. Botibol recalled that people had killed their fellows for far less than six thousand dollars. It was happening every day in the newspapers. So why take a chance on that either? Check on it first. Be sure of your facts. Find out about it by a little polite conversation. Then, provided that the woman appeared also to be a pleasant, kindly human being, the thing was a cinch and he could leap overboard with a light heart.

Mr. Botibol advanced casually toward the woman and took up a position beside her, leaning on the rail. "Hullo," he said pleasantly.

She turned and smiled at him, a surprisingly lovely, almost a beautiful smile, although the face itself was very plain. "Hullo," she answered him.

Check, Mr. Botibol told himself, on the first question. She is neither blind nor deaf. "Tell me," he said, coming straight to the point, "what did you think of the auction last night?"

"Auction?" she asked, frowning. "Auction? What auction?"

"You know, that silly old thing they have in the lounge after dinner, selling numbers on the ship's daily run. I just wondered what you thought about it."

She shook her head, and again she smiled, a sweet and pleasant smile that had in it perhaps the trace of an apology. "I'm very lazy," she said. "I always go to bed early. I have my dinner in bed. It's so restful to have dinner in bed."

Mr. Botibol smiled back at her and began to edge away. "Got to go and get my exercise now," he said.

"Never miss my exercise in the morning. It was nice seeing you. Very nice seeing you . . ." He retreated about ten paces, and the woman let him go without looking around.

Everything was now in order. The sea was calm, he was lightly dressed for swimming, there were almost certainly no man-eating sharks in this part of the Atlantic, and there was this pleasant kindly old woman to give the alarm. It was a question now only of whether the ship would be delayed long enough to swing the balance in his favor. Almost certainly it would. In any event, he could do a little to help in that direction himself. He could make a few difficulties about getting hauled up into the lifeboat. Swim around a bit, back away from them surreptitiously as they tried to come up close to fish him out. Every minute, every second gained would help him win. He began to move forward again to the rail, but now a new fear assailed him. Would he get caught in the propeller? He had heard about that happening to persons falling off the sides of big ships. But then, he wasn't going to fall, he was going to jump, and that was a very different thing. Provided he jumped out far enough he would be sure to clear the propeller.

Mr. Botibol advanced slowly to a position at the rail about twenty yards away from the woman. She wasn't looking at him now. So much the better. He didn't want her watching him as he jumped off. So long as no one was watching he would be able to say afterward that he had slipped and fallen by accident. He peered over the side of the ship. It was a long, long drop. Come to think of it now, he might easily hurt himself badly if he hit the water flat. Wasn't there someone who once split his stomach open that way, doing a belly flop from the high dive? He must jump straight and land feet first. Go in like a knife. Yes sir. The water seemed cold and deep and gray and it made him shiver to look at it. But it was now or never. Be a man, William Botibol, be a man. All right then . . . now . . . here goes . . .

He climbed up onto the wide wooden toprail, stood there poised, balancing for three terrifying seconds, then he leaped—he leaped up and out as far as he could go and at the same time he shouted *"Help!"*

"Help! Help!" he shouted as he fell. Then he hit the water and went under.

When the first shout for help sounded, the woman who was leaning on the rail started up and gave a little jump of surprise. She looked around quickly and saw sailing past her through the air this small man dressed in white shorts and tennis shoes, spread-eagled and shouting as he went. For a moment she looked as though she weren't quite sure what she ought to do: throw a life belt, run away and give the alarm, or simply turn and yell. She drew back a pace from the rail and swung half around facing up to the bridge, and for this brief moment she remained motionless, tense, undecided. Then almost at once she seemed to relax, and she leaned forward far over the rail, staring at the water where it was turbulent in the ship's wake. Soon a tiny round black head appeared in the foam, an arm was raised about it, once, twice, vigorously waving, and a small faraway voice was heard calling something that was difficult to understand. The woman leaned still farther over the rail, trying to keep the little bobbing black speck in sight, but soon, so very soon, it was such a long way away that she couldn't even be sure it was there at all.

After a while another woman came out on deck. This one was bony and angular, and she wore horn-rimmed spectacles. She spotted the first woman and walked over to her, treading the deck in the deliberate, military fashion of all spinsters.

"So *there* you are," she said.

The woman with the fat ankles turned and looked at her, but said nothing.

"I've been searching for you," the bony one continued. "Searching all over."

"It's very odd," the woman with the fat ankles said. "A man dived overboard just now, with his clothes on."

"Nonsense!"

"Oh yes. He said he wanted to get some exercise and he dived in and didn't even bother to take his clothes off."

"You better come down now," the bony woman said. Her mouth had suddenly become firm, her whole face sharp and alert, and she spoke less kindly than before. "And don't you ever go wandering about on deck alone like this again. You know quite well you're meant to wait for me."

"Yes, Maggie," the woman with the fat ankles answered, and again she smiled, a tender, trusting smile, and she took the hand of the other one and allowed herself to be led away across the deck.

"Such a nice man," she said. "He waved to me."

GALLOPING FOXLEY

FIVE days a week, for thirty-six years, I have travelled the eight-twelve train to the City. It is never unduly crowded, and it takes me right in to Cannon Street Station, only an eleven and a half minute walk from the door of my office in Austin Friars.

I have always liked the process of commuting; every phase of the little journey is a pleasure to me. There is a regularity about it that is agreeable and comforting to a person of habit, and in addition, it serves as a sort of slipway along which I am gently but firmly launched into the waters of daily business routine.

Ours is a smallish country station and only nineteen or twenty people gather there to catch the eight-twelve. We are a group that rarely changes, and when occasionally a new face appears on the platform it causes a certain disclamatory, protestant ripple, like a new bird in a cage of canaries.

But normally, when I arrive in the morning with my

usual four minutes to spare, there they all are, these good, solid, steadfast people, standing in their right places with their right umbrellas and hats and ties and faces and their newspapers under their arms, as unchanged and unchangeable through the years as the furniture in my own living-room. I like that.

I like also my corner seat by the window and reading *The Times* to the noise and motion of the train. This part of it lasts thirty-two minutes and it seems to soothe both my brain and my fretful old body like a good long massage. Believe me, there's nothing like routine and regularity for preserving one's peace of mind. I have now made this morning journey nearly ten thousand times in all, and I enjoy it more and more every day. Also (irrelevant, but interesting), I have become a sort of clock. I can tell at once if we are running two, three, or four minutes late, and I never have to look up to know which station we are stopped at.

The walk at the other end from Cannon Street to my office is neither too long nor too short—a healthy little perambulation along streets crowded with fellow commuters all proceeding to their places of work on the same orderly schedule as myself. It gives me a sense of assurance to be moving among these dependable, dignified people who stick to their jobs and don't go gadding about all over the world. Their lives, like my own, are regulated nicely by the minute hand of an accurate watch, and very often our paths cross at the same times and places on the street each day.

For example, as I turn the corner into St. Swithin's

Lane, I invariably come head on with a genteel middle-aged lady who wears silver pince-nez and carries a black briefcase in her hand—a first-rate accountant, I should say, or possibly an executive in the textile industry. When I cross over Threadneedle Street by the traffic lights, nine times out of ten I pass a gentleman who wears a different garden flower in his button-hole each day. He dresses in black trousers and grey spats and is clearly a punctual and meticulous person, probably a banker, or perhaps a solicitor like myself; and several times in the last twenty-five years, as we have hurried past one another across the street, our eyes have met in a fleeting glance of mutual approval and respect.

At least half the faces I pass on this little walk are now familiar to me. And good faces they are too, my kind of faces, my kind of people—sound, sedulous, businesslike folk with none of that restlessness and glittering eye about them that you see in all these so-called clever types who want to tip the world upside down with their Labour Governments and socialized medicines and all the rest of it.

So you can see that I am, in every sense of the words, a contented commuter. Or would it be more accurate to say that I *was* a contented commuter? At the time when I wrote the little autobiographical sketch you have just read—intending to circulate it among the staff of my office as an exhortation and an example—I was giving a perfectly true account of my feelings. But that was a whole week ago, and since then something rather peculiar has happened. As a matter of fact, it started to happen last Tuesday, the very morning that I was carrying the rough draft up to Town in my pocket; and this, to me, was so timely and coincidental that I can only believe it to have been the work of God. God had read my little essay and he had said to himself, "This man Perkins is becoming over-complacent. It is high time I taught him a lesson." I honestly believe that's what happened.

As I say, it was last Tuesday, the Tuesday after Easter, a warm yellow spring morning, and I was striding onto the platform of our small country station with *The Times* tucked under my arm and the draft of "The Contented Commuter" in my pocket, when I immediately became aware that something was wrong. I could actually *feel* that curious little ripple of protest running along the ranks of my fellow commuters. I stopped and glanced around.

The stranger was standing plumb in the middle of the platform, feet apart and arms folded, looking for all the world as though he owned the whole place. He was a biggish, thickset man, and even from behind he somehow managed to convey a powerful impression of arrogance and oil. Very definitely, he was not one of us. He carried a cane instead of an umbrella, his shoes were brown instead of black, the grey hat was cocked at a ridiculous angle, and in one way and another there seemed to be an excess of silk and polish about his person. More than this I did not care to observe. I walked straight past him with my face to the sky, adding, I sincerely hope, a touch of real frost to an atmosphere that was already cool.

The train came in. And now, try if you can to imagine my horror when the new man actually followed me into *my own* compartment! Nobody has done this to me for fifteen years. My colleagues always respect my seniority. One of my special little pleasures is to have the place to myself for at least one, sometimes two or even three stations. But here, if you please, was this fellow, this stranger, straddling the seat opposite and blowing his nose and rustling *The Daily Mail* and lighting a disgusting pipe.

I lowered my *Times* and stole a glance at his face. I suppose he was about the same age as me—sixty-two or three—but he had one of those unpleasantly handsome, brown, leathery countenances that you see nowadays in advertisements for men's shirts—the lion shooter and the polo player and the Everest climber and the tropical explorer and the racing yachtsman all rolled into one; dark eyebrows, steely eyes, strong white teeth clamping the stem of a pipe. Personally, I mistrust all handsome men. The superficial pleasures of this life come too easily to them, and they seem to walk the world as though they themselves were personally responsible for their own good looks. I don't mind a *woman* being pretty. That's different. But in a man, I'm sorry, but somehow or other I find it downright offensive. Anyway, here was this one sitting right opposite me in the carriage, and I was looking at him over the top of my *Times* when suddenly he glanced up and our eyes met.

"D'you mind the pipe?" he asked, holding it up in his fingers. That was all he said. But the sound of his voice had a sudden and extraordinary effect upon me. In fact, I think I jumped. Then I sort of froze up and sat staring at him for at least a minute before I got a hold of myself and made an answer.

"This is a smoker," I said, "so you may do as you please."

"I just thought I'd ask."

There it was again, that curiously crisp, familiar voice, clipping its words and spitting them out very hard and small like a little quick-firing gun shooting out raspberry seeds. Where had I heard it before? And why did every word seem to strike upon some tiny tender spot far back in my memory? Good heavens, I thought. Pull yourself together. What sort of nonsense is this?

The stranger returned to his paper. I pretended to do the same. But by this time I was properly put out and I couldn't concentrate at all. Instead, I kept stealing glances at him over the top of the editorial page. It was really an intolerable face, vulgarly, almost lasciviously handsome, with an oily salacious sheen all over the skin. But had I or had I not seen it before sometime in my life? I began to think I had, because now, even when I looked at it I felt a peculiar kind of discomfort that I cannot quite describe—something to do with pain and with violence, perhaps even with fear.

We spoke no more during the journey, but you can well imagine that by then my whole routine had been thoroughly upset. My day was ruined; and more than one of my clerks at the office felt the sharper edge of my tongue, particularly after luncheon when my digestion started acting up on me as well.

The next morning, there he was again standing in the middle of the platform with his cane and his pipe and his silk scarf and his nauseatingly handsome face. I walked past him and approached a certain Mr. Grummitt, a stockbroker who has been commuting with me for over twenty-eight years. I can't say I've ever had an actual conversation with him before—we are rather a reserved lot on our station—but a crisis like this will usually break the ice.

"Grummitt," I whispered. "Who's this bounder?"

"Search me," Grummitt said.

"Pretty unpleasant."

"Very."

"Not going to be a regular, I trust."

"Oh God," Grummitt said.

Then the train came in.

This time, to my great relief, the man got into another compartment.

But the following morning I had him with me again.

"Well," he said, settling back in the seat directly opposite. "It's a *topping* day." And once again I felt that slow uneasy stirring of the memory, stronger than ever this time, closer to the surface but not yet quite within my reach.

Then came Friday, the last day of the week. I re-member it had rained as I drove to the station, but it was one of those warm sparkling April showers that last only five or six minutes, and when I walked onto the platform, all the umbrellas were rolled up and the sun was shining and there were big white clouds floating in the sky. In spite of this, I felt depressed. There was no pleasure in this journey for me any longer. I knew the stranger would be there. And sure enough, he was, stand-ing with his legs apart just as though he owned the place and this time swinging his cane casually back and forth through the air.

The cane! That did it! I stopped like I'd been shot.

"It's Foxley!" I cried under my breath. "Galloping Foxley! And still swinging his cane!"

I stepped closer to get a better look. I tell you I've never had such a shock in all my life. It was Foxley all-right. Bruce Foxley or Galloping Foxley as we used to call him. And the last time I'd seen him, let me see—it was at school and I was no more than twelve or thirteen years old.

At that point the train came in, and heaven help me if he didn't get into my compartment once again. He put his hat and cane up on the rack, then turned and sat down and began lighting his pipe. He glanced up at me through the smoke with those rather small cold eyes and he said, "*Ripping* day, isn't it. Just like summer."

There was no mistaking the voice now. It hadn't changed at all. Except that the things I had been used to hearing it say were different.

"Allright Perkins," it used to say. "Allright you nasty little boy. I am about to beat you again."

How long ago was that? It must be nearly fifty years. Extraordinary, though, how little the features had altered. Still the same arrogant tilt of the chin, the flaring nostrils, the contemptuous staring eyes that were too small and a shade too close together for comfort; still the same habit·of thrusting his face forward at you, impinging on you, pushing you into a corner, and even the hair I could remember—coarse and slightly wavy, with just a trace of oil all over it, like a well-tossed salad. He used to keep a bottle of green hair mixture on the side table in his study—when you have to dust a room you get to know and to hate all the objects in it—and this bottle had the royal coat of arms on the label and the name of a shop in Bond Street, and under that, in small print, it said "By Appointment—Hairdressers To His Majesty King Edward VII." I can remember that particularly because it seemed so funny that a shop should want to boast about being hairdresser to someone who was practically bald—even a monarch.

And now I watched Foxley settle back in his seat and begin reading his paper. It was a curious sensation, sitting only a yard away from this man who fifty years before had made me so miserable that I had once contemplated suicide. He hadn't recognized *me;* there wasn't much danger of that because of my mustache. I felt fairly sure I was safe and could sit there and watch him all I wanted.

Looking back on it, there seems little doubt that I suffered very badly at the hands of Bruce Foxley my first year in school, and strangely enough, the unwitting cause of it all was my father. I was twelve and a half when I first went off to this fine old Public School. That was, let me see, in 1907. My father, who wore a silk topper and morning coat, escorted me to the station, and I can remember how we were standing on the platform among piles of wooden tuck-boxes and trunks and what seemed like thousands of very large boys milling about and talking and shouting at one another, when suddenly somebody who was wanting to get by us gave my father a great push from behind and nearly knocked him off his feet.

My father, who was a small, courteous, dignified person, turned around with surprising speed and seized the culprit by the wrist.

"Don't they teach you better manners than that at this school, young man," he said.

The boy, at least a head taller than my father, looked down at him with a cold, arrogant-laughing glare, and said nothing.

"It seems to me," my father said, staring back at him, "that an apology would be in order."

But the boy just kept on looking down his nose at my father with this funny little arrogant smile at the corners of his mouth, and his chin kept coming further and further out.

"You strike me as being an impudent and ill-mannered boy," my father went on. "And I can only pray that you are an exception in your school. I would not wish for any son of mine to pick up such habits."

At this point, the big boy inclined his head slightly in my direction, and a pair of small, cold, rather close together eyes looked down into mine. I was not particularly frightened at the time; I knew nothing about the power of senior boys over junior boys at Public Schools; and I can remember that I looked straight back at him in support of my father, whom I adored and respected.

When my father started to say something more, the boy simply turned away and sauntered slowly down the platform into the crowd.

Bruce Foxley never forgot this episode; and of course the really unlucky thing about it for me was that when I arrived at school I found myself in the same "house" as him. Even worse than that—I was in his study. He was doing his last year, and he was a prefect—a "boazer" we called it—and as such he was officially permitted to beat any of the fags in the house. But being in his study, I automatically became his own particular, personal slave. I was his valet and cook and maid and errand-boy, and it was my duty to see that he never lifted a finger for himself unless absolutely necessary. In no society that I know of in the world is a servant imposed upon to the extent that we wretched little fags were imposed upon by the boazers at school. In frosty or snowy weather I even had to sit on the seat of the lavatory (which was in an unheated outhouse) every morning after breakfast to warm it before Foxley came along.

I could remember how he used to saunter across the room in his loose-jointed, elegant way, and if a chair were in his path he would knock it aside and I would have to run over and pick it up. He wore silk shirts and always had a silk handkerchief tucked up his sleeve, and his shoes were made by someone called Lobb (who also had a Royal crest). They were pointed shoes, and it was my duty to rub the leather with a bone for fifteen minutes each day to make it shine.

But the worst memories of all had to do with the changing-room.

I could see myself now, a small pale shrimp of a boy standing just inside the door of this huge room in my pyjamas and bedroom slippers and brown camel hair dressing-gown. A single bright electric bulb was hanging on a flex from the ceiling, and all around the walls the black and yellow football shirts with their sweaty smell filling the room, and the voice, the clipped, pip-spitting voice was saying, "So which is it to be this time? Six with the dressing-gown on—or four with it off?"

I never could bring myself to answer this question. I would simply stand there staring down at the dirty floor-planks, dizzy with fear and unable to think of anything except that this other larger boy would soon start smashing away at me with his long, thin, white stick, slowly, scientifically, skillfully, legally, and with apparent relish, and I would bleed. Five hours earlier, I had failed to get the fire to light in his study. I had spent my pocket money on a box of special firelighters and I had held a newspaper across the chimney opening to make a draught and I had knelt down in front of it and blown my guts out into the bottom of the grate; but the coals would not burn.

"If you're too obstinate to answer," the voice was saying, "then I'll have to decide for you."

I wanted desperately to answer because I knew which one I had to choose. It's the first thing you learn when you arrive. Always keep the dressing-gown *on* and take the extra strokes. Otherwise you're almost certain to get cut. Even three with it on is better than one with it off.

"Take it off then and get into the far corner and touch your toes. I'm going to give you four."

Slowly I would take it off and lay it on the ledge above the boot-lockers. And slowly I would walk over to the far corner, cold and naked now in my cotton pyjamas, treading softly and seeing everything around me suddenly very bright and flat and far away, like a magic lantern picture, and very big, and very unreal, and sort of swimming through the water in my eyes.

"Go on and touch your toes. Tighter—much tighter than that."

Then he would walk down to the far end of the changing-room and I would be watching him upside down between my legs, and he would disappear through a doorway that led down two steps into what we called "the basin-passage." This was a stone-floored corridor with wash basins along one wall, and beyond it was the bathroom. When Foxley disappeared I knew he was walking down to the far end of the basin-passage. Foxley always did that. Then, in the distance, but echoing loud among the basins and the tiles, I would hear the noise of his shoes on the stone floor as he started galloping forward, and through my legs I would see him leaping up the two steps into the changing-room and come bounding toward me with his face thrust forward and the cane held high in the air. This was the moment when I shut my eyes and waited for the crack and told myself that whatever happened I must not straighten up.

Anyone who has been properly beaten will tell you that the real pain does not come until about eight or ten seconds after the stroke. The stroke itself is merely a loud crack and a sort of blunt thud against your backside, numbing you completely. (I'm told a bullet wound does the same). But later on, oh my heavens, it feels like someone is laying a red hot poker right across your naked buttocks and it is absolutely impossible to prevent yourself from reaching back and clutching it with your fingers.

Foxley knew all about this time lag, and the slow walk back over a distance that must altogether have been fifteen yards gave each stroke plenty of time to reach the peak of its pain before the next one was delivered.

On the fourth stroke I would invariably straighten up. I couldn't help it. It was an automatic defense reaction from a body that had had as much as it could stand.

"You flinched," Foxley would say. "That one doesn't count. Go on—down you get."

The next time I would remember to grip my ankles.

Afterwards, he would watch me as I walked over—very stiff now and holding by backside—to put on my dressing-gown, but I would always try to keep turned away from him so he couldn't see my face. And when I went out, it would be, "Hey you! Come back!"

I was in the passage then, and I would stop and turn and stand in the doorway, waiting.

"Come here. Come on, come back here. Now—haven't you forgotten something?"

All I could think of at that moment was the excruciating burning pain in my behind.

"You strike me as being an impudent and ill-mannered boy," he would say, imitating my father's voice. "Don't they teach you better manners than that at this school?"

"Thank . . . you," I would stammer. "Thank . . . you . . . for the beating."

And then back up the dark stairs to the dormitory and it became much better then because it was all over and the pain was going and the others were clustering round and treating me with a certain rough sympathy born of having gone through the same thing themselves, many times.

"Hey Perkins, let's have a look."

"How many d'you get?"

"Five, wasn't it. We heard them easily from here."

"Come on, man. Let's see the marks."

I would take down my pyjamas and stand there while this group of experts solemnly examined the damage.

"Rather far apart, aren't they? Not quite up to Foxley's usual standard."

"Two of them are close. Actually touching. Look—these two are beauties!"

"That low one was a rotten shot."

"Did he go right down the basin-passage to start his run?"

"You got an extra one for flinching, didn't you?"

"By golly, old Foxley's really got it in for *you*, Perkins."

"Bleeding a bit too. Better wash it, you know."

Then the door would open and Foxley would be there, and everyone would scatter and pretend to be doing his teeth or saying his prayers while I was left standing in the centre of the room with my pants down.

"What's going on here?" Foxley would say, taking a quick look at his own handiwork. "You—Perkins! Put your pyjamas on properly and get into bed."

And that was the end of a day.

Through the week, I never had a moment of time to myself. If Foxley saw me in the study taking up a novel or perhaps opening my stamp album, he would immediately find something for me to do. One of his favourites, especially when it was raining outside, was, "Oh Perkins, I think a bunch of wild irises would look rather nice on my desk, don't you?"

Wild irises grew only around Orange Ponds. Orange Ponds was two miles down the road and half a mile across the fields. I would get up from my chair, put on my raincoat and my straw hat, take my umbrella—my brolly—and set off on this long and lonely trek. The straw hat had to be worn at all times outdoors, but it was easily destroyed by rain; therefore the brolly was necessary to protect the hat. On the other hand, you can't keep a brolly over your head while scrambling about on a woody bank looking for irises, so to save my hat from ruin I would put it on the ground under my brolly while I searched for the flowers. In this way, I caught many colds.

But the most dreaded day was Sunday. Sunday was for cleaning the study, and how well I can remember the terror of those mornings, the frantic dusting and scrubbing, and then the waiting for Foxley to come in to inspect.

"Finished?" he would ask.

"I . . . I think so."

Then he would stroll over to the drawer of his desk and take out a single white glove, fitting it slowly onto his right hand, pushing each finger well home, and I would stand there watching and trembling as he moved around the room running his white-gloved forefinger along the picture tops, the skirting, the shelves, the window sills, the lamp shades. I never took my eyes off that finger. For me it was an instrument of doom. Nearly always, it managed to discover some tiny crack that I had overlooked or perhaps hadn't even thought about; and when this happened Foxley would turn slowly around, smiling that dangerous little smile that wasn't a smile, holding up the white finger so that I should see for myself the thin smudge of dust that lay along the side of it.

"Well," he would say. "So you're a lazy little boy. Aren't you?"

No answer.

"Aren't you?"

"I thought I dusted it all."

"Are you or are you not a nasty, lazy little boy?"

"Y-yes."

"But your father wouldn't want you to grow up like that, would he? Your father is very particular about manners, is he not?"

No answer.

"I asked you, is your father particular about manners?"

"Perhaps—yes."

"Therefore I will be doing him a favour if I punish you, won't I?"

"I don't know."

"Won't I?"

"Y-yes."

"We will meet later then, after prayers, in the changing-room."

The rest of the day would be spent in an agony of waiting for the evening to come.

Oh my goodness, how it was all coming back to me now. Sunday was also letter-writing time. "Dear Mummy and Daddy—thank you very much for your letter. I hope you are both well. I am, except I have got a cold because I got caught in the rain but it will soon be over. Yesterday we played Shrewsbury and beat them 4–2. I watched and Foxley who you know is the head of our house scored one of our goals. Thank you very much for the cake. With love from William."

I usually went to the lavatory to write my letter, or to the boot-hole, or the bathroom—any place out of Foxley's way. But I had to watch the time. Tea was at four-thirty and Foxley's toast had to be ready. Every day I had to make toast for Foxley, and on weekdays there were no fires allowed in the studies so all the fags, each making toast for his own studyholder, would have to crowd around the one small fire in the library, jockeying for position with his toasting-fork. Under these conditions, I still had to see that Foxley's toast was (1) very crisp (2) not burned at all (3) hot and ready exactly on time. To fail in any one of these requirements was a "beatable offense."

"Hey you! What's this?"

"It's toast."

"Is this really your idea of toast?"

"Well . . ."

"You're too idle to make it right, aren't you?"

"I try to make it."

"You know what they do to an idle horse, Perkins?"

"No."

"Are you a horse?"

"No."

"Well—anyway you're an ass—ha, ha—so I think you qualify. I'll be seeing you later."

Oh, the agony of those days. To burn Foxley's toast was a "beatable offense." So was forgetting to take the mud off Foxley's football boots. So was failing to hang up Foxley's football clothes. So was rolling up Foxley's brolly the wrong way round. So was banging the study door when Foxley was working. So was filling Foxley's bath too hot for him. So was not cleaning the buttons properly on Foxley's O.T.C. uniform. So was making those blue metal-polish smudges on the uniform itself. So was failing to shine the *soles* of Foxley's shoes. So was leaving

Foxley's study untidy at any time. In fact, so far as Foxley was concerned, I was practically a beatable offense myself.

I glanced out the window. My goodness, we were nearly there. I must have been dreaming away like this for quite a while, and I hadn't even opened my *Times*. Foxley was still leaning back in the corner seat opposite me reading his *Daily Mail*, and through a cloud of blue smoke from his pipe I could see the top half of his face over the newspaper, the small bright eyes, the corrugated forehead, the wavy, slightly oily hair.

Looking at him now, after all that time, was a peculiar and rather exciting experience. I knew he was no longer dangerous, but the old memories were still there and I didn't feel altogether comfortable in his presence. It was something like being inside the cage with a tame tiger.

What nonsense is this? I asked myself. Don't be so stupid. My heavens, if you wanted to you could go ahead and tell him exactly what you thought of him and he couldn't touch you. Hey—that was an idea!

Except that—well—after all, was it worth it? I was too old for that sort of thing now, and I wasn't sure that I really felt much anger toward him anyway.

So what should I do? I couldn't sit there staring at him like an idiot.

At that point, a little impish fancy began to take a hold of me. What I would like to do, I told myself, would be to lean across and tap him lightly on the knee and tell him who I was. Then I would watch his face. After that, I would begin talking about our schooldays together, making it just loud enough for the other people in the carriage to hear. I would remind him playfully of some of the things he used to do to me, and perhaps even describe the changing-room beatings so as to embarrass him a trifle. A bit of teasing and discomfort wouldn't do him any harm. And it would do *me* an awful lot of good.

Suddenly he glanced up and caught me staring at him. It was the second time this had happened, and I noticed a flicker of irritation in his eyes.

All right, I told myself. Here we go. But keep it pleasant and sociable and polite. It'll be much more effective that way, more embarrassing for him.

So I smiled at him and gave him a courteous little nod. Then, raising my voice, I said, "I do hope you'll excuse me. I'd like to introduce myself." I was leaning forward, watching him closely so as not to miss the reaction. "My name is Perkins—William Perkins—and I was at Repton in 1907."

The others in the carriage were sitting very still, and I could sense that they were all listening and waiting to see what would happen next.

"I'm glad to meet you," he said, lowering the paper to his lap. "Mine's Fortescue—Jocelyn Fortescue. Eton, 1916."

SKIN

THAT year—1946—winter was a long time going. Although it was April, a freezing wind blew through the streets of the city, and overhead the snow clouds moved across the sky.

The old man who was called Drioli shuffled painfully along the sidewalk of the Rue de Rivoli. He was cold and miserable, huddled up like a hedgehog in a filthy black coat, only his eyes and the top of his head visible above the turned-up collar.

The door of a cafe opened and the faint whiff of roasting chicken brought a pain of yearning to the top of his stomach. He moved on, glancing without any interest at the things in the shopwindows—perfume, silk ties and shirts, diamonds, porcelain, antique furniture, finely bound books. Then a picture gallery. He had always liked picture galleries. This one had a single canvas on display in the window. He stopped to look at it. He turned to go on. He checked, looked back; and now,

suddenly, there came to him a slight uneasiness, a movement of the memory, a distant recollection of something,
somewhere, he had seen before. He looked again. It was
a landscape, a clump of trees leaning madly over to one
side as if blown by a tremendous wind, the sky swirling
and twisting all around. Attached to the frame there was
a little plaque, and on this it said: "CHAÏM SOUTINE
(1894–1943)."

Drioli stared at the picture, wondering vaguely what
there was about it that seemed familiar. Crazy painting,
he thought. Very strange and crazy—but I like it . . .
Chaïm Soutine . . . Soutine . . . "By God!" he cried
suddenly. "My little Kalmuck, that's who it is! My little
Kalmuck with a picture in the finest shop in Paris! Just
imagine that!"

The old man pressed his face closer to the window.
He could remember the boy—yes, quite clearly he could
remember him. But when? When? The rest of it was
not so easy to recollect. It was so long ago. How long?
Twenty—no, more like thirty years, wasn't it? Wait a
minute. Yes—it was the year before the war, the first
war, 1913. That was it. And this Soutine, this ugly little
Kalmuck, a sullen brooding boy whom he had liked—
almost loved—for no reason at all that he could think of
except that he could paint.

And how he could paint! It was coming back more
clearly now—the street, the line of refuse cans along the
length of it, the rotten smell, the brown cats walking
delicately over the refuse, and then the women, moist
fat women sitting on the doorsteps with their feet upon

the cobblestones of the street. Which street? Where was it the boy had lived?

The Cité Falguière, that was it! The old man nodded his head several times, pleased to have remembered the name. Then there was the studio with the single chair in it, and the filthy red couch that the boy had used for sleeping; the drunken parties, the cheap white wine, the furious quarrels, and always, always the bitter sullen face of the boy brooding over his work.

It was odd, Drioli thought, how easily it all came back to him now, how each single small remembered fact seemed instantly to remind him of another.

There was that nonsense with the tattoo, for instance. Now, *that* was a mad thing if ever there was one. How had it started? Ah, yes—he had got rich one day, that was it, and he had bought lots of wine. He could see himself now as he entered the studio with the parcel of bottles under his arm—the boy sitting before the easel, and his (Drioli's) own wife standing in the center of the room, posing for her picture.

"Tonight we shall celebrate," he said. "We shall have a little celebration, us three."

"What is it that we celebrate?" the boy asked, without looking up. "Is it that you have decided to divorce your wife so she can marry me?"

"No," Drioli said. "We celebrate because today I have made a great sum of money with my work."

"And I have made nothing. We can celebrate that also."

"If you like." Drioli was standing by the table unwrapping the parcel. He felt tired and he wanted to get at the wine. Nine clients in one day was all very nice, but it could play hell with a man's eyes. He had never done as many as nine before. Nine boozy soldiers—and the remarkable thing was that no fewer than seven of them had been able to pay in cash. This had made him extremely rich. But the work was terrible on the eyes. Drioli's eyes were half closed from fatigue, the whites streaked with little connecting lines of red; and about an inch behind each eyeball there was a small concentration of pain. But it was evening now and he was wealthy as a pig, and in the parcel there were three bottles—one for his wife, one for his friend, and one for him. He had found the corkscrew and was drawing the corks from the bottles, each making a small plop as it came out.

The boy put down his brush. "Oh Christ," he said. "How can one work with all this going on?"

The girl came across the room to look at the painting. Drioli came over also, holding a bottle in one hand, a glass in the other.

"No!" the boy shouted, blazing up suddenly. "Please —no!" He snatched the canvas from the easel and stood it against the wall. But Drioli had seen it.

"I like it."

"It's terrible."

"It's marvellous. Like all the others that you do, it's marvellous. I love them all."

"The trouble is," the boy said, scowling, "that in themselves they are not nourishing. I cannot eat them."

"But still they are marvellous." Drioli handed him a

tumbler full of the pale-yellow wine. "Drink it," he said. "It will make you happy."

Never, he thought, had he known a more unhappy person, or one with a gloomier face. He had spotted him in a café some seven months before, drinking alone, and because he had looked like a Russian or some sort of an Asiatic, Drioli had sat down at his table and talked.

"You are a Russian?"

"Yes."

"Where from?"

"Minsk."

Drioli had jumped up and embraced him, crying that he too had been born in that city.

"It wasn't actually Minsk," the boy had said. "But quite near."

"Where?"

"Smilovichi, about twelve miles away."

"Smilovichi!" Drioli had shouted, embracing him again. "I walked there several times when I was a boy." Then he had sat down again, staring affectionately at the other's face. "You know," he had said, "you don't look like a western Russian. You're like a Tartar, or a Kalmuck. You look exactly like a Kalmuck."

Now, standing in the studio, Drioli looked again at the boy as he took the glass of wine and tipped it down his throat in one swallow. Yes, he did have a face like a Kalmuck—very broad and high-cheeked, with a wide coarse nose. This broadness of the cheeks was accentuated by the ears which stood out sharply from the head. And then he had the narrow eyes, the black hair, the thick sullen mouth of a Kalmuck; but the hands—the hands were always a surprise, so small and white like a lady's, with tiny thin fingers.

"Give me some more," the boy said. "If we are to celebrate, then let us do it properly."

Drioli distributed the wine and sat himself on a chair. The boy sat on the old couch with Drioli's wife. The three bottles were placed on the floor between them.

"Tonight we shall drink as much as we possibly can," Drioli said. "I am exceptionally rich. I think perhaps I should go out now and buy some more bottles. How many shall I get?"

"Six more," the boy said. "Two for each."

"Good. I shall go now and fetch them."

"And I will help you."

In the nearest café Drioli bought six bottles of white wine, and they carried them back to the studio. They placed them on the floor in two rows, and Drioli fetched the corkscrew and pulled the corks, all six of them; then they sat down again and continued to drink.

"It is only the very wealthy," Drioli said, "who can afford to celebrate in this manner."

"That is true," the boy said. "Isn't that true, Josie?"

"Of course."

"How do you feel, Josie?"

"Fine."

"Will you leave Drioli and marry me?"

"No."

"Beautiful wine," Drioli said. "It is a privilege to drink it."

Slowly, methodically, they set about getting themselves drunk. The process was routine, but all the same there was a certain ceremony to be observed, and a gravity to be maintained, and a great number of things to be said, then said again—and the wine must be praised, and the slowness was important too, so that there would be time to savour the three delicious stages of transition, especially (for Drioli) the one when he began to float and his feet did not really belong to him. That was the best period of them all—when he could look down at his feet and they were so far away that he would wonder what crazy person they might belong to and why they were lying around on the floor like that, in the distance.

After a while, he got up to switch on the light. He was surprised to see that the feet came with him when he did this, especially because he couldn't feel them touching the ground. It gave him a pleasant sensation of walking on air. Then he began wandering around the room, peeking slyly at the canvases stacked against the walls.

"Listen," he said at length. "I have an idea." He came across and stood before the couch, swaying gently. "Listen, my little Kalmuck."

"What?"

"I have a tremendous idea. Are you listening?"

"I'm listening to Josie."

"Listen to me, *please*. You are my friend—my ugly little Kalmuck from Minsk—and to me you are such an artist that I would like to have a picture, a lovely picture—"

"Have them all. Take all you can find, but do not interrupt me when I am talking with your wife."

"No, no. Now listen. I mean a picture that I can have with me always . . . forever . . . wherever I go . . . whatever happens . . . but always with me . . . a picture by you." He reached forward and shook the boy's knee. "Now listen to me, *please*."

"Listen to him," the girl said.

"It is this. I want you to paint a picture on my skin, on my back. Then I want you to tattoo over what you have painted so that it will be there always."

"You have crazy ideas."

"I will teach you how to use the tattoo. It is easy. A child could do it."

"I am not a child."

"*Please* . . ."

"You are quite mad. What is it you want?" The painter looked up into the slow, dark, wine-bright eyes of the other man. "What in heaven's name is it you want?"

"You could do it easily! You could! You could!"

"You mean with the tattoo?"

"Yes, with the tattoo! I will teach you in two minutes!"

"Impossible!"

"Are you saying I don't know what I'm talking about?"

No, the boy could not possibly be saying that because if anyone knew about the tattoo it was he—Drioli. Had he not, only last month, covered a man's whole belly with the most wonderful and delicate design composed entirely of flowers? What about the client who had had so much hair upon his chest that he had done him a picture of a grizzly bear so designed that the hair on the chest became the furry coat of the bear? Could he not draw the likeness of a lady and position it with such subtlety upon a man's arm that when the muscle of the arm was flexed the lady came to life and performed some astonishing contortions?

"All I am saying," the boy told him, "is that you are drunk and this is a drunken idea."

"We could have Josie for a model. A study of Josie upon my back. Am I not entitled to a picture of my wife upon my back?"

"Of Josie?"

"Yes." Drioli knew he only had to mention his wife and the boy's thick brown lips would loosen and begin to quiver.

"No," the girl said.

"Darling Josie, *please*. Take this bottle and finish it, then you will feel more generous. It is an enormous idea. Never in my life have I had such an idea before."

"What idea?"

"That he should make a picture of you upon my back. Am I not entitled to that?"

"A picture of me?"

"A nude study," the boy said. "It is an agreeable idea."

"Not nude," the girl said.

"It is an enormous idea," Drioli said.

"It's a damn crazy idea," the girl said.

"It is in any event an idea," the boy said. "It is an idea that calls for a celebration."

They emptied another bottle among them. Then the boy said, "It is no good. I could not possibly manage the tattoo. Instead, I will paint this picture on your back and you will have it with you so long as you do not take a bath and wash it off. If you never take a bath again in your life then you will have it always, as long as you live."

"No," Drioli said.

"Yes—and on the day that you decide to take a bath I will know that you do not any longer value my picture. It will be a test of your admiration for my art."

"I do not like the idea," the girl said. "His admiration for your art is so great that he would be unclean for many years. Let us have the tattoo. But not nude."

"Then just the head," Drioli said.

"I could not manage it."

"It is immensely simple. I will undertake to teach you in two minutes. You will see. I shall go now and fetch the instruments. The needles and the inks. I have inks of many different colors—as many different colors as you have paints, and far more beautiful. . . ."

"It is impossible."

"I have many inks. Have I not many different colors of inks, Josie?"

"Yes."

"You will see," Drioli said. "I will go now and fetch them." He got up from his chair and walked unsteadily, but with determination, out of the room.

In half an hour Drioli was back. "I have brought everything," he cried, waving a brown suitcase. "All the necessities of the tattooist are here in this bag."

He placed the bag on the table, opened it, and laid out the electric needles and the small bottles of colored inks. He plugged in the electric needle, then he took the instrument in his hand and pressed a switch. It made a buzzing sound and the quarter inch of needle that projected from the end of it began to vibrate swiftly up and down. He threw off his jacket and rolled up his left sleeve. "Now look. Watch me and I will show you how easy it is. I will make a design on my arm, here."

His forearm was already covered with blue markings, but he selected a small clear patch of skin upon which to demonstrate.

"First, I choose my ink—let us use ordinary blue—and I dip the point of my needle in the ink . . . so . . . and I hold the needle up straight and I run it lightly over the surface of the skin . . . like this . . . and with the little motor and the electricity, the needle jumps up and down and punctures the skin and the ink goes in and there you are . . . See how easy it is . . . see how I draw a picture of a greyhound here upon my arm . . ."

The boy was intrigued. "Now let *me* practice a little—on your arm."

With the buzzing needle he began to draw blue lines upon Drioli's arm. "It is simple," he said. "It is like drawing with pen and ink. There is no difference except that it is slower."

"There is nothing to it. Are you ready? Shall we begin?"

"At once."

"The model!" cried Drioli. "Come on, Josie!" He was in a bustle of enthusiasm now, tottering around the room arranging everything, like a child preparing for some exciting game. "Where will you have her? Where shall she stand?"

"Let her be standing there, by my dressing table. Let her be brushing her hair. I will paint her with her hair down over her shoulders and her brushing it."

"Tremendous. You are a genius."

Reluctantly, the girl walked over and stood by the dressing table, carrying her glass of wine with her.

Drioli pulled off his shirt and stepped out of his trousers. He retained only his underpants and his socks and shoes, and he stood there swaying gently from side to side, his small body firm, white-skinned, almost hairless. "Now," he said, "I am the canvas. Where will you place your canvas?"

"As always, upon the easel."

"Don't be crazy. I am the canvas."

"Then place yourself upon the easel. That is where you belong."

"How can I?"

"Are you the canvas or are you not the canvas?"

"I am the canvas. Already I begin to feel like a canvas."

"Then place yourself upon the easel. There should be no difficulty."

"Truly, it is not possible."

"Then sit on the chair. Sit back to front, then you can lean your drunken head against the back of it. Hurry now, for I am about to commence."

"I am ready. I am waiting."

"First," the boy said, "I shall make an ordinary painting. Then, if it pleases me, I shall tattoo over it." With a wide brush he began to paint upon the naked skin of the man's back.

"Ayee! Ayee!" Drioli screamed. "A monstrous centipede is marching down my spine!"

"Be still now! Be still!" The boy worked rapidly, applying the paint only in a thin blue wash so that it would not afterward interfere with the process of tattooing. His concentration, as soon as he began to paint, was so great that it appeared somehow to supersede his drunkenness. He applied the brush strokes with quick short jabs of the arm, holding the wrist stiff, and in less than half an hour it was finished.

"All right. That's all," he said to the girl, who immediately returned to the couch, lay down, and fell asleep.

Drioli remained awake. He watched the boy take up the needle and dip it in the ink; then he felt the sharp tickling sting as it touched the skin of his back. The pain, which was unpleasant but never extreme, kept him from going to sleep. By following the track of the needle and by watching the different colors of ink that the boy was using, Drioli amused himself trying to visualize what was going on behind him. The boy worked with an astonishing intensity. He appeared to have become completely absorbed in the little machine and in the unusual effects it was able to produce.

Far into the small hours of the morning the machine buzzed and the boy worked. Drioli could remember that when the artist finally stepped back and said, "It is finished," there was daylight outside and the sound of people walking in the street.

"I want to see it," Drioli said. The boy held up a mirror, at an angle, and Drioli craned his neck to look.

"Good God!" he cried. It was a startling sight. The whole of his back, from the top of the shoulders to the base of the spine, was a blaze of color—gold and green and blue and black and scarlet. The tattoo was applied so heavily it looked almost like an impasto. The boy had followed as closely as possible the original brush strokes, filling them in solid, and it was marvellous the way he had made use of the spine and the protrusion of the shoulder blades so that they became part of the composition. What is more, he had somehow managed to achieve—even with this slow process—a certain spontaneity. The portrait was quite alive; it contained much of that twisted, tortured, quality so characteristic of Soutine's other work. It was not a good likeness. It was a mood rather than a likeness, the model's face vague and tipsy, the background swirling around her head in a mass of dark-green curling strokes.

"It's tremendous!"

"I rather like it myself." The boy stood back, examining it critically. "You know," he added, "I think it's good enough for me to sign." And taking up the buzzer again, he inscribed his name in red ink on the right-hand side, over the place where Drioli's kidney was.

The old man who was called Drioli was standing in a sort of trance, staring at the painting in the window of the picture-dealer's shop. It had been so long ago, all that—almost as though it had happened in another life.

And the boy? What had become of him? He could remember now that after returning from the war—the first war—he had missed him and had questioned Josie.

"Where is my little Kalmuck?"

"He is gone," she had answered. "I do not know where, but I heard it said that a dealer had taken him up and sent him away to Céret to make more paintings."

"Perhaps he will return."

"Perhaps he will. Who knows?"

That was the last time they had mentioned him. Shortly afterward they had moved to Le Havre where there were more sailors and business was better. The old man smiled as he remembered Le Havre. Those were the pleasant years, the years between the wars, with the small shop near the docks and the comfortable rooms and always enough work, with every day three, four, five sailors coming and wanting pictures on their arms. Those were truly the pleasant years.

Then had come the second war, and Josie being killed, and the German's arriving, and that was the finish of his business. No one had wanted pictures on their arms any more after that. And by that time he was too old for any other kind of work. In desperation he had made his way back to Paris, hoping vaguely that things would be easier in the big city. But they were not.

And now, after the war was over, he possessed neither the means nor the energy to start up his small business again. It wasn't very easy for an old man to know what to do, especially when one did not like to beg. Yet how else could he keep alive?

Well, he thought, still staring at the picture. So that is my little Kalmuck. And how quickly the sight of one small object such as this can stir the memory. Up to a few moments ago he had even forgotten that he had a tattoo on his back. It had been ages since he had thought about it. He put his face closer to the window and looked into the gallery. On the walls he could see many other pictures and all seemed to be the work of the same artist. There were a great number of people strolling around. Obviously it was a special exhibition.

On a sudden impulse, Drioli turned, pushed open the door of the gallery and went in.

It was a long room with a thick wine-colored carpet, and by God how beautiful and warm it was! There were all these people strolling about looking at the pictures, well-washed, dignified people, each of whom held a catalogue in the hand. Drioli stood just inside the door, nervously glancing around, wondering whether he dared go forward and mingle with this crowd. But before he had had time to gather his courage, he heard a voice beside him saying, "What is it you want?"

The speaker wore a black morning coat. He was plump and short and had a very white face. It was a flabby face with so much flesh upon it that the cheeks hung down on either side of the mouth in two fleshy collops, spanielwise. He came up close to Drioli and said again, "What is it you want?"

Drioli stood still.

"If you please," the man was saying, "take yourself out of my gallery."

"Am I not permitted to look at the pictures?"

"I have asked you to leave."

Drioli stood his ground. He felt suddenly, overwhelmingly outraged.

"Let us not have trouble," the man was saying. "Come on now, this way." He put a fat white paw on Drioli's arm and began to push him firmly to the door.

That did it. "Take your goddam hands off me!" Drioli shouted. His voice rang clear down the long gallery and all the heads jerked around as one—all the startled faces stared down the length of the room at the person who had made this noise. A flunky came running over to help, and the two men tried to hustle Drioli through the door. The people stood still, watching the struggle. Their faces expressed only a mild interest, and seemed to be saying, "It's all right. There's no danger to us. It's being taken care of."

"I, too!" Drioli was shouting. "I, too, have a picture by this painter! He was my friend and I have a picture which he gave me!"

"He's mad."

"A lunatic. A raving lunatic."

"Someone should call the police."

With a rapid twist of the body Drioli suddenly jumped clear of the two men, and before anyone could stop him he was running down the gallery shouting, "I'll show you! I'll show you! I'll show you!" He flung off his overcoat, then his jacket and shirt, and he turned so that his naked back was toward the people.

"There!" he cried, breathing quickly. "You see? There it is!"

There was a sudden absolute silence in the room, each person arrested in what he was doing, standing motionless in a kind of shocked, uneasy bewilderment. They were staring at the tattooed picture. It was still there, the colors as bright as ever, but the old man's back was thinner now, the shoulder blades protruded more sharply, and the effect, though not great, was to give the picture a curiously wrinkled, squashed appearance.

Somebody said, "My God, but it is!"

Then came the excitement and the noise of voices as the people surged forward to crowd around the old man.

"It is unmistakable!"

"His early manner, yes?"

"It is fantastic, fantastic!"

"And look, it is signed!"

"Bend your shoulders forward, my friend, so that the picture stretches out flat."

"Old one, when was this done?"

"In 1913," Drioli said, without turning around. "In the autumn of 1913."

"Who taught Soutine to tattoo?"

"I taught him."

"And the woman?"

"She was my wife."

The gallery owner was pushing through the crowd toward Drioli. He was calm now, deadly serious, making a smile with his mouth. "Monsieur," he said, "I will buy it." Drioli could see the loose fat upon the face vibrating as he moved his jaw. "I said I will buy it, Monsieur."

"How can you buy it?" Drioli asked softly.

"I will give two hundred thousand francs for it." The dealer's eyes were small and dark, the wings of his broad nose-base were beginning to quiver.

"Don't do it!" someone murmured in the crowd. "It is worth twenty times as much."

Drioli opened his mouth to speak. No words came, so he shut it; then he opened it again and said slowly, "But how can I sell it?" He lifted his hands, let them drop loosely to his sides. "Monsieur, how can I possibly sell it?" All the sadness in the world was in his voice.

"Yes!" they were saying in the crowd. "How can he sell it? It is a part of himself!"

"Listen," the dealer said, coming up close. "I will help you. I will make you rich. Together we shall make some private arrangement over this picture, no?"

Drioli watched him with slow, apprehensive eyes. "But how can you buy it, Monsieur? What will you do with it when you have bought it? Where will you keep it? Where will you keep it tonight? And where tomorrow?"

"Ah, where will I keep it? Yes, where will I keep it? Now, where will I keep it? Well, now . . ." The dealer stroked the bridge of his nose with a fat white finger. "It would seem," he said, "that if I take the picture, I take you also. That is a disadvantage." He paused and stroked his nose again. "The picture itself is of no value until you are dead. How old are you, my friend?"

"Sixty-one."

"But you are perhaps not very robust, no?" The dealer lowered the hand from his nose and looked Drioli up and down, slowly, like a farmer appraising an old horse.

"I do not like this," Drioli said, edging away. "Quite honestly, Monsieur, I do not like it." He edged straight into the arms of a tall man who put out his hands and caught him gently by the shoulders. Drioli glanced around and apologized. The man smiled down at him, patting one of the old fellow's naked shoulders reassuringly with a hand encased in a canary-colored glove.

"Listen, my friend," the stranger said, still smiling. "Do you like to swim and to bask yourself in the sun?"

Drioli looked up at him, rather startled.

"Do you like fine food and red wine from the great châteaux of Bordeaux?" The man was still smiling, showing strong white teeth with a flash of gold among them. He spoke in a soft coaxing manner, one gloved hand still resting on Drioli's shoulder. "Do you like such things?"

"Well—yes," Drioli answered, still greatly perplexed. "Of course."

"And the company of beautiful women?"

"Why not?"

"And a cupboard full of suits and shirts made to your own personal measurements? It would seem that you are a little lacking for clothes."

Drioli watched this suave man, waiting for the rest of the proposition.

"Have you ever had a shoe constructed especially for your own foot?"

"No."

"You would like that?"

"Well . . ."

"And a man who will shave you in the mornings and trim your hair?"

Drioli simply stood and gaped.

"And a plump attractive girl to manicure the nails of your fingers?"

Someone in the crowd giggled.

"And a bell beside your bed to summon a maid to bring your breakfast in the morning? Would you like these things, my friend? Do they appeal to you?"

Drioli stood still and looked at him.

"You see, I am the owner of the Hotel Bristol in Cannes. I now invite you to come down there and live as my guest for the rest of your life in luxury and comfort." The man paused, allowing his listener time to savor this cheerful prospect.

"Your only duty—shall I call it your pleasure—will be to spend your time on my beach in bathing trunks, walking among my guests, sunning yourself, swimming, drinking cocktails. You would like that?"

There was no answer.

"Don't you see—all the guests will thus be able to observe this fascinating picture by Soutine. You will become famous, and men will say, 'Look, there is the fellow with ten million francs upon his back.' You like this idea, Monsieur? It pleases you?"

Drioli looked up at the tall man in the canary gloves, still wondering whether this was some sort of a joke. "It is a comical idea," he said slowly. "But do you really mean it?"

"Of course I mean it."

"Wait," the dealer interrupted. "See here, old one. Here is the answer to our problem. I will buy the picture, and I will arrange with a surgeon to remove the skin from

your back, and then you will be able to go off on your
own and enjoy the great sum of money I shall give you
for it."

"With no skin on my back?"

"No, no, please! You misunderstand. This surgeon will
put a new piece of skin in the place of the old one. It is
simple."

"Could he do that?"

"There is nothing to it."

"Impossible!" said the man with the canary gloves.
"He's too old for such a major skin-grafting operation. It
would kill him. It would kill you, my friend."

"It would kill me?"

"Naturally. You would never survive. Only the picture
would come through."

"In the name of God!" Drioli cried. He looked around
aghast at the faces of the people watching him, and in the
silence that followed, another man's voice, speaking
quietly from the back of the group, could be heard saying, "Perhaps, if one were to offer this old man enough
money, he might consent to kill himself on the spot. Who
knows?" A few people sniggered. The dealer moved his
feet uneasily on the carpet.

Then the hand in the canary glove was tapping Drioli
again upon the shoulder. "Come on," the man was saying,
smiling his broad white smile. "You and I will go and have
a good dinner and we can talk about it some more while
we eat. How's that? Are you hungry?"

Drioli watched him, frowning. He didn't like the man's

long flexible neck, or the way he craned it forward at you when he spoke, like a snake.

"Roast duck and Chambertin," the man was saying. He put a rich succulent accent on the words, splashing them out with his tongue. "And perhaps a soufflé aux marrons, light and frothy."

Drioli's eyes turned up toward the ceiling, his lips became loose and wet. One could see the poor old fellow beginning literally to drool at the mouth.

"How do you like your duck?" the man went on. "Do you like it very brown and crisp outside, or shall it be . . ."

"I am coming," Drioli said quickly. Already he had picked up his shirt and was pulling it frantically over his head. "Wait for me, Monsieur. I am coming." And within a minute he had disappeared out of the gallery with his new patron.

It wasn't more than a few weeks later that a picture by Soutine, of a woman's head, painted in an unusual manner, nicely framed and heavily varnished, turned up for sale in Buenos Aires. That—and the fact that there is no hotel in Cannes called Bristol—causes one to wonder a little, and to pray for the old man's health, and to hope fervently that wherever he may be at this moment, there is a plump attractive girl to manicure the nails of his fingers, and a maid to bring him his breakfast in bed in the mornings.

POISON

I<small>T</small> must have been around midnight when I drove home, and as I approached the gates of the bungalow I switched off the head-lamps of the car so the beam wouldn't swing in through the window of the side bedroom and wake Harry Pope. But I needn't have bothered. Coming up the drive I noticed his light was still on, so he was awake anyway—unless perhaps he'd dropped off while reading.

I parked the car and went up the five steps to the balcony, counting each step carefully in the dark so I wouldn't take an extra one which wasn't there when I got to the top. I crossed the balcony, pushed through the screen doors into the house itself and switched on the light in the hall. I went across to the door of Harry's room, opened it quietly, and looked in.

He was lying on the bed and I could see he was awake. But he didn't move. He didn't even turn his head toward me, but I heard him say, "Timber, Timber, come here."

He spoke slowly, whispering each word carefully, separately, and I pushed the door right open and started to go quickly across the room.

"Stop. Wait a moment, Timber." I could hardly hear what he was saying. He seemed to be straining enormously to get the words out.

"What's the matter, Harry?"

"Sshhh!" he whispered. "Sshhh! For God's sake don't make a noise. Take your shoes off before you come nearer. *Please* do as I say, Timber."

The way he was speaking reminded me of George Barling after he got shot in the stomach when he stood leaning against a crate containing a spare airplane engine, holding both hands on his stomach and saying things about the German pilot in just the same hoarse straining half whisper Harry was using now.

"Quickly, Timber, but take your shoes off first."

I couldn't understand about taking off the shoes but I figured that if he was as ill as he sounded I'd better humor him, so I bent down and removed the shoes and left them in the middle of the floor. Then I went over to his bed.

"Don't touch the bed! For God's sake don't touch the bed!" He was still speaking like he'd been shot in the stomach and I could see him lying there on his back with a single sheet covering three quarters of his body. He was wearing a pair of pyjamas with blue, brown, and white stripes, and he was sweating terribly. It was a hot night and I was sweating a little myself, but not like Harry. His whole face was wet and the pillow around his head was sodden with moisture. It looked like a bad go of malaria to me.

"What is it, Harry?"

"A krait," he said.

"A *krait*! Oh, my God! Where'd it bite you? How long ago?"

"Shut up," he whispered.

"Listen, Harry," I said, and I leaned forward and touched his shoulder. "We've got to be quick. Come on now, quickly, tell me where it bit you." He was lying there very still and tense as though he were holding on to himself hard because of sharp pain.

"I haven't been bitten," he whispered. "Not yet. It's on my stomach. Lying there asleep."

I took a quick pace backward; I couldn't help it, and I stared at his stomach or rather at the sheet that covered it. The sheet was rumpled in several places and it was impossible to tell if there was anything underneath.

"You don't really mean there's a krait lying on your stomach now?"

"I swear it."

"How did it get there?" I shouldn't have asked the question because it was easy to see he wasn't fooling. I should have told him to keep quiet.

"I was reading," Harry said, and he spoke very slowly, taking each word in turn and speaking it carefully so as not to move the muscles of his stomach. "Lying on my back reading and I felt something on my chest, behind the book. Sort of tickling. Then out of the corner of my eye saw this little krait sliding over my pajamas. Small, about ten inches. Knew I mustn't move. Couldn't have anyway. Lay there watching it. Thought it would go over top of

the sheet." Harry paused and was silent for a few moments. His eyes looked down along his body toward the
place where the sheet covered his stomach, and I could see
he was watching to make sure his whispering wasn't disturbing the thing that lay there.

"There was a fold in the sheet," he said, speaking more
slowly than ever now and so softly I had to lean close to
hear him. "See it, it's still there. It went under that. I
could feel it through my pajamas, moving on my stomach.
Then it stopped moving and now it's lying there in the
warmth. Probably asleep. I've been waiting for you." He
raised his eyes and looked at me.

"How long ago?"

"Hours," he whispered. "Hours and bloody hours and
hours. I can't keep still much longer. I've been wanting to
cough."

There was not much doubt about the truth of Harry's
story. As a matter of fact it wasn't a surprising thing for a
krait to do. They hang around people's houses and they
go for the warm places. The surprising thing was that
Harry hadn't been bitten. The bite is quite deadly except
sometimes when you catch it at once and they kill a fair
number of people each year in Bengal, mostly in the vil-
lages.

"All right, Harry," I said, and now I was whispering
too. "Don't move and don't talk any more unless you have
to. You know it won't bite unless it's frightened. We'll fix
it in no time."

I went softly out of the room in my stocking feet and
fetched a small sharp knife from the kitchen. I put it in

my trouser pocket ready to use instantly in case something went wrong while we were still thinking out a plan. If Harry coughed or moved or did something to frighten the krait and got bitten, I was going to be ready to cut the bitten place and try to suck the venom out. I came back to the bedroom and Harry was still lying there very quiet and sweating all over his face. His eyes followed me as I moved across the room to his bed and I could see he was wondering what I'd been up to. I stood beside him, trying to think of the best thing to do.

"Harry," I said, and now when I spoke I put my mouth almost on his ear so I wouldn't have to raise my voice above the softest whisper, "I think the best thing to do is for me to draw the sheet back very, very gently. Then we could have a look first. I think I could do that without disturbing it."

"Don't be a damn' fool." There was no expression in his voice. He spoke each word too slowly, too carefully, and too softly for that. The expression was in the eyes and around the corners of the mouth.

"Why not?"

"The light would frighten him. It's dark under there now."

"Then how about whipping the sheet back quick and brushing it off before it has time to strike?"

"Why don't you get a doctor?" Harry said. The way he looked at me told me I should have thought of that myself in the first place.

"A doctor. Of course. That's it. I'll get Ganderbai."

I tiptoed out to the hall, looked up Ganderbai's number in the book, lifted the phone and told the operator to hurry.

"Doctor Ganderbai," I said. "This is Timber Woods."

"Hello, Mr. Woods. You not in bed yet?"

"Look, could you come round at once? And bring serum—for a krait bite."

"Who's been bitten?" The question came so sharply it was like a small explosion in my ear.

"No one. No one yet. But Harry Pope's in bed and he's got one lying on his stomach—asleep under the sheet on his stomach."

For about three seconds there was silence on the line. Then speaking slowly, not like an explosion now but slowly, precisely, Ganderbai said, "Tell him to keep quite still. He is not to move or to talk. Do you understand?"

"Of course."

"I'll come at once!" He rang off and I went back to the bedroom. Harry's eyes watched me as I walked across to his bed.

"Ganderbai's coming. He said for you to lie still."

"What in God's name does he think I'm doing!"

"Look, Harry, he said no talking. Absolutely no talking. Either of us."

"Why don't you shut up then?" When he said this, one side of his mouth started twitching with rapid little downward movements that continued for a while after he finished speaking. I took out my handkerchief and very gently I wiped the sweat off his face and neck, and I could feel the slight twitching of the muscle—the one he used for smiling—as my fingers passed over it with the handkerchief.

I slipped out to the kitchen, got some ice from the ice-box, rolled it up in a napkin, and began to crush it small. That business of the mouth, I didn't like that. Or the way he talked, either. I carried the ice pack back to the bedroom and laid it across Harry's forehead.

"Keep you cool."

He screwed up his eyes and drew breath sharply through his teeth. "Take it away," he whispered. "Make me cough." His smiling-muscle began to twitch again.

The beam of a head-lamp shone through the window as Ganderbai's car swung around to the front of the bungalow. I went out to meet him, holding the ice pack with both hands.

"How is it?" Ganderbai asked, but he didn't stop to talk; he walked on past me across the balcony and through the screen doors into the hall. "Where is he? Which room?"

He put his bag down on a chair in the hall and followed me into Harry's room. He was wearing soft-soled bedroom slippers and he walked across the floor noiselessly, delicately, like a careful cat. Harry watched him out of the sides of his eyes. When Ganderbai reached the bed he looked down at Harry and smiled, confident and reassuring, nodding his head to tell Harry it was a simple matter and he was not to worry but just to leave it to Doctor Ganderbai. Then he turned and went back to the hall and I followed him.

"First thing is to try to get some serum into him," he said, and he opened his bag and started to make preparations. "Intravenously. But I must do it neatly. Don't want to make him flinch."

We went into the kitchen and he sterilized a needle. He had a hypodermic syringe in one hand and a small bottle in the other and he stuck the needle through the rubber top of the bottle and began drawing a pale yellow liquid up into the syringe by pulling out the plunger. Then he handed the syringe to me.

"Hold that till I ask for it."

He picked up the bag and together we returned to the room. Harry's eyes were bright now and wide open. Ganderbai bent over Harry and very cautiously, like a man handling sixteenth-century lace, he rolled up the pyjama sleeve to the elbow without moving the arm. I noticed he stood well away from the bed.

He whispered, "I'm going to give you an injection. Serum. Just a prick but try not to move. Don't tighten your stomach muscles. Let them go limp."

Harry looked at the syringe.

Ganderbai took a piece of red rubber tubing from his bag and slid one end under and up and around Harry's bicep; then he tied the tubing tight with a knot. He sponged a small area of the bare forearm with alcohol, handed the swab to me and took the syringe from my hand. He held it up to the light, squinting at the calibrations, squirting out some of the yellow fluid. I stood still beside him, watching. Harry was watching too and sweating all over his face so it shone like it was smeared thick with face cream melting on his skin and running down onto the pillow.

I could see the blue vein on the inside of Harry's forearm, swollen now because of the tourniquet, and then I saw the needle above the vein, Ganderbai holding the syringe almost flat against the arm, sliding the needle in sideways through the skin into the blue vein, sliding it slowly but so firmly it went in smooth as into cheese. Harry looked at the ceiling and closed his eyes and opened them again but he didn't move.

When it was finished Ganderbai leaned forward putting his mouth close to Harry's ear. "Now you'll be all right even if you *are* bitten. But don't move. Please don't move. I'll be back in a moment."

He picked up his bag and went out to the hall and I followed.

"Is he safe now?" I asked.

"No."

"How safe is he?"

The little Indian doctor stood there in the hall rubbing his lower lip.

"It must give some protection, mustn't it?" I asked.

He turned away and walked to the screen doors that led onto the veranda. I thought he was going through them but he stopped this side of the doors and stood looking out into the night.

"Isn't the serum very good?" I asked.

"Unfortunately not," he answered without turning round. "It might save him. It might not. I am trying to think of something else to do."

"Shall we draw the sheet back quick and brush it off before it has time to strike?"

"Never! We are not entitled to take a risk." He spoke sharply and his voice was pitched a little higher than usual.

"We can't very well leave him lying there," I said. "He's getting nervous."

"Please! Please!" he said, turning round, holding both hands up in the air. "Not so fast, please. This is not a matter to rush into bald-headed." He wiped his forehead with his handkerchief and stood there, frowning, nibbling his lip.

"You see," he said at last. "There is a way to do this. You know what we must do—we must administer an anesthetic to the creature where it lies."

It was a splendid idea.

"It is not safe," he continued, "because a snake is cold-blooded and anesthetic does not work so well or so quick with such animals, but it is better than any other thing to do. We could use ether . . . chloroform . . ." He was speaking slowly and trying to think the thing out while he talked.

"Which shall we use?"

"Chloroform," he said suddenly. "Ordinary chloroform. That is best. Now quick!" He took my arm and pulled me toward the balcony. "Drive to my house! By the time you get there I will have waked up my boy on the telephone and he will show you my poisons cupboard. Here is the key of the cupboard. Take a bottle of chloroform. It has an orange label and the name is printed on it. I stay here in case anything happens. Be quick now, hurry! No, no, you don't need your shoes!"

I drove fast and in about fifteen minutes I was back with the bottle of chloroform. Ganderbai came out of Harry's room and met me in the hall. "You got it?" he said. "Good, good. I just been telling him what we are going to do. But now we must hurry. It is not easy for him in there like that all this time. I am afraid he might move."

He went back to the bedroom and I followed, carrying the bottle carefully with both hands. Harry was lying on the bed in precisely the same position as before with the sweat pouring down his cheeks. His face was white and wet. He turned his eyes toward me and I smiled at him and nodded confidently. He continued to look at me. I raised my thumb, giving him the okay signal. He closed his eyes. Ganderbai was squatting down by the bed, and on the floor beside him was the hollow rubber tube that he had previously used as a tourniquet, and he'd got a small paper funnel fitted into one end of the tube.

He began to pull a little piece of the sheet out from under the mattress. He was working directly in line with Harry's stomach, about eighteen inches from it, and I watched his fingers as they tugged gently at the edge of the sheet. He worked so slowly it was almost impossible to discern any movement either in his fingers or in the sheet that was being pulled.

Finally he succeeded in making an opening under the sheet and he took the rubber tube and inserted one end of it in the opening so that it would slide under the sheet along the mattress toward Harry's body. I do not know how long it took him to slide that tube in a few inches. It may have been twenty minutes, it may have been forty. I never once saw the tube move. I knew it was going in because the visible part of it grew gradually shorter, but I doubted that the krait could have felt even the faintest vibration. Ganderbai himself was sweating now, large pearls of sweat standing out all over his forehead and along his upper lip. But his hands were steady and I noticed that his eyes were watching, not the tube in his hands, but the area of crumpled sheet above Harry's stomach.

Without looking up, he held out a hand to me for the chloroform. I twisted out the ground-glass stopper and put the bottle right into his hand, not letting go till I was sure he had a good hold on it. Then he jerked his head for me to come closer and he whispered, "Tell him I'm going to soak the mattress and that it will be very cold under his body. He must be ready for that and he must not move. Tell him now."

I bent over Harry and passed on the message.

"Why doesn't he get on with it?" Harry said.

"He's going to now, Harry. But it'll feel very cold, so be ready for it."

"Oh, God Almighty, get on, get on!" For the first time he raised his voice, and Ganderbai glanced up sharply, watched him for a few seconds, then went back to his business.

Ganderbai poured a few drops of chloroform into the paper funnel and waited while it ran down the tube. Then he poured some more. Then he waited again, and the heavy sickening smell of chloroform spread out over the room bringing with it faint unpleasant memories of white-coated nurses and white surgeons standing in a white room around a long white table. Ganderbai was pouring steadily now and I could see the heavy vapor of the chloroform swirling slowly like smoke above the paper funnel. He paused, held the bottle up to the light, poured one more funnelful and handed the bottle back to me. Slowly he drew out the rubber tube from under the sheet; then he stood up.

The strain of inserting the tube and pouring the chloroform must have been great, and I recollect that when Ganderbai turned and whispered to me, his voice was small and tired. "We'll give it fifteen minutes. Just to be safe."

I leaned over to tell Harry. "We're going to give it fifteen minutes, just to be safe. But it's probably done for already."

"Then why for God's sake don't you look and see!" Again he spoke loudly and Ganderbai sprang round, his small brown face suddenly very angry. He had almost pure black eyes and he stared at Harry and Harry's smiling-muscle started to twitch. I took my handkerchief and wiped his wet face, trying to stroke his forehead a little for comfort as I did so.

Then we stood and waited beside the bed, Ganderbai watching Harry's face all the time in a curious intense manner. The little Indian was concentrating all his will power on keeping Harry quiet. He never once took his eyes from the patient and although he made no sound, he seemed somehow to be shouting at him all the time, saying: Now listen, you've got to listen, you're not going to go spoiling this now, d'you hear me; and Harry lay there twitching his mouth, sweating, closing his eyes, opening them, looking at me, at the sheet, at the ceiling, at me again, but never at Ganderbai. Yet somehow Ganderbai was holding him. The smell of chloroform was oppressive and it made me feel sick, but I couldn't leave the room now. I had the feeling someone was blowing up a huge balloon and I could see it was going to burst but I couldn't look away.

At length Ganderbai turned and nodded and I knew he was ready to proceed. "You go over to the other side of the bed," he said. "We will each take one side of the sheet and draw it back together, but very slowly please, and very quietly."

"Keep still now, Harry," I said and I went around to the other side of the bed and took hold of the sheet. Ganderbai stood opposite me, and together we began to draw back the sheet, lifting it up clear of Harry's body, taking it back very slowly, both of us standing well away but at the same time bending forward, trying to peer underneath it. The smell of chloroform was awful. I remember trying to hold my breath and when I couldn't do that any longer I tried to breathe shallow so the stuff wouldn't get into my lungs.

The whole of Harry's chest was visible now, or rather the striped pyjama top which covered it, and then I saw the white cord of his pyjama trousers, neatly tied in a bow. A little farther and I saw a button, a mother-of-pearl button, and that was something I had never had on my pyjamas, a fly button, let alone a mother-of-pearl one. This Harry, I thought, he is very refined. It is odd how one sometimes has frivolous thoughts at exciting moments, and I distinctly remember thinking about Harry being very refined when I saw that button.

Apart from the button there was nothing on his stomach.

We pulled the sheet back faster then, and when we had uncovered his legs and feet we let the sheet drop over the end of the bed onto the floor.

"Don't move," Ganderbai said, "don't move, Mr. Pope"; and he began to peer around along the side of Harry's body and under his legs.

"We must be careful," he said. "It may be anywhere. It could be up the leg of his pyjamas."

When Ganderbai said this, Harry quickly raised his head from the pillow and looked down at his legs. It was the first time he had moved. Then suddenly he jumped up, stood on his bed and shook his legs one after the other violently in the air. At that moment we both thought he had been bitten and Ganderbai was already reaching down into his bag for a scalpel and a tourniquet when Harry ceased his caperings and stood still and looked at the mattress he was standing on and shouted, "It's not there!"

Ganderbai straightened up and for a moment he too looked at the mattress; then he looked up at Harry. Harry was all right. He hadn't been bitten and now he wasn't going to get bitten and he wasn't going to be killed and everything was fine. But that didn't seem to make anyone feel any better.

"Mr. Pope, you are of course *quite* sure you saw it in the first place?" There was a note of sarcasm in Ganderbai's voice that he would never have employed in ordinary circumstances. "You don't think you might possibly have been dreaming, do you, Mr. Pope?" The way Ganderbai was looking at Harry, I realized that the sarcasm was not seriously intended. He was only easing up a bit after the strain.

Harry stood on his bed in his striped pyjamas, glaring at Ganderbai, and the color began to spread out over his cheeks.

"Are you telling me I'm a liar?" he shouted.

Ganderbai remained absolutely still, watching Harry. Harry took a pace forward on the bed and there was a shining look in his eyes."

"Why, you dirty little Hindu sewer rat!"

"Shut up, Harry!" I said.

"You dirty black—"

"Harry!" I called. "Shut up, Harry!" It was terrible, the things he was saying.

Ganderbai went out of the room as though neither of us was there and I followed him and put my arm around his shoulder as he walked across the hall and out onto the balcony.

"Don't you listen to Harry," I said. "This thing's made him so he doesn't know what he's saying."

We went down the steps from the balcony to the drive

and across the drive in the darkness to where his old Morris car was parked. He opened the door and got in.

"You did a wonderful job," I said. "Thank you so very much for coming."

"All he needs is a good holiday," he said quietly, without looking at me, then he started the engine and drove off.

THE WISH

UNDER the palm of one hand the child became aware of the scab of an old cut on his knee-cap. He bent forward to examine it closely. A scab was always a fascinating thing; it presented a special challenge he was never able to resist.

Yes, he thought, I will pick it off, even if it isn't ready, even if the middle of it sticks, even if it hurts like anything.

With a fingernail he began to explore cautiously around the edges of the scab. He got the nail underneath it, and when he raised it, but ever so slightly, it suddenly came off, the whole hard brown scab came off beautifully, leaving an interesting little circle of smooth red skin.

Nice. Very nice indeed. He rubbed the circle and it didn't hurt. He picked up the scab, put it on his thigh and flipped it with a finger so that it flew away and landed on the edge of the carpet, the enormous red and black and yellow carpet that stretched the whole length of the hall from the stairs on which he sat to the front door in the distance. A tremendous carpet. Bigger than the tennis lawn. Much bigger than that. He regarded it gravely, settling his eyes upon it with mild pleasure. He had never really noticed it before, but now, all of a sudden, the colours seemed to brighten mysteriously and spring out at him in a most dazzling way.

You see, he told himself, I know how it is. The red parts of the carpet are red-hot lumps of coal. What I must do is this: I must walk all the way along it to the front door without touching them. If I touch the red I will be burnt. As a matter of fact, I will be burnt up completely. And the black parts of the carpet . . . . . yes, the black parts are snakes, poisonous snakes, adders mostly, and co-bras, thick like tree-trunks round the middle, and if I touch one of *them*, I'll be bitten and I'll die before tea time. And if I get across safely, without being burnt and without being bitten, I will be given a puppy for my birthday tomorrow.

He got to his feet and climbed higher up the stairs to obtain a better view of this vast tapestry of colour and death. Was it possible? Was there enough yellow? Yellow was the only colour he was allowed to walk on. Could it be done? This was not a journey to be undertaken lightly; the risks were too great for that. The child's face—a fringe of white-gold hair, two large blue eyes, a small pointed chin—peered down anxiously over the banisters. The yellow was a bit thin in places and there were one or two widish gaps, but it did seem to go all the way along to the other end. For someone who had only yesterday triumphantly travelled the whole length of the brick path from the stables to the summer-house without touching the cracks, this carpet thing should not be too difficult. Except for the snakes. The mere thought of snakes sent a fine electricity of fear running like pins down the backs of his legs and under the soles of his feet.

He came slowly down the stairs and advanced to the edge of the carpet. He extended one small sandaled foot and placed it cautiously upon a patch of yellow. Then he brought the other foot up, and there was just enough room for him to stand with the two feet together. There! He had started! His bright oval face was curiously intent, a shade whiter perhaps than before, and he was holding his arms out sideways to assist his balance. He took another step, lifting his foot high over a patch of black, aiming carefully with his toe for a narrow channel of yellow on the other side. When he had completed the second step he paused to rest, standing very stiff and still. The narrow channel of yellow ran forward unbroken for at least five yards and he advanced gingerly along it, bit by bit, as though walking a tight-rope. Where it finally curled off sideways, he had to take another long stride, this time over a vicious looking mixture of black and red. Halfway across he began to wobble. He waved his arms around wildly, windmill fashion, to keep his balance, and he got across safely and rested again on the other side. He was quite breathless now, and so tense he stood high on his toes all the time, arms out sideways, fists clenched. He was on a big safe island of yellow. There was lots of room on it, he couldn't possibly fall off, and he stood there resting.

hesitating, waiting, wishing he could stay for ever on this big safe yellow island. But the fear of not getting the puppy compelled him to go on.

Step by step, he edged further ahead, and between each one he paused to decide exactly where next he should put his foot. Once, he had a choice of ways, either to left or right, and he chose the left because although it seemed the more difficult, there was not so much black in that direction. The black was what made him nervous. He glanced quickly over his shoulder to see how far he had come. Nearly halfway. There could be no turning back now. He was in the middle and he couldn't turn back and he couldn't jump off sideways either because it was too far, and when he looked at all the red and all the black that lay ahead of him, he felt that old sudden sickening surge of panic in his chest—like last Easter time, that afternoon when he got lost all alone in the darkest part of Piper's Wood.

He took another step, placing his foot carefully upon the only little piece of yellow within reach, and this time the point of the foot came within a centimetre of some black. It wasn't touching the black, he could see it wasn't touching, he could see the small line of yellow separating the toe of his sandal from the black; but the snake stirred as though sensing the nearness, and raised its head and gazed at the foot with bright beady eyes, watching to see if it was going to touch.

"*I'm not touching you! You mustn't bite me! You know I'm not touching you!*"

Another snake slid up noiselessly beside the first, raised

its head, two heads now, two pairs of eyes staring at the foot, gazing at a little naked place just below the sandal strap where the skin showed through. The child went high up on his toes and stayed there, frozen stiff with terror. It was minutes before he dared to move again.

The next step would have to be a really long one. There was this deep curling river of black that ran clear across the width of the carpet, and he was forced by his position to cross it at its widest part. He thought first of trying to jump it, but decided he couldn't be sure of landing accurately on the narrow band of yellow the other side. He took a deep breath, lifted one foot, and inch by inch he pushed it out in front of him, far far out, then down and down until at last the tip of his sandal was across and resting safely on the edge of the yellow. He leaned forward, transferring his weight to this front foot. Then he tried to bring the back foot up as well. He strained and pulled and jerked his body, but the legs were too wide apart and he couldn't make it. He tried to get back again. He couldn't do that either. He was doing the splits and he was properly stuck. He glanced down and saw this deep curling river of black underneath him. Parts of it were stirring now, and uncoiling and sliding and beginning to shine with a dreadful oily glister. He wobbled, waved his arms frantically to keep his balance, but that seemed to make it worse. He was starting to go over. He was going over to the right, quite slowly he was going over, then faster and faster, and at the last moment, instinctively he put out a hand to break the fall and the next thing he saw was this bare hand of his going right into the middle of a great glistening mass of black and he gave one piercing cry of terror as it touched.

Outside in the sunshine, far away behind the house, the mother was looking for her son.

NECK

WHEN, about eight years ago, old Sir William Turton died and his son Basil inherited "The Turton Press" (as well as the title), I can remember how they started laying bets around Fleet Street as to just how long it would be before some nice young woman managed to persuade the little fellow that she must look after him. That is to say, him and his money.

The new Sir Basil Turton was maybe forty years old at the time, a bachelor, a man of mild and simple character who up to then had shown no interest in anything at all except his collection of modern paintings and sculpture. No woman had disturbed him; no scandal or gossip had ever touched his name. But now that he had become the proprietor of quite a large newspaper and magazine empire, it was necessary for him to emerge from the calm of his father's country house and come up to London.

Naturally, the vultures started gathering at once, and I believe that not only Fleet Street but very nearly the whole of the city was looking on eagerly as they scrambled for the body. It was slow motion, of course, deliberate and deadly slow motion, and therefore not so much like vultures as a bunch of agile crabs clawing for a piece of horsemeat under water.

But to everyone's surprise the little chap proved to to remarkably elusive, and the chase dragged on right through the spring and early summer of that year. I did not know Sir Basil personally, nor did I have any reason to feel friendly toward him, but I couldn't help taking the side of my own sex and found myself cheering loudly every time he managed to get himself off the hook.

Then, round about the beginning of August, apparently at some secret female signal, the girls declared a sort of truce among themselves while they went abroad, and rested, and regrouped, and made fresh plans for the winter kill. This was a mistake because precisely at that moment a dazzling creature called Natalia something or other, who nobody had heard of before, swept in from the Continent, took Sir Basil firmly by the wrist and led him off in a kind of swoon to the Registry Office at Caxton Hall where she married him before anyone else, least of all the bridegroom, realized what was happening.

You can imagine that the London ladies were indignant, and naturally they started disseminating a vast amount of fruity gossip about the new Lady Turton ("That dirty poacher," they called her). But we don't have to go into that. In fact, for the purposes of this story we can skip the next six years, which brings us right up to the present, to an occasion exactly one week ago today when I myself had the pleasure of meeting her ladyship for the first time. By now, as you must have guessed, she was not only running the whole of "The Turton Press," but as a result had become a considerable political force in the country. I realize that other women have done this sort of thing before, but what made her particular case unusual was the fact that she was a foreigner and that nobody seemed to know precisely what country she came from, Yugoslavia, Bulgaria, or Russia.

So last Thursday I went to this small dinner party at a friend's in London, and while we were standing around in the drawing-room before the meal, sipping good martinis and talking about the atom bomb and Mr. Bevan, the maid popped her head in to announce the last guest.

"Lady Turton," she said.

Nobody stopped talking; we were too well-mannered for that. No heads were turned. Only our eyes swung round to the door, waiting for the entrance.

She came in fast—tall and slim in a red-gold dress with sparkles on it—the mouth smiling, the hand outstretched toward her hostess, and my heavens, I must say she was a beauty.

"Mildred, good evening!"

"My dear Lady Turton! How nice!"

I believe we *did* stop talking then, and we turned and stared and stood waiting quite meekly to be introduced, just like she might have been the queen or a famous filmstar. But she was better looking than either of those. The hair was black, and to go with it she had one of those pale, oval, innocent fifteenth-century Flemish faces, almost exactly a Madonna by Memling or Van Eyck. At least that was the first impression. Later, when my turn came to shake hands, I got a closer look and saw that except for the outline and colouring it wasn't really a Madonna at all —far, far from it.

The nostrils for example were very odd, somehow more open, more flaring than any I had seen before, and excessively arched. This gave the whole nose a kind of open, snorting look that had something of the wild animal about it—the mustang.

And the eyes, when I saw them close, were not wide and round the way the Madonna painters used to make them, but long and half closed, half smiling, half sullen, and slightly vulgar, so that in one way and another they gave her a most delicately dissipated air. What's more, they didn't look at you directly. They came to you slowly from over on one side with a curious sliding motion that made me nervous. I tried to see their colour, thought it was pale grey, but couldn't be sure.

Then she was led away across the room to meet other people. I stood watching her. She was clearly conscious of her success and of the way these Londoners were deferring to her. "Here am I," she seemed to be saying, "and I only came over a few years ago, but already I am richer and more powerful than any of you." There was a little prance of triumph in her walk.

A few minutes later we went in to dinner, and to my surprise I found myself seated on her ladyship's right. I presumed that our hostess had done this as a kindness to me, thinking I might pick up some material for the social column I write each day in the evening paper, and I settled myself down ready for an interesting meal. But the famous lady took no notice of me at all; she spent her time talking to the man on her left, the host. Until at last, just as I was finishing my ice-cream, she suddenly turned, reached over, picked up my place card and read the name. Then, with that queer sliding motion of the eyes she looked into my face. I smiled and made a little bow. She didn't smile back, but started shooting questions at me, rather personal questions—job, age, family, things like that —in a peculiar lapping voice, and I found myself answering as best I could.

During this inquisition it came out among other things that I was a lover of painting and sculpture.

"Then you should come down to the country some time and see my husband's collection." She said it casually, merely as a form of conversation, but you must realize that in my job I cannot afford to lose an opportunity like this.

"How kind of you, Lady Turton. But I'd simply love to. When shall I come?"

Her head went up and she hesitated, frowned, shrugged her shoulders, and then said, "Oh, I don't care. Any time."

"How about this next week-end? Would that be all right?"

The slow narrow eyes rested a moment on mine, then travelled away. "I suppose so, if you wish. I don't care."

And that was how on the following Saturday afternoon I came to be driving down to Wooton with my suitcase in the back of the car. You may think that perhaps I forced the invitation a bit, but I couldn't have gotten it any other way. And apart from the professional aspect, I personally wanted very much to see the house. As you know, Wooton is one of the truly great stone houses of the early English Renaissance. Like its sisters, Longleat, Wollaton, and Montacute, it was built in the latter half of the sixteenth century when for the first time a great man's house could be designed as a comfortable dwelling, not as a castle, and when a new group of architects such as John Thorpe and the Smithsons were starting to do marvellous things all over the country. It lies south of Oxford, near a small town called Princes Risborough—not a long trip from London—and as I swung in through the main gates the sky was closing overhead and the early winter evening was beginning.

I went slowly up the long drive, trying to see as much of the grounds as possible, especially the famous topiary which I had heard such a lot about. And I must say it was an impressive sight. On all sides there were massive yew trees, trimmed and clipped into many different comical shapes—hens, pigeons, bottles, boots, arm-chairs, castles, egg-cups, lanterns, old women with flaring petticoats, tall pillars, some crowned with a ball, others with big rounded roofs and stemless mushroom finials—and in the half dark-ness the greens had turned to black so that each figure, each tree, took on a dark, smooth, sculptural quality. At one point I saw a lawn covered with gigantic chess-men, each a live yew tree, marvellously fashioned. I stopped the car, got out and walked among them, and they were twice as tall as me. What's more, the set was complete, kings, queens, bishops, knights, rooks and pawns, standing in position as for the start of a game.

Around the next bend I saw the great gray house itself, and in front of it the large entrance forecourt enclosed by a high balustraded wall with small pillared pavilions at its outer angles. The piers of the balustrades were surmounted by stone obelisks—the Italian influence on the Tudor mind—and a flight of steps at least a hundred feet wide led up to the house.

As I drove into the forecourt I noticed with rather a shock that the fountain basin in the middle supported a large statue by Epstein. A lovely thing, mind you, but surely not quite in sympathy with its surroundings. Then, looking back as I climbed the stairway to the front door, I saw that on all the little lawns and terraces round about there were other modern statues and many kinds of curious sculpture. In the distance, I thought I recognized Gaudier Breska, Brancusi, Saint-Gaudens, Henry Moore, and Epstein again.

The door was opened by a young footman who led me up to a bedroom on the first floor. Her ladyship, he explained, was resting, so were the other guests, but they would all be down in the main drawing-room in an hour or so, dressed for dinner.

Now in my job it is necessary to do a lot of week-ending. I suppose I spend around fifty Saturdays and Sundays a year in other peoples' houses, and as a result I have become fairly sensitive to unfamiliar atmospheres. I can tell good or bad almost by sniffing with my nose the moment I get in the front door; and this one I was in now I did not

like. The place smelled wrong. There was the faint, des-
sicated whiff of something troublesome in the air; I was
conscious of it even as I lay steaming luxuriously in my
great marble bath; and I couldn't help hoping that no unpleasant things were going to happen before Monday
came.

The first of them—though more of a surprise than an
unpleasantness—occurred ten minutes later. I was sitting
on the bed putting on my socks when softly the door
opened, and an ancient lopsided gnome in black tails slid
into the room. He was the butler, he explained, and his
name was Jelks, and he did so hope I was comfortable and
had everything I wanted.

I told him I was and had.

He said he would do all he could to make my week-end
agreeable. I thanked him and waited for him to go. He
hesitated, and then, in a voice dripping with unction, he
begged permission to mention a rather delicate matter. I
told him to go ahead.

To be quite frank, he said, it was about tipping. The
whole business of tipping made him acutely miserable.

Oh? And why was that?

Well, if I really wanted to know, he didn't like the idea
that his guests felt under an obligation to tip him when
they left the house—as indeed they did. It was an undignified proceeding both for the tipper and the tipped.
Moreover, he was well aware of the anguish that was often created in the minds of guests such as myself, if I
would pardon the liberty, who might feel compelled by
convention to give more than they could really afford.

He paused, and two small crafty eyes watching my face for a sign. I murmured that he needn't worry himself about such things so far as I was concerned.

On the contrary, he said, he hoped sincerely that I would agree from the beginning to give him no tip at all.

"Well," I said. "Let's not fuss about it now, and when the time comes we'll see how we feel."

"No, sir!" he cried. "Please, I really must insist."

So I agreed.

He thanked me, and shuffled a step or two closer. Then, laying his head on one side and clasping his hands before him like a priest, he gave a tiny apologetic shrug of the shoulders. The small sharp eyes were still watching me, and I waited, one sock on, the other in my hands, trying to guess what was coming next.

All that he would ask, he said softly, so softly now that his voice was like music heard faintly in the street outside a great concert hall, all that he would ask was that instead of a tip I should give him thirty-three and a third percent of my winnings at cards over the week-end. If I lost, there would be nothing to pay.

It was all so soft and smooth and sudden that I was not even surprised.

"Do they play a lot of cards, Jelks?"

"Yes, sir, a great deal."

"Isn't thirty-three and a third a bit steep?"

"I don't think so, sir."

"I'll give you ten percent."

"No, sir, I couldn't do that." He was now examining the finger-nails of his left hand, and patiently frowning.

"Then we'll make it fifteen. All right?"

"Thirty-three and a third, sir. It's very reasonable. After all, sir, seeing that I don't even know if you are a good player, what I'm actually doing, not meaning to be personal, is backing a horse and I've never even seen it run."

No doubt you think that I should never have started bargaining with the butler in the first place, and perhaps you are right. But being a liberal-minded person, I always try my best to be affable with the lower classes. Apart from that, the more I thought about it, the more I had to admit to myself that it was an offer no sportsman had the right to reject.

"All right then, Jelks. As you wish."

"Thank you, sir." He moved toward the door, walking slowly sideways like a crab; but once more he hesitated, a hand on the knob. "If I may give you a little advice, sir —may I?"

"Yes?"

"It's simply that her ladyship tends to overbid her hand."

Now *this was* going too far. I was so startled I dropped my sock. After all, it's one thing to have a harmless little sporting arrangement with the butler about tipping, but when he begins conniving with you to take money away from the hostess then it's time to call a halt.

"All right Jelks. Now that'll do."

"No offense, sir, I hope. All I mean is you're bound to be playing against her ladyship. She always partners Major Haddock."

"Major Haddock? You mean Major Jack Haddock?"

"Yes, sir."

I noticed there was the trace of a sneer around the corners of Jelks's nose when he spoke about this man. And it was worse with Lady Turton. Each time he said "her ladyship" he spoke the words with the outsides of his lips as though he were nibbling a lemon, and there was a subtle, mocking inflection in his voice.

"You'll excuse me now, sir. *Her ladyship* will be down at seven o'clock. So will *Major Haddock* and the others." He slipped out the door leaving behind him a certain dampness in the room and a faint smell of embrocation.

Shortly after seven, I found my way to the main drawing-room, and Lady Turton, as beautiful as ever, got up to greet me.

"I wasn't even sure you were coming," she said in that peculiar lilting voice. "What's your name again?"

"I'm afraid I took you at your word, Lady Turton. I hope it's all right."

"Why not?" she said. "There's forty-seven bedrooms in the house. This is my husband."

A small man came around the back of her and said, "You know, I'm so glad you were able to come." He had a lovely warm smile and when he took my hand I felt instantly a touch of friendship in his fingers.

"And Carmen La Rosa," Lady Turton said.

This was a powerfully built woman who looked as though she might have something to do with horses. She nodded at me, and although my hand was already halfway out she didn't give me hers, thus forcing me to convert the movement into a noseblow.

"You have a cold?" she said. "I'm sorry."

I did not like Miss Carmen La Rosa.

"And this is Jack Haddock."

I knew this man slightly. He was a director of companies (whatever that may mean), and a well-known member of society. I had used his name a few times in my column, but I had never liked him, and this I think was mainly because I have a deep suspicion of all people who carry their military titles back with them into private life —especially majors and colonels. Standing there in his dinner-jacket with his full-blooded animal face and black eyebrows and large white teeth, he looked so handsome there was almost something indecent about it. He had a way of raising his upper lip when he smiled, baring the teeth, and he was smiling now as he gave me a hairy brown hand.

"I hope you're going to say some nice things about us in your column."

"He better had," Lady Turton said, "or I'll say some nasty ones about him on my front page."

I laughed, but the three of them, Lady Turton, Major Haddock, and Carmen La Rosa had already turned away and were settling themselves back in the sofa. Jelks gave me a drink, and Sir Basil drew me gently aside for a quiet chat at the other end of the room. Every now and again Lady Turton would call to her husband to fetch her something—another martini, a cigarette, an ashtray, a handkerchief—and he, half rising from his chair, would be forestalled by the watchful Jelks who fetched it for him.

Clearly, Jelks loved his master; and just as clearly he hated the wife. Each time he did something for her he made a little sneer with his nose and drew his lips together so they puckered like a turkey's bottom.

At dinner, our hostess sat her two friends, Haddock and La Rosa, on either side of her. This unconventional arrangement left Sir Basil and me at the other end of the table where we were able to continue our pleasant talk about painting and sculpture. Of course it was obvious to me by now that the Major was infatuated with her ladyship. And again, although I hate to say it, it seemed as though the La Rosa woman was hunting the same bird.

All this foolishness appeared to delight the hostess. But it did not delight her husband. I could see that he was conscious of the little scene all the time we were talking; and often his mind would wander from our subject and he would stop short in mid-sentence, his eyes travelling down to the other end of the table to settle pathetically for a moment on that lovely head with the black hair and the curiously flaring nostrils. He must have noticed then how exhilarated she was, how the hand that gestured as she spoke rested every now and again on the Major's arm, and how the other woman, the one who perhaps had something to do with horses, kept saying "Nata-*li*-a! Now Nata-*li*-a, listen to me!"

"Tomorrow," I said, "you must take me round and show me the sculptures you've put up in the garden."

"Of course," he said, "with pleasure." He glanced again at the wife, and his eyes had a sort of supplicating look that was piteous beyond words. He was so mild and passive a man in every way that even now I could see there was no anger in him, no danger, no chance of an explosion.

After dinner I was ordered straight to the card table to partner Miss Carmen La Rosa against Major Haddock and Lady Turton. Sir Basil sat quietly on the sofa with a book.

There was nothing unusual about the game itself; it was routine and rather dull. But Jelks was a nuisance. All evening he prowled around us, emptying ashtrays and asking about drinks and peering at our hands. He was obviously short-sighted and I doubt he saw much of what was going on because as you may or may not know, here in England no butler has ever been permitted to wear spectacles— nor, for that matter, a moustache. This is the golden, unbreakable rule, and a very sensible one it is too, although I'm not quite sure what lies behind it. I presume that a moustache would make him look too much like a gentleman, and spectacles too much like an American, and where would we be then I should like to know? In any event Jelks was a nuisance all evening; and so was Lady Turton who was constantly being called to the phone on newspaper business.

At eleven o'clock she looked up from her cards and said, "Basil, it's time you went to bed."

"Yes, my dear, perhaps it is." He closed the book, got up, and stood for a minute watching the play. "Are you having a good game?" he asked.

The others didn't answer him, so I said, "It's a nice game."

"I'm so glad. And Jelks will look after you and get any-thing you want."

"Jelks can go to bed too," the wife said.

I could hear Major Haddock breathing through his nose beside me, and the soft drop of the cards one by one onto the table, and then the sound of Jelks's feet shuffling over the carpet toward us.

"You wouldn't prefer me to stay, m'lady?"

"No. Go to bed. You too, Basil."

"Yes, my dear. Goodnight. Goodnight all."

Jelks opened the door for him, and he went slowly out followed by the butler.

As soon as the next rubber was over, I said that I too wanted to go to bed.

"All right," Lady Turton said. "Goodnight."

I went up to my room, locked the door, took a pill, and went to sleep.

The next morning, Sunday, I got up and dressed around ten o'clock and went down to the breakfast room. Sir Basil was there before me, and Jelks was serving him with grilled kidneys and bacon and fried tomatoes. He was de-lighted to see me and suggested that as soon as we had finished eating we should take a long walk around the grounds. I told him nothing would give me more pleasure.

Half an hour later we started out, and you've no idea what a relief it was to get away from that house and into the open air. It was one of those warm shining days that come occasionally in midwinter after a night of heavy rain, with a bright surprising sun and no breath of wind.

Bare trees seemed beautiful in the sunlight, water still drip-dripping from the branches, and wet places all around were sparkling with diamonds. The sky had small faint clouds.

"*What* a lovely day!"

"Yes—isn't it a lovely day!"

We spoke hardly another word during the walk; it wasn't necessary. But he took me everywhere and I saw it all—the huge chess-men and all the rest of the topiary. The elaborate garden houses, the pools, the fountains, the children's maze whose hedges were hornbeam and lime so that it was only good in summer when the leaves were out, and the parterres, the rockeries, the greenhouses with their vines and nectarine trees. And of course, the sculpture. Most of the contemporary European sculptors were there, in bronze, granite, limestone, and wood; and although it was a pleasure to see them warming and glowing in the sun, to me they still looked a trifle out of place in these vast formal surroundings.

"Shall we rest here now a little while?" Sir Basil said after we had walked for more than an hour. So we sat down on a white bench beside a water-lily pond full of carp and goldfish, and lit cigarettes. We were some way from the house, on a piece of ground that was raised above its surroundings, and from where we sat the gardens were spread out below us like a drawing in one of those old books on garden architecture, with the hedges and lawns and terraces and fountains making a pretty pattern of squares and rings.

"My father bought this place just before I was born,"

Sir Basil said. "I've lived here ever since, and I know every inch of it. Each day I grow to love it more."

"It must be wonderful in summer."

"Oh, but it is. You should come down and see it in May and June. Will you promise to do that?"

"Of course," I said. "I'd love to come," and as I spoke I was watching the figure of a woman dressed in red moving among the flower-beds in the far distance. I saw her cross over a wide expanse of lawn, and there was a lilt in her walk, a little shadow attending her, and when she was over the lawn, she turned left and went along one side of a high wall of clipped yew until she came to another smaller lawn that was circular and had in its centre a piece of sculpture.

"This garden is younger than the house," Sir Basil said. "It was laid out early in the eighteenth century by a Frenchman called Beaumont, the same fellow who did Levens, in Westmoreland. For at least a year he had two hundred and fifty men working on it."

The woman in the red dress had been joined now by a man, and they were standing face to face, about a yard apart, in the very centre of the whole garden panorama, on this little circular patch of lawn, apparently conversing. The man had some small black object in his hand.

"If you're interested, I'll show you the bills that Beaumont put in to the old Duke while he was making it."

"I'd like very much to see them. They must be fascinating."

"He paid his labourers a shilling a day and they worked ten hours."

In the clear sunlight it was not difficult to follow the movements and gestures of the two figures on the lawn. They had turned now toward the piece of sculpture, and were pointing at it in a sort of mocking way, apparently laughing and making jokes about its shape. I recognized it as being one of the abstract Henry Moores, done in wood, a thin smooth object of singular beauty that had two or three holes in it and a number of strange limbs protruding.

"When Beaumont planted the yew trees for the chessmen and the other things, he knew they wouldn't amount to much for at least a hundred years. We don't seem to possess that sort of patience in our planning these days, do we? What do you think?"

"No," I said. "We don't."

The black object in the man's hand turned out to be a camera, and now he had stepped back and was taking pictures of the woman beside the Henry Moore. She was striking a number of different poses, all of them, so far as I could see, ludicrous and meant to be amusing. Once she put her arms around one of the protruding wooden limbs and hugged it, and another time she climbed up and sat sidesaddle on the thing, holding imaginary reins in her hands. A great wall of yew hid these two people from the house, and indeed from all the rest of the garden except the little hill on which we sat. They had every right to believe that they were not overlooked, and even if they had happened to glance our way—which was into the sun —I doubt they would have noticed the two small motionless figures sitting on the bench beside the pond.

"You know, I love these yews," Sir Basil said. "The colour of them is so wonderful in a garden because it rests the eye. And in the summer it breaks up the areas of brilliance into little patches and makes them more comfortable to admire. Have you noticed the different shades of green on the planes and facets of each clipped tree?"

"It's lovely, isn't it."

The man now seemed to be explaining something to the woman, and pointing at the Henry Moore, and I could tell by the way they threw back their heads that they were laughing again. The man continued to point, and then the woman walked around the back of the wood carving, bent down and poked her head through one of its holes. The thing was about the size, shall I say, of a small horse, but thinner than that, and from where I sat I could see both sides of it—to the left, the woman's body, to the right, her head protruding through. It was very much like one of those jokes at the seaside where you put your head through a hole in a board and get photographed as a fat lady. Then man was photographing her now.

"There's another thing about yews," Sir Basil said. "In the early summer when the young shoots come out . . ." At that moment he paused and sat up straighter and leaned slightly forward, and I could sense his whole body suddenly stiffening.

"Yes," I said, "when the young shoots come out?"

The man had taken the photograph, but the woman still had her head through the hole, and now I saw him put both hands (as well as the camera) behind his back and advance toward her. Then he bent forward so his face was close to hers, touching it, and he held it there while he gave her, I suppose, a few kisses or something like that. In the stillness that followed, I fancied I heard a faint far-away tinkle of female laughter coming to us through the sunlight across the garden.

"Shall we go back to the house?" I asked.

"Back to the house?"

"Yes, shall we go back and have a drink before lunch?"

"A drink? Yes, we'll have a drink." But he didn't move. He sat very still, gone far away from me now, staring intently at the two figures. I also was staring at them. I couldn't take my eyes away; I *had* to look. It was like seeing a dangerous little ballet in miniature from a great distance, and you knew the dancers and the music but not the end of the story, not the choreography, nor what they were going to do next, and you were fascinated, and you *had* to look.

"Gaudier Breska," I said. "How great do you think he might've become if he hadn't died so young?"

"Who?"

"Gaudier Breska."

"Yes," he said. "Of course."

I noticed now that something queer was happening. The woman still had her head through the hole, but she was beginning to wriggle her body from side to side in a slow unusual manner, and the man was standing motionless, a pace or so away, watching her. He seemed suddenly uneasy the way he stood there, and I could tell by the drop of the head and by the stiff intent set of the body that there was no laughter in him any more. For a while he re-

mained still, then I saw him place his camera on the
ground and go forward to the woman, taking her head in
his hands; and all at once it was more like a puppet show
than a ballet, with tiny wooden figures performing tiny
jerky movements, crazy and unreal, on a faraway sunlit
stage.

We sat quietly together on the white bench, and we
watched while the tiny puppet man began to manipulate
the woman's head with his hands. He was doing it gently,
there was no doubt about that, slowly and gently, stepping
back every now and then to think about it some more,
and several times crouching down to survey the situation
from another angle. Whenever he left her alone the
woman would again start to wriggle her body, and the
peculiar way she did it reminded me of a dog that feels
a collar round its neck for the first time.

"She's stuck," Sir Basil said.

And now the man was walking to the other side of the
carving, the side where the woman's body was, and he put
out his hands and began trying to do something with her
neck. Then, as though suddenly exasperated, he gave the
neck two or three quick jerky pulls, and this time the
sound of the woman's voice, raised high in anger, or pain,
or both, came back to us small and clear through the sunlight.

Out of the corner of one eye I could see Sir Basil nodding his head quietly up and down. "I got my fist caught
in a jar of boiled sweets once," he said, "and I couldn't
get it out."

The man had retreated a few yards, and was standing

with hands on hips, head up, looking furious and sullen. The woman, from her uncomfortable position, appeared to be talking to him, or rather shouting at him, and although the body itself was pretty firmly fixed and could only wriggle, the legs were free and did a good deal of moving and stamping.

"I broke the jar with a hammer and told my mother I'd knocked it off the shelf by mistake." He seemed calmer now, not tense at all, although his voice was curiously flat. "I suppose we'd better go down and see if we can help."

"Perhaps we should."

But still he didn't move. He took out a cigarette and lit it, putting the used match carefully back in the box.

"I'm sorry," he said. "Will you have one?"

"Thanks, I think I will." He made a little ceremony of giving me the cigarette and lighting it for me, and again he put the used match back in the box. Then we got up and walked slowly down the grass slope.

We came upon them silently, through an archway in the yew hedge, and it was naturally quite a surprise.

"What's the matter here?" Sir Basil asked. He spoke softly, with a dangerous softness that I'm sure his wife had never heard before.

"She's gone and put her head through the hole and now she can't get it out," Major Haddock said. "Just for a lark you know."

"For a what?"

"Basil!" Lady Turton shouted. "Don't be such a damn fool! Do something can't you!" She may not have been able to move much, but she could still talk.

"Pretty obvious we're going to have to break up this

lump of wood," the Major said. There was a small smudge of red on his grey moustache, and this, like the single extra touch of colour that ruins a perfect painting, managed somehow to destroy all his manly good looks. It made him comic.

"You mean break the Henry Moore?"

"My dear sir, there's no other way of setting the lady free. God knows how she managed to squeeze it in, but I know for a fact she can't pull it out. It's the ears get in the way."

"Oh dear," Sir Basil said. "What a terrible pity. My beautiful Henry Moore."

At this stage Lady Turton began abusing her husband in a most unpleasant manner, and there's no knowing how long it would have gone on had not Jelks suddenly appeared out of the shadows. He came sidling silently on to the lawn and stationed himself at a respectful distance from Sir Basil, as though awaiting instructions. His black clothes looked perfectly ridiculous in the morning sunlight, and with his ancient pink-white face and white hands he was like some small crabby animal that has lived all its life in a hole under the ground.

"Is there anything I can do, Sir Basil?" He kept his voice level, but I didn't think his face was quite straight. When he looked at Lady Turton there was a little exulting glimmer in his eyes.

"Yes Jelks, there is. Go back and get me a saw or something so I can cut out a section of this wood."

"Shall I call one of the men, Sir Basil? William is a good carpenter."

"No, I'll do it myself. Just get the tools—and hurry."

While they were waiting for Jelks, I strolled away because I didn't wish to hear any more of the things that
Lady Turton was saying to her husband. But I was back
in time to see the butler returning, followed now by the
other woman, Carmen La Rosa, who made a rush for the
hostess.

"Nata-*li*-a! My dear Nata-*li*-a! What *have* they done to
you?"

"Oh shut up," the hostess said. "And get out of the way,
will you."

Sir Basil took up a position close to his lady's head, waiting for Jelks. Jelks advanced slowly, carrying a saw in one
hand, an axe in the other, and he stopped maybe a yard
away. He then held out both implements in front of him
so his master could choose, and there was a brief moment
—no more than two or three seconds—of silence, and of
waiting, and it just happened that I was watching Jelks at
this time. I saw the hand that was carrying the axe come
forward an extra fraction of an inch toward Sir Basil. It
was so slight a movement it was barely noticeable—a tiny
pushing forward of the hand, slow and secret, a little offer, a little coaxing offer that was accompanied perhaps by
an infinitesimal lift of the eyebrows.

I'm not sure whether Sir Basil saw it, but he hesitated,
and again the hand that held the axe came edging forward,
and it was almost exactly like that card trick where the
man says "Take one, whichever one you want," and you
always get the one he means you to have. Sir Basil got the
axe. I saw him reach out in a dreamy sort of way, accept-
ing it from Jelks, and then, the instant he felt the handle

in his grasp he seemed to realize what was required of him and he sprang to life.

For me, after that, it was like the awful moment when you see a child running out into the road and a car is coming and all you can do is shut your eyes tight and wait until the noise tells you it has happened. The moment of waiting becomes a long lucid period of time with yellow and red spots dancing on a black field, and even if you open your eyes again and find that nobody has been killed or hurt, it makes no difference because so far as you and your stomach were concerned you saw it all.

I saw this one all right, every detail of it, and I didn't open my eyes again until I heard Sir Basil's voice, even softer than usual, calling in gentle protest to the butler.

"Jelks," he was saying, and I looked and saw him standing there as calm as you please, still holding the axe. Lady Turton's head was there too, still sticking through the hole, but her face had turned a terrible ashy grey, and the mouth was opening and shutting and making a kind of gurgling sound.

"Look here, Jelks," Sir Basil was saying. "What on earth are you thinking about. This thing's much too dangerous. Give me the saw." And as he exchanged implements I noticed for the first time two little warm roses of colour appearing on his cheeks, and above them, all around the corners of his eyes, the twinkling tiny wrinkles of a smile.

NUNC DIMITTIS

It is nearly midnight, and I can see that if I don't make a start with writing this story now, I never shall. All evening I have been sitting here trying to force myself to begin, but the more I have thought about it, the more appalled and ashamed and distressed I have become by the whole thing.

My idea—and I believe it was a good one—was to try, by a process of confession and analysis, to discover a reason or at any rate some justification for my outrageous behavior toward Janet de Pelagia. I wanted, essentially, to address myself to an imaginary and sympathetic listener, a kind of mythical *you*, someone gentle and understanding to whom I might tell unashamedly every detail of this unfortunate episode. I can only hope that I am not too upset to make a go of it.

If I am to be quite honest with myself, I suppose I shall have to admit that what is disturbing me most is not so much the sense of my own shame, or even the hurt that

I have inflicted upon poor Janet; it is the knowledge that I have made a monstrous fool of myself and that all my friends—if I can still call them that—all those warm and lovable people who used to come so often to my house, must now be regarding me as nothing but a vicious, vengeful old man. Yes, that surely hurts. When I say to you that my friends were my whole life—everything, absolutely everything in it—then perhaps you will begin to understand.

Will you? I doubt it—unless I digress for a minute to tell you roughly the sort of person I am.

Well—let me see. Now that I come to think of it, I suppose I am, after all, a type; a rare one, mark you, but nevertheless a quite definite type—the wealthy, leisurely, middle-aged man of culture, adored (I choose the word carefully) by his many friends for his charm, his money, his air of scholarship, his generosity and, I sincerely hope, for himself also. You will find him (this type) only in the big capitals, London, Paris, New York; of that I am certain. The money he has was earned by his dead father whose memory he is inclined to despise. This is not his fault, for there is something in his make-up that compels him secretly to look down upon all people who never had the wit to learn the difference between Rockingham and Spode, Waterford and Venetian, Sheraton and Chippendale, Monet and Manet, or even Pommard and Montrachet.

He is, therefore, a connoisseur, possessing above all things an exquisite taste. His Constables, Boningtons, Lautrecs, Redons, Viuillards, Mathew Smiths are as fine as anything in the Tate; and because they are so fabulous and beautiful, they create an atmosphere of suspense around him in the home, something tantalizing, breathtaking, faintly frightening—frightening to think that he has the power and the right, if he feels inclined, to slash, tear, plunge his fist right through a superb Dedham Vale, a Mont Saint-Victoire, an Arles cornfield, a Tahiti maiden, a portrait of Madame Cézanne. And from the walls on which these wonders hang there issues a little golden glow of splendour, a subtle emanation of grandeur in which he lives and moves and entertains with a sly nonchalance that is not entirely unpracticed.

He is invariably a bachelor, yet he never appears to get entangled with the women who surround him, who love him so dearly. It is just possible—and this you may or may not have noticed—that there is a frustration, a discontent, a regret somewhere inside him. Even a slight aberration.

I don't think I need say any more. I have been very frank. You should know me well enough by now to judge me fairly—and dare I hope it?—to sympathize with me when you hear my story. You may even decide that much of the blame for what has happened should be placed, not upon me, but upon a lady called Gladys Ponsonby. After all, she was the one who started it. Had I not escorted Gladys Ponsonby back to her house that night nearly six months ago, and had she not spoken so freely to me about certain people, certain things, then this tragic business could never have taken place.

It was last December, if I remember rightly, and I had

been dining with the Ashendens in that lovely house of theirs that overlooks the southern fringe of Regents Park. There were a fair number of people there, but Gladys Ponsonby was the only one beside myself who had come alone. So when it was time for us to leave, I naturally offered to see her safely back to her house. She accepted and we left together in my car; but unfortunately, when we arrived at her place she insisted that I come in and have "one for the road," as she put it. I didn't wish to seem stuffy, so I told the chauffeur to wait and followed her in.

Gladys Ponsonby is an unusually short woman, certainly not more than four feet nine or ten, maybe even less than that—one of those tiny persons who gives me, when I am beside her, the comical, rather wobbly feeling that I am standing on a chair. She is a widow, a few years younger than me—maybe fifty-three or four, and it is possible that thirty years ago she was quite a fetching little thing. But now the face is loose and puckered with nothing distinctive about it whatsoever. The individual features, the eyes, the nose, the mouth, the chin, are buried in the folds of fat around the puckered little face and one does not notice them. Except perhaps the mouth, which reminds me—I cannot help it—of a salmon.

In the living-room, as she gave me my brandy, I noticed that her hand was a trifle unsteady. The lady is tired, I told myself, so I mustn't stay long. We sat down together on the sofa and for a while discussed the Ashendens' party and the people who were there. Finally I got up to go.

"Sit down, Lionel," she said. "Have another brandy."

"No, really, I must go."

"Sit down and don't be so stuffy. *I'm* having another one, and the least you can do is keep me company while I drink it."

I watched her as she walked over to the sideboard, this tiny woman, faintly swaying, holding her glass out in front of her with both hands as though it were an offering; and the sight of her walking like that, so incredibly short and squat and stiff, suddenly gave me the ludicrous notion that she had no legs at all above the knees.

"Lionel, what are you chuckling about?" She half turned to look at me as she poured the drink, and some of it slopped over the side of the glass.

"Nothing, my dear. Nothing at all."

"Well, stop it, and tell me what you think of my new portrait." She indicated a large canvas hanging over the fireplace that I had been trying to avoid with my eye ever since I entered the room. It was a hideous thing, painted, as I well knew, by a man who was now all the rage in London, a very mediocre painter called John Royden. It was a full length portrait of Gladys Lady Ponsonby, painted with a certain technical cunning that made her out to be a tall and quite alluring creature.

"Charming," I said.

"Isn't it, though! I'm so glad you like it."

"Quite charming."

"I think John Royden is a genius. Don't you think he's a genius, Lionel?"

"Well—that might be going a bit far."

"You mean it's a little early to say for sure?"

"Exactly."

"But listen, Lionel—and I think this will surprise you. John Royden is so sought after now that he won't even *consider* painting anyone for less than a thousand guineas!"

"Really?"

"Oh yes! And everyone's queuing up, simply *queuing up* to get themselves done."

"Most interesting."

"Now take your Mr. Cézanne or whatever his name is. I'll bet *he* never got that sort of money in *his* lifetime."

"Never."

"And you say *he* was a genius?"

"Sort of—yes."

"Then so is Royden," she said, settling herself again on the sofa. "The money proves it."

She sat silent for a while, sipping her brandy, and I couldn't help noticing how the unsteadiness of her hand was causing the rim of the glass to jog against her lower lip. She knew I was watching her, and without turning her head she swivelled her eyes and glanced at me cautiously out of the corners of them. "A penny for your thoughts?"

Now, if there is one phrase in the world I cannot abide, it is this. It gives me an actual physical pain in the chest and I begin to cough.

"Come on, Lionel. A penny for them."

I shook my head, quite unable to answer. She turned away abruptly and placed the brandy glass on a small table to her left; and the manner in which she did this seemed to suggest—I don't know why—that she felt rebuffed and was now clearing the decks for action. I waited, rather uncomfortable in the silence that followed, and because I had no conversation left in me, I made a great play about smoking my cigar, studying the ash intently and blowing the smoke up slowly toward the ceiling. But she made no move. There was beginning to be something about this lady I did not much like, a mischievous, brooding air that made me want to get up quickly and go away. When she looked around again, she was smiling at me slyly with those little buried eyes of hers, but the mouth—oh, just like a salmon's—was absolutely rigid.

"Lionel, I think I'll tell you a secret."

"Really, Gladys, I simply must get home."

"Don't be frightened, Lionel. I won't embarrass you. You look so frightened all of a sudden."

"I'm not very good at secrets."

"I've been thinking," she said, "you're such a great expert on pictures, this ought to interest you." She sat quite still except for her fingers which were moving all the time. She kept them perpetually twisting and twisting around each other, and they were like a bunch of small white snakes wriggling in her lap.

"Don't you want to hear my secret, Lionel?"

"It isn't that, you know. It's just that it's so awfully late . . ."

"This is probably the best kept secret in London. A woman's secret. I suppose it's known to about—let me see—about thirty or forty women altogether. And not a single man. Except him, of course—John Royden."

I didn't wish to encourage her, so I said nothing.

"But first of all, promise—*promise* you won't tell a soul?"

"Dear me!"

"You *promise*, Lionel?"

"Yes, Gladys, allright, I promise."

"Good! Now listen." She reached for the brandy glass and settled back comfortably in the far corner of the sofa. "I suppose you know John Royden paints only women?"

"I didn't."

"And they're always full-length portraits, either standing or sitting—like mine there. Now take a good look at it, Lionel. Do you see how beautifully the dress is painted?"

"Well . . ."

"Go over and look carefully, please."

I got up reluctantly and went over and examined the painting. To my surprise I noticed that the paint of the dress was laid on so heavily it was actually raised out from the rest of the picture. It was a trick, quite effective in its way, but neither difficult to do nor entirely original.

"You see?" she said. "It's thick, isn't it, where the dress is?"

"Yes."

"But there's a bit more to it than that, you know, Lionel. I think the best way is to describe what happened the very first time I went along for a sitting."

Oh, what a bore this woman, is, I thought, and how can I get away?

"That was about a year ago, and I remember how excited I was to be going in to the studio of the great painter. I dressed myself up in a wonderful new thing I'd just got from Norman Hartnell, and a special little red hat, and off I went. Mr. Royden met me at the door, and of course I was fascinated by him at once. He had a small pointed beard and thrilling blue eyes, and he wore a black velvet jacket. The studio was huge, with red velvet sofas and velvet chairs—he loves velvet—and velvet curtains and even a velvet carpet on the floor. He sat me down, gave me a drink and came straight to the point. He told me about how he painted quite differently from other artists. In his opinion, he said, there was only one method of attaining perfection when painting a woman's body and I mustn't be shocked when I heard what it was.

" 'I don't think I'll be shocked, Mr. Royden,' I told him.

" 'I'm sure you won't either,' he said. He had the most marvellous white teeth and they sort of shone through his beard when he smiled. 'You see, it's like this,' he went on. 'You examine any painting you like of a woman—I don't care who it's by—and you'll see that although the dress may be well painted, there is an effect of artificiality, of flatness about the whole thing, as though the dress were draped over a log of wood. And you know why?'

" 'No, Mr. Royden, I don't.'

" 'Because the painters themselves didn't really know what was underneath! ' "

Gladys Ponsonby paused to take a few more sips of brandy. "Don't look so startled, Lionel," she said to me. "There's nothing wrong about this. Keep quiet and let me finish. So then Mr. Royden said, 'That's why I insist on painting my subjects first of all in the nude.'

" 'Good Heavens, Mr. Royden!' I exclaimed.

" 'If you object to that, I don't mind making a slight concession, Lady Ponsonby,' he said. 'But I prefer it the other way.'

" 'Really, Mr. Royden, I don't know.'

" 'And when I've done you like that,' he went on, 'we'll have to wait a few weeks for the paint to dry. Then you come back and I paint on your underclothing. And when that's dry, I paint on the dress. You see, it's quite simple.' "

"The man's an absolute bounder!" I cried.

"No, Lionel, no! You're quite wrong. If only you could have heard him, so charming about it all, so genuine and sincere. Anyone could see he really *felt* what he was saying."

"I tell you, Gladys, the man's a bounder!"

"Don't be so silly, Lionel. And anyway, let me finish. The first thing I told him was that my husband (who was alive then) would never agree.

" 'Your husband need never know,' he answered. 'Why trouble him. No one knows my secret except the women I've painted.'

"And when I protested a bit more, I remember he

said, 'My dear Lady Ponsonby, there's nothing immoral about this. Art is only immoral when practiced by amateurs. It's the same with medicine. You wouldn't refuse to undress before your doctor, would you?'

"I told him I would if I'd gone to him for earache. That made him laugh. But he kept on at me about it and I must say he was very convincing, so after a while I gave in and that was that. So now Lionel, my sweet, you know the secret." She got up and went over to fetch herself some more brandy.

"Gladys, is this really true?"

"Of course it's true."

"You mean to say that's the way he paints all his subjects?"

"Yes. And the joke is the husbands never know anything about it. All they see is a nice fully clothed portrait of their wives. Of course, there's nothing wrong with being painted in the nude; artists do it all the time. But our silly husbands have a way of objecting to that sort of thing."

"By gad, the fellow's got a nerve!"

"I think he's a genius."

"I'll bet he got the idea from Goya."

"Nonsense, Lionel."

"Of course he did. But listen, Gladys. I want you to tell me something. Did you by any chance know about this . . . this peculiar technique of Royden's before you went to him?"

When I asked the question she was in the act of pouring the brandy, and she hesitated and turned her head to look at me, a little silky smile moving the corners of her mouth. "Damn you, Lionel," she said. "You're far too clever. You never let me get away with a single thing."

"So you knew?"

"Of course. Hermione Girdlestone told me."

"Exactly as I thought!"

"There's still nothing wrong."

"Nothing," I said. "Absolutely nothing." I could see it all quite clearly now. This Royden was indeed a bounder, practicing as neat a piece of psychological trickery as ever I'd seen. The man knew only too well that there was a whole set of wealthy indolent women in the city who got up at noon and spent the rest of the day trying to relieve their boredom with bridge and canasta and shopping until the cocktail hour came along. All they craved was a little excitement, something out of the ordinary, and the more expensive the better. Why—the news of an entertainment like this would spread through their ranks like smallpox. I could just see the great plump Hermione Girdlestone leaning over the canasta table and telling them about it . . . "But my dear, it's *simp*-ly fascinating . . . I can't *tell* you how intriguing it is . . . *much* more fun than going to your doctor . . ."

"You won't tell anyone, Lionel, will you? You promised."

"No, of course not. But now I must go, Gladys, I really must."

"Don't be so silly. I'm just beginning to enjoy myself. Stay till I've finished this drink anyway."

I sat patiently on the sofa while she went on with her

interminable brandy sipping. The little buried eyes still watching me out of their corners in that mischievous, canny way, and I had a strong feeling that the woman was now hatching out some further unpleasantness or scandal. There was the look of serpents in those eyes and a queer curl around the mouth; and in the air—although maybe I only imagined it—the faint smell of danger.

Then suddenly, so suddenly that I jumped, she said "Lionel, what's this I hear about you and Janet de Pelagia?"

"Now Gladys, please . . ."

"Lionel, you're blushing!"

"Nonsense."

"Don't tell me the old bachelor has really taken a tumble at last?"

"Gladys, this is too absurd." I began making movements to go, but she put a hand on my knee and stopped me.

"Don't you know by now, Lionel, that there *are* no secrets?"

"Janet is a fine girl."

"You can hardly call her a *girl*." Gladys Ponsonby paused, staring down into the large brandy glass that she held cupped in both hands. "But of course, I agree with you, Lionel, she's a wonderful person in every way. Except," and now she spoke very slowly, "except that she *does* say some rather peculiar things occasionally."

"What sort of things?"

"Just things, you know—things about people. About you."

"What did she say about me?"

"Nothing at all, Lionel. It wouldn't interest you."

"What did she say about me?"

"It's not even worth repeating, honestly it isn't. It's only that it struck me as being rather odd at the time."

"Gladys—what did she say?" While I waited for her to answer, I could feel the sweat breaking out all over my body.

"Well now, let me see. Of course, she was only joking or I couldn't dream of telling you, but I suppose she *did* say how it was all a wee bit of a bore."

"What was?"

"Sort of going out to dinner with you nearly every night—that kind of thing."

"She said it was a bore?"

"Yes." Gladys Ponsonby drained the brandy glass with one last big gulp, and sat up straight. "If you really want to know, she said it was a crashing bore. And then . . ."

"What did she say then?"

"Now look, Lionel—there's no need to get excited. I'm only telling you this for your own good."

"Then please hurry up and tell it."

"It's just that I happened to be playing canasta with Janet this afternoon and I asked her if she was free to dine with me tomorrow. She said no, she wasn't."

"Go on."

"Well—actually what she said was 'I'm dining with that crashing old bore Lionel Lampson.'"

"Janet said that?"

"Yes, Lionel dear."

"What else?"

"Now, that's enough. I don't think I should tell the rest."

"Finish it, please!"

"Why Lionel, don't keep shouting at me like that. Of course I'll tell you if you insist. As a matter of fact, I wouldn't consider myself a true friend if I didn't. Don't you think it's the sign of true friendship when two people like us . . ."

"Gladys! *Please* hurry."

"Good Heavens, you must give me time to *think*. Let me see now—so far as I can remember, what she *actually* said was this . . ."—and Gladys Ponsonby, sitting upright on the sofa with her feet not quite touching the floor, her eyes away from me now, looking at the wall, began cleverly to mimic the deep tone of that voice I knew so well—" 'Such a bore, my dear, because with Lionel one can *always* tell exactly what will happen *right* from beginning to end. For dinner we'll go to the Savoy Grill—it's *always* the Savoy Grill—and for two hours I'll have to listen to the pompous old . . . I mean I'll have to listen to him droning away about pictures and porcelain—*always* pictures and porcelain. Then in the taxi going home he'll reach out for my hand, and he'll lean closer, and I'll get a whiff of stale cigar smoke and brandy, and he'll start burbling about how he wished—oh how he wished he was just twenty years younger. And I will say "Could you open a window, do you mind?" And when we arrive at my house I'll tell him to keep the taxi, but he'll pretend he hasn't heard and pay it off quickly. And then at the front door, while I fish for my key, he'll stand beside me with a sort of silly spaniel look in his eyes, and I'll slowly put the key in the lock, and slowly turn it, and then—very quickly, before he has time to move—I'll say goodnight and skip inside and shut the door behind me . . .' Why Lionel! What's the matter, dear? You look positively ill . . ."

At that point, mercifully, I must have swooned clear away. I can remember practically nothing of the rest of that terrible night except for a vague and disturbing suspicion that when I regained consciousness I broke down completely and permitted Gladys Ponsonby to comfort me in a variety of different ways. Later, I believe I walked out of the house and was driven home, but I remained more or less unconscious of everything around me until I woke up in my bed the next morning.

I awoke feeling weak and shaken. I lay still with my eyes closed, trying to piece together the events of the night before—Gladys Ponsonby's living-room, Gladys on the sofa sipping brandy, the little puckered face, the mouth that was like a salmon's mouth, the things she had said . . . What was it she had said. Ah yes. About me. My God, yes! About Janet and me! Those outrageous, unbelievable remarks! Could Janet really have made them? Could she?

I can remember with what terrifying swiftness my hatred of Janet de Pelagia now began to grow. It all happened in a few minutes—a sudden, violent welling up of a hatred that filled me till I thought I was going to burst. I tried to dismiss it but it was on me like a fever, and in no time at all I was hunting around, as would some filthy gangster, for a method of revenge.

A curious way to behave, you may say, for a man such as me; to which I would answer—no, not really, if you consider the circumstances. To my mind, this was the sort of thing that could drive a man to murder. As a matter of fact, had it not been for a small sadistic streak that caused me to seek a more subtle and painful punishment for my victim, I might well have become a murderer myself. But mere killing, I decided, was too good for this woman, and far too crude for my own taste. So I began looking for a superior alternative.

I am not normally a scheming person; I consider it an odious business and have had no practice in it whatsoever. But fury and hate can concentrate a man's mind to an astonishing degree, and in no time at all a plot was forming and unfolding in my head—a plot so superior and exciting that I began to be quite carried away at the idea of it. By the time I had filled in the details and overcome one or two minor objections, my brooding vengeful mood had changed to one of extreme elation, and I remember how I started bouncing up and down absurdly on my bed and clapping my hands. The next thing I knew I had the telephone directory on my lap and was searching eagerly for a name. I found it, picked up the phone, and dialled the number.

"Hello," I said. "Mr. Royden? Mr. John Royden?"

"Speaking."

Well—it wasn't difficult to persuade the man to call

around and see me for a moment. I had never met him, but of course he knew my name, both as an important collector of paintings and as a person of some consequence in society. I was a big fish for him to catch.

"Let me see now, Mr. Lampson," he said, "I think I ought to be free in about a couple of hours. Will that be allright?"

I told him it would be fine, gave my address, and rang off.

I jumped out of bed. It was really remarkable how exhilarated I felt all of a sudden. One moment I had been in agony of despair, contemplating murder and suicide and I don't know what; the next, I was whistling an aria from Puccini in my bath. Every now and again I caught myself rubbing my hands together in a devilish fashion, and once, during my exercises, when I over-balanced doing a double-knee-bend, I sat on the floor and giggled like a schoolboy.

At the appointed time Mr. John Royden was shown in to my library and I got up to meet him. He was a small neat man with a slightly ginger goatee beard. He wore a black velvet jacket, a rust-brown tie, a red pullover, and black suède shoes. I shook his small neat hand.

"Good of you to come along so quickly, Mr. Royden."

"Not at all, sir." The man's lips—like the lips of nearly all bearded men—looked wet and naked, a trifle indecent, shining pink in among all that hair. After telling him again how much I admired his work, I got straight down to business.

"Mr. Royden," I said. "I have a rather unusual request to make of you, something quite personal in its way."

"Yes, Mr. Lampson?" He was sitting in the chair opposite me and he cocked his head over to one side, quick and perky like a bird.

"Of course, I know I can trust you to be discreet about anything I say."

"Absolutely, Mr. Lampson."

"Allright. Now my proposition is this: there is a certain lady in town here whose portrait I would like you to paint. I very much want to possess a fine painting of her. But there are certain complications. For example, I have my own reasons for not wishing her to know that it is I who am commissioning the portrait."

"You mean . . ."

"Exactly, Mr. Royden. That is exactly what I mean. As a man of the world I'm sure you will understand."

He smiled, a crooked little smile that only just came through his beard, and he nodded his head knowingly up and down.

"Is it not possible," I said, "that a man might be—how shall I put it?—extremely fond of a lady and at the same time have his own good reasons for not wishing her to know about it yet?"

"More than possible, Mr. Lampson."

"Sometimes a man has to stalk his quarry with great caution, waiting patiently for the right moment to reveal himself."

"Precisely, Mr. Lampson."

"There are better ways of catching a bird than by chasing it through the woods."

"Yes indeed, Mr. Lampson."

"Putting salt in its tail, for instance."

"Ha-ha!"

"Allright, Mr. Royden. I think you understand. Now—do you happen by any chance to know a lady called Janet de Pelagia?"

"Janet de Pelagia? Let me see now—yes. At least, what I mean is I've heard of her. I couldn't exactly say I know her."

"That's a pity. It makes it a little more difficult. Do you think you could get to meet her—perhaps at a cocktail party or something like that?"

"Shouldn't be too tricky, Mr. Lampson."

"Good, because what I suggest is this: that you go up to her and tell her she's the sort of model you've been searching for for years—just the right face, the right figure, the right coloured eyes. You know the sort of thing. Then ask her if she'd mind sitting for you free of charge. Say you'd like to do a picture of her for next year's Academy. I feel sure she'd be delighted to help you, and honoured too, if I may say so. Then you will paint her and exhibit the picture and deliver it to me after the show is over. No one but you need know that I have bought it."

The small round eyes of Mr. John Royden were watching me shrewdly, I thought, and the head was again cocked over to one side. He was sitting on the edge of his chair, and in this position, with the pullover making a flash of red down his front, he reminded me of a robin on a twig listening for a suspicious noise.

"There's really nothing wrong about it at all," I said. "Just call it—if you like—a harmless little conspiracy being perpetrated by a . . . well . . . by a rather romantic old man."

"I know, Mr. Lampson, I know . . ." He still seemed to be hesitating, so I said quickly, "I'll be glad to pay you double your usual fee."

That did it. The man actually licked his lips. "Well, Mr. Lampson, I must say this sort of thing's not really in my line, you know. But all the same, it'd be a very heartless man who refused such a—shall I say such a romantic assignment?"

"I should like a full length portrait, Mr. Royden, please. A large canvas—let me see—about twice the size of that Manet on the wall there."

"About sixty by thirty-six?"

"Yes. And I should like her to be standing. That, to my mind, is her most graceful attitude."

"I quite understand, Mr. Lampson. And it'll be a pleasure to paint such a lovely lady."

I expect it will, I told myself. The way you go about it, my boy, I'm quite sure it will. But I said, "Allright, Mr. Royden, then I'll leave it all to you. And don't forget, please—this is a little secret between ourselves."

When he had gone I forced myself to sit still and take twenty-five deep breaths. Nothing else would have restrained me from jumping up and shouting for joy like an idiot. I have never in my life felt so exhilarated. My plan was working! The most difficult part was already accomplished. There would be a wait now, a long wait. The way this man painted, it would take him several months to finish the picture. Well, I would just have to be patient, that's all.

I now decided on the spur of the moment that it would be best if I were to go abroad in the interim; and the very next morning, after sending a message to Janet (with whom, you will remember, I was due to dine that night) telling her I had been called away, I left for Italy.

There, as always, I had a delightful time, marred only by a constant nervous excitement caused by the thought of returning to the scene of action.

I eventually arrived back, four months later, in July, on the day after the opening of the Royal Academy, and I found to my relief that everything had gone according to plan during my absence. The picture of Janet de Pelagia had been painted and hung in the Exhibition, and it was already the subject of much favourable comment both by the critics and the public. I myself refrained from going to see it but Royden told me on the telephone that there had been several inquiries by persons who wished to buy it, all of whom had been informed that it was not for sale. When the show was over, Royden delivered the picture to my house and received his money.

I immediately had it carried up to my work-room, and with mounting excitement I began to examine it closely. The man had painted her standing up in a black evening dress and there was a red-plush sofa in the background. Her left hand was resting on the back of a heavy chair, also of red-plush, and there was a huge crystal chandelier hanging from the ceiling.

My God, I thought, what a hideous thing! The portrait itself wasn't so bad. He had caught the woman's expression—the forward drop of the head, the wide blue eyes, the large, ugly-beautiful mouth with the trace of a smile in one corner. He had flattered her, of course. There wasn't a wrinkle on her face or the slightest suggestion of fat under her chin. I bent forward to examine the painting of the dress. Yes—here the paint was thicker, much thicker. At this point, unable to wait another moment, I threw off my coat and prepared to go to work.

I should mention here that I am myself an expert cleaner and restorer of paintings. The cleaning, particularly, is a comparatively simple process provided one has patience and a gentle touch, and those professionals who make such a secret of their trade and charge such shocking prices get no business from me. Where my own pictures are concerned I always do the job myself.

I poured out the turpentine and added a few drops of alcohol. I dipped a small wad of cotton-wool in the mixture, squeezed it out, and then gently, so very gently, with a circular motion, I began to work upon the black paint of the dress. I could only hope that Royden had allowed each layer to dry thoroughly before applying the next, otherwise the two would merge and the process I had in mind would be impossible. Soon I would know. I was working on one square inch of black dress somewhere around the lady's stomach and I took plenty of time, cautiously testing and teasing the paint, adding a drop or two more of alcohol to my mixture, testing again, adding another drop until finally it was just strong enough to loosen the pigment.

For perhaps a whole hour I worked away on this little square of black, proceeding more and more gently as I came closer to the layer below. Then, a tiny pink spot appeared, and gradually it spread and spread until the whole of my square inch was a clear shining patch of pink. Quickly I neutralized with pure turps.

So far so good. I knew now that the black paint could be removed without disturbing what was underneath. So long as I was patient and industrious I would easily be able to take it all off. Also, I had discovered the right mixture to use and just how hard I could safely rub, so things should go much quicker now.

I must say it was rather an amusing business. I worked first from the middle of her body downward, and as the lower half of her dress came away bit by bit onto my little wads of cotton, a queer pink undergarment began to reveal itself. I didn't for the life of me know what the thing was called, but it was a formidable apparatus constructed of what appeared to be a strong thick elastic material, and its purpose was apparently to contain and to compress the woman's bulging figure into a neat streamlined shape, giving a quite false impression of slimness. As I travelled lower and lower down, I came upon a striking arrangement of suspenders, also pink, which were attached to this elastic armour and hung downward four or five inches to grip the tops of the stockings.

Quite fantastic the whole thing seemed to me as I

stepped back a pace to survey it. It gave me a strong sense of having somehow been cheated; for had I not, during all these past months, been admiring the sylphlike figure of this lady? She was a faker. No question about it. But do many other females practice this sort of deception, I wondered. I knew, of course, that in the days of stays and corsets it was usual for ladies to strap themselves up; yet for some reason I was under the impression that nowadays all they had to do was diet.

When the whole of the lower half of the dress had come away, I immediately turned my attention to the upper portion, working my way slowly upward from the lady's middle. Here, around the midriff, there was an area of naked flesh; then higher up upon the bosom itself and actually containing it, I came upon a contrivance made of some heavy black material edged with frilly lace. This, I knew very well, was the brassière—another formidable appliance upheld by an arrangement of black straps as skillfully and scientifically rigged as the supporting cables of a suspension bridge.

Dear me, I thought. One lives and learns.

But now at last the job was finished, and I stepped back again to take a final look at the picture. It was truly an astonishing sight! This woman, Janet de Pelagia, almost life size, standing there in her underwear—in a sort of drawing room, I suppose it was—with a great chandelier above her head and a red-plush chair by her side; and she herself—this was the most disturbing part of all—looking so completely unconcerned, with the wide placid blue eyes, the faintly smiling, ugly-beautiful mouth. Also I noticed, with something of a shock, that she was exceedingly bow-legged, like a jockey. I tell you frankly, the whole thing embarrassed me. I felt as though I had no right to be in the room, certainly no right to stare. So after a while I went out and shut the door behind me. It seemed like the only decent thing to do.

Now, for the next and final step! And do not imagine simply because I have not mentioned it lately that my thirst for revenge had in any way diminished during the last few months. On the contrary, it had if anything increased; and with the last act about to be performed, I can tell you I found it hard to contain myself. That night, for example, I didn't even go to bed.

You see, I couldn't wait to get the invitations out. I sat up all night preparing them and addressing the envelopes. There were twenty-two of them in all, and I wanted each to be a personal note. "I'm having a little dinner on Friday night, the twenty-second, at eight. I do hope you can come along . . . I'm so looking forward to seeing you again . . ."

The first, the most carefully phrased, was to Janet de Pelagia. In it I regretted not having seen her for so long . . . I had been abroad . . . It was time we got together again, etc. etc. The next was to Gladys Ponsonby. Then one to Hermione Lady Girdlestone, another to Princess Bicheno, Mrs. Cudbird, Sir Hubert Kaul, Mrs. Galbally, Peter Euan-Thomas, James Pisker, Sir Eustace Piegrome, Peter van Santen, Elizabeth Moynihan, Lord Mulherrin, Bertram Sturt, Phillip Cornelius, Jack Hill, Lady Akeman, Mrs. Icely, Humphrey King-Howard,

Johnny O'Coffey, Mrs. Uvary, and the Dowager Countess of Waxworth.

It was a carefully selected list, containing as it did the most distinguished men, the most brilliant and influential women in the top crust of our society.

I was well aware that a dinner at my house was regarded as quite an occasion; everybody liked to come. And now, as I watched the point of my pen moving swiftly over the paper, I could almost see the ladies in their pleasure picking up their bedside telephones the morning the invitations arrived, shrill voices calling to shriller voices over the wires . . . "Lionel's giving a party . . . he's asked you too? My dear, how nice . . . his food is always *so* good . . . and *such* a lovely man, isn't he though, yes . . ."

Is that really what they would say? It suddenly occurred to me that it might not be like that at all. More like this perhaps: "I agree, my dear, yes, not a bad old man . . . but a bit of a bore, don't you think? . . . What did you say? . . . dull? But desperately, my dear. You've hit the nail right on the head . . . did you ever hear what Janet de Pelagia once said about him? . . . Ah yes, I thought you'd heard that one . . . screamingly funny, don't you think? . . . poor Janet . . . how she stood it as long as she did I don't know . . ."

Anyway, I got the invitations off, and within a couple of days everybody with the exception of Mrs. Cudbird and Sir Hubert Kaul, who were away, had accepted with pleasure.

At eight-thirty on the evening of the twenty-second,

my large drawing-room was filled with people. They stood about the room admiring the pictures, drinking their martinis, talking with loud voices. The women smelled strongly of scent, the men were pink-faced and carefully buttoned up in their dinner-jackets. Janet de Pelagia was wearing the same black dress she had used for the portrait, and every time I caught sight of her, a kind of huge bubble-vision—as in those absurd cartoons—would float up above my head, and in it I would see Janet in her underclothes, the black brassière, the pink elastic belt, the suspenders, the jockey's legs.

I moved from group to group, chatting aimiably with them all, listening to their talk. Behind me I could hear Mrs. Galbally telling Sir Eustace Piegrome and James Pisker how the man at the next table to hers at Claridges the night before had had red lipstick on his white moustache. "Simply *plastered* with it," she kept saying, "and the old boy was ninety if he was a day . . ." On the other side, Lady Girdlestone was telling somebody where one could get truffles cooked in brandy, and I could see Mrs. Icely whispering something to Lord Mulherrin while his Lordship kept shaking his head slowly from side to side like an old and dispirited metronome.

Dinner was announced, and we all moved out.

"My goodness!" they cried as they entered the dining-room. "How dark and sinister!"

"I can hardly see a thing!"

"What divine little candles!"

"But Lionel, how romantic!"

There were six very thin candles set about two feet

apart from each other down the centre of the long table. Their small flames made a little glow of light around the table itself, but left the rest of the room in darkness. It was an amusing arrangement and apart from the fact that it suited my purpose well, it made a pleasant change. The guests soon settled themselves in their right places and the meal began.

They all seemed to enjoy the candle-light and things went famously, though for some reason the darkness caused them to speak much louder than usual. Janet de Pelagia's voice struck me as being particularly strident. She was sitting next to Lord Mulherrin, and I could hear her telling him about the boring time she had had at Cap Ferrat the week before. "Nothing but Frenchmen," she kept saying. "Nothing but Frenchmen in the whole place . . ."

For my part, I was watching the candles. They were so thin that I knew it would not be long before they burned down to their bases. Also I was mighty nervous—I will admit that—but at the same time intensely exhilarated, almost to the point of drunkenness. Every time I heard Janet's voice or caught sight of her face shadowed in the light of the candles, a little ball of excitement exploded inside me and I felt the fire of it running under my skin.

They were eating their strawberries when at last I decided the time had come. I took a deep breath and in a loud voice I said, "I'm afraid we'll have to have the lights on now. The candles are nearly finished. Mary," I called, "Oh Mary, switch on the lights will you please."

There was a moment of silence after my announcement.

I heard the maid walking over to the door, then the gentle click of the switch and the room was flooded with a blaze of light. They all screwed up their eyes, opened them again, gazed about them.

At that point I got up from my chair and slid quietly from the room, but as I went I saw a sight that I shall never forget as long as I live. It was Janet, with both hands in mid-air, stopped, frozen rigid, caught in the act of gesticulating toward someone across the table. Her mouth had dropped open two inches and she wore the surprised, not-quite-understanding look of a person who precisely one second before has been shot dead right through the heart.

In the hall outside I paused and listened to the beginning of the uproar, the shrill cries of the ladies and the outraged unbelieving exclamations of the men; and soon there was a great hum of noise with everybody talking or shouting at the same time. Then—and this was the sweetest moment of all—I heard Lord Mulherrin's voice, roaring above the rest, "Here! Someone! Hurry! Give her some water quick!"

Out in the street the chauffeur helped me into my car, and soon we were away from London and bowling merrily along the Great North Road toward this, my other house, which is only ninety-five miles from Town anyway.

The next two days I spent in gloating. I mooned around in a dream of ecstasy, half drowned in my own complacency and filled with a sense of pleasure so great that it constantly gave me pins and needles all along the lower parts of my legs. It wasn't until this morning when Gladys Ponsonby called me on the phone that I suddenly came to my senses and realized I was not a hero at all but an outcast. She informed me—with what I thought was just a trace of relish—that everybody was up in arms, that all of them, all my old and loving friends were saying the most terrible things about me and had sworn never never to speak to me again. Except her, she kept saying. Everybody except her. And didn't I think it would be rather cosy, she asked, if she were to come down and stay with me a few days to cheer me up?

I'm afraid I was too upset by that time even to answer her politely. I put the phone down and went away to weep.

Then at noon today came the final crushing blow. The post arrived, and with it—I can hardly bring myself to write about it, I am so ashamed—came a letter, the sweetest, most tender little note imaginable from none other than Janet de Pelagia herself. She forgave me completely, she wrote, for everything I had done. She knew it was only a joke and I must not listen to the horrid things other people were saying about me. She loved me as she always had and always would to her dying day.

Oh, what a cad, what a brute I felt when I read this! The more so when I found that she had actually sent me by the same post a small present as an added sign of her affection—a half pound jar of my favorite food of all, fresh caviar.

I can never under any circumstances resist good caviar. It is perhaps my greatest weakness. So although I naturally had no appetite whatsoever for food at dinner-time this evening, I must confess I took a few spoonfuls of the stuff in an effort to console myself in my misery. It is even possible that I took a shade too much, because I haven't been feeling any too chipper this last hour or so. Perhaps I ought to go up right away and get myself some bicarbonate of soda. I can easily come back and finish this later, when I'm in better trim.

You know—now I come to think of it, I really do feel rather ill all of a sudden.

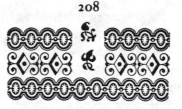

THE GREAT AUTOMATIC
GRAMMATISATOR

"WELL, Knipe, my boy. Now that it's all finished, I just called you in to tell you I think you've done a fine job."

Adolph Knipe stood still in front of Mr. Bohlen's desk. There seemed to be no enthusiasm in him at all.

"Aren't you pleased?"

"Oh yes, Mr. Bohlen."

"Did you see what the papers said this morning."

"No sir, I didn't."

The man behind the desk pulled a folded newspaper toward him, and began to read: "The building of the great automatic computing engine, ordered by the government some time ago, is now complete. It is probably the fastest electronic calculating machine in the world today. Its function is to satisfy the ever-increasing need of science, industry, and administration for rapid mathematical calculation which, in the past, by traditional methods, would have been physically impossible, or would have required more time than the problems justified. The speed with which the new engine works, said Mr. John Bohlen, head of the firm of electrical engineers mainly responsible for its construction, may be grasped by the fact that it can provide the correct answer in five seconds to a problem that would occupy a mathematician for a month. In three minutes, it can produce a calculation that by hand (if it were possible) would fill half a million sheets of foolscap paper. The automatic computing engine uses pulses of electricity, generated at the rate of a million a second, to solve all calculations that resolve themselves into addition, subtraction, multiplication, and division. For practical purposes there is no limit to what it can do . . ."

Mr. Bohlen glanced up at the long, melancholy face of the younger man. "Aren't you proud, Knipe? Aren't you pleased?"

"Of course, Mr. Bohlen."

"I don't think I have to remind you that your own contribution, especially to the original plans, was an important one. In fact, I might go so far as to say that without you and some of your ideas, this project might still be on the drawing-boards today."

Adolph Knipe moved his feet on the carpet, and he watched the two small white hands of his chief, the nervous fingers playing with a paper-clip, unbending it, straightening out the hairpin curves. He didn't like the man's hands. He didn't like his face either, with the tiny mouth and the narrow purple-coloured lips. It was unpleasant the way only the lower lip moved when he talked.

"Is anything bothering you, Knipe? Anything on your mind?"

"Oh no, Mr. Bohlen. No."

"How would you like to take a week's holiday? Do you good. You've earned it."

"Oh, I don't know, sir."

The older man waited, watching this tall, thin person who stood so sloppily before him. He was a difficult boy. Why couldn't he stand up straight? Always drooping and untidy, with spots on his jacket, and hair falling all over his face.

"I'd like you to take a holiday, Knipe. You need it."

"All right, sir. If you wish."

"Take a week. Two weeks if you like. Go somewhere warm. Get some sunshine. Swim. Relax. Sleep. Then come back, and we'll have another talk about the future."

Adolph Knipe went home by bus to his two-room apartment. He threw his coat on the sofa, poured himself a drink of whiskey, and sat down in front of the typewriter that was on the table. Mr. Bohlen was right. Of course he was right. Except that he didn't know the half of it. He probably thought it was a woman. Whenever a young man gets depressed, everybody thinks it's a woman.

He leaned forward and began to read through the half-finished sheet of typing still in the machine. It was headed "A Narrow Escape," and it began *"The night was dark and stormy, the wind whistled in the trees, the rain poured down like cats and dogs . . ."*

Adolph Knipe took a sip of whiskey, tasting the malty-bitter flavour, feeling the trickle of cold liquid as it travelled down his throat and settled in the top of his stomach, cool at first, then spreading and becoming warm, making a little area of warmness in the gut. To hell with Mr. John Bohlen anyway. And to hell with the great electrical computing machine. To hell with . . .

At exactly that moment, his eyes and mouth began slowly to open, in a sort of wonder, and slowly he raised his head and became still, absolutely motionless, gazing at the wall opposite with this look that was more perhaps of astonishment than of wonder, but quite fixed now, unmoving, and remaining thus for forty, fifty, sixty seconds. Then gradually (the head still motionless), a subtle change spreading over the face, astonishment becoming pleasure, very slight at first, only around the corners of the mouth, increasing gradually, spreading out until at last the whole face was open wide and shining with extreme delight. It was the first time Adolph Knipe had smiled in many, many months.

"Of course," he said, speaking aloud, "it's completely ridiculous." Again he smiled, raising his upper lip and baring his teeth in a queerly sensual manner.

"It's a delicious idea, but so impracticable it doesn't really bear thinking about at all."

From then on, Adolph Knipe began to think about nothing else. The idea fascinated him enormously, at first because it gave him a promise—however remote—of revenging himself in a most devilish manner upon his greatest enemies. From this angle alone, he toyed idly with it for perhaps ten or fifteen minutes; then all at once he found himself examining it quite seriously as a practical possibility. He took paper and made some preliminary notes. But he didn't get far. He found himself, almost immediately, up against the old truth that a machine, however ingenious, is incapable of original thought. It can handle no problems except those that resolve themselves into mathematical terms—problems that contain one, and only one, correct answer.

This was a stumper. There didn't seem any way around it. A machine cannot have a brain. On the other hand, it *can* have a memory, can it not? Their own electronic calculator had a marvellous memory. Simply by converting electric pulses, through a column of mercury, into supersonic waves, it could store away at least a thousand numbers at a time, extracting any one of them at the precise moment it was needed. Would it not be possible, therefore, on this principle, to build a memory section of almost unlimited size?

Now what about that?

Then suddenly, he was struck by a powerful but simple little truth, and it was this: *That English grammar is governed by rules that are almost mathematical in their strictness!* Given the words, and given the sense of what is to be said, then there is only one correct order in which those words can be arranged.

No, he thought, that isn't quite accurate. In many sentences there are several alternative positions for words and phrases, all of which may be grammatically correct. But what the hell. The theory itself is basically true. Therefore, it stands to reason that an engine built along the lines of the electric computer could be adjusted to arrange words (instead of numbers) in their right order according to the rules of grammar. Give it the verbs, the nouns, the adjectives, the pronouns, store them in the memory section as a vocabulary, and arrange for them to be extracted as required. Then feed it with plots and leave it to write the sentences.

There was no stopping Knipe now. He went to work immediately, and there followed during the next few days a period of intense labour. The living-room became littered with sheets of paper: formulae and calculations; lists of words, thousands and thousands of words; the plots of stories, curiously broken up and subdivided; huge extracts from *Roget's Thesaurus;* pages filled with the first names of men and women; hundreds of surnames taken from the telephone directory; intricate drawings of wires and circuits and switches and thermionic valves; drawings of machines that could punch holes of different shapes in little cards, and of a strange electrical typewriter that could type ten thousand words a minute. Also, a kind of control panel with a series of small push-buttons, each one labelled with the name of a famous American magazine.

He was working in a mood of exultation, prowling around the room amidst this littering of paper, rubbing his hands together, talking out loud to himself; and sometimes, with a sly curl of the nose, he would mutter a series of murderous imprecations in which the word 'editor' seemed always to be present. On the fifteenth day of continuous work, he collected the papers into two large folders which he carried—almost at a run—to the offices of John Bohlen Inc., electrical engineers.

Mr. Bohlen was pleased to see him back.

"Well Knipe, good gracious me, you look a hundred per cent better. You have a good holiday? Where'd you go?"

He's just as ugly and untidy as ever, Mr. Bohlen thought. Why doesn't he stand up straight? He looks like a bent stick. "You look a hundred per cent better, my boy." I wonder what he's grinning about. Every time I see him, his ears seem to have got larger.

Adolph Knipe placed the folders on the desk. "Look, Mr. Bohlen!" he cried. "Look at these!"

Then he poured out his story. He opened the folders and pushed the plans in front of the astonished little man. He talked for over an hour, explaining everything, and when he had finished, he stepped back, breathless, flushed, waiting for the verdict.

"You know what I think, Knipe? I think you're nuts." Careful now, Mr. Bohlen told himself. Treat him carefully. He's valuable, this one is. If only he didn't look so awful, with that long horse face and the big teeth. The fellow had ears as big as rhubarb leaves.

"But Mr. Bohlen! It'll work! I've proved to you it'll work! You can't deny that!"

"Take it easy now, Knipe. Take it easy, and listen to me." Adolph Knipe watched his man, disliking him more every second.

"This idea," Mr. Bohlen's lower lip was saying, "is very

ingenious—I might almost say brilliant—and it only goes to confirm my high opinion of your abilities, Knipe. But don't take it too seriously. After all, my boy, what possible use can it be to us? Who on earth wants a machine for writing stories? And where's the money in it, anyway? Just tell me that."

"May I sit down, sir?"

"Sure, take a seat."

Adolph Knipe seated himself on the edge of a chair. The older man watched him with alert brown eyes, wondering what was coming now.

"I would like to explain something, Mr. Bohlen, if I may, about how I came to do all this."

"Go right ahead, Knipe." He would have to be humoured a little now, Mr. Bohlen told himself. The boy was really valuable—a sort of genius, almost—worth his weight in gold to the firm. Just look at these papers here. Darndest thing you ever saw. Astonishing piece of work. Quite useless, of course. No commercial value. But it proved again the boy's ability.

"It's a sort of confession, I suppose, Mr. Bohlen. I think it explains why I've always been so . . . so kind of worried."

"You tell me anything you want, Knipe. I'm here to help you—you know that."

The young man clasped his hands together tight on his lap, hugging himself with his elbows. It seemed as though suddenly he was feeling very cold.

"You see, Mr. Bohlen, to tell the honest truth, I don't really care much for my work here. I know I'm good at it and all that sort of thing, but my heart's not in it. It's not what I want to do most."

Up went Mr. Bohlen's eyebrows, quick like a spring. His whole body became very still.

"You see, sir, all my life I've wanted to be a writer."

"A writer!"

"Yes, Mr. Bohlen. You may not believe it, but every bit of spare time I've had, I've spent writing stories. In the last ten years I've written hundreds, literally hundreds of short stories. Five hundred and sixty-six, to be precise. Approximately one a week."

"Good heavens, man! What on earth did you do that for?"

"All I know, sir, is I have the urge."

"What sort of urge?"

"The creative urge, Mr. Bohlen." Every time he looked up he saw Mr. Bohlen's lips. They were growing thinner and thinner, more and more purple.

"And may I ask you what you do with these stories, Knipe?"

"Well sir, that's the trouble. No one will buy them. Each time I finish one, I send it out on the rounds. It goes to one magazine after another. That's all that happens, Mr. Bohlen, and they simply send them back. It's very depressing."

Mr. Bohlen relaxed. "I can see quite well how you feel, my boy." His voice was dripping with sympathy. "We all go through it one time or another in our lives. But now—now that you've had proof—positive proof—from the experts themselves, from the editors, that your stories are—

what shall I say—rather unsuccessful, it's time to leave off. Forget it, my boy. Just forget all about it."

"No, Mr. Bohlen! No! That's not true! I *know* my stories are good. My heavens, when you compare them with the stuff some of those magazines print—oh my word, Mr. Bohlen!—the sloppy, boring stuff that you see in the magazines week after week—why, it drives me mad!"

"Now wait a minute, my boy . . ."

"Do you ever read the magazines, Mr. Bohlen?"

"You'll pardon me, Knipe, but what's all this got to do with your machine?"

"Everything, Mr. Bohlen, absolutely everything! What I want to tell you is, I've made a study of the magazines, and it seems that each one tends to have its own particular type of story. The writers—the successful ones—know this, and they write accordingly."

"Just a minute, my boy. Calm yourself down, will you. I don't think all this is getting us anywhere."

"*Please*, Mr. Bohlen, hear me through. It's all terribly important." He paused to catch his breath. He was properly worked up now, throwing his hands around as he talked. The long, toothy face, with the big ears on either side, simply shone with enthusiasm, and there was an excess of saliva in his mouth which caused him to speak his words wet. "So you see, on my machine, by having an adjustable co-ordinator between the 'plot-memory' section and the 'word-memory' section, I am able to produce any type of story I desire simply by pressing the required button."

"Yes, I know, Knipe, I know. This is all very interesting, but what's the point of it?"

"Just this, Mr. Bohlen. The market is limited. We've got to be able to produce the right stuff, at the right time, whenever we want it. It's a matter of business, that's all. I'm looking at it from *your* point of view now—as a commercial proposition."

"My dear boy, it can't possibly be a commercial proposition—ever. You know as well as I do what it costs to build one of these machines."

"Yes sir, I do. But with due respect, I don't believe you know what the magazines pay writers for stories."

"What do they pay?"

"Anything up to twenty-five hundred dollars. It probably averages around a thousand."

Mr. Bohlen jumped.

"Yes *sir*, it's true."

"Absolutely impossible, Knipe! Ridiculous!"

"No sir, it's true."

"You mean to sit there and tell me that these magazines pay out money like that to a man for . . . just for scribbling off a story! Good heavens, Knipe! Whatever next! Writers must all be millionaires!"

"That's exactly it, Mr. Bohlen! That's where the machine comes in. Listen a minute, sir, while I tell you some more. I've got it all worked out. The big magazines are carrying approximately three fiction stories in each issue. Now, take the fifteen most important magazines—the ones paying the most money. A few of them are monthlies, but most of them come out every week. All right. That makes, let us say, around forty big money stories being bought each week. That's forty thousand dollars. So with our machine—when we get it working properly—we can collar nearly the whole of this market!"

"My dear boy, you're mad!"

"No sir, honestly, it's true what I say. Don't you see that with volume alone we'll completely overwhelm them! This machine can produce a five-thousand word story, all typed and ready for despatch, in thirty seconds. How can the writers compete with that? I ask you, Mr. Bohlen, *how?*"

At that point, Adolph Knipe noticed a slight change in the man's expression, an extra brightness in the eyes, the nostrils distending, the whole face becoming still, almost rigid. Quickly, he continued. "Nowadays, Mr. Bohlen, the hand-made article hasn't a hope. It can't possibly compete with mass-production, especially in this country—you know that. Carpets . . . chairs . . . shoes . . . bricks . . . crockery . . . anything you like to mention—they're all made by machinery now. The quality may be inferior, but that doesn't matter. It's the cost of production that counts. And stories—well—they're just another product, like carpets or chairs, and no one cares how you produce them so long as you deliver the goods. We'll sell them wholesale, Mr. Bohlen! We'll undercut every writer in the country! We'll corner the market!"

Mr. Bohlen edged up straighter in his chair. He was leaning forward now, both elbows on the desk, the face alert, the small brown eyes resting on the speaker.

"I still think it's impracticable, Knipe."

"Forty thousand a week!" cried Adolph Knipe. "And if we halve the price, making it twenty thousand a week, that's still a million a year!" And softly he added, "You didn't get any million a year for building the old electronic calculator, did you, Mr. Bohlen?"

"But seriously now, Knipe. D'you really think they'd buy them?"

"Listen, Mr. Bohlen. Who on earth is going to want custom-made stories when they can get the other kind at half the price? It stands to reason, doesn't it?"

"And how will you sell them? Who will you say has written them?"

"We'll set up our own literary agency, and we'll distribute them through that. And we'll invent all the names we want for the writers."

"I don't like it, Knipe. To me, that smacks of trickery, does it not?"

"And another thing, Mr. Bohlen. There's all manner of valuable by-products once you've got started. Take advertising, for example. Beer manufacturers and people like that are willing to pay good money these days if famous writers will lend their names to their products. Why, my heavens, Mr. Bohlen! This isn't any children's play-thing we're talking about. It's big business."

"Don't get too ambitious, my boy."

"And another thing. There isn't any reason why we shouldn't put *your* name, Mr. Bohlen, on some of the better stories, if you wished it."

"My goodness, Knipe. What should I want that for?"

"I don't know, sir, except that some writers get to be

very much respected—like Mr. Erle Gardner or Kathleen Norris, for example. We've got to have names, and I was certainly thinking of using my own on one or two stories, just to help out."

"A writer, eh?" Mr. Bohlen said, musing. "Well, it would surely surprise them over at the club when they saw my name in the magazines—the good magazines."

"That's right, Mr. Bohlen."

For a moment, a dreamy, faraway look came into Mr. Bohlen's eyes, and he smiled. Then he stirred himself and began leafing through the plans that lay before him.

"One thing I don't quite understand, Knipe. Where do the plots come from? The machine can't possibly invent plots."

"We feed those in, sir. That's no problem at all. Everyone has plots. There's three or four hundred of them written down in that folder there on your left. Feed them straight into the 'plot-memory' section of the machine."

"Go on."

"There are many other little refinements too, Mr. Bohlen. You'll see them all when you study the plans carefully. For example, there's a trick that nearly every writer uses, of inserting at least one long, obscure word into each story. This makes the reader think that the man is very wise and clever. So I have the machine do the same thing. There'll be a whole stack of long words stored away just for this purpose."

"Where?"

"In the 'word-memory' section," he said, epexegetically. Through most of that day the two men discussed the possibilities of the new engine. In the end, Mr. Bohlen said he would have to think about it some more. The next morning, he was quietly enthusiastic. Within a week, he was completely sold on the idea.

"What we'll have to do, Knipe, is to say that we're merely building another mathematical calculater, but of a new type. That'll keep the secret."

"Exactly, Mr. Bohlen."

And in six months the machine was completed. It was housed in a separate brick building at the back of the premises, and now that it was ready for action, no one was allowed near it excepting Mr. Bohlen and Adolph Knipe.

It was an exciting moment when the two men—the one, short, plump, breviped—the other tall, thin and toothy—stood in the corridor before the control panel and got ready to run off the first story. All around them were walls dividing up into many small corridors, and the walls were covered with wiring and plugs and switches and huge glass valves. They were both nervous, Mr. Bohlen hopping from one foot to the other, quite unable to keep still.

"Which button?" Adolph Knipe asked, eyeing a row of small white discs that resembled the keys of a typewriter. "You choose, Mr. Bohlen. Lots of magazines to pick from —*Saturday Evening Post*, *Collier's*, *Ladies' Home Journal* —any one you like."

"Goodness me, boy! How do I know." He was jumping up and down like a man with hives.

"Mr. Bohlen," Adolph Knipe said gravely, "do you realize that at this moment, with your little finger alone, you have it in your power to become the most versatile writer on this continent?"

"Listen Knipe, just get on with it, will you please—and cut out the preliminaries."

"Okay, Mr. Bohlen. Then we'll make it . . . let me see—this one. How's that?" He extended one finger and pressed down a button with the name *TODAY'S WOMAN* printed across it in diminutive black type. There was a sharp click, and when he took his finger away, the button remained down, below the level of the others.

"So much for the selection," he said. "Now—here we go!" He reached up and pulled a switch on the panel. Immediately, the room was filled with a loud humming noise, and a crackling of electric sparks, and the jingle of many, tiny, quickly-moving levers; and almost in the same instant, sheets of quarto paper began sliding out from a slot to the right of the control panel and dropping into a basket below. They came out quick, one sheet a second, and in less than half a minute it was all over. The sheets stopped coming.

"That's it!" Adolph Knipe cried. "There's your story!"

They grabbed the sheets and began to read. The first one they picked up started as follows: "Aifkjmbsaoe-gwcztpplnvoqudskigt&,fuhpekanvbertyuiolkjhgfdsazxcv-bnm,peruitrehdjkgmvnb,wmsuy . . ." They looked at the others. The style was roughly similar in all of them. Mr. Bohlen began to shout. The younger man tried to calm him down.

"It's all right, sir. Really it is. It only needs a little adjustment. We've got a connection wrong somewhere, that's all. You must remember, Mr. Bohlen, there's over a million feet of wiring in this room. You can't expect everything to be right first time."

"It'll never work," Mr. Bohlen said.

"Be patient, sir. Be patient."

Adolph Knipe set out to discover the fault, and in four days time he announced that all was ready for the next try.

"It'll never work," Mr. Bohlen said. "I know it'll never work."

Knipe smiled and pressed the selector button marked *Reader's Digest*. Then he pulled the switch, and again the strange, exciting, humming sound filled the room. One page of typescript flew out of the slot into the basket.

"Where's the rest?" Mr. Bohlen cried. "It's stopped! It's gone wrong!"

"No sir, it hasn't. It's exactly right. It's for the Digest, don't you see?"

This time, it began: "Fewpeopleyetknowthatarevolutionarynewcurehasbeendiscoveredwhichmaywellbringpermanentrelieftosufferersofthemostdreadeddiseaseofour time . . ." And so on.

"It's gibberish!" Mr. Bohlen shouted.

"No sir, it's fine. Can't you see? It's simply that she's not breaking up the words. That's an easy adjustment. But the story's there. Look, Mr. Bohlen, look! It's all there except that the words are joined together."

And indeed it was.

On the next try a few days later, everything was perfect, even the punctuation. The first story they ran off, for a famous women's magazine, was a solid, plotty story of a boy who wanted to better himself with his rich employer. This boy arranged, so the story went, for a friend to hold up the rich man's daughter on a dark night when she was driving home. Then the boy himself, happening by, knocked the gun out of his friend's hand and rescued the girl. The girl was grateful. But the father was suspicious. He questioned the boy sharply. The boy broke down and confessed. Then the father, instead of kicking him out of the house, said that he admired the boy's resourcefulness. The girl admired his honesty—and his looks. The father promised him to be head of the Accounts Department. The girl married him.

"It's tremendous, Mr. Bohlen! It's exactly right!"

"Seems a bit sloppy to me, my boy."

"No sir, it's a seller, a real seller!"

In his excitement, Adolph Knipe promptly ran off six more stories in as many minutes. All of them—except one, which for some reason came out a trifle lewd—seemed entirely satisfactory.

Mr. Bohlen was now mollified. He agreed to set up a literary agency in an office downtown, and to put Knipe in charge. In a couple of weeks, this was accomplished. Then Knipe mailed out the first dozen stories. He put his own name to four of them, Mr. Bohlen's to one, and for the others he simply invented names.

Five of these stories were promptly accepted. The one with Mr. Bohlen's name on it was turned down with a letter from the fiction editor saying, "This is a skilful job, but in our opinion it doesn't quite come off. We would like to see more of this writer's work . . ." Adolph Knipe took a cab out to the factory and ran off another story for the same magazine. He again put Mr. Bohlen's name to it, and mailed it out immediately. That one they bought.

The money started pouring in. Knipe slowly and carefully stepped up the output, and in six months' time he was delivering thirty stories a week, and selling about half.

He began to make a name for himself in literary circles as a prolific and successful writer. So did Mr. Bohlen; but not quite such a good name, although he didn't know it. At the same time, Knipe was building up a dozen or more fictitious persons as promising young authors. Everything was going fine.

At this point it was decided to adapt the machine for writing novels as well as stories. Mr. Bohlen, thirsting now for greater honours in the literary world, insisted that Knipe go to work at once on this prodigous task.

"I want to do a novel," he kept saying. "I want to do a novel."

"And so you will, sir. And so you will. But please be patient. This is a very complicated adjustment I have to make."

"Everyone tells me I ought to do a novel," Mr. Bohlen cried. "All sorts of publishers are chasing after me day and night begging me to stop fooling around with stories and do something really important instead. A novel's the only thing that counts—that's what they say."

"We're all going to do novels," Knipe told him. "Just as many as we want. But please be patient."

"Now listen to me, Knipe. What I'm going to do is a *serious* novel, something that'll make 'em sit up and take notice. I've been getting rather tired of the sort of stories you've been putting my name to lately. As a matter of fact, I'm none too sure you haven't been trying to make a monkey out of me."

"A monkey, Mr. Bohlen?"

"Keeping all the best ones for yourself, that's what you've been doing."

"Oh no, Mr. Bohlen! No!"

"So this time I'm going to make damn sure I write a high class intelligent book. You understand that."

"Look, Mr. Bohlen. With the sort of switchboard I'm rigging up, you'll be able to write any sort of book you want."

And this was true, for within another couple of months, the genius of Adolph Knipe had not only adapted the machine for novel writing, but had constructed a marvellous new control system which enabled the author to pre-select literally any type of plot and any style of writing he desired. There were so many dials and levers on the thing, it looked like the instrument panel of some enormous airplane.

First, by depressing one of a series of master buttons, the writer made his primary decision: historical, satirical, philosophical, political, romantic, erotic, humorous, or straight. Then, from the second row (the basic buttons), he chose his theme: army life, pioneer days, civil war, world war, racial problem, wild west, country life, childhood memories, seafaring, the sea bottom, and many, many more. The third row of buttons gave a choice of literary style: classical, whimsical, racy, Hemingway, Faulkner, Joyce, feminine, etc. The fourth row was for characters, the fifth for wordage—and so on and so on—ten long rows of pre-selector buttons.

But that wasn't all. Control had also to be exercised during the actual writing process (which took about fifteen minutes per novel), and to do this the author had to sit, as it were, in the driver's seat, and pull (or push) a battery of labelled stops, as on an organ. By so doing, he was able continually to modulate or merge fifty different and variable qualities such as tension, surprise, humor, pathos, and mystery. Numerous dials and gauges on the dashboard itself told him throughout exactly how far along he was with his work.

Finally, there was the question of "passion." From a careful study of the books at the top of the best-seller lists for the past year, Adolph Knipe had decided that this was the most important ingredient of all—a magical catalyst that somehow or other could transform the dullest novel into a howling success—at any rate financially. But Knipe also knew that passion was powerful, heady stuff, and must be prudently dispensed—the right proportions at the right moments; and to ensure this, he had devised an independent control consisting of two sensitive sliding adjustors operated by footpedals, similar to the throttle and brake in a car. One pedal governed the percentage of passion to be injected, the other regulated its intensity. There was no doubt, of course—and this was the only drawback —that the writing of a novel by the Knipe method was going to be rather like flying a plane and driving a car and playing an organ all at the same time, but this did not trouble the inventor. When all was ready, he proudly escorted Mr. Bohlen into the machine house and began to explain the operating procedure for the new wonder.

"Good God, Knipe! I'll never be able to do all that! Dammit, man, it'd be easier to write the thing by hand!"

"You'll soon get used to it, Mr. Bohlen, I promise you. In a week or two, you'll be doing it without hardly thinking. It's just like learning to drive."

Well, it wasn't quite as easy as that, but after many hours of practice, Mr. Bohlen began to get the hang of it, and finally, late one evening, he told Knipe to make ready for running off the first novel. It was a tense moment, with the fat little man crouching nervously in the driver's seat, and the tall toothy Knipe fussing excitedly around him.

"I intend to write an important novel, Knipe."

"I'm sure you will, sir. I'm sure you will."

With one finger, Mr. Bohlen carefully pressed the necessary pre-selector buttons:

> Master button—*satirical*
> Subject—*racial problem*
> Style—*classical*
> Characters—*six men, four women, one infant*
> Length—*fifteen chapters*.

At the same time he had his eye particularly upon three organ stops marked *power, mystery, profundity*.

"Are you ready, sir?"

"Yes, yes, I'm ready."

Knipe pulled the switch. The great engine hummed. There was a deep whirring sound from the oiled movement of fifty thousand cogs and rods and levers; then came the drumming of the rapid electrical typewriter, setting up a shrill, almost intolerable clatter. Out into the basket flew the typewritten pages—one every two seconds. But what with the noise and the excitement, and having to play upon the stops, and watch the chapter-counter and the pace-indicator and the passion-gauge, Mr. Bohlen began to panic. He reacted in precisely the way a learner driver does in a car—by pressing both feet hard down on the pedals and keeping them there until the thing stopped.

"Congratulations on your first novel," Knipe said, picking up the great bundle of typed pages from the basket.

Little pearls of sweat were oozing out all over Mr. Bohlen's face. "It sure was hard work, my boy."

"But you got it done, sir. You got it done."

"Let me see it, Knipe. How does it read?"

He started to go through the first chapter, passing each finished page to the younger man.

"Good heavens, Knipe! What's this!" Mr. Bohlen's thin purple fish-lip was moving slightly as it mouthed the words, his cheeks were beginning slowly to inflate.

"But look here, Knipe! This is outrageous!"

"I must say it's a bit fruity, sir."

"*Fruity!* It's perfectly revolting! I can't possibly put my name to this!"

"Quite right, sir. Quite right."

"Knipe! Is this some nasty trick you've been playing on me?"

"Oh no, sir! No!"

"It certainly looks like it."

"You don't think, Mr. Bohlen, that you mightn't have been pressing a little hard on the passion-control pedals, do you?"

"My dear boy, how should *I* know."

"Why don't you try another?"

So Mr. Bohlen ran off a second novel, and this time it went according to plan.

Within a week, the manuscript had been read and accepted by an enthusiastic publisher. Knipe followed with one in his own name, then made a dozen more for good measure. In no time at all, Adolph Knipe's Literary Agency had become famous for its large stable of promising young novelists. And once again the money started rolling in.

It was at this stage that young Knipe began to display a real talent for big business.

"See here, Mr. Bohlen," he said. "We still got too much competition. Why don't we just absorb all the other writers in the country?"

Mr. Bohlen, who now sported a bottle-green velvet jacket and allowed his hair to cover two-thirds of his ears, was quite content with things the way they were. "Don't know what you mean, my boy. You can't just absorb writers."

"Of course you can, sir. Exactly like Rockefeller did with his oil companies. Simply buy 'em out, and if they won't sell, squeeze 'em out. It's easy!"

"Careful now, Knipe. Be careful."

"I've got a list here, sir, of fifty of the most successful writers in the country, and what I intend to do is offer each one of them a lifetime contract with pay. All *they* have to do is undertake never to write another word; and, of course, to let us use their names on our own stuff. How about that?"

"They'll never agree."

"You don't know writers, Mr. Bohlen. You watch and see."

"What about that creative urge, Knipe?"

"It's bunk! All they're really interested in is the money —just like everybody else."

In the end, Mr. Bohlen reluctantly agreed to give it a try, and Knipe, with his list of writers in his pocket, went off in a large chauffeur-driven Cadillac to make his calls.

He journeyed first to the man at the top of the list, a very great and wonderful writer, and he had no trouble getting into the house. He told his story and produced a suitcase full of sample novels, and a contract for the man to sign which guaranteed him so much a year for life. The man listened politely, decided he was dealing with a lunatic, gave him a drink, then firmly showed him to the door.

The second writer on the list, when he saw Knipe was serious, actually attacked him with a large metal paperweight, and the inventor had to flee down the garden followed by such a torrent of abuse and obscenity as he had never heard before.

But it took more than this to discourage Adolph Knipe. He was disappointed but not dismayed, and off he went in his big car to seek his next client. This one was a female, famous and popular, whose fat romantic books sold by the million across the country. She received Knipe graciously, gave him tea, and listened attentively to his story.

"It all sounds very fascinating," she said. "But of course I find it a little hard to believe."

"Madam," Knipe answered. "Come with me and see it with your own eyes. My car awaits you."

So off they went, and in due course, the astonished lady was ushered into the machine house where the wonder was kept. Eagerly, Knipe explained its workings, and after a while he even permitted her to sit in the driver's seat and practice with the buttons.

"All right," he said suddenly, "You want to do a book now?"

"Oh yes!" she cried. "Please!"

She was very competent and seemed to know exactly what she wanted. She made her own pre-selections, then ran off a long, romantic, passion-filled novel. She read through the first chapter and became so enthusiastic that she signed up on the spot.

"That's one of them out of the way," Knipe said to Mr. Bohlen afterwards. "A pretty big one too."

"Nice work, my boy."

"And you know *why* she signed?"

"Why?"

"It wasn't the money. She's got plenty of that."

"Then why?"

Knipe grinned, lifting his lip and baring a long pale upper gum. "Simply because she saw the machine-made stuff was better than her own."

Thereafter, Knipe wisely decided to concentrate only upon mediocrity. Anything better than that—and there were so few it didn't matter much—was apparently not quite so easy to seduce.

In the end, after several months of work, he had persuaded something like seventy per cent of the writers on his list to sign the contract. He found that the older ones, those who were running out of ideas and had taken to drink, were the easiest to handle. The younger people were more troublesome. They were apt to become abusive, sometimes violent when he approached them; and more than once Knipe was slightly injured on his rounds.

But on the whole, it was a satisfactory beginning. This last year—the first full year of the machine's operation—it was estimated that at least one half of all the novels and stories published in the English language were produced by Adolph Knipe upon the Great Automatic Grammatisator.

Does this surprise you?

I doubt it.

And worse is yet to come. Today, as the secret spreads, many more are hurrying to tie up with Mr. Knipe. And all the time the screw turns tighter for those who hesitate to sign their names.

This very moment, as I sit here listening to the howling of my nine starving children in the other room, I can feel my own hand creeping closer and closer to that golden contract that lies over on the other side of the desk.

Give us strength, oh Lord, to let our children starve.

CLAUD'S DOG

The Ratcatcher

In the afternoon the ratcatcher came to the filling station. He came sidling up the driveway with a stealthy, soft-treading gait, making no noise at all with his feet on the gravel. He had an army knapsack slung over one shoulder and he was wearing an old-fashioned black jacket with large pockets. His brown corduroy trousers were tied around the knees with pieces of white string.

"Yes?" Claud asked, knowing very well who he was.

"Rodent operative." His small dark eyes moved swiftly over the premises.

"The ratcatcher?"

"That's me."

The man was lean and brown with a sharp face and two long sulphur-coloured teeth that protruded from the upper jaw, overlapping the lower lip, pressing it inward. The ears were thin and pointed and set far back on the head, near the nape of the neck. The eyes were almost black, but when they looked at you there was a flash of yellow somewhere inside them.

"You've come very quick."

"Special orders from the Health Officer."

"And now you're going to catch all the rats?"

"Yep."

The kind of dark furtive eyes he had were those of an animal that lives its life peering out cautiously and forever from a hole in the ground.

"How are you going to catch em?"

"Ah-h-h," the ratman said darkly. "That's all accordin to where they is."

"Trap em, I suppose."

"Trap em!" he cried, disgusted. "You won't catch many rats that way! Rats isn't rabbits you know."

He held his face up high, sniffing the air with a nose that twitched perceptibly from side to side.

"No," he said, scornfully. "Trappin's no way to catch a rat. Rats is clever, let me tell you that. If you want to catch em, you got to know em. You got to know rats on this job."

I could see Claud staring at him with a certain fascination.

"They're more clever'n dogs, rats is."

"Get away."

"You know what they do? They watch you! All the time you're goin round preparin to catch em, they're sittin quietly in dark places, watchin you." The man crouched, stretching his stringy neck far forward.

"So what do you do?" Claud asked, fascinated.

"Ah! That's it you see. That's where you got to know rats."

"How d'you catch em?"

"There's ways," the ratman said, leering. "There's various ways."

He paused, nodding his repulsive head sagely up and down. "It's all dependin," he said, "on where they is. This ain't a sewer job, is it?"

"No, it's not a sewer job."

"Tricky things, sewer jobs. Yes," he said, delicately sniffing the air to the left of him with his mobile nose-end, "sewer jobs is very tricky things."

"Not especially, I shouldn't think."

"Oh-ho. You shouldn't, shouldn't you! Well, I'd like to see *you* do a sewer job! Just exackly how would *you* set about it, I'd like to know?"

"Nothing to it. I'd just poison em, that's all."

"And where exackly would you put the poison, might I ask?"

"Down the sewer. Where the hell you think I put it!"

"There!" the ratman cried, triumphant. "I knew it! Down the sewer! And you know what'd happen then? Get washed away, that's all. Sewer's like a river, y'know."

"That's what *you* say," Claud answered. "That's only what *you* say."

"It's facts."

"All right then, all right. So what would *you* do, Mr. Know-all?"

"That's exackly where you got to know rats, on a sewer job."

"Come on then, let's have it."

"Now listen. I'll tell you." The ratman advanced a step closer, his voice became secretive and confidential, the voice of a man divulging fabulous professional secrets. "You works on the understandin that a rat is a gnawin animal, see. Rats *gnaws*. Anythin you give em, don't matter what it is, anythin new they never seen before, and what do they do? They *gnaws* it. So now! There you are! You got a sewer job on your hands. And what d'you do?"

His voice had the soft throaty sound of a croaking frog and he seemed to speak all his words with an immense wet-lipped relish, as though they tasted good on the tongue. The accent was similar to Claud's, the broad soft accent of the Buckinghamshire countryside, but his voice was more throaty, the words more fruity in his mouth.

"All you do is you go down the sewer and you take along some ordinary paper bags, just ordinary brown paper bags, and these bags is filled with plaster of Paris powder. Nothin else. Then you suspend the bags from the roof of the sewer so they hang down not quite touchin the water. See? Not quite touchin, and just high enough so a rat can reach em."

Claud was listening, rapt.

"There you are, y'see. Old rat comes swimmin along the sewer and sees the bag. He stops. He takes a sniff at it and it don't smell so bad anyway. So what's he do then?"

"He *gnaws* it," Claud cried, delighted.

"There! That's it! That's exackly it! He starts *gnawin* away at the bag and the bag breaks and the old rat gets a mouthful of powder for his pains."

"Well?"

"That does him."

"What? Kills him?"

"Yep. Kills him stony!"

"Plaster of Paris ain't poisonous, you know."

"Ah! There you are! That's exackly where you're wrong, see. This powder swells. When you wet it, it swells. Gets into the rat's tubes and swells right up and kills him quicker'n anythin in the world."

"*No!*"

"That's where you got to know rats."

The ratman's face glowed with a stealthy pride, and he rubbed his stringy fingers together, holding the hands up close to the face. Claud watched him, fascinated.

"Now—where's them rats?" The word "rats" came out of his mouth soft and throaty, with a rich fruity relish as though he were gargling with melted butter. "Let's take a look at them *rraats.*"

"Over there in the hayrick across the road."

"Not in the house?" he asked, obviously disappointed.

"No. Only around the hayrick. Nowhere else."

"I'll wager they're in the house too. Like as not gettin in all your food in the night and spreadin disease and sickness. You got any disease here?" he asked, looking first at me, then at Claud.

"Everyone fine here."

"Quite sure?"

"Oh yes."

"You never know, you see. You could be sickenin for it weeks and weeks and not feel it. Then all of a sudden—

bang!—and it's got you. That's why Doctor Arbuthnot's so particular. That's why he sent me out so quick, see. To stop the spreadin of disease."

He had now taken upon himself the mantle of the Health Officer. A most important rat he was now, deeply disappointed that we were not suffering from bubonic plague.

"I feel fine," Claud said, nervously.

The ratman searched his face again, but said nothing.

"And how are you goin to catch em in the hayrick?"

The ratman grinned, a crafty toothy grin. He reached down into his knapsack and withdrew a large tin which he held up level with his face. He peered around one side of it at Claud.

"Poison!" he whispered. But he pronounced it *pye-zn*, making it into a soft, dark, dangerous word. "Deadly *pye-zn*, that's what this is!" He was weighing the tin up and down in his hands as he spoke. "Enough here to kill a million men!"

"Terrifying," Claud said.

"Exackly it! They'd put you inside for six months if they caught you with even a spoonful of this," he said, wetting his lips with his tongue. He had a habit of craning his head forward on his neck as he spoke.

"Want to see?" he asked, taking a penny from his pocket, prising open the lid. "There now! There it is!" He spoke fondly, almost lovingly of the stuff, and he held it forward for Claud to look.

"Corn? Or barley is it?"

"It's oats. Soaked in deadly *pye-zn*. You take just one of

them grains in your mouth and you'd be a gonner in five minutes!"

"Honest?"

"Yep. Never out of me sight, this tin."

He caressed it with his hands and gave it a little shake so that the oat grains rustled softly inside.

"But not today. Your rats don't get this today. They wouldn't have it anyway. That they wouldn't. There's where you got to know rats. Rats is suspicious. Terrible suspicious, rats is. So today they gets some nice clean tasty oats as'll do em no harm in the world. Fatten em, that's all it'll do. And tomorrow they gets the same again. And it'll taste so good there'll be all the rats in the districk comin along after a couple of days."

"Rather clever."

"You got to be clever on this job. You got to be cleverer'n a rat and that's sayin somethin."

"You've almost got to be a rat yourself," I said. It slipped out in error, before I had time to stop myself, and I couldn't really help it because I was looking at the man at the time. But the effect upon him was surprising.

"There!" he cried. "Now you got it! Now you really said somethin! A good ratter's got to be more like a rat than anythin else in the world! Cleverer even than a rat, and that's not an easy thing to be, let me tell you!"

"Quite sure it's not."

"All right then, let's go. I haven't got all day, you know. There's Lady Leonora Benson asking for me urgent up there at the Manor."

"She got rats, too?"

"Everybody's got rats," the ratman said, and he ambled off down the driveway, across the road to the hayrick and we watched him go. The way he walked was so like a rat it made you wonder—that slow, almost a delicate ambling walk with a lot of give at the knees and no sound at all from the footsteps on the gravel. He hopped nimbly over the gate into the field, then walked quickly round the hayrick scattering handfuls of oats onto the ground.

The next day he returned and repeated the procedure.

The day after that he came again and this time he put down the poisoned oats. But he didn't scatter these; he placed them carefully in little piles at each corner of the rick.

"You got a dog?" he asked when he came back across the road on the third day after putting down the poison.

"Yes."

"Now if you want to see your dog die an orrible twistin death, all you got to do is let him in that gate sometime."

"We'll take care," Claud told him. "Don't you worry about that."

The next day he returned once more, this time to collect the dead.

"You got an old sack?" he asked. "Most likely we goin to need a sack to put em in."

He was puffed up and important now, the black eyes gleaming with pride. He was about to display the sensational results of his craft to the audience.

Claud fetched a sack and the three of us walked across the road, the ratman leading. Claud and I leaned over the gate, watching. The ratman prowled around the hayrick, bending over to inspect his little piles of poison.

"Somethin wrong here," he muttered. His voice was soft and angry.

He ambled over to another pile and got down on his knees to examine it closely.

"Somethin bloody wrong here."

"What's the matter?"

He didn't answer, but it was clear that the rats hadn't touched his bait.

"These are very clever rats here," I said.

"Exactly what I told him, Gordon. These aren't just no ordinary kind of rats you're dealing with here."

The ratman walked over to the gate. He was very annoyed and showed it on his face and around the nose and by the way the two yellow teeth were pressing down into the skin of his lower lip. "Don't give me that crap," he said, looking at me. "There's nothin wrong with these rats except somebody's feedin em. They got somethin juicy to eat somewhere and plenty of it. There's no rats in the world'll turn down oats unless their bellies is full to burstin."

"They're clever," Claud said.

The man turned away, disgusted. He knelt down again and began to scoop up the poisoned oats with a small shovel, tipping them carefully back into the tin. When he had done, all three of us walked back across the road.

The ratman stood near the petrol-pumps, a rather sorry, humble ratman now whose face was beginning to take on a brooding aspect. He had withdrawn into himself and

was brooding in silence over his failure, the eyes veiled
and wicked, the little tongue darting out to one side of the
two yellow teeth, keeping the lips moist. It appeared to be
essential that the lips should be kept moist. He looked up
at me, a quick surreptitious glance, then over at Claud.
His nose-end twitched, sniffing the air. He raised himself
up and down a few times on his toes, swaying gently, and
in a voice soft and secretive, he said: "Want to see
somethin?" He was obviously trying to retrieve his reputation.

"What?"

"Want to see somethin *amazin*?" As he said this he put
his right hand into the deep poacher's pocket of his jacket
and brought out a large live rat clasped tight between his
fingers.

"Good God!"

"Ah! That's it, y'see!" He was crouching slightly now
and craning his neck forward and leering at us and holding this enormous brown rat in his hands, one finger and
thumb making a tight circle around the creature's neck,
clamping its head rigid so it couldn't turn and bite.

"D'you usually carry rats around in your pockets?"

"Always got a rat or two about me somewhere."

With that he put his free hand into the other pocket and
produced a small white ferret.

"Ferret," he said, holding it up by the neck.

The ferret seemed to know him and stayed still in his
grasp.

"There's nothin'll kill a rat quicker'n a ferret. And
there's nothin a rat's more frightened of either."

He brought his hands close together in front of him so that the ferret's nose was within six inches of the rat's face. The pink beady eyes of the ferret stared at the rat. The rat struggled, trying to edge away from the killer.

"Now," he said. "Watch!"

His khaki shirt was open at the neck and he lifted the rat and slipped it down inside his shirt, next to his skin. As soon as his hand was free, he unbuttoned his jacket at the front so that the audience could see the bulge the body of the rat made under his shirt. His belt prevented it from going down lower than his waist.

Then he slipped the ferret in after the rat.

Immediately there was a great commotion inside the shirt. It appeared that the rat was running around the man's body, being chased by the ferret. Six or seven times they went around, the small bulge chasing the larger one, gaining on it slightly each circuit and drawing closer and closer until at last the two bulges seemed to come together and there was a scuffle and a series of shrill shrieks.

Throughout this performance the ratman had stood absolutely still with legs apart, arms hanging loosely, the dark eyes resting on Claud's face. Now he reached one hand down into his shirt and pulled out the ferret; with the other he took out the dead rat. There were traces of blood around the white muzzle of the ferret.

"Not sure I liked that very much."

"You never seen anythin like it before, I'll bet you that."

"Can't really say I have."

"Like as not you'll get yourself a nasty little nip in the guts one of these days," Claud told him. But he was clearly impressed, and the ratman was becoming cocky again.

"Want to see somethin far more *amazin'n* that?" he asked. "You want to see somethin you'd never even *believe* unless you seen it with your own eyes?"

"Well?"

We were standing in the driveway out in front of the pumps and it was one of those pleasant warm November mornings. Two cars pulled in for petrol, one right after the other, and Claud went over and gave them what they wanted.

"You want to see?" the ratman asked.

I glanced at Claud, slightly apprehensive. "Yes," Claud said. "Come on then, let's see."

The ratman slipped the dead rat back into one pocket, the ferret into the other. Then he reached down into his knapsack and produced—if you please—a second live rat.

"Good Christ!" Claud said.

"Always got one or two rats about me somewhere," the man announced calmly. "You got to know rats on this job and if you want to know em you got to have em round you. This is a sewer rat, this is. An old sewer rat, clever as buggery. See him watchin me all the time, wonderin what I'm goin to do? See him?"

"Very unpleasant."

"What are you going to do?" I asked. I had a feeling I was going to like this one even less than the last.

"Fetch me a piece of string."

Claud fetched him a piece of string.

With his left hand, the man looped the string around

one of the rat's hind legs. The rat struggled, trying to turn its head to see what was going on, but he held it tight around the neck with finger and thumb.

"Now!" he said, looking about him. "You got a table inside."

"We don't want the rat inside the house," I said.

"Well—I need a table. Or somethin flat like a table."

"What about the bonnet of that car?" Claud said.

We walked over to the car and the man put the old sewer rat on the bonnet. He attached the string to the windshield wiper so that the rat was now tethered.

At first it crouched, unmoving and suspicious, a big-bodied grey rat with bright black eyes and a scaly tail that lay in a long curl upon the car's bonnet. It was looking away from the ratman, but watching him sideways to see what he was going to do. The man stepped back a few paces and immediately the rat relaxed. It sat up on its haunches and began to lick the grey fur on its chest. Then it scratched its muzzle with both front paws. It seemed quite unconcerned about the three men standing nearby.

"Now—how about a little bet?" the ratman asked.

"We don't bet," I said.

"Just for fun. It's more fun if you bet."

"What d'you want to bet on?"

"I'll bet you I can kill that rat without usin my hands. I'll put my hands in my pockets and not use em."

"You'll kick it with your feet," Claud said.

It was apparent that the ratman was out to earn some money. I looked at the rat that was going to be killed and began to feel slightly sick, not so much because it was going to be killed but because it was going to be killed in a special way, with a considerable degree of relish.

"No," the ratman said. "No feet."

"Nor arms?" Claud asked.

"Nor arms. Nor legs, nor hands neither."

"You'll sit on it."

"No. No squashin."

"Let's see you do it."

"You bet me first. Bet me a quid."

"Don't be so bloody daft," Claud said. "Why should we give you a quid?"

"What'll you bet?"

"Nothin."

"All right. Then it's no go."

He made as if to untie the string from the windshield wiper.

"I'll bet you a shilling," Claud told him. The sick gastric sensation in my stomach was increasing, but there was an awful magnetism about this business and I found myself quite unable to walk away or even move.

"You too?"

"No," I said.

"What's the matter with you?" the ratman asked.

"I just don't want to bet you, that's all."

"So you want me to do this for a lousy shillin?"

"I don't want you to do it."

"Where's the money?" he said to Claud.

Claud put a shilling piece on the bonnet, near the radiator. The ratman produced two sixpences and laid them beside Claud's money. As he stretched out his hand to do this, the rat cringed, drawing its head back and flattening itself against the bonnet.

"Bet's on," the ratman said.

Claud and I stepped back a few paces. The ratman stepped forward. He put his hands in his pockets and inclined his body from the waist so that his face was on a level with the rat, about three feet away.

His eyes caught the eyes of the rat and held them. The rat was crouching, very tense, sensing extreme danger, but not yet frightened. The way it crouched, it seemed to me it was preparing to spring forward at the man's face; but there must have been some power in the ratman's eyes that prevented it from doing this, and subdued it, and then gradually frightened it so that it began to back away, dragging its body backward with slow crouching steps until the string tautened on its hind leg. It tried to struggle back further against the string, jerking its leg to free it. The man leaned forward toward the rat, following it with his face, watching it all the time with his eyes, and suddenly the rat panicked and leaped sideways in the air. The string pulled it up with a jerk that must almost have dislocated its leg.

It crouched again, in the middle of the bonnet, as far away as the string would allow, and it was properly frightened now, whiskers quivering, the long grey body tense with fear.

At this point, the ratman again began to move his face closer. Very slowly he did it, so slowly there wasn't really any movement to be seen at all except that the face just happened to be a fraction closer each time you looked.

He never took his eyes from the rat. The tension was considerable and I wanted suddenly to cry out and tell him to stop. I wanted him to stop because it was making me feel sick inside, but I couldn't bring myself to say the word. Something extremely unpleasant was about to happen—I was sure of that. Something sinister and cruel and ratlike, and perhaps it really would make me sick. But I had to see it now.

The ratman's face was about eighteen inches from the rat. Twelve inches. Then ten, or perhaps it was eight, and soon there was not more than the length of a man's hand separating their faces. The rat was pressing its body flat against the car-bonnet, tense and terrified. The ratman was also tense, but with a dangerous active tensity that was like a tight-wound spring. The shadow of a smile flickered around the skin of his mouth.

Then suddenly he struck.

He struck as a snake strikes, darting his head forward with one swift knifelike stroke that originated in the muscles of the lower body, and I had a momentary glimpse of his mouth opening very wide and two yellow teeth and the whole face contorted by the effort of mouth-opening.

More than that I did not care to see. I closed my eyes, and when I opened them again the rat was dead and the ratman was slipping the money into his pocket and spitting to clear his mouth.

"That's what they makes lickerish out of," he said. "Rat's blood is what the big factories and the chocolate-people use to make lickerish."

Again the relish, the wet-lipped, lip-smacking relish as he spoke the words, the throaty richness of his voice and the thick syrupy way he pronounced the word *lickerish*.

"No," he said, "There's nothin wrong with a drop of rat's blood."

"Don't talk so absolutely disgusting," Claud told him.

"Ah! But that's it, you see. You eaten it many a time. Penny sticks and lickerish bootlaces is all made from rat's blood."

"We don't want to hear about it, thank you."

"Boiled up, it is, in great cauldrons, bubblin and steamin and men stirrin it with long poles. That's one of the big secrets of the chocolate-makin factories, and no one knows about it—no one except the ratters supplyin the stuff."

Suddenly he noticed that his audience was no longer with him, that our faces were hostile and sick-looking and crimson with anger and disgust. He stopped abruptly, and without another word he turned and sloped off down the driveway out on to the road, moving with the slow, that almost delicate ambling walk that was like a rat prowling, making no noise with his footsteps even on the gravel of the driveway.

CLAUD'S DOG

Rummins

THE SUN was up over the hills now and the mist had cleared and it was wonderful to be striding along the road with the dog in the early morning, especially when it was autumn, with the leaves changing to gold and yellow and sometimes one of them breaking away and falling slowly, turning slowly over in the air, dropping noiselessly right in front of him onto the grass beside the road. There was a small wind up above, and he could hear the beeches rustling and murmuring like a crowd of people.

This was always the best time of the day for Claud Cubbage. He gazed approvingly at the rippling velvety hindquarters of the greyhound trotting in front of him.

"Jackie," he called softly. "Hey, Jackson. How you feeling, boy?"

The dog half turned at the sound of its name and gave a quick acknowledging wag of the tail.

There would never be another dog like this Jackie, he told himself. How beautiful the slim streamlining, the small pointed head, the yellow eyes, the black mobile nose. Beautiful the long neck, the way the deep brisket curved back and up out of sight into no stomach at all.

See how he walked upon his toes, noiselessly, hardly touching the surface of the road at all.

"Jackson," he said. "Good old Jackson."

In the distance, Claud could see Rummins's farmhouse, small, narrow, and ancient, standing back behind the hedge on the right hand side.

I'll turn round there, he decided. That'll be enough for today.

Rummins, carrying a pail of milk across the yard, saw him coming down the road. He set the pail down slowly and came forward to the gate, leaning both arms on the topmost bar, waiting.

"Morning Mr. Rummins," Claud said. It was necessary to be polite to Rummins because of eggs.

Rummins nodded and leaned over the gate, looking critically at the dog.

"Looks well," he said.

"He is well."

"When's he running?"

"I don't know, Mr. Rummins."

"Come on. When's he running?"

"He's only ten months yet, Mr. Rummins. He's not even schooled properly, honest."

The small beady eyes of Rummins peered suspiciously over the top of the gate. "I wouldn't mind betting a couple of quid you're having it off with him somewhere secret soon."

Claud moved his feet uncomfortably on the black road surface. He disliked very much this man with the wide frog mouth, the broken teeth, the shifty eyes; and most of all he disliked having to be polite to him because of eggs.

"That hayrick of yours opposite," he said, searching desperately for another subject. "It's full of rats."

"All hayrick's got rats."

"Not like this one. Matter of fact we've been having a touch of trouble with the authorities about that."

Rummins glanced up sharply. He didn't like trouble with the authorities. Any man who sells eggs blackmarket and kills pigs without a permit is wise to avoid contact with that sort of people.

"What kind of trouble?"

"They sent the ratcatcher along."

"You mean just for a few rats?"

"A few! Blimey, it's *swarming*!"

"Never."

"Honest it is, Mr. Rummins. There's hundreds of em."

"Didn't the ratcatcher catch em?"

"No."

"Why?"

"I reckon they're too artful."

Rummins began thoughtfully to explore the inner rim of one nostril with the end of his thumb, holding the noseflap between thumb and finger as he did so.

"I wouldn't give thank you for no ratcatchers," he said. "Ratcatchers is government men working for the soddin government and I wouldn't give thank you for em."

"Nor me, Mr. Rummins. All ratcatchers is slimy cunning creatures."

"Well," Rummins said, sliding fingers under his cap to scratch the head, "I was coming over soon anyway to fetch in that rick. Reckon I might just as well do it today as any other time. I don't want no government men nosing around my stuff thank you very much."

"Exactly, Mr. Rummins."

"We'll be over later—Bert and me." With that he turned and ambled off across the yard.

Around three in the afternoon, Rummins and Bert were seen riding slowly up the road in a cart drawn by a ponderous and magnificent black carthorse. Opposite the filling station the cart turned off into the field and stopped near the hayrick.

"This ought to be worth seeing," I said. "Get the gun."

Claud fetched the rifle and slipped a cartridge into the breech.

I strolled across the road and leaned against the open gate. Rummins was on the top of the rick now and cutting away at the cord that bound the thatching. Bert remained in the cart, fingering the four-foot-long knife.

Bert had something wrong with one eye. It was pale grey all over, like a boiled fish-eye, and although it was motionless in its socket it appeared always to be looking at you and following you round the way the eyes of the people in some of those portraits do, in the museums. Wherever you stood and wherever Bert was looking, there was this faulty eye fixing you sideways with a cold stare, boiled and misty pale with a little black dot in the centre, like a fish-eye on a plate.

In his build he was the opposite of his father who was short and squat like a frog. Bert was a tall, reedy, boneless boy, loose at the joints, even the head loose upon the shoulders, falling sideways as though perhaps it was too heavy for the neck.

"You only made this rick last June," I said to him. "Why take it away so soon?"

"Dads wants it."

"Funny time to cut a new rick, November."

"Dad wants it," Bert repeated, and both his eyes, the sound one and the other stared down at me with a look of absolute vacuity.

"Going to all that trouble stacking it and thatching it and then pulling it down five months later."

"Dad wants it." Bert's nose was running and he kept wiping it with the back of his hand and wiping the back of the hand on his trousers.

"Come on Bert," Rummins called, and the boy climbed up onto the rick and stood in the place where the thatch had been removed. He took the knife and began to cut down into the tight-packed hay with an easy-swinging, sawing movement, holding the handle with both hands and rocking his body like a man sawing wood with a big saw. I could hear the crisp cutting noise of the blade against the dry hay and the noise becoming softer as the knife sank deeper into the rick.

"Claud's going to take a pot at the rats as they come out."

The man and the boy stopped abruptly and looked

across the road at Claud who was leaning against the red pump with rifle in hand.

"Tell him to put that bloody rifle away," Rummins said.

"He's a good shot. He won't hit you."

"No one's potting no rats alongside of me, don't matter how good they are."

"You'll insult him."

"Tell him to put it away," Rummins said, slow and hostile. "I don't mind dogs nor sticks but I'll be buggered if I'll have rifles."

The two on the hayrick watched while Claud did as he was told, then they resumed their work in silence. Soon Bert came down into the cart, and reaching out with both hands he pulled a slice of solid hay away from the rick so that it dropped neatly into the cart beside him.

A rat, grey-black, with a long tail, came out of the base of the rick and ran into the hedge.

"A rat," I said.

"Kill it," Rummins said. "Why don't you get a stick and kill it?"

The alarm had been given now and the rats were coming out quicker, one or two of them every minute, fat and long-bodied, crouching close to the ground as they ran through the grass into the hedge. Whenever the horse saw one of them it twitched its ears and followed it with uneasy rolling eyes.

Bert had climbed back on top of the rick and was cutting out another bale. Watching him, I saw him suddenly stop, hesitate for perhaps a second, then again begin to cut, but very cautiously this time; and now I could hear a different sound, a muffled rasping noise as the blade of the knife grated against something hard.

Bert pulled out the knife and examined the blade, testing it with his thumb. He put it back, letting it down gingerly into the cut, feeling gently downward until it came again upon the hard object; and once more, when he made another cautious little sawing movement, there came that grating sound.

Rummins turned his head and looked over his shoulder at the boy. He was in the act of lifting an armful of loosened thatch, bending forward with both hands grasping the straw, but he stopped dead in the middle of what he was doing and looked at Bert. Bert remained still, hands holding the handle of the knife, a look of bewilderment on his face. Behind, the sky was a pale clear blue and the two figures up there on the hayrick stood out sharp and black like an etching against the paleness.

Then Rummins' voice, louder than usual, edged with an unmistakable apprehension that the loudness did nothing to conceal: "Some of them haymakers is too bloody careless what they put on a rick these days."

He paused, and again the silence, the men motionless, and across the road Claud leaning motionless against the red pump. It was so quiet suddenly we could hear a woman's voice far down the valley on the next farm calling the men to food.

Then Rummins again, shouting where there was no

need to shout: "Go on, then! Go on an cut through it, Bert! A little stick of wood won't hurt the soddin knife!"

For some reason, as though perhaps scenting trouble, Claud came strolling across the road and joined me leaning on the gate. He didn't say anything, but both of us seemed to know that there was something disturbing about these two men, about the stillness that surrounded them and especially about Rummins himself. Rummins was frightened. Bert was frightened too. And now as I watched them, I became conscious of a small vague image moving just below the surface of my memory. I tried desperately to reach back and grasp it. Once I almost touched it, but it slipped away and when I went after it I found myself travelling back and back through many weeks, back into the yellow days of summer—the warm wind blowing down the valley from the south, the big beech trees heavy with their foliage, the fields turning to gold, the harvesting, the hay making, the rick—the building of the rick.

Instantly, I felt a fine electricity of fear running over the skin of my stomach.

Yes—the building of the rick. When was it we had built it? June? That was it, of course—a hot muggy day in June with the clouds low overhead and the air thick with the smell of thunder.

And Rummins had said, "Let's for God's sake get it in quick before the rain comes."

And Ole Jimmy had said, "There ain't going to be no rain. And there ain't no hurry either. You know very well when thunder's in the south it don't cross over into the valley."

Rummins, standing up in the cart handing out the pitchforks had not answered him. He was in a furious brooding temper because of his anxiety about getting in the hay before it rained.

"There ain't goin to be no rain before evenin," Ole Jimmy had repeated, looking at Rummins; and Rummins had stared back at him, the eyes glimmering with a slow anger.

All through the morning we had worked without a pause, loading the hay into the cart, trundling it across the field, pitching it out onto the slowly growing rick that stood over by the gate opposite the filling station. We could hear the thunder in the south as it came toward us and moved away again. Then it seemed to return and remain stationary somewhere beyond the hills, rumbling intermittently. When we looked up we could see the clouds overhead moving and changing shape in the turbulence of the upper air; but on the ground it was hot and muggy and there was no breath of wind. We worked slowly, listlessly in the heat, shirts wet with sweat, faces shining.

Claud and I had worked beside Rummins on the rick itself, helping to shape it, and I could remember how very hot it had been and the flies around my face and the sweat pouring out everywhere; and especially I could remember the grim scowling presence of Rummins beside me, working with a desperate urgency and watching the sky and shouting at the men to hurry.

At noon, in spite of Rummins, we had knocked off for lunch.

Claud and I had sat down under the hedge with Ole Jimmy and another man called Wilson who was a soldier home on leave, and it was too hot to do much talking. Wilson had some bread and cheese and a canteen of cold tea. Ole Jimmy had a satchel that was an old gas-mask container, and in this, closely packed, standing upright with their necks protruding, were six pint bottles of beer.

"Come on," he said, offering a bottle to each of us.

"I'd like to buy one from you," Claud said, knowing very well the old man had little money.

"Take it."

"I must pay you."

"Don't be so daft. Drink it."

He was a very good old man, good and clean, with a clean pink face that he shaved each day. He had used to be a carpenter, but they retired him at the age of seventy and that was some years before. Then the Village Council, seeing him still active, had given him the job of looking after the newly built children's playground, of maintaining the swings and see-saws in good repair and also of acting as a kind of gentle watchdog, seeing that none of the kids hurt themselves or did anything foolish.

That was a fine job for an old man to have and everybody seemed pleased with the way things were going— until a certain Saturday night. That night Ole Jimmy had got drunk and gone reeling and singing down the middle of the High Street with such a howling noise that people got out of their beds to see what was going on below. The next morning they had sacked him saying he was a bum and a drunkard not fit to associate with young children on the playground.

But then an astonishing thing happened. The first day that he stayed away—a Monday it was—not one single child came near the playground.

Nor the next day, nor the one after that.

All week the swings and the see-saws and the high slide with steps going up to it stood deserted. Not a child went near them. Instead they followed Ole Jimmy out into a field behind the Rectory and played their games there with him watching; and the result of all this was that after a while the Council had had no alternative but to give the old man back his job.

He still had it now and he still got drunk and no one said anything about it any more. He left it only for a few days each year, at haymaking time. All his life Ole Jimmy had loved to go haymaking and he wasn't going to give it up yet.

"You want one?" he asked now, holding a bottle out to Wilson, the soldier.

"No thanks. I got tea."

"They say tea's good on a hot day."

"It is. Beer makes me sleepy."

"If you like," I said to Ole Jimmy, "we could walk across to the filling-station and I'll do you a couple of nice sandwiches? Would you like that?"

"Beer's plenty. There's more food in one bottle of beer, me lad, than twenty sandwiches."

He smiled at me, showing two rows of pale-pink, toothless gums, but it was a pleasant smile and there was nothing repulsive about the way the gums showed.

We sat for a while in silence. The soldier finished his bread and cheese and lay back on the ground, tilting his hat forward over his face. Ole Jimmy had drunk three bottles of beer, and now he offered the last to Claud and me.

"No thanks."

"No thanks. One's plenty for me."

The old man shrugged, unscrewed the stopper, tilted his head back and drank, pouring the beer into his mouth with the lips held open so the liquid ran smoothly without gurgling down his throat. He wore a hat that was of no colour at all and of no shape, and it did not fall off when he tilted back his head.

"Ain't Rummins goin to give that old horse a drink?" he asked, lowering the bottle, looking across the field at the great cart-horse that stood steaming between the shafts of the cart.

"Not Rummins."

"Horses is thirsty, just the same as us." Ole Jimmy paused, still looking at the horse. "You got a bucket of water in that place of yours there?"

"Of course."

"No reason why we shouldn't give the old horse a drink then, is there?"

"That's a very good idea. We'll give him a drink."

Claud and I both stood up and began walking toward the gate and I remember turning and calling back to the old man: "You quite sure you wouldn't like me to bring you a nice sandwich? Won't take a second to make."

He shook his head and waved the bottle at us and said something about taking himself a little nap. We went on through the gate over the road to the filling station.

I suppose we stayed away for about an hour attending to customers and getting ourselves something to eat, and when at length we returned, Claud carrying the bucket of water, I noticed that the rick was at least six foot high.

"Some water for the old horse," Claud said, looking hard at Rummins who was up in the cart pitching hay onto the rick.

The horse put its head in the bucket, sucking and blowing gratefully at the water.

"Where's Ole Jimmy?" I asked. We wanted the old man to see the water because it had been his idea.

When I asked the question there was a moment, a brief moment when Rummins hesitated, pitchfork in mid-air, looking around him.

"I brought him a sandwich," I added.

"Bloody old fool drunk to much beer and gone off home to sleep," Rummins said.

I strolled along the hedge back to the place where we had been sitting with Ole Jimmy. The five empty bottles were lying there in the grass. So was the satchel. I picked up the satchel and carried it back to Rummins.

"I don't think Ole Jimmy's gone home, Mr. Rummins," I said, holding up the satchel by the long shoulder-band. Rummins glanced at it but made no reply. He was in a frenzy of haste now because the thunder was closer, the clouds blacker, the heat more oppressive than ever.

Carrying the satchel, I started back to the filling station where I remained for the rest of the afternoon, serving customers. Toward evening, when the rain came, I glanced across the road and noticed that they had got the hay in and were laying a tarpaulin over the rick.

In a few days the thatcher arrived and took the tarpaulin off and made a roof of straw instead. He was a good thatcher and he made a fine roof with long straw, thick and well packed. The slope was nicely angled, the edges cleanly clipped, and it was a pleasure to look at it from the road or from the door of the filling station.

All this came flooding back to me now as clearly as if it were yesterday—the building of the rick on that hot thundery day in June, the yellow field, the sweet woody smell of the hay; and Wilson the soldier, with tennis shoes on his feet, Bert with the boiled eye, Ole Jimmy with the clean old face, the pink naked gums; and Rummins, the broad dwarf, standing up in the cart scowling at the sky because he was anxious about the rain.

At this very moment, there he was again, this Rummins, crouching on top of the rick with a sheaf of thatch in his arms looking round at the son, the tall Bert, motionless also, both of them black like silhouettes against the sky, and once again I felt the fine electricity of fear as it came and went in little waves over the skin of my stomach.

"Go on and cut through it, Bert," Rummins said, speaking loudly.

Bert put pressure on the big knife and there was a high grating noise as the edge of the blade sawed across something hard. It was clear from Bert's face that he did not like what he was doing.

It took several minutes before the knife was through—then again at last the softer sound of the blade slicing the tight-packed hay and Bert's face turned sideways to the father, grinning with relief, nodding inanely.

"Go on and cut it out," Rummins said, and still he did not move.

Bert made a second vertical cut the same depth as the first; then he got down and pulled the bale of hay so it came away cleanly from the rest of the rick like a chunk of cake, dropping into the cart at his feet.

Instantly, the boy seemed to freeze, staring stupidly at the newly exposed face of the rick, unable to believe or perhaps refusing to believe what this thing was that he had cut in two.

Rummins, who knew very well what it was, had turned away and was climbing quickly down the other side of the rick. He moved so fast he was through the gate and halfway across the road before Bert started to scream.

CLAUD'S DOG

Mr. Hoddy

THEY got out of the car and went in the front door of Mr. Hoddy's house.

"I've an idea dad's going to question you rather sharp tonight," Clarice whispered.

"About what, Clarice?"

"The usual stuff. Jobs and things like that. And whether you can support me in a fitting way."

"Jackie's going to do that," Claud said. "When Jackie wins there won't even be any need for any jobs . . ."

"Don't you ever mention Jackie to my dad, Claud Cubbage, or that'll be the end of it. If there's one thing in the world he can't abide it's greyhounds. Don't you ever forget that."

"Oh Christ," Claud said.

"Tell him something else—anything—anything to make him happy, see?" And with that she led Claud into the parlour.

Mr. Hoddy was a widower, a man with a prim sour mouth and an expression of eternal disapproval all over his face. He had the small, close-together teeth of his daughter Clarice, the same suspicious, inward look about the eyes, but none of her freshness and vitality, none of her warmth. He was a small sour apple of a man, grey-skinned and shrivelled, with a dozen or so surviving strands of black hair pasted across the dome of his bald head. But a very superior man was Mr. Hoddy, a grocer's assistant, one who wore a spotless white gown at his work, who handled large quantities of such precious commodities as butter and sugar, who was deferred to, even smiled at by every housewife in the village.

Claud Cubbage was never quite at his ease in this house and that was precisely as Mr. Hoddy intended it. They were sitting round the fire in the parlour with cups of tea in their hands, Mr. Hoddy in the best chair to the right of the fireplace, Claud and Clarice on the sofa, decorously separated by a wide space. The younger daughter, Ada, was on a hard upright chair to the left; and they made a little circle round the fire, a stiff, tense little circle, primly tea-sipping.

"Yes Mr. Hoddy," Claud was saying, "you can be quite sure both Gordon and me's got quite a number of nice little ideas up our sleeves this very moment. It's only a question of taking our time and making sure which is going to be the most profitable."

"What sort of ideas?" Mr. Hoddy asked, fixing Claud with his small, disapproving eyes.

"Ah, there you are now. That's it, you see." Claud shifted uncomfortably on the sofa. His blue lounge suit was tight around his chest, and it was especially tight between his legs, up in the crutch. The tightness in his crutch was actually painful to him and he wanted terribly to hitch it downward.

"This man you call Gordon, I thought he had a profitable business out there as it is," Mr. Hoddy said. "Why does he want to change?"

"Absolutely right, Mr. Hoddy. It's a first-rate business. But it's a good thing to keep expanding, see. New ideas is what we're after. Something I can come in on as well and take a share of the profits."

"Such as what?"

Mr. Hoddy was eating a slice of currant cake, nibbling it round the edges, and his small mouth was like the mouth of a caterpillar biting a tiny curved slice out of the edge of a leaf.

"Such as what?" he asked again.

"There's long conferences, Mr. Hoddy, takes place every day between Gordon and me about these different matters of business."

"Such as what?" he repeated, relentless.

Clarice glanced sideways at Claud, encouraging. Claud turned his large slow eyes upon Mr. Hoddy, and he was silent. He wished Mr. Hoddy wouldn't push him around like this, always shooting questions at him and glaring at him and acting just exactly like he was the bloody adjutant or something.

"Such as what?" Mr. Hoddy said, and this time Claud knew that he was not going to let go. Also, his instinct warned him that the old man was trying to create a crisis.

"Well now," he said, breathing deep. "I don't really want to go into details until we got it properly worked out. All we're doing so far is turning our ideas over in our minds, see."

"All I'm asking," Mr. Hoddy said irritably, "is what *sort* of business are you contemplating? I presume that it's respectable?"

"Now *please*, Mr. Hoddy. You don't for one moment think we'd even so much as *consider* anything that wasn't absolutely and entirely respectable, do you?"

Mr. Hoddy grunted, stirring his tea slowly, watching Claud. Clarice sat mute and fearful on the sofa, gazing into the fire.

"I've never been in favour of starting a business," Mr. Hoddy pronounced, defending his own failure in that line. "A good respectable job is all a man should wish for. A respectable job in respectable surroundings. Too much hokey-pokey in business for my liking."

"The thing is this," Claud said, desperate now. "All I want is to provide my wife with everything she can possibly desire. A house to live in and furniture and a flower-garden and a washing-machine and all the best things in the world. That's what I want to do, and you can't do that on an ordinary wage, now can you? It's impossible to get enough money to do that unless you go into business, Mr. Hoddy. You'll surely agree with me there?"

Mr. Hoddy, who had worked for an ordinary wage all his life, didn't much like this point of view.

"And don't you think *I* provide everything my family wants, might I ask?"

"Oh yes and more!" Claud cried fervently. "But *you've* got a very superior job, Mr. Hoddy, and that makes all the difference."

"But what *sort* of business are you thinking of," the man persisted.

Claud sipped his tea to give himself a little more time and he couldn't help wondering how the miserable old bastard's face would look if he simply up and told him the truth right there and then, if he'd said what we've got, Mr. Hoddy, if you really want to know, is a couple of greyhounds and one's a perfect ringer for the other and we're going to bring off the biggest goddam gamble in the history of flapping, see. He'd like to watch the old bastard's face if he said that, he really would.

They were all waiting for him to proceed now, sitting there with cups of tea in their hands staring at him and waiting for him to say something good. "Well," he said, speaking very slowly because he was thinking deep. "I've been pondering something a long time now, something as'll make more money even than Gordon's second hand cars or anything else come to that, and practically no expense involved." That's better, he told himself. Keep going along like that.

"And what might that be?"

"Something so queer, Mr. Hoddy, there isn't one in a million would even believe it."

"Well, what is it?" Mr. Hoddy placed his cup carefully on the little table beside him and leaned forward to listen. And Claud, watching him, knew more than ever that this man and all those like him were his enemies. It was the Mr. Hoddys were the trouble. They were all the same. He knew them all, with their clean ugly hands, their grey skin, their acrid mouths, their tendency to develop little round bulging bellies just below the waist-coat; and always the unctuous curl of the nose, the weak chin, the suspicious eyes that were dark and moved too quick. The Mr. Hoddys. Oh Christ.

"Well, what is it?"

"It's an absolute gold-mine Mr. Hoddy, honestly it is."

"I'll believe that when I hear it."

"It's a thing so simple and amazing most people wouldn't even bother to do it." He had it now—something he *had* actually been thinking seriously about for a long time, something he'd always wanted to do. He leaned across and put his tea-cup carefully on the table beside Mr. Hoddy's, then, not knowing what to do with his hands, placed them on his knees, palms down-ward.

"Well, come on man, what is it?"

"It's maggots," Claud answered softly.

Mr. Hoddy jerked back as though someone had squirted water in his face. "Maggots!" he said, aghast. "*Maggots?* What on earth do you mean, maggots?" Claud had forgotten that this word was almost unmentionable in any self-respecting grocer's shop. Ada began to giggle, but Clarice glanced at her so malignantly the giggle died on her mouth.

"That's where the money is, starting a maggot-factory."

"Are you trying to be funny?"

"Honestly Mr. Hoddy, it may sound a bit queer, and that's simply because you never heard of it before, but it's a little gold mine."

"A *maggot-factory*! Really now Cubbage! Please be sensible!"

Clarice wished her father wouldn't call him Cubbage.

"You never heard speak of a maggot-factory, Mr. Hoddy?"

"I certainly have not!"

"There's maggot-factories going now, real big companies with managers and directors and all, and you know what, Mr. Hoddy? They're making millions!"

"Nonsense, man."

"And you know why they're making millions?" Claud paused, but he did not notice now that his listener's face was slowly turning yellow. "It's because of the enormous demand for maggots, Mr. Hoddy."

At that moment, Mr. Hoddy was listening also to other voices, the voices of his customers across the counter—Mrs. Rabbits for instance, as he sliced off her ration of butter, Mrs. Rabbits with her brown moustache and always talking so loud and saying well well well; he could hear her now saying well well well Mr. Hoddy, so your Clarice got married last week, did she. Very nice too, I must say, and what was it you said her husband does, Mr. Hoddy?

He owns a maggot-factory, Mrs. Rabbits.

No thank you, he told himself, watching Claud with his small, hostile eyes. No thank you very much indeed. I don't want that.

"I can't say," he announced primly, "that I myself have ever had occasion to purchase a maggot."

"Now you come to mention it, Mr. Hoddy, nor have I.

Nor has many other people we know. But let me ask you something else. How many times you had occasion to purchase . . . a crown wheel and pinion, for instance?"

This was a shrewd question and Claud permitted himself a slow mawkish smile.

"What's that got to do with maggots?"

"Exactly this—that certain people buy certain things, see. You never bought a crown wheel and pinion in your life, but that don't say there isn't men getting rich this very moment making them—because there is. It's the same with maggots!"

"Would you mind telling me who these unpleasant people are who buy maggots?"

"Maggots are bought by fishermen, Mr. Hoddy. Amateur fishermen. There's thousands and thousands of fishermen all over the country going out every weekend fishing the rivers and all of them wanting maggots. Willing to pay good money for them, too. You go along the river there anywhere you like above Marlow on a Sunday and you'll see them *lining* the banks. Sitting there one beside the other simply *lining* the banks on both sides."

"Those men don't buy maggots. They go down the bottom of the garden and dig worms."

"Now that's just where you're wrong, Mr. Hoddy, if you'll allow me to say so. That's just where you're absolutely wrong. They want maggots, not worms."

"In that case they get their own maggots."

"They don't *want* to get their own maggots. Just imagine, Mr. Hoddy, it's Saturday afternoon and you're going out fishing and a nice clean tin of maggots arrives by post and all you've got to do is slip it in the fishing bag and away you go. You don't think fellers is going out digging for worms and hunting for maggots when they can have them delivered right to their very doorsteps like that just for a bob or two, do you?"

"And might I ask how you propose to run this maggot-factory of yours?" When he spoke the word maggot, it seemed as if he were spitting out a sour little pip from his mouth.

"Easiest thing in the world to run a maggot-factory." Claud was gaining confidence now and warming to his subject. "All you need is a couple of old oil drums and a few lumps of rotten meat or a sheep's head, and you put them in the oil drums and that's all you do. The flies do the rest."

Had he been watching Mr. Hoddy's face he would probably have stopped there.

"Of course, it's not quite as easy as it sounds. What you've got to do next is feed up your maggots with special diet. Bran and milk. And then when they get big and fat you put them in pint tins and post them off to your customers. Five shillings a pint they fetch. *Five shillings a pint!*" he cried, slapping his knee. "You just imagine that, Mr. Hoddy! And they say one bluebottle'll lay twenty pints easy!"

He paused again, but merely to marshal his thoughts, for there was no stopping him now.

"And there's another thing, Mr. Hoddy. A good maggot-factory don't just breed ordinary maggots, you know.

Every fisherman's got his own tastes. Maggots are commonest, but also there's lug worms. Some fishermen won't have nothing but lug worms. And of course there's coloured maggots. Ordinary maggots are white, but you get them all sorts of different colours by feeding them special foods, see. Red ones and green ones and black ones and you can even get blue ones if you know what to feed them. The most difficult thing of all in a maggot-factory is a blue maggot, Mr. Hoddy."

Claud stopped to catch his breath. He was having a vision now—the same vision that accompanied all his dreams of wealth—of an immense factory building with tall chimneys and hundreds of happy workers streaming in through the wide wrought iron gates and Claud himself sitting in his luxurious office directing operations with a calm and splendid assurance.

"There's people with brains studying these things this very minute," he went on. "So you got to jump in quick unless you want to get left out in the cold. That's the secret of big business, jumping in quick before all the others, Mr. Hoddy."

Clarice, Ada, and the father sat absolutely still looking straight ahead. None of them moved or spoke. Only Claud rushed on.

"Just so long as you make sure your maggots is alive when you post em. They've got to be wiggling, see. Maggots is no good unless they're wiggling. And when we really get going, when we've built up a little capital, then we'll put up some glasshouses."

Another pause, and Claud stroked his chin. "Now I expect you're all wondering why a person should want glass-houses in a maggot-factory. Well—I'll tell you. It's for the flies in the winter, see. Most important to take care of your flies in the winter."

"I think that's enough, thank you, Cubbage," Mr. Hoddy said suddenly.

Claud looked up and for the first time he saw the expression on the man's face. It stopped him cold.

"I don't want to hear any more about it," Mr. Hoddy said.

"All I'm trying to do, Mr. Hoddy," Claud cried, "is give your little girl everything she can possibly desire. That's all I'm thinking of night and day, Mr. Hoddy."

"Then all I hope is you'll be able to do it without the help of maggots."

"Dad!" Clarice cried, alarmed. "I simply won't have you talking to Claud like that."

"I'll talk to him how I wish, thank you miss."

"I think it's time I was getting along," Claud said. "Goodnight."

CLAUD'S DOG

Mr. Feasey

WE were both up early when the big day came.

I wandered into the kitchen for a shave but Claud got dressed right away and went outside to arrange about the straw. The kitchen was a front room and through the window I could see the sun just coming up behind the line of trees on top of the ridge the other side of the valley.

Each time Claud came past the window with an arm-load of straw I noticed over the rim of the mirror the intent, breathless expression on his face, the great round bullet-head thrusting forward and the forehead wrinkled into deep corrugations right up to the hairline. I'd only seen this look on him once before and that was the evening he'd asked Clarice to marry him. Today he was so excited he even walked funny, treading softly as though the concrete around the filling-station were a shade too hot for the soles of his feet; and he kept packing more and more straw into the back of the van to make it comfortable for Jackie.

Then he came into the kitchen to fix breakfast, and I watched him put the pot of soup on the stove and begin stirring it. He had a long metal spoon and he kept on stirring and stirring all the time it was coming to the boil, and about every half minute he leaned forward and stuck his nose into that sickly-sweet steam of cooking horseflesh. Then he started putting extras into it—three peeled onions, a few young carrots, a cupful of stinging-nettle tops, a teaspoon of Valentines Meatjuice, twelve drops of cod-liver oil—and everything he touched was handled very gently with the ends of his big fat fingers as though it might have been a little fragment of Venetian glass. He took some minced horsemeat from the icebox, measured one handful into Jackie's bowl, three into the other, and when the soup was ready he shared it out between the two, pouring it over the meat.

It was the same ceremony I'd seen performed each morning for the past five months, but never with such intense and breathless concentration as this. There was no talk, not even a glance my way, and when he turned and went out again to fetch the dogs, even the back of his neck and the shoulders seemed to be whispering, "Oh Jesus, don't let anything go wrong, and especially don't let me *do* anything wrong today."

I heard him talking softly to the dogs in the pen as he put the leashes on them, and when he brought them around into the kitchen, they came in prancing and pulling to get at the breakfast, treading up and down with their front feet and waving their enormous tails from side to side, like whips.

"All right," Claud said, speaking at last. "Which is it?"

Most mornings he'd offer to bet me a pack of cigarettes, but there were bigger things at stake today and I knew all he wanted for the moment was a little extra reassurance.

He watched me as I walked once around the two beautiful, identical, tall, velvety-black dogs, and he moved aside, holding the leashes at arms' length to give me a better view.

"Jackie!" I said, trying the old trick that never worked. "Hey Jackie!" Two identical heads with identical expressions flicked around to look at me, four bright, identical, deep-yellow eyes stared into mine. There'd been a time when I fancied the eyes of one were a slightly darker yellow than those of the other. There'd also been a time when I thought I could recognise Jackie because of a deeper brisket and a shade more muscle on the hindquarters. But it wasn't so.

"Come on," Claud said. He was hoping that today of all days I would make a bad guess.

"This one," I said. "This is Jackie."

"Which?"

"This one on the left."

"There!" he cried, his whole face suddenly beaming. "You're wrong again!"

"I don't think I'm wrong."

"You're about as wrong as you could possibly be. And now listen, Gordon, and I'll tell you something. All these last weeks, every morning while you've been trying to pick him out—you know what?"

"What?"

"I've been keeping count. And the result is you haven't been right even *one-half* the time! You'd have done better tossing a coin!"

What he meant was that if I (who saw them every day

and side by side) couldn't do it, why the hell should we be frightened of Mr. Feasey. Claud knew Mr. Feasey was famous for spotting ringers, but he knew also that it could be very difficult to tell the difference between two dogs when there wasn't any.

He put the bowls of food on the floor, giving Jackie the one with the least meat because he was running today. When he stood back to watch them eat, the shadow of deep concern was back again on his face and the large pale eyes were staring at Jackie with the same rapt and melting look of love that up till recently had been reserved only for Clarice.

"You see, Gordon," he said. "It's just what I've always told you. For the last hundred years there's been all manner of ringers, some good and some bad, but in the whole history of dog-racing there's never been a ringer like this."

"I hope you're right," I said, and my mind began travelling back to that freezing afternoon just before Christmas, four months ago, when Claud had asked to borrow the van and had driven away in the direction of Aylesbury without saying where he was going. I had assumed he was off to see Clarice, but late in the afternoon he had returned bringing with him this dog he said he'd bought off a man for thirty-five shillings.

"Is he fast?" I had said. We were standing out by the pumps and Claud was holding the dog on a leash and looking at him, and a few snowflakes were falling and settling on the dog's back. The motor of the van was still running.

"Fast!" Claud had said. "He's just about the slowest dog you ever saw in your whole life!"

"Then what you buy him for?"

"Well," he had said, the big bovine face secret and cunning, "it occurred to me that maybe he might possibly look a little bit like Jackie. What d'you think?"

"I suppose he does a bit, now you come to mention it."

He had handed me the leash and I had taken the new dog inside to dry him off while Claud had gone round to the pen to fetch his beloved. And when he returned and we put the two of them together for the first time, I can remember him stepping back and saying, "Oh, Jesus!" and standing dead still in front of them like he was seeing a phantom. Then he became very quick and quiet. He got down on his knees and began comparing them carefully point by point, and it was almost like the room was getting warmer and warmer the way I could feel his excitement growing every second through this long silent examination in which even the toenails and the dewclaws, eighteen on each dog, were matched alongside one another for colour.

"Look," he said said at last, standing up. "Walk them up and down the room a few times, will you?" And then he had stayed there for quite five or six minutes leaning against the stove with his eyes half closed and his head on one side, watching them and frowning and chewing his lips. After that, as though he didn't believe what he had seen the first time, he had gone down again on his knees to recheck everything once more; but suddenly, in the middle of it he had jumped up and looked at me, his face fixed and tense, with a curious whiteness around the nostrils and the eyes. "All right," he had said, a little tremor in his voice. "You know what? We're home. We're rich."

And then the secret conferences between us in the kitchen, the detailed planning, the selection of the most suitable track, and finally every other Saturday, eight times in all, locking up my filling-station (losing a whole afternoon's custom) and driving the ringer all the way up to Oxford to a scruffy little track out in the fields near Headingley where the big money was played but which was actually nothing except a line of old posts and cord to mark the course, an upturned bicycle for pulling the dummy hare, and at the far end, in the distance, six traps and the starter. We had driven this ringer up there eight times over a period of sixteen weeks and entered him with Mr. Feasey and stood around on the edge of the crowd in freezing raining cold, waiting for his name to go up on the blackboard in chalk. The Black Panther we called him. And when his time came, Claud would always lead him down to the traps and I would stand at the finish to catch him and keep him clear of the fighters, the gypsy dogs that the gypsies so often slipped in specially to tear another one to pieces at the end of a race.

But you know, there was something rather sad about taking this dog all the way up there so many times and letting him run and watching him and hoping and praying that whatever happened he would always come last. Of course the praying wasn't necessary and we never really had a moment's worry because the old fellow simply couldn't gallop and that's all there was to it. He run exactly like a crab. The only time he didn't come last was when a big fawn dog by the name of Amber Flash put his foot in a hole and broke a hock and finished on three legs. But even then ours only just beat him. So this way we got him right down to bottom grade with the scrubbers, and the last time we were there all the bookies were laying him twenty or thirty to one and calling his name and begging people to back him.

Now at last, on this sunny April day, it was Jackie's turn to go instead. Claud said we mustn't run the ringer any more or Mr. Feasey might begin to get tired of him and throw him out altogether, he was so slow. Claud said this was the exact psychological time to have it off, and that Jackie would win it anything between thirty and fifty lengths.

He had raised Jackie from a pup and the dog was only fifteen months now, but he was a good fast runner. He'd never raced yet, but we knew he was fast from clocking him round the little private schooling track at Uxbridge where Claud had taken him every Sunday since he was seven months old—except once when he was having some inoculations. Claud said he probably wasn't fast enough to win top grade at Mr. Feasey's, but where we'd got him now, in bottom grade with the scrubbers, he could fall over and get up again and still win it twenty—well, anyway ten or fifteen lengths, Claud said.

So all I had to do this morning was go to the bank in the village and draw out fifty pounds for myself and fifty for Claud which I would lend him as an advance against wages, and then at twelve o'clock lock up the filling-station and hang the notice on one of the pumps saying "GONE FOR THE DAY." Claud would shut the ringer in the pen at the back and put Jackie in the van and off we'd go. I won't say I was as excited as Claud, but there again, I didn't have all sorts of important things depending on it either, like buying a house and being able to get married. Nor was I almost *born* in a kennel with greyhounds like he was, walking about thinking of absolutely nothing else all day—except perhaps Clarice in the evenings. Personally, I had my own career as a filling-station owner to keep me busy, not to mention second-hand cars, but if Claud wanted to fool around with dogs that was all right with me, especially a thing like today—if it came off. As a matter of fact, I don't mind admitting that every time I thought about the money we were putting on and the money we might win, my stomach gave a little lurch.

The dogs had finished their breakfast now and Claud took them out for a short walk across the field opposite while I got dressed and fried the eggs. Afterwards, I went to the bank and drew out the money (all in ones), and the rest of the morning seemed to go very quickly serving customers.

At twelve sharp I locked up and hung the notice on the pump. Claud came around from the back leading Jackie and carrying a large suitcase made of reddish-brown cardboard.

"Suitcase?"

"For the money," Claud answered. "You said yourself no man can carry two thousand pound in his pockets."

It was a lovely yellow spring day with the buds burst-

ing all along the hedges and the sun shining through the
new pale green leaves on the big beech tree across the
road. Jackie looked wonderful, with two big hard muscles
the size of melons bulging on his hindquarters, his coat
glistening like black velvet. While Claud was putting the
suitcase in the van, the dog did a little prancing jig on
his toes to show how fit he was, then he looked up at me
and grinned, just like he knew he was off to the races to
win two thousand pounds and a heap of glory. This Jackie
had the widest most human-smiling grin I ever saw. Not
only did he lift his upper lip, but he actually stretched the
corners of his mouth so you could see every tooth in his
head except perhaps one or two of the molars right at the
back; and every time I saw him do it I found myself waiting to hear him start laughing out loud as well.

We got in the van and off we went. I was doing the
driving. Claud was beside me and Jackie was standing up
on the straw in the rear looking over our shoulders
through the windshield. Claud kept turning round and
trying to make him lie down so he wouldn't get thrown
whenever we went round the sharp corners, but the dog
was too excited to do anything except grin back at him
and wave his enormous tail.

"You got the money, Gordon?" Claud was chain-smok-
ing cigarettes and quite unable to sit still.

"Yes."

"Mine as well?"

"I got a hundred and five altogether. Five for the winder
like you said, so he won't stop the hare and make it a no-
race."

"Good," Claud said, rubbing his hands together hard as though he were freezing cold. "Good good good."

We drove through the little narrow High Street of Great Missenden and caught a glimpse of old Rummins going into The Nag's Head for his morning pint, then outside the village we turned left and climbed over the ridge of the Chilterns toward Princes Risborough, and from there it would only be twenty odd miles to Oxford.

And now a silence and a kind of tension began to come over us both. We sat very quiet, not speaking at all, each nursing his own fears and excitements, containing his anxiety. And Claud kept smoking his cigarettes and throwing them half finished out the window. Usually, on these trips, he talked his head off all the way there and back, all the things he'd done with dogs in his life, the jobs he'd pulled, the places he'd been, the money he'd won; and all the things other people had done with dogs, the thievery, the cruelty, the unbelievable trickery and cunning of owners at the flapping tracks. But today I don't think he was trusting himself to speak very much. At this point, for that matter, nor was I. I was sitting there watching the road and trying to keep my mind off the immediate future by thinking back on all that stuff Claud had told me about this curious greyhound racing racket.

I swear there wasn't a man alive who knew more about it than Claud did, and ever since we'd got the ringer and decided to pull this job, he'd taken it upon himself to give me an education in the business. By now, in theory at any rate, I suppose I knew nearly as much as him.

It had started during the very first strategy conference

we'd had in the kitchen. I can remember it was the day after the ringer arrived and we were sitting there watching for customers through the window, and Claud was explaining to me all about what we'd have to do, and I was trying to follow him as best I could until finally there came one question I had to ask.

"What I don't see," I had said, "is why you use the ringer at all. Wouldn't it be safer if we use Jackie all the time and simply stop him the first half dozen races so he come last? Then when we're good and ready, we can let him go. Same result in the end, wouldn't it be, if we do it right? And no danger of being caught."

Well, as I say, that did it. Claud looked up at me quickly and said, "Hey! None of that! I'd just like you to know 'stopping's' something I never do. What's come over you, Gordon?" He seemed genuinely pained and shocked by what I had said.

"I don't see anything wrong with it."

"Now listen to me, Gordon. Stopping a good dog breaks his heart. A good dog knows he's fast, and seeing all the others out there in front and not being able to catch them—it breaks his heart, I tell you. And what's more, you wouldn't be making suggestions like that if you knew some of the tricks them fellers do to stop their dogs at the flapping tracks."

"Such as what, for example?" I had asked.

"Such as anything in the world almost, so long as it makes the dog go slower. And it takes a lot of stopping, a good greyhound does. Full of guts and so mad keen you can't even let them watch a race they'll tear the leash right out of your hand rearing to go. Many's the time I've seen one with a broken leg insisting on finishing the race."

He had paused then, looking at me thoughtfully with those large pale eyes, serious as hell and obviously thinking deep. "Maybe," he had said, "if we're going to do this job properly I'd better tell you a thing or two so's you'll know what we're up against."

"Go ahead and tell me," I had said. "I'd like to know."

For a moment he stared in silence out the window. "The main thing you got to remember," he had said darkly, "is that all these fellers going to the flapping tracks with dogs —they're artful. They're more artful than you could possibly imagine." Again he paused, marshalling his thoughts.

"Now take for example the different ways of stopping a dog. The first, the commonest, is strapping."

"Strapping?"

"Yes. Strapping em up. That's commonest. Pulling the muzzle-strap tight around their necks so they can't hardly breathe, see. A clever man knows just which hole on the strap to use and just how many lengths it'll take off his dog in a race. Usually a couple of notches is good for five or six lengths. Do it up real tight and he'll come last. I've known plenty of dogs collapse and die from being strapped up tight on a hot day. Strangulated, absolutely strangulated, and a very nasty thing it was too. Then again, some of em just tie two of the toes together with black cotton. Dog never runs well like that. Unbalances him."

"That doesn't sound too bad."

"Then there's others that put a piece of fresh-chewed gum up under their tails, right up close where the tail joins the body. And there's nothing funny about that," he had said, indignant. "The tail of a running dog goes up and down ever so slightly and the gum on the tail keeps sticking to the hairs on the backside, just where it's tenderest. No dog likes that, you know. Then there's sleeping pills. That's used a lot nowadays. They do it by weight, exactly like a doctor, and they measure the powder according to whether they want to slow him up five or ten or fifteen lengths. Those are just a few of the ordinary ways," he had said. "Actually they're nothing. Absolutely nothing compared with some of the other things that's done to hold a dog back in a race, especially by the gypsies. There's things the gypsies do that are almost too disgusting to mention, such as when they're just putting the dog in the trap, things you wouldn't hardly do to your worst enemies."

And when he had told me about those—which were, indeed, terrible things because they had to do with physical injury, quickly, painfully inflicted—then he had gone on to tell me what they did when they wanted the dog to win.

"There's just as terrible things done to make em go fast as to make em go slow," he had said softly, his face veiled and secret. "And perhaps the commonest of all is wintergreen. Whenever you see a dog going around with no hair on his back or little bald patches all over him—that's wintergreen. Just before the race they rub it hard into the skin. Sometimes it's Sloane's Liniment, but mostly it's wintergreen. Stings terrible. Stings so bad that all the old dog wants to do is run run run as fast as he possibly can to get away from the pain.

"Then there's special drugs they give with the needle. Mind you, that's the modern method and most of the spivs at the track are too ignorant to use it. It's the fellers coming down from London in the big cars with stadium dogs they've borrowed for the day by bribing the trainer —they're the ones use the needle."

I could remember him sitting there at the kitchen table with a cigarette dangling from his mouth and dropping his eyelids to keep out the smoke and looking at me through his wrinkled, nearly closed eyes, and saying, "What you've got to remember, Gordon, is this. There's nothing they won't do to make a dog win if they want him to. On the other hand, no dog can run faster than he's built, no matter what they do to him. So if we can get Jackie down into bottom grade, then we're home. No dog in bottom grade can get near him, not even with winter-green and needles. Not even with ginger."

"Ginger?"

"Certainly. That's a common one, ginger is. What they do, they take a piece of raw ginger about the size of a walnut, and about five minutes before the off they slip it into the dog."

"You mean in his mouth? He eats it?"

"No," he had said. "Not in his mouth."

And so it had gone on. During each of the eight long trips we had subsequently made to the track with the ringer I had heard more and more about this charming sport—more, especially, about the methods of stopping

them and making them go (even the names of the drugs
and the quantities to use). I heard about "the rat treatment" (for non-chasers, to make them chase the dummy
hare), where a rat is placed in a can which is then tied
around the dog's neck. There's a small hole in the lid of
the can just large enough for the rat to poke its head out
and nip the dog. But the dog can't get at the rat, and so
naturally he goes half crazy running around and being
bitten in the neck, and the more he shakes the can the
more the rat bites him. Finally, someone releases the rat,
and the dog, who up to then was a nice docile tail-
wagging animal who wouldn't hurt a mouse, pounces on
it in a rage and tears it to pieces. Do this a few times,
Claud had said— "mind you, I don't hold with it myself"
—and the dog becomes a real killer who will chase anything, even the dummy hare.

We were over the Chilterns now and running down out
of the beechwoods into the flat elm and oak-tree country
south of Oxford. Claud sat quietly beside me, nursing his
nervousness and smoking cigarettes, and every two or
three minutes he would turn round to see if Jackie was all
right. The dog was at last lying down, and each time
Claud turned round, he whispered something to him
softly, and the dog acknowledged his words with a faint
movement of the tail that made the straw rustle.

Soon we would be coming into Thame, the broad High
Street where they penned the pigs and cows and sheep on
market day, and where the Fair came once a year with the
swings and roundabouts and bumping cars and gypsy cara-
vans right there in the street in the middle of the town.

Claud was born in Thame, and we'd never driven through it yet without him mentioning this fact.

"Well," he said as the first houses came into sight, "here's Thame. I was born and bred in Thame, you know, Gordon."

"You told me."

"Lots of funny things we used to do around here when we was nippers," he said, slightly nostalgic.

"I'm sure."

He paused, and I think more to relieve the tension building up inside him than anything else, he began talking about the years of his youth.

"There was a boy next door," he said. "Gilbert Gomm his name was. Little sharp ferrety face and one leg a bit shorter'n the other. Shocking things him and me used to do together. You know one thing we done, Gordon?"

"What?"

"We'd go into the kitchen Saturday nights when mum and dad were at the pub, and we'd disconnect the pipe from the gas-ring and bubble the gas into a milk bottle full of water. Then we'd sit down and drink it out of teacups."

"Was that so good?"

"Good! It was absolutely disgusting! But we'd put lashings of sugar in and then it didn't taste so bad."

"Why did you drink it?"

Claud turned and looked at me, incredulous. "You mean you never drunk 'Snakes Water'!"

"Can't say I have."

"I thought everyone done that when they was kids! It

intoxicates you, just like wine only worse, depending on how long you let the gas bubble through. We used to get reeling drunk together there in the kitchen Saturday nights and it was marvellous. Until one night dad comes home early and catches us. I'll never forget that night as long as I live. There was me holding the milk bottle, and the gas bubbling through it lovely, and Gilbert kneeling on the floor ready to turn off the tap the moment I give the word, and in walks dad."

"What did he say?"

"Oh Christ, Gordon, that was terrible. He didn't say one word, but he stands there by the door and he starts feeling for his belt, undoing the buckle very slow and pulling the belt slow out of his trousers, looking at me all the time. Great big feller he was, with great big hands like coalhammers and a black moustache and them little purple veins running all over his cheeks. Then he comes over quick and grabs me by the coat and lets me have it, hard as he can, using the end with the buckle on it and honest to God, Gordon, I thought he was going to kill me. But in the end he stops and then he puts on the belt again, slow and careful, buckling it up and tucking in the flap and belching with the beer he'd drunk. And then he walks out again back to the pub, still without saying a word. Worst hiding I ever had in my life."

"How old were you then?"

"Round about eight, I should think," Claud said.

As we drew closer to Oxford, he became silent again. He kept twisting his neck to see if Jackie was all right, to touch him, to stroke his head, and once he turned around and knelt on the seat to gather more straw around the dog, murmuring something about a draft. We drove around the fringe of Oxford and into a network of narrow country roads, and after a while we turned into a small bumpy lane and along this we began to overtake a thin stream of men and women all walking and cycling in the same direction. Some of the men were leading greyhounds. There was a large saloon car in front of us and through the rear window we could see a dog sitting on the back seat between two men.

"They come from all over," Claud said darkly. "That one there's probably come up special from London. Probably slipped him out from one of the big stadium kennels just for the afternoon. That could be a Derby dog probably, for all we know."

"Hope he's not running against Jackie."

"Don't worry," Claud said. "All new dogs automatically go in top grade. That's one rule Mr. Feasey's very particular about."

There was an open gate leading into a field, and Mr. Feasey's wife came forward to take our admission money before we drove in.

"He'd have her winding the bloody pedals too if she had the strength," Claud said. "Old Feasey don't employ more people than he has to."

I drove across the field and parked at the end of a line of cars along the top hedge. We both got out and Claud went quickly round the back to fetch Jackie. I stood beside the car, waiting. It was a very large field with a steepish slope on it, and we were at the top of the slope, looking down. In the distance I could see the six starting traps and the wooden posts marking the track which ran along the bottom of the field and turned sharp at right angles and came on up the hill toward the crowd, to the finish. Thirty yards beyond the finishing line stood the upturned bicycle for driving the hare. Because it is portable, this is the standard machine for hare-driving used at all flapping tracks. It comprises a flimsy wooden platform about eight feet high, supported on four poles knocked into the ground. On top of the platform there is fixed, upside down with wheels in the air, an ordinary old bicycle. The rear wheel is to the front, facing down the track, and from it the tire has been removed, leaving a concave metal rim. One end of the cord that pulls the hare is attached to this rim, and the winder (or hare driver), by straddling the bicycle at the back and turning the pedals with his hands, revolves the wheel and winds in the cord around the rim. This pulls the dummy hare toward him at any speed he likes up to forty miles an hour. After each race someone takes the dummy hare (with cord attached) all the way down to the starting traps again, thus unwinding the cord on the wheel, ready for a fresh start. From his high platform, the winder can watch the race and regulate the speed of the hare to keep it just ahead of the leading dog. He can also stop the hare any time he wants and make it a "no race" (if the wrong dog looks like winning) by suddenly turning the pedals backwards and getting the cord tangled up in the hub of the wheel. The other way of doing it is to slow down the hare suddenly, for perhaps one second, and that makes the lead dog automatically check a little so that the others catch up with him. He is an important man, the winder.

I could see Mr. Feasey's winder already standing atop his platform, a powerful looking man in a blue sweater, leaning on the bicycle and looking down at the crowd through the smoke of his cigarette.

There is a curious law in England which permits race meetings of this kind to be held only seven times a year over one piece of ground. That is why all Mr. Feasey's equipment was movable, and after the seventh meeting he would simply transfer to the next field. The law didn't bother him at all.

There was already a good crowd and the bookmakers were erecting their stands in a line over to the right. Claud had Jackie out of the van now and was leading him over to a group of people clustered around a small stocky man dressed in riding-breeches—Mr. Feasey himself. Each person in the group had a dog on a leash and Mr. Feasey kept writing names in a notebook that he held folded in his left hand. I sauntered over to watch.

"Which you got there?" Mr. Feasey said, pencil poised above the notebook.

"Midnight," a man said who was holding a black dog.

Mr. Feasey stepped back a pace and looked most carefully at the dog.

"Midnight. Right. I got him down."

"Jane," the next man said.

"Let me look. Jane . . . Jane . . . yes, all right."

"Soldier." This dog was led by a tall man with long teeth who wore a dark-blue, double-breasted lounge suit, shiny with wear, and when he said "Soldier" he began slowly to scratch the seat of his trousers with the hand that wasn't holding the leash.

Mr. Feasey bent down to examine the dog. The other man looked up at the sky.

"Take him away," Mr. Feasey said.

The man looked down quick and stopped scratching.

"Go on, take him away."

"Listen, Mr. Feasey," the man said, lisping slightly through his long teeth. "Now don't talk so bloody silly, *please*."

"Go on and beat it, Larry, and stop wasting my time. You know as well as I do the Soldier's got two white toes on his off fore."

"Now look, Mr. Feasey," the man said. "You ain't even seen Soldier for six months at least."

"Come on now, Larry, and beat it. I haven't got time arguing with you." Mr. Feasey didn't appear the least angry. "Next," he said.

I saw Claud step forward leading Jackie. The large bovine face was fixed and wooden, the eyes staring at something about a yard above Mr. Feasey's head, and he was holding the leash so tight his knuckles were like a row of little white onions. I knew just how he was feeling. I felt the same way myself at that moment, and it was even worse when Mr. Feasey suddenly started laughing.

"Hey!" he cried. "Here's the Black Panther. Here's the champion."

"That's right, Mr. Feasey," Claud said.

"Well, I'll tell you," Mr. Feasey said, still grinning.

"You can take him right back home where he come from. I don't want him."

"But look here, Mr. Feasey . . ."

"Six or eight times at least I've run him for you now and that's enough. Look—why don't you shoot him and have done with it?"

"Now listen, Mr. Feasey, *please.* Just once more and I'll never ask you again."

"Not even once! I got more dogs than I can handle here today. There's no room for crabs like that."

I thought Claud was going to cry.

"Now honest, Mr. Feasey," he said. "I been up at six every morning this past two weeks giving him road-work and massage and buying him beefsteaks, and be-lieve me he's a different dog absolutely than what he was last time he run."

The words "different dog" caused Mr. Feasey to jump like he'd been pricked with a hatpin. "What's that!" he cried. "Different dog!"

I'll say this for Claud, he kept his head. "See here, Mr. Feasey," he said. "I'll thank you not to go implying things to me. You know very well I didn't mean that."

"All right, all right. But just the same, you can take him away. There's no sense running dogs as slow as him. Take him home now, will you please, and don't hold up the whole meeting."

I was watching Claud. Claud was watching Mr. Feasey. Mr. Feasey was looking round for the next dog to enter up. Under his brown tweedy jacket he wore a yellow pullover, and this streak of yellow on his breast and his thin gaitered legs and the way he jerked his head from side to side made him seem like some sort of a little perky bird—a goldfinch, perhaps.

Claud took a step forward. His face was beginning to purple slightly with the outrage of it all and I could see his Adam's apple moving up and down as he swallowed.

"I'll tell you what I'll do, Mr. Feasey. I'm so absolutely sure this dog's improved I'll bet you a quid he don't finish last. There you are."

Mr. Feasey turned slowly around and looked at Claud. "You crackers?" he asked.

"I'll bet you a quid, there you are, just to prove what I'm saying."

It was a dangerous move, certain to cause suspicion, but Claud knew it was the only thing left to do. There was silence while Mr. Feasey bent down and examined the dog. I could see the way his eyes were moving slowly over the animal's whole body, part by part. There was something to admire in the man's thoroughness, and in his memory; something to fear also in this self-confident little rogue who held in his head the shape and colour and markings of perhaps several hundred different but very similar dogs. He never needed more than one little clue—a small scar, a splay toe, a trifle in at the hocks, a less pronounced wheelback, a slightly darker brindle—Mr. Feasey always remembered.

So I watched him now as he bent down over Jackie. His face was pink and fleshy, the mouth small and tight as though it couldn't stretch enough to make a smile, and the eyes were like two little cameras focussed sharply on the dog.

"Well," he said, straightening up. "It's the same dog anyway."

"I should hope so too!" Claud cried. "Just what sort of a fellow you think I am, Mr. Feasey?"

"I think you're crackers, that's what I think. But it's a nice easy way to make a quid. I suppose you forgot how Amber Flash nearly beat him on three legs last meeting?"

"This one wasn't fit then," Claud said. "He hadn't had beefsteak and massage and roadwork like I've been giving him lately. But look, Mr. Feasey, you're not to go sticking him in top grade just to win the bet. This is a bottom grade dog, Mr. Feasey. You know that."

Mr. Feasey laughed. The small button mouth opened into a tiny circle and he laughed and looked at the crowd who laughed with him. "Listen," he said, laying a hairy hand on Claud's shoulder. "I know my dogs. I don't have to do any fiddling around to win *this* quid. He goes in bottom."

"Right," Claud said. "That's a bet." He walked away with Jackie and I joined him.

"Jesus, Gordon, that was a near one!"

"Shook me."

"But we're in now," Claud said. He had that breathless look on his face again and he was walking about quick and funny, like the ground was burning his feet.

People were still coming through the gate into the

field and there were easily three hundred of them now. Not a very nice crowd. Sharpnosed men and women with dirty faces and bad teeth and quick shifty eyes. The dregs of the big town. Oozing out like sewage from a cracked pipe and trickling along the road through the gate and making a smelly little pond of sewage at the top end of the field. They were all there, all the spivs and the gypsies and the touts and the dregs and the sewage and the scrapings and the scum from the cracked drainpipes of the big town. Some with dogs, some without. Dogs led about on pieces of string, miserable dogs with hanging heads, thin mangy dogs with sores on their quarters (from sleeping on board), sad old dogs with grey muzzles, doped dogs, dogs stuffed with porridge to stop them winning, dogs walking stiff-legged—one especially, a white one. "Claud, why is that white one walking so stiff-legged?"

"Which one?"

"That one over there."

"Ah yes, I see. Very probably because he's been hung."

"Hung?"

"Yes, hung. Suspended in a harness for twenty-four hours with his legs dangling."

"Good God, but why?"

"To make him run slow, of course. Some people don't hold with dope or stuffing or strapping up. So they hang em."

"I see."

"Either that," Claud said, "or they sandpaper them.

Rub their pads with rough sandpaper and take the skin off so it hurts when they run."

"Yes, I see."

And then the fitter, brighter looking dogs, the better fed ones who get horsemeat every day, not pigswill or rusk and cabbage water, their coats shinier, their tails moving, pulling at their leads, undoped, unstuffed, awaiting perhaps a more unpleasant fate, the muzzle-strap to be tightened an extra four notches. *But make sure he can breathe now, Jock. Don't choke him completely. Don't let's have him collapse in the middle of the race. Just so he wheezes a bit, see. Go on tightening it up an extra notch at a time until you can hear him wheezing. You'll see his mouth open and he'll start breathing heavy. Then it's just right, but not if his eyeballs is bulging. Watch out for that, will you? Okay?*

Okay.

"Let's get away from the crowd, Gordon. It don't do Jackie no good getting excited by all these other dogs."

We walked up the slope to where the cars were parked, then back and forth in front of the line of cars, keeping the dog on the move. Inside some of the cars I could see men sitting with their dogs, and the men scowled at us through the windows as we went by.

"Watch out now, Gordon. We don't want any trouble."

"No, all right."

These were the best dogs of all, the secret ones kept in the cars and taken out quick just to be entered up

(under some invented name) and put back again quick
and held there till the last minute, then straight down
to the traps and back again into the cars after the race
so no nosey bastard gets too close a look. The trainer
at the big stadium said so. *All right, he said. You can
have him, but for Christsake don't let anybody recognise him. There's thousands of people know this dog,
so you've got to be careful, see. And it'll cost you fifty
pound.*

Very fast dogs these, but it doesn't much matter how
fast they are they probably get the needle anyway, just
to make sure. One and a half ccs. of ether, subcutaneous,
done in the car, injected very slow. That'll put ten
lengths on any dog. Or sometimes it's caffein, caffein
in oil, or camphor. That makes them go too. The men
in the big cars know all about that. And some of them
know about whiskey. But that's intravenous. Not so
easy when it's intravenous. Might miss the vein. All
you got to do is miss the vein and it don't work and
where are you then? So it's ether, or it's caffein, or it's
camphor. *Don't give her too much of that stuff now,
Jock. What does she weigh? Fifty-eight pounds. All
right then, you know what the man told us. Wait a
minute now. I got it written down on a piece of paper.
Here it is. Point 1 of a cc. per 10 pounds bodyweight
equals 5 lengths over 300 yards. Wait a minute now
while I work it out. Oh Christ, you better guess it.
Just guess it, Jock. It'll be all right you'll find. Shouldn't
be any trouble anyway because I picked the others in*

the race myself. Cost me a tenner to old Feasey. A
bloody tenner I give him, and dear Mr. Feasey, I says,
that's for your birthday and because I love you.

Thank you ever so much, Mr. Feasey says. Thank
you, my good and trusted friend.

And for stopping them, for the men in the big cars,
it's chlorbutal. That's a beauty, chlorbutal, because you
can give it the night before, especially to someone else's
dog. Or Pethidine. Pethidine and Hyoscine mixed, whatever that may be.

"Lot of fine old English sporting gentry here," Claud
said.

"Certainly are."

"Watch your pockets, Gordon. You got that money
hidden away?"

We walked around the back of the line of cars—between the cars and the hedge—and I saw Jackie stiffen
and begin to pull forward on the leash, advancing with a
stiff crouching tread. About thirty yards away there were
two men. One was holding a large fawn greyhound, the
dog stiff and tense like Jackie. The other was holding a
sack in his hands.

"Watch," Claud whispered, "they're giving him a
kill."

Out of the sack onto the grass tumbled a small white
rabbit, fluffy white, young, tame. It righted itself and
sat still, crouching in the hunched up way rabbits
crouch, its nose close to the ground. A frightened
rabbit. Out of the sack so suddenly onto the grass with

such a bump. Into the bright light. The dog was going mad with excitement now, jumping up against the
leash, pawing the ground, throwing himself forward,
whining. The rabbit saw the dog. It drew in its head
and stayed still, paralyzed with fear. The man transferred his hold to the dog's collar, and the dog twisted
and jumped and tried to get free. The other man pushed
the rabbit with his foot but it was too terrified to move.
He pushed it again, flicking it forward with his toe
like a football, and the rabbit rolled over several times,
righted itself and began to hop over the grass away from
the dog. The other man released the dog which pounced
with one huge pounce upon the rabbit, and then came
the squeals, not very loud but shrill and anguished and
lasting rather a long time.

"There you are," Claud said. "That's a kill."

"Not sure I liked it very much."

"I told you before, Gordon. Most of em does it.
Keens the dog up before a race."

"I still don't like it."

"Nor me. But they all do it. Even in the big stadiums
the trainers do it. Proper barbary I call it."

We strolled away, and below us on the slope of the
hill the crowd was thickening and the bookies' stands
with the names written on them in red and gold and blue
were all erected now in a long line back of the crowd,
each bookie already stationed on an upturned box beside his stand, a pack of numbered cards in one hand, a
piece of chalk in the other, his clerk behind him with
book and pencil. Then we saw Mr. Feasey walking over

to a blackboard that was nailed to a post stuck in the ground.

"He's chalking up the first race," Claud said. "Come on, quick!"

We walked rapidly down the hill and joined the crowd. Mr. Feasey was writing the runners on the blackboard, copying names from his soft-covered notebook, and a little hush of suspense fell upon the crowd as they watched.

1. SALLY
2. THREE QUID
3. SNAILBOX LADY
4. BLACK PANTHER
5. WHISKEY
6. ROCKIT

"He's in it!" Claud whispered. "First race! Trap four! Now Listen, Gordon! Give me a fiver quick to show the winder."

Claud could hardly speak from excitement. That patch of whiteness had returned around his nose and eyes, and when I handed him a five pound note, his whole arm was shaking as he took it. The man who was going to wind the bicycle pedals was still standing on top of the wooden platform in his blue jersey, smoking. Claud went over and stood below him, looking up.

"See this fiver," he said, talking softly, holding it folded small in the palm of his hand.

The man glanced at it without moving his head.

"Just so long as you wind her true this race, see. No stopping and no slowing down and run her fast. Right?"

The man didn't move but there was a slight, almost imperceptible lifting of the eyebrows. Claud turned away.

"Now look, Gordon. Get the money on gradual, all in little bits like I told you. Just keep going down the line putting on little bits so you don't kill the price, see. And I'll be walking Jackie down very slow, as slow as I dare, to give you plenty of time. Right?"

"Right."

"And don't forget to be standing ready to catch him at the end of the race. Get him clear away from all them others when they start fighting for the hare. Grab a hold of him tight and don't let go till I come running up with the collar and lead. That Whiskey's a gypsy dog and he'll tear the leg off anything as gets in his way."

"Right," I said. "Here we go."

I saw Claud lead Jackie over to the finishing post and collect a yellow jacket with 4 written on it large. Also a muzzle. The other five runners were there too, the owners fussing around them, putting on their numbered jackets, adjusting their muzzles. Mr. Feasey was officiating, hopping about in his tight riding-breeches like an anxious perky bird, and once I saw him say something to Claud and laugh. Claud ignored him. Soon they would all start to lead the dogs down the track, the long walk down the hill and across to the far corner of the field to the starting-traps. It would take them ten minutes to walk it. I've got at least ten minutes, I told myself, and then I began to push my way through the crowd standing six or seven deep in front of the line of bookies.

"Even money Whiskey! Even money Whiskey! Five to Two Sally! Even money Whiskey! Four to one Snail-box! Come on now! Hurry up, hurry up! Which is it?"

On every board all down the line the Black Panther was chalked up at twenty-five to one. I edged forward to the nearest book.

"Three pounds Black Panther," I said, holding out the money.

The man on the box had an inflamed magenta face and traces of some white substance around the corners of his mouth. He snatched the money and dropped it in his satchel. "Seventy-five pound to three Black Panther," he said. "Number forty-two." He handed me a ticket and his clerk recorded the bet.

I stepped back and wrote rapidly on the back of the ticket 75 to 3, then slipped it into the inside pocket of my jacket, with the money.

So long as I continued to spread the cash out thin like this, it ought to be all right. And anyway, on Claud's instructions, I'd made a point of betting a few pounds on the ringer every time he'd run so as not to arouse any suspicion when the real day arrived. Therefore, with some confidence, I went all the way down the line staking three pounds with each book. I didn't hurry, but I didn't waste any time either, and after each bet I wrote the amount on the back of the card before slipping it into my pocket. There were seventeen bookies. I had seventeen tickets and had laid out fifty-one pounds without disturbing the price one point. Forty-nine pounds left to get on. I glanced quickly down the hill. One owner and his dog had already reached the traps. The others were only twenty or thirty yards away. Except for Claud. Claud and Jackie were only halfway there. I could see Claud in his old khaki greatcoat sauntering slowly along with Jackie pulling ahead keenly on the leash, and once I saw him stop completely and bend down pretending to pick something up. When he went on again he seemed to have developed a limp so as to go slower still. I hurried back to the other end of the line to start again.

"Three pounds Black Panther."

The bookmaker, the one with the magenta face and the white substance around the mouth, glanced up sharply, remembering the last time, and in one swift almost graceful movement of the arm he licked his fingers and wiped the figure twenty-five neatly off the board. His wet fingers left a small dark patch opposite Black Panther's name.

"All right, you got one more seventy-five to three," he said. "But that's the lot." Then he raised his voice and shouted, "Fifteen to one Black Panther! Fifteens the Panther!"

All down the line the twenty-fives were wiped out and it was fifteen to one the Panther now. I took it quick, but by the time I was through the bookies had had enough and they weren't quoting him any more. They'd only taken six pounds each, but they stood to lose a hundred and fifty, and for them—small times bookies at a little country flapping-track—that was quite enough for one race, thank you very much. I felt pleased the way I'd managed it. Lots of tickets now. I took them out of my pockets and counted them and they were like a thin pack of cards in my hand. Thirty-three tickets in all. And what did we stand to win? Let me see . . . something over two thousand pounds. Claud had said he'd win it thirty lengths. Where was Claud now?

Far away down the hill I could see the khaki great-coat standing by the traps and the big black dog along-side. All the other dogs were already in and the owners were beginning to walk away. Claud was bending down now, coaxing Jackie into number four, and then he was closing the door and turning away and beginning to run up the hill toward the crowd, the greatcoat flapping around him. He kept looking back over his shoulder as he ran.

Beside the traps the starter stood, and his hand was up waving a handkerchief. At the other end of the track, beyond the winning-post, quite close to where I stood, the man in the blue jersey was straddling the up-turned bicycle on top of the wooden platform and he saw the signal and waved back and began to turn the pedals with his hands. Then a tiny white dot in the dis-tance—the artificial hare that was in reality a football with a piece of white rabbit-skin tacked onto it—began to move away from the traps, accelerating fast. The traps went up and the dogs flew out. They flew out in a single dark lump, all together, as though it were one wide dog instead of six, and almost at once I saw Jackie drawing away from the field. I knew it was Jackie because of the colour. There weren't any other black dogs in the race.

It was Jackie all right. Don't move, I told myself. Don't move a muscle or an eyelid or a toe or a fingertip. Stand quite still and don't move. Watch him going. Come on Jackson, boy! No, don't shout. It's unlucky to shout. And don't move. Be all over in twenty seconds. Round the sharp bend now and coming up the hill and he must be fifteen or twenty lengths clear. Easy twenty lengths. Don't count the lengths, it's unlucky. And don't move. Don't move your head. Watch him out of your eye-corners. Watch that Jackson go! He's really laying down to it now up that hill. He's won it now! He can't lose it now . . .

When I got over to him he was fighting the rabbit-skin and trying to pick it up in his mouth, but his muzzle wouldn't allow it, and the other dogs were pounding up behind him and suddenly they were all on top of him grabbing for the rabbit and I got hold of him round the neck and dragged him clear like Claud had said and knelt down on the grass and held him tight with both arms round his body. The other catchers were having a time all trying to grab their own dogs.

Then Claud was beside me, blowing heavily, unable to speak from blowing and excitement, removing Jackie's muzzle, putting on the collar and lead, and Mr. Feasey was there too, standing with hands on hips, the button mouth pursed up tight like a mushroom, the two little cameras staring at Jackie all over again.

"So that's the game, is it?" he said.

Claud was bending over the dog and acting like he hadn't heard.

"I don't want you here no more after this, you understand that?"

Claud went on fiddling with Jackie's collar.

I heard someone behind us saying, "That flat-faced bastard with the frown swung it properly on old Feasey this time." Someone else laughed. Mr. Feasey walked away. Claud straightened up and went over with Jackie to the hare driver in the blue jersey who had dismounted from his platform.

"Cigarette," Claud said, offering the pack.

The man took one, also the five pound note that was folded up small in Claud's fingers.

"Thanks," Claud said. "Thanks very much."

"Don't mention," the man said.

Then Claud turned to me. "You get it all on, Gordon?" He was jumping up and down and rubbing his hands and patting Jackie, and his lips trembled as he spoke.

"Yes. Half at twenty-fives, half at fifteens."

"Oh Christ, Gordon, that's marvellous. Wait here till I get the suitcase."

"You take Jackie," I said, "and go and sit in the car. I'll see you later."

There was nobody around the bookies now. I was the only one with anything to collect, and I walked slowly with a sort of dancing stride and a wonderful bursting feeling in my chest, toward the first one in the line, the man with the magenta face and the white substance on his mouth. I stood in front of him and I took all the time I wanted going through my pack of tickets to find the two that were his. The name was Syd Pratchett. It was written up large across his board in gold letters on a scarlet field—"SYD PRATCHETT. THE BEST ODDS IN THE MIDLANDS. PROMPT SETTLEMENT."

I handed him the first ticket and said, "Seventy-eight pounds to come." It sounded so good I said it again, making a delicious little song of it. "Seventy-eight pounds to come on this one." I didn't mean to gloat over Mr. Pratchett. As a matter of fact, I was beginning to like him quite a lot. I even felt sorry for him having to fork out so much money. I hoped his wife and kids wouldn't suffer.

"Number forty-two," Mr. Pratchett said, turning to his clerk who held the big book. "Forty-two wants seventy-eight pound."

There was a pause while the clerk ran his finger down the column of recorded bets. He did this twice, then he looked up at the boss and began to shake his head.

"No," he said. "Don't pay. That ticket backed Snailbox Lady."

Mr. Pratchett, standing on his box, leaned over and peered down at the book. He seemed to be disturbed by what the clerk had said, and there was a look of genuine concern on the huge magenta face.

That clerk is a fool, I thought, and any moment now Mr. Pratchett's going to tell him so.

But when Mr. Pratchett turned back to me, the eyes had become narrow and hostile. "Now look Charley," he said softly. "Don't let's have any of that. You know very well you bet Snailbox. What's the idea?"

"I bet Black Panther," I said. "Two separate bets of

three pounds each at twenty-five to one. Here's the second ticket."

This time he didn't even bother to check it with the book. "You bet Snailbox, Charley," he said. "I remember you coming round." With that, he turned away from me and started wiping the names of the last race runners off his board with a wet rag. Behind him, the clerk had closed the book and was lighting himself a cigarette. I stood watching them, and I could feel the sweat beginning to break through the skin all over my body.

"Let me see the book."

Mr. Pratchett blew his nose in the wet rag and dropped it to the ground. "Look," he said, "why don't you go away and stop annoying me?"

The point was this: a bookmaker's ticket, unlike a parimutuel ticket, never has anything written on it regarding the nature of your bet. This is normal practice, the same at every racetrack in the country, whether it's the Silver Ring at Newmarket, the Royal Enclosure at Ascot, or a tiny country flapping track near Oxford. All you receive is a card bearing the bookie's name and a serial number. The wager is (or should be) recorded by the bookie's clerk in his book alongside the number of the ticket, but apart from that there is no evidence at all of how you betted.

"Go on," Mr. Pratchett was saying. "Hop it."

I stepped back a pace and glanced down the long line of bookmakers. None of them was looking my way. Each was standing motionless on his little wooden box beside his wooden placard, staring straight ahead into the crowd. I went up to the next one and presented a ticket.

"I had three pounds on Black Panther at twenty-five to one," I said firmly. "Seventy-eight pounds to come."

This man, who had a soft inflamed face, went through exactly the same routine as Mr. Pratchett, questioning his clerk, peering at the book, and giving me the same answers.

"Whatever's the matter with you?" he said quietly, speaking to me as though I were eight years old. "Trying such a silly thing as that."

This time I stepped well back. "You dirty thieving bastards!" I cried. "The whole lot of you!"

Automatically, as though they were puppets, all the heads down the line flicked round and looked at me. The expressions didn't alter. It was just the heads that moved, all seventeen of them, and seventeen pairs of cold glassy eyes looked down at me. There was not the faintest flicker of interest in any of them.

"Somebody spoke," they seemed to be saying. "We didn't hear it. It's quite a nice day today."

The crowd, sensing excitement, was beginning to mov in around me. I ran back to Mr. Pratchett, right up clos to him and poked him in the stomach with my finger. "You're a thief! A lousy rotten little thief!" I shouted.

The extraordinary thing was, Mr. Pratchett didn't seem to resent this at all.

"Well I never," he said. "*Look* who's talking."

Then suddenly the big face broke into a wide, frog-like grin, and he looked over at the crowd and shouted. "*Look* who's talking!"

All at once, everybody started to laugh. Down the line the bookies were coming to life and turning to each other and laughing and pointing at me and shouting, "*Look* who's talking! *Look* who's talking!" The crowd began to take up the cry as well, and I stood there on the grass alongside Mr. Pratchett with this wad of tickets as thick as a pack of cards in my hand, listening to them and feeling slightly hysterical. Over the heads of the people I could see Mr. Feasey beside his blackboard already chalking up the runners for the next race; and then beyond him, far away up the top of the field, I caught sight of Claud standing by the van, waiting for me with the suitcase in his hand.

It was time to go home.

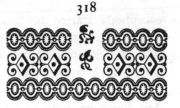

THE LANDLADY

BILLY WEAVER had travelled down from London on the slow afternoon train, with a change at Reading on the way, and by the time he got to Bath it was about nine o'clock in the evening and the moon was coming up out of a clear starry sky over the houses opposite the station entrance. But the air was deadly cold and the wind was like a flat blade of ice on his cheeks.

"Excuse me," he said, "but is there a fairly cheap hotel not too far away from here?"

"Try The Bell and Dragon," the porter answered, pointing down the road. "They might take you in. It's about a quarter of a mile along on the other side."

Billy thanked him and picked up his suitcase and set out to walk the quarter-mile to The Bell and Dragon. He had never been to Bath before. He didn't know anyone who lived there. But Mr. Greenslade at the Head Office in London had told him it was a splendid town. "Find your own lodgings," he had said, "and then go along and report to the Branch Manager as soon as you've got yourself settled."

Billy was seventeen years old. He was wearing a new navy-blue overcoat, a new brown trilby hat, and a new brown suit, and he was feeling fine. He walked briskly down the street. He was trying to do everything briskly these days. Briskness, he had decided, was *the* one common characteristic of all successful businessmen. The big shots up at Head Office were absolutely fantastically brisk all the time. They were amazing.

There were no shops on this wide street that he was walking along, only a line of tall houses on each side, all of them identical. They had porches and pillars and four or five steps going up to their front doors, and it was obvious that once upon a time they had been very swanky residences. But now, even in the darkness, he could see that the paint was peeling from the woodwork on their doors and windows, and that the handsome white façades were cracked and blotchy from neglect.

Suddenly, in a downstairs window that was brilliantly illuminated by a street-lamp not six yards away, Billy caught sight of a printed notice propped up against the glass in one of the upper panes. It said BED AND BREAKFAST. There was a vase of pussy-willows, tall and beautiful, standing just underneath the notice.

He stopped walking. He moved a bit closer. Green curtains (some sort of velvety material) were hanging down on either side of the window. The pussy-willows looked wonderful beside them. He went right up and peered through the glass into the room, and the first thing he saw was a bright fire burning in the hearth. On the carpet in front of the fire, a pretty little dachshund was curled up asleep with its nose tucked into its belly. The room itself, so far as he could see in the half-darkness, was filled with pleasant furniture. There was a baby-grand piano and a big sofa and several plump armchairs; and in one corner he spotted a large parrot in a cage. Animals were usually a good sign in a place like this, Billy told himself; and all in all, it looked to him as though it would be a pretty decent house to stay in. Certainly it would be more comfortable than The Bell and Dragon.

On the other hand, a pub would be more congenial than a boarding-house. There would be beer and darts in the evenings, and lots of people to talk to, and it would probably be a good bit cheaper, too. He had stayed a couple of nights in a pub once before and he had liked it. He had never stayed in any boarding-houses, and, to be perfectly honest, he was a tiny bit frightened of them. The name itself conjured up images of watery cabbage, rapacious landladies, and a powerful smell of kippers in the living-room.

After dithering about like this in the cold for two or three minutes, Billy decided that he would walk on and take a look at The Bell and Dragon before making up his mind. He turned to go.

And now a queer thing happened to him. He was in the act of stepping back and turning away from the window when all at once his eye was caught and held in the most peculiar manner by the small notice that was there. BED AND BREAKFAST, it said. BED AND BREAKFAST, BED AND BREAKFAST, BED AND BREAKFAST. Each word was like a large black eye staring at him through the glass, holding him, compelling him, forcing him to stay where he was and not to walk away from that house, and the next thing he knew, he was actually moving across from the window to the front door of the house, climbing the steps that led up to it, and reaching for the bell.

He pressed the bell. Far away in a back room he heard it ringing, and then *at once*—it must have been at once because he hadn't even had time to take his finger from the bell-button—the door swung open and a woman was standing there.

Normally you ring the bell and you have at least a half-minute's wait before the door opens. But this dame was like a jack-in-the-box. He pressed the bell—and out she popped! It made him jump.

She was about forty-five or fifty years old, and the moment she saw him, she gave him a warm welcoming smile.

"*Please* come in," she said pleasantly. She stepped aside, holding the door wide open, and Billy found himself automatically starting forward. The compulsion or, more accurately, the desire to follow after her into that house was extraordinarily strong.

"I saw the notice in the window," he said, holding himself back.

"Yes, I know."

"I was wondering about a room."

"It's *all* ready for you, my dear," she said. She had a round pink face and very gentle blue eyes.

"I was on my way to The Bell and Dragon," Billy told

her. "But the notice in your window just happened to catch my eye."

"My dear boy," she said, "why don't you come in out of the cold?"

"How much do you charge?"

"Five and sixpence a night, including breakfast."

It was fantastically cheap. It was less than half of what he had been willing to pay.

"If that is too much," she added, "then perhaps I can reduce it just a tiny bit. Do you desire an egg for breakfast? Eggs are expensive at the moment. It would be sixpence less without the egg."

"Five and sixpence is fine," he answered. "I should like very much to stay here."

"I knew you would. Do come in."

She seemed terribly nice. She looked exactly like the mother of one's best school-friend welcoming one into the house to stay for the Christmas holidays. Billy took off his hat, and stepped over the threshold.

"Just hang it there," she said, "and let me help you with your coat."

There were no other hats or coats in the hall. There were no umbrellas, no walking-sticks—nothing.

"We have it *all* to ourselves," she said, smiling at him over her shoulder as she led the way upstairs. "You see, it isn't very often I have the pleasure of taking a visitor into my little nest."

The old girl is slightly dotty, Billy told himself. But at five and sixpence a night, who gives a damn about that?

"I should've thought you'd be simply swamped with applicants," he said politely.

"Oh, I am, my dear, I am, of course I am. But the trouble is that I'm inclined to be just a teeny weeny bit choosy and particular—if you see what I mean."

"Ah, yes."

"But I'm always ready. Everything is always ready day and night in this house just on the off-chance that an acceptable young gentleman will come along. And it is such a pleasure, my dear, such a very great pleasure when now and again I open the door and I see someone standing there who is just *exactly* right." She was halfway up the stairs, and she paused with one hand on the stair-rail, turning her head and smiling down at him with pale lips. "Like you," she added, and her blue eyes travelled slowly all the way down the length of Billy's body, to his feet, and then up again.

On the second-floor landing she said to him, "This floor is mine."

They climbed up another flight. "And this one is *all* yours," she said. "Here's your room. I do hope you'll like it." She took him into a small but charming front bedroom, switching on the light as she went in.

"The morning sun comes right in the window, Mr. Perkins. It *is* Mr. Perkins, isn't it?"

"No," he said. "It's Weaver."

"Mr. Weaver. How nice. I've put a water-bottle between the sheets to air them out, Mr. Weaver. It's such a comfort to have a hot water-bottle in a strange bed with clean sheets, don't you agree? And you may light the gas fire at any time if you feel chilly."

"Thank you," Billy said. "Thank you ever so much." He noticed that the bedspread had been taken off the bed, and that the bedclothes had been neatly turned back on one side, all ready for someone to get in.

"I'm so glad you appeared," she said, looking earnestly into his face. "I was beginning to get worried."

"That's all right," Billy answered brightly. "You mustn't worry about me." He put his suitcase on the chair and started to open it.

"And what about supper, my dear? Did you manage to get anything to eat before you came here?"

"I'm not a bit hungry, thank you," he said. "I think I'll just go to bed as soon as possible because tomorrow I've got to get up rather early and report to the office."

"Very well, then. I'll leave you now so that you can unpack. But before you go to bed, would you be kind enough to pop into the sitting-room on the ground floor and sign the book? Everyone has to do that because it's the law of the land, and we don't want to go breaking any laws at *this* stage in the proceedings, do we?" She gave him a little wave of the hand and went quickly out of the room and closed the door.

Now, the fact that his landlady appeared to be slightly off her rocker didn't worry Billy in the least. After all, she not only was harmless—there was no question about that —but she was also quite obviously a kind and generous soul. He guessed that she had probably lost a son in the war, or something like that, and had never gotten over it.

So a few minutes later, after unpacking his suitcase and washing his hands, he trotted downstairs to the ground floor and entered the living-room. His landlady wasn't there, but the fire was glowing in the hearth, and the little dachshund was still sleeping soundly in front of it. The room was wonderfully warm and cosy. I'm a lucky fellow, he thought, rubbing his hands. This is a bit of all right.

He found the guest-book lying open on the piano, so he took out his pen and wrote down his name and address. There were only two other entries above his on the page, and, as one always does with guest-books, he started to read them. One was a Christopher Mulholland from Cardiff. The other was Gregory W. Temple from Bristol.

That's funny, he thought suddenly. Christopher Mulholland. It rings a bell.

Now where on earth had he heard that rather unusual name before?

Was it a boy at school? No. Was it one of his sister's numerous young men, perhaps, or a friend of his father's? No, no, it wasn't any of those. He glanced down again at the book.

Christopher Mulholland   231 Cathedral Road, Cardiff

Gregory W. Temple   27 Sycamore Drive, Bristol

As a matter of fact, now he came to think of it, he wasn't at all sure that the second name didn't have almost as much of a familiar ring about it as the first.

"Gregory Temple?" he said aloud, searching his memory. "Christopher Mulholland? . . ."

"Such charming boys," a voice behind him answered, and he turned and saw his landlady sailing into the room with a large silver tea-tray in her hands. She was holding it well out in front of her, and rather high up, as though the tray were a pair of reins on a frisky horse.

"They sound somehow familiar," he said.

"They do? How interesting."

"I'm almost positive I've heard those names before somewhere. Isn't that odd? Maybe it was in the newspapers. They weren't famous in any way, were they? I mean famous cricketers or footballers or something like that?"

"Famous," she said, setting the tea-tray down on the low table in front of the sofa. "Oh no, I don't think they were famous. But they were incredibly handsome, both of them, I can promise you that. They were tall and young and handsome, my dear, just exactly like you."

Once more, Billy glanced down at the book. "Look here," he said, noticing the dates. "This last entry is over two years old."

"It is?"

"Yes, indeed. And Christopher Mulholland's is nearly a year before that—more than *three years* ago."

"Dear me," she said, shaking her head and heaving a dainty little sigh. "I would never have thought it. How time does fly away from us all, doesn't it, Mr. Wilkins?"

"It's Weaver," Billy said. "W-e-a-v-e-r."

"Oh, of course it is!" she cried, sitting down on the sofa. "How silly of me. I do apologize. In one ear and out the other, that's me, Mr. Weaver."

"You know something?" Billy said. "Something that's really quite extraordinary about all this?"

"No, dear, I don't."

"Well, you see, both of these names—Mulholland and Temple—I not only seem to remember each one of them separately, so to speak, but somehow or other, in some peculiar way, they both appear to be sort of connected together as well. As though they were both famous for the same sort of thing, if you see what I mean—like . . . well . . . like Dempsey and Tunney, for example, or Churchill and Roosevelt."

"How amusing," she said. "But come over here now, dear, and sit down beside me on the sofa and I'll give you a nice cup of tea and a ginger biscuit before you go to bed."

"You really shouldn't bother," Billy said. "I didn't mean you to do anything like that." He stood by the piano, watching her as she fussed about with the cups and saucers. He noticed that she had small, white, quickly moving hands, and red finger-nails.

"I'm almost positive it was in the newspapers I saw them," Billy said. "I'll think of it in a second. I'm sure I will."

There is nothing more tantalizing than a thing like this that lingers just outside the borders of one's memory. He hated to give up.

"Now wait a minute," he said. "Wait just a minute. Mulholland . . . Christopher Mulholland . . . wasn't *that* the name of the Eton schoolboy who was on a walking-tour through the West Country, and then all of a sudden . . ."

"Milk?" she said. "And sugar?"

"Yes, please. And then all of a sudden . . ."

"Eton schoolboy?" she said. "Oh no, my dear, that can't possibly be right because *my* Mr. Mulholland was certainly not an Eton schoolboy when he came to me. He was a Cambridge undergraduate. Come over here now and sit next to me and warm yourself in front of this lovely fire. Come on. Your tea's all ready for you." She patted the empty place beside her on the sofa, and she sat there smiling at Billy and waiting for him to come over.

He crossed the room slowly, and sat down on the edge of the sofa. She placed his teacup on the table in front of him.

"*There* we are," she said. "How nice and cosy this is, isn t it?"

Billy started sipping his tea. She did the same. For half a minute or so, neither of them spoke. But Billy knew that she was looking at him. Her body was half turned toward him, and he could feel her eyes resting on his face, watching him over the rim of her teacup. Now and again, he caught a whiff of a peculiar smell that seemed to emanate directly from her person. It was not in the least unpleasant, and it reminded him—well, he wasn't quite sure what it reminded him of. Pickled walnuts? New leather? Or was it the corridors of a hospital?

At length, she said, "Mr. Mulholland was a great one for his tea. Never in my life have I seen anyone drink as much tea as dear, sweet Mr. Mulholland."

"I suppose he left fairly recently," Billy said. He was still puzzling his head about the two names. He was positive now that he had seen them in the newspapers—in the headlines.

"Left?" she said, arching her brows. "But my dear boy, he never left. He's still here. Mr. Temple is also here. They're on the fourth floor, both of them together."

Billy set his cup down slowly on the table and stared at his landlady. She smiled back at him, and then she put out one of her white hands and patted him comfortingly on the knee. "How old are you, my dear?" she asked.

"Seventeen."

"Seventeen!" she cried. "Oh, it's the perfect age! Mr. Mulholland was also seventeen. But I think he was a trifle shorter than you are; in fact I'm sure he was, and his teeth weren't *quite* so white. You have the most beautiful teeth, Mr. Weaver, did you know that?"

"They're not as good as they look," Billy said. "They've got simply masses of fillings in them at the back."

"Mr. Temple, of course, was a little older," she said, ignoring his remark. "He was actually twenty-eight. And yet I never would have guessed it if he hadn't told me, never in my whole life. There wasn't a *blemish* on his body."

"A what?" Billy said.

"His skin was *just* like a baby's."

There was a pause. Billy picked up his teacup and took another sip of his tea, then he set it down again gently in its saucer. He waited for her to say something else, but she seemed to have lapsed into another of her silences. He sat there staring straight ahead of him into the far corner of the room, biting his lower lip.

"That parrot," he said at last. "You know something? It had me completely fooled when I first saw it through the window. I could have sworn it was alive."

"Alas, no longer."

"It's most terribly clever the way it's been done," he said. "It doesn't look in the least bit dead. Who did it?"

"I did."

"*You* did?"

"Of course," she said. "And have you met my little Basil as well?" She nodded toward the dachshund curled up so comfortably in front of the fire. Billy looked at it. And suddenly, he realized that this animal had all the time been just as silent and motionless as the parrot. He put out a hand and touched it gently on the top of its back. The back was hard and cold, and when he pushed the hair to one side with his fingers, he could see the skin underneath, greyish-black and dry and perfectly preserved.

"Good gracious me," he said. "How absolutely fascinating." He turned away from the dog and stared with deep admiration at the little woman beside him on the sofa. "It must be most awfully difficult to do a thing like that."

"Not in the least," she said. "I stuff *all* my little pets myself when they pass away. Will you have another cup of tea?"

"No, thank you," Billy said. The tea tasted faintly of bitter almonds, and he didn't much care for it.

"You did sign the book, didn't you?"

"Oh, yes."

"That's good. Because later on, if I happen to forget what you were called, then I could always come down here and look it up. I still do that almost every day with Mr. Mulholland and Mr. . . . Mr. . . ."

"Temple," Billy said. "Gregory Temple. Excuse my asking, but haven't there been *any* other guests here except them in the last two or three years?"

Holding her teacup high in one hand, inclining her head slightly to the left, she looked up at him out of the corners of her eyes and gave him another gentle little smile.

"No, my dear," she said. "Only you."

WILLIAM AND MARY

WILLIAM PEARL did not leave a great deal of money when he died, and his will was a simple one. With the exception of a few small bequests to relatives, he left all his property to his wife.

The solicitor and Mrs. Pearl went over it together in the solicitor's office, and when the business was completed, the widow got up to leave. At that point, the solicitor took a sealed envelope from the folder on his desk and held it out to his client.

"I have been instructed to give you this," he said. "Your husband sent it to us shortly before he passed away." The solicitor was pale and prim, and out of respect for a widow he kept his head on one side as he spoke, looking downward. "It appears that it might be something personal, Mrs. Pearl. No doubt you'd like to take it home with you and read it in privacy."

Mrs. Pearl accepted the envelope and went out into the

street. She paused on the pavement, feeling the thing with her fingers. A letter of farewell from William? Probably, yes. A formal letter. It was bound to be formal—stiff and formal. The man was incapable of acting otherwise. He had never done anything informal in his life.

My dear Mary, I trust that you will not permit my departure from this world to upset you too much, but that you will continue to observe those precepts which have guided you so well during our partnership together. Be diligent and dignified in all things. Be thrifty with your money. Be very careful that you do not . . . et cetera, et cetera.

A typical William letter.

Or was it possible that he might have broken down at the last moment and written her something beautiful? Maybe this was a beautiful tender message, a sort of love letter, a lovely warm note of thanks to her for giving him thirty years of her life and for ironing a million shirts and cooking a million meals and making a million beds, something that she could read over and over again, once a day at least, and she would keep it for ever in the box on her dressing-table together with her brooches.

There is no knowing what people will do when they are about to die, Mrs. Pearl told herself, and she tucked the envelope under her arm and hurried home.

She let herself in the front door and went straight to the living-room and sat down on the sofa without removing her hat or coat. Then she opened the envelope and drew out the contents. These consisted, she saw, of some fifteen or twenty sheets of lined white paper, folded over once and held together at the top left-hand corner by a clip. Each sheet was covered with the small, neat, forward-sloping writing that she knew so well, but when she noticed how much of it there was, and in what a neat businesslike manner it was written, and how the first page didn't even begin in the nice way a letter should, she began to get suspicious.

She looked away. She lit herself a cigarette. She took one puff and laid the cigarette in the ashtray.

If this is about what I am beginning to suspect it is about, she told herself, then I don't want to read it.

Can one refuse to read a letter from the dead?

Yes.

Well . . .

She glanced over at William's empty chair on the other side of the fireplace. It was a big brown leather armchair, and there was a depression on the seat of it, made by his buttocks over the years. Higher up, on the backrest, there was a dark oval stain on the leather where his head had rested. He used to sit reading in that chair and she would be opposite him on the sofa, sewing on buttons or mending socks or putting a patch on the elbow of one of his jackets, and every now and then a pair of eyes would glance up from the book and settle on her, watchful, but strangely impersonal, as if calculating something. She had never liked those eyes. They were ice blue, cold, small, and rather close together, with two deep vertical lines of disapproval dividing them. All her life they had been watching her. And even now, after a week alone in the house, she sometimes had an uneasy feeling that they were still there, following her around, staring at her from doorways, from empty chairs, through a window at night.

Slowly she reached into her handbag and took out her spectacles and put them on. Then, holding the pages up high in front of her so that they caught the late afternoon light from the window behind, she started to read:

THIS NOTE, *my dear Mary*, is entirely for you, and will be given you shortly after I am gone.

Do not be alarmed by the sight of all this writing. It is nothing but an attempt on my part to explain to you precisely what Landy is going to do to me, and why I have agreed that he should do it, and what are his theories and his hopes. You are my wife and you have a right to know these things. In fact you *must* know them. During the past few days I have tried very hard to speak with you about Landy, but you have steadfastly refused to give me a hearing. This, as I have already told you, is a very foolish attitude to take, and I find it not entirely an unselfish one either. It stems mostly from ignorance, and I am absolutely convinced that if only you were made aware of all the facts, you would immediately change your view. That is why I am hoping that when I am no longer with you, and your mind is less distracted, you will consent to listen to me more carefully through these pages. I swear to you that when you have read my story, your sense of antipathy will vanish, and enthusiasm will take its place. I even dare to hope that you will become a little proud of what I have done.

As you read on, you must forgive me, if you will, for the coolness of my style, but this is the only way I know of getting my message over to you clearly. You see, as my time draws near, it is natural that I begin to brim with every kind of sentimentality under the sun. Each day I grow more extravagantly wistful, especially in the evenings, and unless I watch myself closely my emotions will be overflowing onto these pages.

I have a wish, for example, to write something about you and what a satisfactory wife you have been to me through the years, and I am promising myself that if there is time, and I still have the strength, I shall do that next.

I have a yearning also to speak about this Oxford of mine where I have been living and teaching for the past seventeen years, to tell something about the glory of the place and to explain, if I can, a little of what it has meant to have been allowed to work in its midst. All the things and places that I loved so well keep crowding in on me now in this gloomy bedroom. They are bright and beautiful as they always were, and today, for some reason, I can see them more clearly than ever. The path around the lake in the gardens of Worcester College, where Lovelace used to walk. The gateway at Pembroke. The view westward over the town from Magdalen Tower. The great hall at Christchurch. The little rockery at St. Johns where I have counted more than a dozen varieties of campanula, including the rare and dainty C. Waldsteiniana. But there, you see! I haven't even begun and already I'm falling into the trap. So let me get started now; and let you read it slowly, my dear, without any of that sense of sorrow or disapproval that might otherwise embarrass your under-standing. Promise me now that you will read it slowly, and that you will put yourself in a cool and patient frame of mind before you begin.

The details of the illness that struck me down so sud-denly in my middle life are known to you. I need not waste time upon them—except to admit at once how fool-ish I was not to have gone earlier to my doctor. Cancer is one of the few remaining diseases that these modern drugs cannot cure. A surgeon can operate if it has not spread too far; but with me, not only did I leave it too late, but the thing had the effrontery to attack me in the pancreas, making both surgery and survival equally impossible.

So here I was with somewhere between one and six months left to live, growing more melancholy every hour—and then, all of a sudden, in comes Landy.

That was six weeks ago, on a Tuesday morning, very early, long before your visiting time, and the moment he entered I knew there was some sort of madness in the wind. He didn't creep in on his toes, sheepish and em-barrassed, not knowing what to say, like all my other visi-tors. He came in strong and smiling, and he strode up to the bed and stood there looking down at me with a wild bright glimmer in his eyes, and he said, "William, my boy, this is perfect. You're just the one I want!"

Perhaps I should explain to you here that although John Landy has never been to our house, and you have seldom if ever met him, I myself have been friendly with him for at least nine years. I am, of course, primarily a teacher of philosophy, but as you know I've lately been dabbling a good deal in psychology as well. Landy's interests and mine have therefore slightly overlapped. He is a magnificent neurosurgeon, one of the finest, and recently he has been kind enough to let me study the results of some of his work, especially the varying effects of prefrontal lobotomies upon different types of psychopath. So you can see that when he suddenly burst in on me Tuesday morning, we were by no means strangers to one another.

"Look," he said, pulling up a chair beside the bed. "In a few weeks you're going to be dead. Correct?"

Coming from Landy, the question didn't seem especially unkind. In a way it was refreshing to have a visitor brave enough to touch upon the forbidden subject.

"You're going to expire right here in this room, and then they'll take you out and cremate you."

"Bury me," I said.

"That's even worse. And then what? Do you believe you'll go to heaven?"

"I doubt it," I said, "though it would be comforting to think so."

"Or hell, perhaps?"

"I don't really see why they should send me there."

"You never know, my dear William."

"What's all this about?" I asked.

"Well," he said, and I could see him watching me carefully, "personally, I don't believe that after you're dead you'll ever hear of yourself again—unless . . ." and here he paused and smiled and leaned closer ". . . unless, of course, you have the sense to put yourself into my hands. Would you care to consider a proposition?"

The way he was staring at me, and studying me, and appraising me with a queer kind of hungriness, I might have been a piece of prime beef on the counter and he had bought it and was waiting for them to wrap it up.

"I'm really serious about it, William. Would you care to consider a proposition?"

"I don't know what you're talking about."

"Then listen and I'll tell you. Will you listen to me?"

"Go on then, if you like. I doubt I've got very much to lose by hearing it."

"On the contrary, you have a great deal to gain—especially *after you're dead*."

I am sure he was expecting me to jump when he said this, but for some reason I was ready for it. I lay quite still, watching his face and that slow white smile of his that always revealed the gold clasp of an upper denture curled around the canine on the left side of his mouth.

"This is a thing, William, that I've been working on quietly for some years. One or two others here at the hospital have been helping me, especially Morrison, and we've completed a number of fairly successful trials with laboratory animals. I'm at the stage now where I'm ready to have a go with a man. It's a big idea, and it may sound a bit farfetched at first, but from a surgical point of view there doesn't seem to be any reason why it shouldn't be more or less practicable."

Landy leaned forward and placed both his hands on the edge of my bed. He has a good face, handsome in a bony sort of way, and with none of the usual doctor's look about it. You know that look, most of them have it. It glimmers at you out of their eyeballs like a dull electric sign and it reads *Only I can save you.* But John Landy's eyes were wide and bright and little sparks of excitement were dancing in the centres of them.

"Quite a long time ago," he said, "I saw a short medical film that had been brought over from Russia. It was a rather gruesome thing, but interesting. It showed a dog's head completely severed from the body, but with the normal blood supply being maintained through the arteries and veins by means of an artificial heart. Now the thing is this: that dog's head, sitting there all alone on a sort of tray, was *alive.* The brain was functioning. They proved it by several tests. For example, when food was smeared on the dog's lips, the tongue would come out and lick it away; and the eyes would follow a person moving across the room.

"It seemed reasonable to conclude from this that the head and the brain did not need to be attached to the rest of the body in order to remain alive—provided, of course, that a supply of properly oxygenated blood could be maintained.

"Now then. My own thought, which grew out of seeing this film, was to remove the brain from the skull of a human and keep it alive and functioning as an independent unit for an unlimited period after he is dead. *Your* brain, for example, after *you* are dead."

"I don't like that," I said.

"Don't interrupt, William. Let me finish. So far as I can tell from subsequent experiments, the brain is a peculiarly self-supporting object. It manufactures its own cerebrospinal fluid. The magic processes of thought and memory which go on inside it are manifestly not impaired by the absence of limbs or trunk or even of skull, provided, as I say, that you keep pumping in the right kind of oxygenated blood under the proper conditions.

"My dear William, just think for a moment of your own brain. It is in perfect shape. It is crammed full of a lifetime of learning. It has taken you years of work to make it what it is. It is just beginning to give out some first-rate original ideas. Yet soon it is going to have to die along with the rest of your body simply because your silly little pancreas is lousy with cancer."

"No thank you," I said to him. "You can stop there. It's a repulsive idea, and even if you could do it, which I doubt, it would be quite pointless. What possible use is there in keeping my brain alive if I couldn't talk or see or hear or feel? Personally, I can think of nothing more unpleasant."

"I believe that you *would* be able to communicate with us," Landy said. "And we might even succeed in giving you a certain amount of vision. But let's take this slowly. I'll come to all that later on. The fact remains that you're going to die fairly soon whatever happens; and my plans would not involve touching you at all until *after* you are dead. Come now, William. No true philosopher could object to lending his dead body to the cause of science."

"That's not putting it quite straight," I answered. "It seems to me there'd be some doubt as to whether I were dead or alive by the time you'd finished with me."

"Well," he said, smiling a little, "I suppose you're right

about that. But I don't think you ought to turn me down quite so quickly, before you know a bit more about it."

"I said I don't want to hear it."

"Have a cigarette," he said, holding out his case.

"I don't smoke, you know that."

He took one himself and lit it with a tiny silver lighter that was no bigger than a shilling piece. "A present from the people who make my instruments," he said. "Ingenious, isn't it?"

I examined the lighter, then handed it back.

"May I go on?" he asked.

"I'd rather you didn't."

"Just lie still and listen. I think you'll find it quite interesting."

There were some blue grapes on a plate beside my bed. I put the plate on my chest and began eating the grapes.

"At the very moment of death," Landy said, "I should have to be standing by so that I could step in immediately and try to keep your brain alive."

"You mean leaving it in the head?"

"To start with, yes. I'd have to."

"And where would you put it after that?"

"If you want to know, in a sort of basin."

"Are you really serious about this?"

"Certainly I'm serious."

"All right. Go on."

"I suppose you know that when the heart stops and the brain is deprived of fresh blood and oxygen, its tissues die very rapidly. Anything from four to six minutes and the whole thing's dead. Even after three minutes you may get a certain amount of damage. So I should have to work rapidly to prevent this from happening. But with the help of the machine, it should all be quite simple."

"What machine?"

"The artificial heart. We've got a nice adaptation here of the one originally devised by Alexis Carrel and Lindbergh. It oxygenates the blood, keeps it at the right temperature, pumps it in at the right pressure, and does a number of other little necessary things. It's really not at all complicated."

"Tell me what you would do at the moment of death," I said. "What is the first thing you would do?"

"Do you know anything about the vascular and venous arrangements of the brain?"

"No."

"Then listen. It's not difficult. The blood supply to the brain is derived from two main sources, the internal carotid arteries and the vertebral arteries. There are two of each, making four arteries in all. Got that?"

"Yes."

"And the return system is even simpler. The blood is drained away by only two large veins, the internal jugulars. So you have four arteries going up—they go up the neck, of course—and two veins coming down. Around the brain itself they naturally branch out into other channels, but those don't concern us. We never touch them."

"All right," I said. "Imagine that I've just died. Now what would you do?"

"I should immediately open your neck and locate the four arteries, the carotids and the vertebrals. I should then perfuse them, which means that I'd stick a large hollow needle into each. These four needles would be connected by tubes to the artificial heart.

"Then, working quickly, I would dissect out both the left and right internal jugular veins and hitch these also to the heart machine to complete the circuit. Now switch on the machine, which is already primed with the right type of blood, and there you are. The circulation through your brain would be restored."

"I'd be like that Russian dog."

"I don't think you would. For one thing, you'd certainly lose consciousness when you died, and I very much doubt whether you would come to again for quite a long time—if indeed you came to at all. But, conscious or not, you'd be in a rather interesting position, wouldn't you? You'd have a cold dead body and a living brain."

Landy paused to savour this delightful prospect. The man was so entranced and bemused by the whole idea that he evidently found it impossible to believe I might not be feeling the same way.

"We could now afford to take our time," he said. "And believe me, we'd need it. The first thing we'd do would be to wheel you to the operating-room, accompanied of course by the machine, which must never stop pumping. The next problem . . ."

"All right," I said. "That's enough. I don't have to hear the details."

"Oh but you must," he said. "It is important that you should know precisely what is going to happen to you all the way through. You see, afterwards, when you regain consciousness, it will be much more satisfactory from your point of view if you are able to remember exactly *where* you are and *how* you came to be there. If only for your own peace of mind you should know that. You agree?"

I lay still on the bed, watching him.

"So the next problem would be to remove your brain, intact and undamaged, from your dead body. The body is useless. In fact it has already started to decay. The skull and the face are also useless. They are both encumbrances and I don't want them around. All I want is the brain, the clean beautiful brain, alive and perfect. So when I get you on the table I will take a saw, a small oscillating saw, and with this I shall proceed to remove the whole vault of your skull. You'd still be unconscious at that point so I wouldn't have to bother with anaesthetic."

"Like hell you wouldn't," I said.

"You'd be out cold, I promise you that, William. Don't forget you *died* just a few minutes before."

"Nobody's sawing off the top of my skull without an anaesthetic," I said.

Landy shrugged his shoulders. "It makes no difference to me," he said. "I'll be glad to give you a little procaine if you want it. If it will make you any happier I'll infiltrate the whole scalp with procaine, the whole head, from the neck up."

"Thanks very much," I said.

"You know," he went on, "it's extraordinary what sometimes happens. Only last week a man was brought in unconscious, and I opened his head without any anaesthetic at all and removed a small blood clot. I was still working inside the skull when he woke up and began talking.

" 'Where am I?' he asked.

" 'You're in hospital.'

" 'Well,' he said. 'Fancy that.'

" 'Tell me,' I asked him, 'is this bothering you, what I'm doing?'

" 'No,' he answered. 'Not at all. What *are* you doing?'

" 'I'm just removing a blood clot from your brain.'

" 'You *are?*'

" 'Just lie still. Don't move. I'm nearly finished.'

" 'So that's the bastard been giving me all those headaches,' the man said."

Landy paused and smiled, remembering the occasion. "That's word for word what the man said," he went on, "although the next day he couldn't even recollect the incident. It's a funny thing, the brain."

"I'll have the procaine," I said.

"As you wish, William. And now, as I say, I'd take a small oscillating saw and carefully remove your complete calvarium—the whole vault of the skull. This would expose the top half of the brain, or rather the outer covering in which it is wrapped. You may or may not know that there are three separate coverings around the brain itself —the outer one called the dura mater or dura, the middle one called the arachnoid, and the inner one called the pia mater or pia. Most laymen seem to have the idea that the brain is a naked thing floating around in fluid in your head. But it isn't. It's wrapped up neatly in these three strong coverings, and the cerebrospinal fluid actually flows within the little gap between the two inner coverings, known as the subarachnoid space. As I told you before, this fluid is manufactured by the brain, and it drains off into the venous system by osmosis.

"I myself would leave all three coverings—don't they have lovely names, the dura, the arachnoid, and the pia?— I'd leave them all intact. There are many reasons for this, not least among them being the fact that within the dura run the venous channels that drain the blood from the brain into the jugular.

"Now," he went on, "we've got the upper half of your skull off so that the top of the brain, wrapped in its outer covering, is exposed. The next step is the really tricky one: to release the whole package so that it can be lifted cleanly away, leaving the stubs of the four supply arteries and the two veins hanging underneath ready to be re-connected to the machine. This is an immensely lengthy and compli-cated business involving the delicate chipping away of much bone, the severing of many nerves, and the cutting and tying of numerous blood vessels. The only way I could do it with any hope of success would be by taking a ron-geur and slowly biting off the rest of your skull, peeling it off downward like an orange until the sides and under-neath of the brain covering are fully exposed. The prob-lems involved are highly technical and I won't go into them, but I feel fairly sure that the work can be done. It's simply a question of surgical skill and patience. And don't forget that I'd have plenty of time, as much as I wanted, because the artificial heart would be continually pumping away alongside the operating-table, keeping the brain alive.

"Now, let's assume that I've succeeded in peeling off your skull and removing everything else that surrounds the sides of the brain. That leaves it connected to the body only at the base, mainly by the spinal column and by the two large veins and the four arteries that are supplying it with blood. So what next?

"I would sever the spinal column just above the first cervical vertebra, taking great care not to harm the two vertebral arteries which are in that area. But you must re-member that the dura or outer covering is open at this place to receive the spinal column, so I'd have to close this opening by sewing the edges of the dura together. There'd be no problem there.

"At this point, I would be ready for the final move. To one side, on a table, I'd have a basin of a special shape, and this would be filled with what we call Ringer's Solution. That is a special kind of fluid we use for irrigation in neurosurgery. I would now cut the brain completely loose by severing the supply arteries and the veins. Then I would simply pick it up in my hands and transfer it to the basin. This would be the only other time during the whole proceeding when the blood flow would be cut off; but once it was in the basin, it wouldn't take a moment to re-connect the stubs of the arteries and veins to the artificial heart.

"So there you are," Landy said. "Your brain is now in the basin, and still alive, and there isn't any reason why it shouldn't stay alive for a very long time, years and years perhaps, provided we looked after the blood and the machine."

"But would it *function?*"

"My dear William, how should I know? I can't even tell you whether it would ever regain consciousness."

"And if it did?"

"There now! That would be fascinating!"

"Would it?" I said, and I must admit I had my doubts.

"Of course it would! Lying there with all your thinking processes working beautifully, and your memory as well . . ."

"And not being able to see or feel or smell or hear or talk," I said.

"Ah!" he cried. "I knew I'd forgotten something! I never told you about the eye. Listen. I am going to try to leave one of your optic nerves intact, as well as the eye itself. The optic nerve is a little thing about the thickness of a clinical thermometer and about two inches in length as it stretches between the brain and the eye. The beauty of it is that it's not really a nerve at all. It's an outpouching of the brain itself, and the dura or brain covering extends along it and is attached to the eyeball. The back of the eye is therefore in very close contact with the brain, and cerebrospinal fluid flows right up to it.

"All this suits my purpose very well, and makes it reasonable to suppose that I could succeed in preserving one of your eyes. I've already constructed a small plastic case to contain the eyeball, instead of your own socket, and when the brain is in the basin, submerged in Ringer's Solution, the eyeball in its case will float on the surface of the liquid."

"Staring at the ceiling," I said.

"I suppose so, yes. I'm afraid there wouldn't be any muscles there to move it around. But it might be sort of fun to lie there so quietly and comfortably peering out at the world from your basin."

"Hilarious," I said. "How about leaving me an ear as well?"

"I'd rather not try an ear this time."

"I want an ear," I said. "I insist upon an ear."

"No."

"I want to listen to Bach."

"You don't understand how difficult it would be," Landy said gently. "The hearing apparatus—the cochlea, as it's called—is a far more delicate mechanism than the eye. What's more, it is encased in bone. So is a part of the auditory nerve that connects it with the brain. I couldn't possibly chisel the whole thing out intact."

"Couldn't you leave it encased in the bone and bring the bone to the basin?"

"No," he said firmly. "This thing is complicated enough already. And anyway, if the eye works, it doesn't matter all that much about your hearing. We can always hold up messages for you to read. You really must leave me to decide what is possible and what isn't."

"I haven't yet said that I'm going to do it."

"I know, William, I know."

"I'm not sure I fancy the idea very much."

"Would you rather be dead, altogether?"

"Perhaps I would. I don't know yet. I wouldn't be able to talk, would I?"

"Of course not."

"Then how would I communicate with you? How would you know that I'm conscious?"

"It would be easy for us to know whether or not you regain consciousness," Landy said. "The ordinary electro-encephalograph could tell us that. We'd attach the electrodes directly to the frontal lobes of your brain, there in the basin."

"And you could actually tell?"

"Oh, definitely. Any hospital could do that part of it."

"But *I* couldn't communicate with *you*."

"As a matter of fact," Landy said, "I believe you could. There's a man up in London called Wertheimer who's doing some interesting work on the subject of thought communication, and I've been in touch with him. You know, don't you, that the thinking brain throws off electrical and chemical discharges? And that these discharges go out in the form of waves, rather like radio waves?"

"I know a bit about it," I said.

"Well, Wertheimer has constructed an apparatus somewhat similar to the encephalograph, though far more sensitive, and he maintains that within certain narrow limits it can help him to interpret the actual things that a brain is thinking. It produces a kind of graph which is apparently decipherable into words or thoughts. Would you like me to ask Wertheimer to come and see you?"

"No," I said. Landy was already taking it for granted that I was going to go through with this business, and I

resented his attitude. "Go away now and leave me alone,"
I told him. "You won't get anywhere by trying to rush
me."

He stood up at once and crossed to the door.

"One question," I said.

He paused with a hand on the doorknob. "Yes, William?"

"Simply this. Do you yourself honestly believe that
when my brain is in that basin, my mind will be able to
function exactly as it is doing at present? Do you believe
that I will be able to think and reason as I can now? And
will the power of memory remain?"

"I don't see why not," he answered. "It's the same brain.
It's alive. It's undamaged. In fact, it's completely un-
touched. We haven't even opened the dura. The big difference, of course, would be that we've severed every single nerve that leads into it—except for the one optic nerve
—and this means that your thinking would no longer be
influenced by your senses. You'd be living in an extraordinarily pure and detached world. Nothing to bother you
at all, not even pain. You couldn't possibly feel pain because there wouldn't be any nerves to feel it with. In a
way, it would be an almost perfect situation. No worries or
fears or pains or hunger or thirst. Not even any desires.
Just your memories and your thoughts, and if the remaining eye happened to function, then you could read books
as well. It all sounds rather pleasant to me."

"It does, does it?"

"Yes, William, it does. And particularly for a Doctor of
Philosophy. It would be a tremendous experience. You'd
be able to reflect upon the ways of the world with a de-

tachment and a serenity that no man had ever attained before. And who knows what might not happen then! Great thoughts and solutions might come to you, great ideas that could revolutionize our way of life! Try to imagine, if you can, the degree of concentration that you'd be able to achieve!"

"And the frustration," I said.

"Nonsense. There couldn't be any frustration. You can't have frustration without desire, and you couldn't possibly have any desire. Not physical desire, anyway."

"I should certainly be capable of remembering my previous life in the world, and I might desire to return to it."

"What, to this mess! Out of your comfortable basin and back into this madhouse!"

"Answer one more question," I said. "How long do you believe you could keep it alive?"

"The brain? Who knows? Possibly for years and years. The conditions would be ideal. Most of the factors that cause deterioration would be absent, thanks to the artificial heart. The blood-pressure would remain constant at all times, an impossible condition in real life. The temperature would also be constant. The chemical composition of the blood would be near perfect. There would be no impurities in it, no virus, no bacteria, nothing. Of course it's foolish to guess, but I believe that a brain might live for two or three hundred years in circumstances like these. Goodbye for now," he said. "I'll drop in and see you tomorrow." He went out quickly, leaving me, as you might guess, in a fairly disturbed state of mind.

My immediate reaction after he had gone was one of

revulsion toward the whole business. Somehow, it wasn't at all nice. There was something basically repulsive about the idea that I myself, with all my mental faculties intact, should be reduced to a small slimy grey blob lying in a pool of water. It was monstrous, obscene, unholy. Another thing that bothered me was the feeling of helplessness that I was bound to experience once Landy had got me into the basin. There could be no going back after that, no way of protesting or explaining. I would be committed for as long as they could keep me alive.

And what, for example, if I could not stand it? What if it turned out to be terribly painful? What if I became hysterical?

No legs to run away on. No voice to scream with. Nothing. I'd just have to grin and bear it for the next two centuries.

No mouth to grin with either.

At this point, a curious thought struck me, and it was this: Does not a man who has had a leg amputated often suffer from the delusion that the leg is still there? Does he not tell the nurse that the toes he doesn't have any more are itching like mad, and so on and so forth? I seemed to have heard something to that effect quite recently.

Very well. On the same premise, was it not possible that my brain, lying there alone in that basin, might not suffer from a similar delusion in regard to my body? In which case, all my usual aches and pains could come flooding over me and I wouldn't even be able to take an aspirin to relieve them. One moment I might be imagining that I had the most excruciating cramp in my leg, or a violent indigestion, and a few minutes later, I might easily get the feeling that my poor bladder—you know me—was so full that if I didn't get to emptying it soon it would burst.

Heaven forbid.

I lay there for a long time thinking these horrid thoughts. Then quite suddenly, round about midday, my mood began to change. I became less concerned with the unpleasant aspect of the affair and found myself able to examine Landy's proposals in a more reasonable light. Was there not, after all, I asked myself, something a bit comforting in the thought that my brain might not necessarily have to die and disappear in a few weeks' time? There was indeed. I am rather proud of my brain. It is a sensitive, lucid, and uberous organ. It contains a prodigious store of information, and it is still capable of producing imaginative and original theories. As brains go, it is a damn good one, though I say it myself. Whereas my body, my poor old body, the thing that Landy wants to throw away—well, even you, my dear Mary, will have to agree with me that there is really nothing about *that* which is worth preserving any more.

I was lying on my back eating a grape. Delicious it was, and there were three little seeds in it which I took out of my mouth and placed on the edge of the plate.

"I'm going to do it," I said quietly. "Yes, by God, I'm going to do it. When Landy comes back to see me tomorrow I shall tell him straight out that I'm going to do it."

It was as quick as that. And from then on, I began to

feel very much better. I surprised everyone by gobbling an enormous lunch, and shortly after that you came in to visit me as usual.

But how well I looked, you told me. How bright and well and chirpy. Had anything happened? Was there some good news?

Yes, I said, there was. And then, if you remember, I bade you sit down and make yourself comfortable, and I started out immediately to explain to you as gently as I could what was in the wind.

Alas, you would have none of it. I had hardly begun telling you the barest details when you flew into a fury and said that the thing was revolting, disgusting, horrible, unthinkable, and when I tried to go on, you marched out of the room.

Well, Mary, as you know, I have tried to discuss this subject with you many times since then, but you have consistently refused to give me a hearing. Hence this note, and I can only hope that you will have the good sense to permit yourself to read it. It has taken me a long time to write. Two weeks have gone by since I started to scribble the first sentence, and I'm now a good deal weaker than I was then. I doubt I have the strength to say much more. Certainly I won't say goodbye, because there's a chance, just a tiny chance, that if Landy succeeds in his work I may actually *see* you again later, that is if you can bring yourself to come and visit me.

I am giving orders that these pages shall not be delivered to you until a week after I am gone. By now, therefore, as you sit reading them, seven days have already elapsed since Landy did the deed. You yourself may even know what the outcome has been. If you don't, if you have purposely kept yourself apart and have refused to have anything to do with it—which I suspect may be the case— please change your mind now and give Landy a call to see how things went with me. That is the least you can do. I have told him that he may expect to hear from you on the seventh day.

> *Your faithful husband*
> *William*

P.S. Be good when I am gone, and always remember that it is harder to be a widow than a wife. Do not drink cocktails. Do not waste money. Do not smoke cigarettes. Do not eat pastry. Do not use lipstick. Do not buy a television apparatus. Keep my rose beds and my rockery well weeded in the summers. And incidentally I suggest that you have the telephone disconnected now that I shall have no further use for it.

> *W.*

Mrs. Pearl laid the last page of the manuscript slowly down on the sofa beside her. Her little mouth was pursed up tight and there was a whiteness around her nostrils.

But really! You would think a widow was entitled to a bit of peace after all these years.

The whole thing was just too awful to think about. Beastly and awful. It gave her the shudders.

She reached for her bag and found herself another cigarette. She lit it, inhaling the smoke deeply and blowing it out in clouds all over the room. Through the smoke she could see her lovely television set, brand new, lustrous, huge, crouching defiantly but also a little self-consciously on top of what used to be William's worktable.

What would he say, she wondered, if he could see that now?

She paused, to remember the last time he had caught her smoking a cigarette. That was about a year ago, and she was sitting in the kitchen by the open window having a quick one before he came home from work. She'd had the radio on loud playing dance music and she had turned round to pour herself another cup of coffee and there he was standing in the doorway, huge and grim, staring down at her with those awful eyes, a little black dot of fury blazing in the centre of each.

For four weeks after that, he had paid the housekeeping bills himself and given her no money at all, but of course he wasn't to know that she had over six pounds stashed away in a soap-flake carton in the cupboard under the sink.

"What is it?" she had said to him once during supper. "Are you worried about me getting lung cancer?"

"I am not," he had answered.

"Then why can't I smoke?"

"Because I disapprove, that's why."

He had also disapproved of children, and as a result they had never had any of them either.

Where was he now, this William of hers, the great disapprover?

Landy would be expecting her to call up. Did she *have* to call Landy?

Well, not really, no.

She finished her cigarette, then lit another one immediately from the old stub. She looked at the telephone that was sitting on the worktable beside the television set. William had asked her to call. He had specifically requested that she telephone Landy as soon as she had read the letter. She hesitated, fighting hard now against that old ingrained sense of duty that she didn't quite yet dare to shake off. Then, slowly, she got to her feet and crossed over to the phone on the worktable. She found a number in the book, dialled it, and waited.

"I want to speak to Dr. Landy, please."

"Who is calling?"

"Mrs. Pearl. Mrs. William Pearl."

"One moment, please."

Almost at once, Landy was on the other end of the wire.

"Mrs. Pearl?"

"This is Mrs. Pearl."

There was a slight pause.

"I am so glad you called at last, Mrs. Pearl. You are quite well, I hope?" The voice was quiet, unemotional, courteous. "I wonder if you would care to come over here to the hospital? Then we can have a little chat. I expect you are very eager to know how it all came out."

She didn't answer.

"I can tell you now that everything went pretty smoothly, one way and another. Far better, in fact, than I was entitled to hope. It is not only alive, Mrs. Pearl, it is conscious. It recovered consciousness on the second day. Isn't that interesting?"

She waited for him to go on.

"And the eye is seeing. We are sure of that because we get an immediate change in the deflections on the encephalograph when we hold something up in front of it. And now we're giving it the newspaper to read every day."

"Which newspaper?" Mrs. Pearl asked sharply.

"*The Daily Mirror*. The headlines are larger."

"He hates *The Mirror*. Give him *The Times*."

There was a pause, then the doctor said, "Very well, Mrs. Pearl. We'll give it *The Times*. We naturally want to do all we can to keep it happy."

"*Him*," she said. "Not *it*. *Him!*"

"Him," the doctor said. "Yes, I beg your pardon. To keep him happy. That's one reason why I suggested you should come along here as soon as possible. I think it would be good for him to see you. You could indicate how delighted you were to be with him again—smile at him and blow him a kiss and all that sort of thing. It's bound to be a comfort to him to know that you are standing by."

There was a long pause.

"Well," Mrs. Pearl said at last, her voice suddenly very meek and tired. "I suppose I had better come on over and see how he is."

"Good. I knew you would. I'll wait here for you. Come straight up to my office on the second floor. Goodbye."

Half an hour later, Mrs. Pearl was at the hospital.

"You mustn't be surprised by what he looks like," Landy said as he walked beside her down a corridor.

"No, I won't."

"It's bound to be a bit of a shock to you at first. He's not very prepossessing in his present state, I'm afraid."

"I didn't marry him for his looks, Doctor."

Landy turned and stared at her. What a queer little woman this was, he thought, with her large eyes and her sullen, resentful air. Her features, which must have been quite pleasant once, had now gone completely. The mouth was slack, the cheeks loose and flabby, and the whole face gave the impression of having slowly but surely sagged to pieces through years and years of joyless married life. They walked on for a while in silence.

"Take your time when you get inside," Landy said. "He won't know you're in there until you place your face directly above his eye. The eye is always open, but he can't move it at all, so the field of vision is very narrow. At present we have it looking straight up at the ceiling. And of course he can't hear anything. We can talk together as much as we like. It's in here."

Landy opened a door and ushered her into a small square room.

"I wouldn't go too close yet," he said, putting a hand on her arm. "Stay back here a moment with me until you get used to it all."

There was a biggish white enamel bowl about the size of a washbasin standing on a high white table in the centre of the room, and there were half a dozen thin plastic tubes coming out of it. These tubes were connected with a whole lot of glass piping in which you could see the blood flowing to and from the heart machine. The machine itself made a soft rhythmic pulsing sound.

"He's in there," Landy said, pointing to the basin, which

was too high for her to see into. "Come just a little closer. Not too near."

He led her two paces forward.

By stretching her neck, Mrs. Pearl could now see the surface of the liquid inside the basin. It was clear and still, and on it there floated a small oval capsule, about the size of a pigeon's egg.

"That's the eye in there," Landy said. "Can you see it?"

"Yes."

"So far as we can tell, it is still in perfect condition. It's his right eye, and the plastic container has a lens on it similar to the one he used in his own spectacles. At this moment he's probably seeing quite as well as he did before."

"The ceiling isn't much to look at," Mrs. Pearl said.

"Don't worry about that. We're in the process of working out a whole programme to keep him amused, but we don't want to go too quickly at first."

"Give him a good book."

"We will, we will. Are you feeling all right, Mrs. Pearl?"

"Yes."

"Then we'll go forward a little more, shall we, and you'll be able to see the whole thing."

He led her forward until they were standing only a couple of yards from the table, and now she could see right down into the basin.

"There you are," Landy said. "That's William."

He was far larger than she had imagined he would be,

and darker in colour. With all the ridges and creases running over his surface, he reminded her of nothing so much as an enormous pickled walnut. She could see the stubs of the four big arteries and the two veins coming out from the base of him and the neat way in which they were joined to the plastic tubes; and with each throb of the heart machine, all the tubes gave a little jerk in unison as the blood was pushed through them.

"You'll have to lean over," Landy said, "and put your pretty face right above the eye. He'll see you then, and you can smile at him and blow him a kiss. If I were you I'd say a few nice things as well. He won't actually hear them, but I'm sure he'll get the general idea."

"He hates people blowing kisses at him," Mrs. Pearl said. "I'll do it my own way if you don't mind." She stepped up to the edge of the table, leaned forward until her face was directly over the basin, and looked straight down into William's eye.

"Hallo, dear," she whispered. "It's me—Mary."

The eye, bright as ever, stared back at her with a peculiar, fixed intensity.

"How are you, dear?" she said.

The plastic capsule was transparent all the way round so that the whole of the eyeball was visible. The optic nerve connecting the underside of it to the brain looked like a short length of grey spaghetti.

"Are you feeling all right, William?"

It was a queer sensation peering into her husband's eye when there was no face to go with it. All she had to look at was the eye, and she kept staring at it, and gradually it grew bigger and bigger, and in the end it was the only thing that she could see—a sort of face in itself. There was a network of tiny red veins running over the white surface of the eyeball, and in the ice-blue of the iris there were three or four rather pretty darkish streaks radiating from the pupil in the centre. The pupil was large and black, with a little spark of light reflecting from one side of it.

"I got your letter, dear, and came over at once to see how you were. Dr. Landy says you are doing wonderfully well. Perhaps if I talk slowly you can understand a little of what I am saying by reading my lips."

There was no doubt that the eye was watching her.

"They are doing everything possible to take care of you, dear. This marvellous machine thing here is pumping away all the time and I'm sure it's a lot better than those silly old hearts all the rest of us have. Ours are liable to break down any moment, but yours will go on for ever."

She was studying the eye closely, trying to discover what there was about it that gave it such an unusual appearance.

"You seem fine, dear, just fine. Really you do."

It looked ever so much nicer, this eye, than either of his eyes used to look, she told herself. There was a softness about it somewhere, a calm, kindly quality that she had never seen before. Maybe it had to do with the dot in the very centre, the pupil. William's pupils used always to be tiny black pinheads. They used to glint at you, stabbing into your brain, seeing right through you, and they always knew at once what you were up to and even what you were thinking. But this one she was looking at now was large and soft and gentle, almost cowlike.

"Are you quite sure he's conscious?" she asked, not looking up.

"Oh yes, completely," Landy said.

"And he *can* see me?"

"Perfectly."

"Isn't that marvellous? I expect he's wondering what happened."

"Not at all. He knows perfectly well where he is and why he's there. He can't possibly have forgotten that."

"You mean he *knows* he's in this basin?"

"Of course. And if only he had the power of speech, he would probably be able to carry on a perfectly normal conversation with you this very minute. So far as I can see, there should be absolutely no difference mentally between this William here and the one you used to know back home."

"Good *gracious* me," Mrs. Pearl said, and she paused to consider this intriguing aspect.

You know what, she told herself, looking behind the eye now and staring hard at the great grey pulpy walnut that lay so placidly under the water. I'm not at all sure that I don't prefer him as he is at present. In fact, I believe that I could live very comfortably with this kind of a William. I could cope with this one.

"Quiet, isn't he?" she said.

"Naturally he's quiet."

No arguments and criticisms, she thought, no constant admonitions, no rules to obey, no ban on smoking cigarettes, no pair of cold disapproving eyes watching me over the top of a book in the evenings, no shirts to wash and iron, no meals to cook—nothing but the throb of the heart machine, which was rather a soothing sound anyway and certainly not loud enough to interfere with television.

"Doctor," she said. "I do believe I'm suddenly getting to feel the most enormous affection for him. Does that sound queer?"

"I think it's quite understandable."

"He looks so helpless and silent lying there under the water in his little basin."

"Yes, I know."

"He's like a baby, that's what he's like. He's exactly like a little baby."

Landy stood still behind her, watching.

"There," she said softly, peering into the basin. "From now on Mary's going to look after you *all* by herself and you've nothing to worry about in the world. When can I have him back home, Doctor?"

"I beg your pardon?"

"I said when can I have him back—back in my own house?"

"You're joking," Landy said.

She turned her head slowly around and looked directly at him. "Why should I joke?" she asked. Her face was bright, her eyes round and bright as two diamonds.

"He couldn't possibly be moved."

"I don't see why not."

"This is an experiment, Mrs. Pearl."

"It's my husband, Dr. Landy."

A funny little nervous half-smile appeared on Landy's mouth. "Well . . ." he said.

"It *is* my husband, you know." There was no anger in her voice. She spoke quietly, as though merely reminding him of a simple fact.

"That's rather a tricky point," Landy said, wetting his lips. "You're a widow now, Mrs. Pearl. I think you must resign yourself to that fact."

She turned away suddenly from the table and crossed over to the window. "I mean it," she said, fishing in her bag for a cigarette. "I want him back."

Landy watched her as she put the cigarette between her lips and lit it. Unless he were very much mistaken, there was something a bit odd about this woman, he thought. She seemed almost pleased to have her husband over there in the basin.

He tried to imagine what his own feelings would be if it were *his* wife's brain lying there and *her* eye staring up at him out of that capsule.

He wouldn't like it.

"Shall we go back to my room now?" he said.

She was standing by the window, apparently quite calm and relaxed, puffing her cigarette.

"Yes, all right."

On her way past the table she stopped and leaned over the basin once more. "Mary's leaving now, sweetheart," she said. "And don't you worry about a single thing, you understand? We're going to get you right back home where we can look after you properly just as soon as we possibly can. And listen, dear . . ." At this point she paused and carried the cigarette to her lips, intending to take a puff. Instantly the eye flashed.

She was looking straight into it at the time, and right in the centre of it she saw a tiny but brilliant flash of light, and the pupil contracted into a minute black pinpoint of absolute fury.

At first she didn't move. She stood bending over the basin, holding the cigarette up to her mouth, watching the eye.

Then very slowly, deliberately, she put the cigarette between her lips and took a long suck. She inhaled deeply, and she held the smoke inside her lungs for three or four seconds; then suddenly, *whoosh*, out it came through her nostrils in two thin jets which struck the water in the basin and billowed out over the surface in a thick blue cloud, enveloping the eye.

Landy was over by the door, with his back to her, waiting. "Come on, Mrs. Pearl," he called.

"Don't look so cross, William," she said softly. "It isn't any good looking cross."

Landy turned his head to see what she was doing.

"Not any more it isn't," she whispered. "Because from now on, my pet, you're going to do just exactly what Mary tells you. Do you understand that?"

"Mrs. Pearl," Landy said, moving toward her.

"So don't be a naughty boy again, will you, my precious," she said, taking another pull at the cigarette. "Naughty boys are liable to get punished most severely nowadays, you ought to know that."

Landy was beside her now, and he took her by the arm

and began drawing her firmly but gently away from the table.

"Goodbye, darling," she called. "I'll be back soon."

"That's enough, Mrs. Pearl."

"Isn't he sweet?" she cried, looking up at Landy with big bright eyes. "Isn't he darling? I just can't wait to get him home."

THE WAY UP TO HEAVEN

ALL her life, Mrs. Foster had had an almost pathological fear of missing a train, a plane, a boat, or even a theatre curtain. In other respects, she was not a particularly nervous woman, but the mere thought of being late on occasions like these would throw her into such a state of nerves that she would begin to twitch. It was nothing much—just a tiny vellicating muscle in the corner of the left eye, like a secret wink—but the annoying thing was that it refused to disappear until an hour or so after the train or plane or whatever it was had been safely caught.

It is really extraordinary how in certain people a simple apprehension about a thing like catching a train can grow into a serious obsession. At least half an hour before it was time to leave the house for the station, Mrs. Foster would step out of the elevator all ready to go, with hat and coat and gloves, and then, being quite unable to sit down, she would flutter and fidget about from room to room until her husband, who must have been well aware of her state, finally emerged from his privacy and suggested in a cool dry voice that perhaps they had better get going now, had they not?

Mr. Foster may possibly have had a right to be irritated by this foolishness of his wife's, but he could have had no excuse for increasing her misery by keeping her waiting unnecessarily. Mind you, it is by no means certain that this is what he did, yet whenever they were to go somewhere, his timing was so accurate—just a minute or two late, you understand—and his manner so bland that it was hard to believe he wasn't purposely inflicting a nasty private little torture of his own on the unhappy lady. And one thing he must have known—that she would never dare to call out and tell him to hurry. He had disciplined her too well for that. He must also have known that if he was prepared to wait even beyond the last moment of safety, he could drive her nearly into hysterics. On one or two special occasions in the later years of their married life, it seemed almost as though he had *wanted* to miss the train simply in order to intensify the poor woman's suffering.

Assuming (though one cannot be sure) that the husband was guilty, what made his attitude doubly unreasonable was the fact that, with the exception of this one small irrepressible foible, Mrs. Foster was and always had been a good and loving wife. For over thirty years, she had served him loyally and well. There was no doubt about this. Even she, a very modest woman, was aware of it, and although she had for years refused to let herself believe that Mr. Foster would ever consciously torment her, there had been times recently when she had caught herself beginning to wonder.

Mr. Eugene Foster, who was nearly seventy years old, lived with his wife in a large six-story house on East Sixty-second Street, and they had four servants. It was a gloomy place, and few people came to visit them. But on this particular morning in January, the house had come alive and there was a great deal of bustling about. One maid was distributing bundles of dust sheets to every room, while another was draping them over the furniture. The butler was bringing down suitcases and putting them in the hall. The cook kept popping up from the kitchen to have a word with the butler, and Mrs. Foster herself, in an old-fashioned fur coat and with a black hat on the top of her head, was flying from room to room and pretending to supervise these operations. Actually, she was thinking of nothing at all except that she was going to miss her plane if her husband didn't come out of his study soon and get ready.

"What time is it, Walker?" she said to the butler as she passed him.

"It's ten minutes past nine, Madam."

"And has the car come?"

"Yes, Madam, it's waiting. I'm just going to put the luggage in now."

"It takes an hour to get to Idlewild," she said. "My plane leaves at eleven. I have to be there half an hour before-hand for the formalities. I shall be late. I just *know* I'm going to be late."

"I think you have plenty of time, Madam," the butler

said kindly. "I warned Mr. Foster that you must leave at nine fifteen. There's still another five minutes."

"Yes, Walker, I know, I know. But get the luggage in quickly, will you please?"

She began walking up and down the hall, and whenever the butler came by, she asked him the time. This, she kept telling herself, was the *one* plane she must not miss. It had taken months to persuade her husband to allow her to go. If she missed it, he might easily decide that she should cancel the whole thing. And the trouble was that he insisted on coming to the airport to see her off.

"Dear God," she said aloud, "I'm going to miss it. I know, I know, I *know* I'm going to miss it." The little muscle beside the left eye was twitching madly now. The eyes themselves were very close to tears.

"What time is it, Walker?"

"It's eighteen minutes past, Madam."

"Now I really *will* miss it!" she cried. "Oh, I wish he would come!"

This was an important journey for Mrs. Foster. She was going all alone to Paris to visit her daughter, her only child, who was married to a Frenchman. Mrs. Foster didn't care much for the Frenchman, but she was fond of her daughter, and, more than that, she had developed a great yearning to set eyes on her three grandchildren. She knew them only from the many photographs that she had received and that she kept putting up all over the house. They were beautiful, these children. She doted on them, and each time a new picture arrived, she would carry it away and sit with it for a long time, staring at it lovingly and search-

ing the small faces for signs of that old satisfying blood
likeness that meant so much. And now, lately, she had
come more and more to feel that she did not really wish
to live out her days in a place where she could not be near
these children, and have them visit her, and take them for
walks, and buy them presents, and watch them grow. She
knew, of course, that it was wrong and in a way disloyal
to have thoughts like these while her husband was still
alive. She knew also that although he was no longer active
in his many enterprises, he would never consent to leave
New York and live in Paris. It was a miracle that he had
ever agreed to let her fly over there alone for six weeks to
visit them. But, oh, how she wished she could live there
always, and be close to them!

"Walker, what time is it?"

"Twenty-two minutes past, Madam."

As he spoke, a door opened and Mr. Foster came into
the hall. He stood for a moment, looking intently at his
wife, and she looked back at him—at this diminutive but
still quite dapper old man with the huge bearded face that
bore such an astonishing resemblance to those old photographs of Andrew Carnegie.

"Well," he said, "I suppose perhaps we'd better get going fairly soon if you want to catch that plane."

"*Yes*, dear—*yes!* Everything's ready. The car's waiting."

"That's good," he said. With his head over to one side,
he was watching her closely. He had a peculiar way of
cocking the head and then moving it in a series of small,
rapid jerks. Because of this and because he was clasping

his hands up high in front of him, near the chest, he was somehow like a squirrel standing there—a quick clever old squirrel from the Park.

"Here's Walker with your coat, dear. Put it on."

"I'll be with you in a moment," he said. "I'm just going to wash my hands."

She waited for him, and the tall butler stood beside her, holding the coat and the hat.

"Walker, will I miss it?"

"No, Madam," the butler said. "I think you'll make it all right."

Then Mr. Foster appeared again, and the butler helped him on with his coat. Mrs. Foster hurried outside and got into the hired Cadillac. Her husband came after her, but he walked down the steps of the house slowly, pausing halfway to observe the sky and to sniff the cold morning air.

"It looks a bit foggy," he said as he sat down beside her in the car. "And it's always worse out there at the airport. I shouldn't be surprised if the flight's cancelled already."

"Don't say that, dear—*please*."

They didn't speak again until the car had crossed over the river to Long Island.

"I arranged everything with the servants," Mr. Foster said. "They're all going off today. I gave them half pay for six weeks and told Walker I'd send him a telegram when we wanted them back."

"Yes," she said. "He told me."

"I'll move into the club tonight. It'll be a nice change staying at the club."

"Yes, dear. I'll write to you."

"I'll call in at the house occasionally to see that everything's all right and to pick up the mail."

"But don't you really think Walker should stay there all the time to look after things?" she asked meekly.

"Nonsense. It's quite unnecessary. And anyway, I'd have to pay him full wages."

"Oh yes," she said. "Of course."

"What's more, you never know what people get up to when they're left alone in a house," Mr. Foster announced, and with that he took out a cigar and, after snipping off the end with a silver cutter, lit it with a gold lighter.

She sat still in the car with her hands clasped together tight under the rug.

"Will you write to me?" she asked.

"I'll see," he said. "But I doubt it. You know I don't hold with letter-writing unless there's something specific to say."

"Yes, dear, I know. So don't you bother."

They drove on, along Queens Boulevard, and as they approached the flat marshland on which Idlewild is built, the fog began to thicken and the car had to slow down.

"Oh dear!" cried Mrs. Foster. "I'm *sure* I'm going to miss it now! What time is it?"

"Stop fussing," the old man said. "It doesn't matter anyway. It's bound to be cancelled now. They never fly in this sort of weather. I don't know why you bothered to come out."

She couldn't be sure, but it seemed to her that there was

suddenly a new note in his voice, and she turned to look at him. It was difficult to observe any change in his expression under all that hair. The mouth was what counted. She wished, as she had so often before, that she could see the mouth clearly. The eyes never showed anything except when he was in a rage.

"Of course," he went on, "if by any chance it *does* go, then I agree with you—you'll be certain to miss it now. Why don't you resign yourself to that?"

She turned away and peered through the window at the fog. It seemed to be getting thicker as they went along, and now she could only just make out the edge of the road and the margin of grassland beyond it. She knew that her husband was still looking at her. She glanced back at him again, and this time she noticed with a kind of horror that he was staring intently at the little place in the corner of her left eye where she could feel the muscle twitching.

"Won't you?" he said.

"Won't I what?"

"Be sure to miss it now if it goes. We can't drive fast in this muck."

He didn't speak to her any more after that. The car crawled on and on. The driver had a yellow lamp directed onto the edge of the road, and this helped him to keep going. Other lights, some white and some yellow, kept coming out of the fog toward them, and there was an especially bright one that followed close behind them all the time.

Suddenly, the driver stopped the car.

"There!" Mr. Foster cried. "We're stuck. I knew it."

"No, sir," the driver said, turning round. "We made it. This is the airport."

Without a word, Mrs. Foster jumped out and hurried through the main entrance into the building. There was a mass of people inside, mostly disconsolate passengers standing around the ticket counters. She pushed her way through and spoke to the clerk.

"Yes," he said. "Your flight is temporarily postponed. But please don't go away. We're expecting this weather to clear any moment."

She went back to her husband who was still sitting in the car and told him the news. "But don't you wait, dear," she said. "There's no sense in that."

"I won't," he answered. "So long as the driver can get me back. Can you get me back, driver?"

"I think so," the man said.

"Is the luggage out?"

"Yes, sir."

"Goodbye, dear," Mrs. Foster said, leaning into the car and giving her husband a small kiss on the coarse grey fur of his cheek.

"Goodbye," he answered. "Have a good trip."

The car drove off, and Mrs. Foster was left alone.

The rest of the day was a sort of nightmare for her. She sat for hour after hour on a bench, as close to the airline counter as possible, and every thirty minutes or so she would get up and ask the clerk if the situation had changed. She always received the same reply—that she must continue to wait, because the fog might blow away at any moment. It wasn't until after six in the evening that the loudspeakers finally announced that the flight had been postponed until eleven o'clock the next morning.

Mrs. Foster didn't quite know what to do when she heard this news. She stayed sitting on her bench for at least another half-hour, wondering, in a tired, hazy sort of way, where she might go to spend the night. She hated to leave the airport. She didn't wish to see her husband. She was terrified that in one way or another he would eventually manage to prevent her from getting to France. She would have liked to remain just where she was, sitting on the bench the whole night through. That would be the safest. But she was already exhausted, and it didn't take her long to realize that this was a ridiculous thing for an elderly lady to do. So in the end she went to a phone and called the house.

Her husband, who was on the point of leaving for the club, answered it himself. She told him the news, and asked whether the servants were still there.

"They've all gone," he said.

"In that case, dear, I'll just get myself a room somewhere for the night. And don't you bother yourself about it at all."

"That would be foolish," he said. "You've got a large house here at your disposal. Use it."

"But, dear, it's *empty*."

"Then I'll stay with you myself."

"There's no food in the house. There's nothing."

"Then eat before you come in. Don't be so stupid, woman. Everything you do, you seem to want to make a fuss about it."

"Yes," she said. "I'm sorry. I'll get myself a sandwich here, and then I'll come on in."

Outside, the fog had cleared a little, but it was still a long, slow drive in the taxi, and she didn't arrive back at the house on Sixty-second Street until fairly late.

Her husband emerged from his study when he heard her coming in. "Well," he said, standing by the study door, "how was Paris?"

"We leave at eleven in the morning," she answered. "It's definite."

"You mean if the fog clears."

"It's clearing now. There's a wind coming up."

"You look tired," he said. "You must have had an anxious day."

"It wasn't very comfortable. I think I'll go straight to bed."

"I've ordered a car for the morning," he said. "Nine o'clock."

"Oh, thank you, dear. And I certainly hope you're not going to bother to come all the way out again to see me off."

"No," he said slowly. "I don't think I will. But there's no reason why you shouldn't drop me at the club on your way."

She looked at him, and at that moment he seemed to be standing a long way off from her, beyond some border-line. He was suddenly so small and far away that she couldn't be sure what he was doing, or what he was thinking, or even what he was.

"The club is downtown," she said. "It isn't on the way to the airport."

"But you'll have plenty of time, my dear. Don't you want to drop me at the club?"

"Oh, yes—of course."

"That's good. Then I'll see you in the morning at nine."

She went up to her bedroom on the third floor, and she was so exhausted from her day that she fell asleep soon after she lay down.

Next morning, Mrs. Foster was up early, and by eight thirty she was downstairs and ready to leave.

Shortly after nine, her husband appeared. "Did you make any coffee?" he asked.

"No, dear. I thought you'd get a nice breakfast at the club. The car is here. It's been waiting. I'm all ready to go."

They were standing in the hall—they always seemed to be meeting in the hall nowadays—she with her hat and coat and purse, he in a curiously cut Edwardian jacket with high lapels.

"Your luggage?"

"It's at the airport."

"Ah yes," he said. "Of course. And if you're going to take me to the club first, I suppose we'd better get going fairly soon, hadn't we?"

"Yes!" she cried. "Oh, yes—*please!*"

"I'm just going to get a few cigars. I'll be right with you. You get in the car."

She turned and went out to where the chauffeur was

standing, and he opened the car door for her as she approached.

"What time is it?" she asked him.

"About nine fifteen."

Mr. Foster came out five minutes later, and watching him as he walked slowly down the steps, she noticed that his legs were like goat's legs in those narrow stovepipe trousers that he wore. As on the day before, he paused halfway down to sniff the air and to examine the sky. The weather was still not quite clear, but there was a wisp of sun coming through the mist.

"Perhaps you'll be lucky this time," he said as he settled himself beside her in the car.

"Hurry, please," she said to the chauffeur. "Don't bother about the rug. I'll arrange the rug. Please get going. I'm late."

The man went back to his seat behind the wheel and started the engine.

"*Just* a moment!" Mr. Foster said suddenly. "Hold it a moment, chauffeur, will you?"

"What is it, dear?" She saw him searching the pockets of his overcoat.

"I had a little present I wanted you to take to Ellen," he said. "Now, where on earth is it? I'm sure I had it in my hand as I came down."

"I never saw you carrying anything. What sort of present?"

"A little box wrapped up in white paper. I forgot to give it to you yesterday. I don't want to forget it today."

"A little box!" Mrs. Foster cried. "I never saw any little

box!" She began hunting frantically in the back of the car. Her husband continued searching through the pockets of his coat. Then he unbuttoned the coat and felt around in his jacket. "Confound it," he said, "I must've left it in my bedroom. I won't be a moment."

"Oh, *please!*" she cried. "We haven't got time! *Please* leave it! You can mail it. It's only one of those silly combs anyway. You're always giving her combs."

"And what's wrong with combs, may I ask?" he said, furious that she should have forgotten herself for once.

"Nothing, dear, I'm sure. But . . ."

"Stay here!" he commanded. "I'm going to get it."

"Be quick, dear! Oh, *please* be quick!"

She sat still, waiting and waiting.

"Chauffeur, what time is it?"

The man had a wristwatch, which he consulted. "I make it nearly nine thirty."

"Can we get to the airport in an hour?"

"Just about."

At this point, Mrs. Foster suddenly spotted a corner of something white wedged down in the crack of the seat on the side where her husband had been sitting. She reached over and pulled out a small paper-wrapped box, and at the same time she couldn't help noticing that it was wedged down firm and deep, as though with the help of a pushing hand.

"Here it is!" she cried. "I've found it! Oh dear, and now he'll be up there forever searching for it! Chauffeur, quickly—run in and call him down, will you please?"

The chauffeur, a man with a small rebellious Irish

mouth, didn't care very much for any of this, but he climbed out of the car and went up the steps to the front door of the house. Then he turned and came back. "Door's locked," he announced. "You got a key?"

"Yes—wait a minute." She began hunting madly in her purse. The little face was screwed up tight with anxiety, the lips pushed outward like a spout.

"Here it is! No—I'll go myself. It'll be quicker. I know where he'll be."

She hurried out of the car and up the steps to the front door, holding the key in one hand. She slid the key into the keyhole and was about to turn it—and then she stopped. Her head came up, and she stood there absolutely motionless, her whole body arrested right in the middle of all this hurry to turn the key and get into the house, and she waited—five, six, seven, eight, nine, ten seconds, she waited. The way she was standing there, with her head in the air and the body so tense, it seemed as though she were listening for the repetition of some sound that she had heard a moment before from a place far away inside the house.

Yes—quite obviously she was listening. Her whole attitude was a *listening* one. She appeared actually to be moving one of her ears closer and closer to the door. Now it was right up against the door, and for still another few seconds she remained in that position, head up, ear to door, hand on key, about to enter but not entering, trying instead, or so it seemed, to hear and to analyze these sounds that were coming faintly from this place deep within the house.

Then, all at once, she sprang to life again. She withdrew the key from the door and came running back down the steps.

"It's too late!" she cried to the chauffeur. "I can't wait for him, I simply can't. I'll miss the plane. Hurry now, driver, hurry! To the airport!"

The chauffeur, had he been watching her closely, might have noticed that her face had turned absolutely white and that the whole expression had suddenly altered. There was no longer that rather soft and silly look. A peculiar hardness had settled itself upon the features. The little mouth, usually so flabby, was now tight and thin, the eyes were bright, and the voice, when she spoke, carried a new note of authority.

"Hurry, driver, hurry!"

"Isn't your husband travelling with you?" the man asked, astonished.

"Certainly not! I was only going to drop him at the club. It won't matter. He'll understand. He'll get a cab. Don't sit there talking, man. *Get going!* I've got a plane to catch for Paris!"

With Mrs. Foster urging him from the back seat, the man drove fast all the way, and she caught her plane with a few minutes to spare. Soon she was high up over the Atlantic, reclining comfortably in her airplane chair, listening to the hum of the motors, heading for Paris at last. The new mood was still with her. She felt remarkably strong and, in a queer sort of way, wonderful. She was a trifle breathless with it all, but this was more from pure astonishment at what she had done than anything else, and as the plane flew farther and farther away from New York and East Sixty-second Street, a great sense of calmness began to settle upon her. By the time she reached Paris, she was just as strong and cool and calm as she could wish.

She met her grandchildren, and they were even more beautiful in the flesh than in their photographs. They were like angels, she told herself, so beautiful they were. And every day she took them for walks, and fed them cakes, and bought them presents, and told them charming stories.

Once a week, on Tuesdays, she wrote a letter to her husband—a nice, chatty letter—full of news and gossip, which always ended with the words "Now be sure to take your meals regularly, dear, although this is something I'm afraid you may not be doing when I'm not with you."

When the six weeks were up, everybody was sad that she had to return to America, to her husband. Everybody, that is, except her. Surprisingly, she didn't seem to mind as much as one might have expected, and when she kissed them all goodbye, there was something in her manner and in the things she said that appeared to hint at the possibility of a return in the not too distant future.

However, like the faithful wife she was, she did not overstay her time. Exactly six weeks after she had arrived, she sent a cable to her husband and caught the plane back to New York.

Arriving at Idlewild, Mrs. Foster was interested to observe that there was no car to meet her. It is possible that she might even have been a little amused. But she was extremely calm and did not overtip the porter who helped her into a taxi with her baggage.

New York was colder than Paris, and there were lumps of dirty snow lying in the gutters of the streets. The taxi drew up before the house on Sixty-second Street, and Mrs. Foster persuaded the driver to carry her two large cases to the top of the steps. Then she paid him off and rang the bell. She waited, but there was no answer. Just to make sure, she rang again, and she could hear it tinkling shrilly far away in the pantry, at the back of the house. But still no one came.

So she took out her own key and opened the door herself.

The first thing she saw as she entered was a great pile of mail lying on the floor where it had fallen after being slipped through the letter hole. The place was dark and cold. A dust sheet was still draped over the grandfather clock. In spite of the cold, the atmosphere was peculiarly oppressive, and there was a faint but curious odor in the air that she had never smelled before.

She walked quickly across the hall and disappeared for a moment around the corner to the left, at the back. There was something deliberate and purposeful about this action; she had the air of a woman who is off to investigate a rumor or to confirm a suspicion. And when she returned a few seconds later, there was a little glimmer of satisfaction on her face.

She paused in the center of the hall, as though wondering what to do next. Then, suddenly, she turned and went across into her husband's study. On the desk she found his address book, and after hunting through it for a while she picked up the phone and dialled a number.

"Hello," she said. "Listen—this is Nine East Sixty-second Street. . . . Yes, that's right. Could you send someone round as soon as possible, do you think? Yes, it seems to be stuck between the second and third floors. At least, that's where the indicator's pointing. . . . Right away? Oh, that's very kind of you. You see, my legs aren't any too good for walking up a lot of stairs. Thank you so much. Goodbye."

She replaced the receiver and sat there at her husband's desk, patiently waiting for the man who would be coming soon to repair the elevator.

ROYAL JELLY

"IT WORRIES me to death, Albert, it really does," Mrs. Taylor said.

She kept her eyes fixed on the baby who was now lying absolutely motionless in the crook of her left arm.

"I just know there's something wrong."

The skin on the baby's face had a pearly translucent quality, and was stretched very tightly over the bones.

"Try again," Albert Taylor said.

"It won't do any good."

"You have to keep trying, Mabel," he said.

She lifted the bottle out of the saucepan of hot water and shook a few drops of milk onto the inside of her wrist, testing for temperature.

"Come on," she whispered. "Come on, my baby. Wake up and take a bit more of this."

There was a small lamp on the table close by that made a soft yellow glow all around her.

"Please," she said. "Take just a weeny bit more."

The husband watched her over the top of his magazine.

She was half dead with exhaustion, he could see that, and the pale oval face, usually so grave and serene, had taken on a kind of pinched and desperate look. But even so, the drop of her head as she gazed down at the child was curiously beautiful.

"You see," she murmured. "It's no good. She won't have it."

She held the bottle up to the light, squinting at the calibrations.

"One ounce again. That's all she's taken. No—it isn't even that. It's only three quarters. It's not enough to keep body and soul together, Albert, it really isn't. It worries me to death."

"I know," he said.

"If only they could *find out* what was wrong."

"There's nothing wrong, Mabel. It's just a matter of time."

"Of course there's something wrong."

"Dr. Robinson says no."

"Look," she said, standing up. "You can't tell me it's natural for a six-weeks-old child to weigh less, less by more than *two whole pounds* than she did when she was born! Just look at those legs! They're nothing but skin and bone!"

The tiny baby lay limply on her arm, not moving.

"Dr. Robinson said you was to stop worrying, Mabel. So did that other one."

"Ha!" she said. "Isn't that wonderful! I'm to stop worrying!"

"Now, Mabel."

"What does he want me to do? Treat it as some sort of a joke?"

"He didn't say that."

"I hate doctors! I hate them all!" she cried, and she swung away from him and walked quickly out of the room toward the stairs, carrying the baby with her.

Albert Taylor stayed where he was and let her go.

In a little while he heard her moving about in the bedroom directly over his head, quick nervous footsteps going tap tap tap on the linoleum above. Soon the footsteps would stop, and then he would have to get up and follow her, and when he went into the bedroom he would find her sitting beside the cot as usual, staring at the child and crying softly to herself and refusing to move.

"She's starving, Albert," she would say.

"Of course she's not starving."

"She *is* starving. I know she is. And Albert?"

"Yes?"

"I believe you know it too, but you won't admit it. Isn't that right?"

Every night now it was like this.

Last week they had taken the child back to the hospital, and the doctor had examined it carefully and told them that there was nothing the matter.

"It took us nine years to get this baby, Doctor," Mabel had said. "I think it would kill me if anything should happen to her."

That was six days ago and since then it had lost another five ounces.

But worrying about it wasn't going to help anybody,

Albert Taylor told himself. One simply had to trust the doctor on a thing like this. He picked up the magazine that was still lying on his lap and glanced idly down the list of contents to see what it had to offer this week:

AMONG THE BEES IN MAY

HONEY COOKERY

THE BEE FARMER AND THE B. PHARM.

EXPERIENCES IN THE CONTROL OF NOSEMA

THE LATEST ON ROYAL JELLY

THIS WEEK IN THE APIARY

THE HEALING POWER OF PROPOLIS

REGURGITATIONS

BRITISH BEEKEEPERS ANNUAL DINNER

ASSOCIATION NEWS

All his life Albert Taylor had been fascinated by anything that had to do with bees. As a small boy he used often to catch them in his bare hands and go running with them into the house to show to his mother, and sometimes he would put them on his face and let them crawl about over his cheeks and neck, and the astonishing thing about it all was that he never got stung. On the contrary, the bees seemed to enjoy being with him. They never tried to fly away, and to get rid of them he would have to brush them off gently with his fingers. Even then they would frequently return and settle again on his arm or hand or knee, any place where the skin was bare.

His father, who was a bricklayer, said there must be

some witch's stench about the boy, something noxious that came oozing out through the pores of the skin, and that no good would ever come of it, hypnotizing insects like that. But the mother said it was a gift given him by God, and even went so far as to compare him with St. Francis and the birds.

As he grew older, Albert Taylor's fascination with bees developed into an obsession, and by the time he was twelve he had built his first hive. The following summer he had captured his first swarm. Two years later, at the age of fourteen, he had no less than five hives standing neatly in a row against the fence in his father's small back yard, and already—apart from the normal task of producing honey— he was practising the delicate and complicated business of rearing his own queens, grafting larvae into artificial cell cups, and all the rest of it.

He never had to use smoke when there was work to do inside a hive, and he never wore gloves on his hands or a net over his head. Clearly there was some strange sympathy between this boy and the bees, and down in the village, in the shops and pubs, they began to speak about him with a certain kind of respect, and people started coming up to the house to buy his honey.

When he was eighteen, he had rented one acre of rough pasture alongside a cherry orchard down the valley about a mile from the village, and there he had set out to establish his own business. Now, eleven years later, he was still in the same spot, but he had six acres of ground instead of one, two hundred and forty well-stocked hives, and a small house that he'd built mainly with his own hands.

He had married at the age of twenty and that, apart from the fact that it had taken them over nine years to get a child, had also been a success. In fact, everything had gone pretty well for Albert until this strange little baby girl came along and started frightening them out of their wits by refusing to eat properly and losing weight every day.

He looked up from the magazine and began thinking about his daughter.

This evening, for instance, when she had opened her eyes at the beginning of the feed, he had gazed into them and seen something that frightened him to death—a kind of misty vacant stare, as though the eyes themselves were not connected to the brain at all but were just lying loose in their sockets like a couple of small grey marbles.

Did those doctors really know what they were talking about?

He reached for an ashtray and started slowly picking the ashes out from the bowl of his pipe with a matchstick.

One could always take her along to another hospital, somewhere in Oxford perhaps. He might suggest that to Mabel when he went upstairs.

He could still hear her moving around in the bedroom, but she must have taken off her shoes now and put on slippers because the noise was very faint.

He switched his attention back to the magazine and went on with his reading. He finished an article called "Experiences in the Control of Nosema," then turned over the page and began reading the next one, "The Latest on

Royal Jelly." He doubted very much whether there would be anything in this that he didn't know already:

What is this wonderful substance called royal jelly?

He reached for the tin of tobacco on the table beside him and began filling his pipe, still reading.

Royal jelly is a glandular secretion produced by the nurse bees to feed the larvae immediately they have hatched from the egg. The pharingeal glands of bees produce this substance in much the same way as the mammary glands of vertebrates produce milk. The fact is of great biological interest because no other insects in the world are known to have evolved such a process.

All old stuff, he told himself, but for want of anything better to do, he continued to read.

Royal jelly is fed in concentrated form to all bee larvae for the first three days after hatching from the egg; but beyond that point, for all those who are destined to become drones or workers, this precious food is greatly diluted with honey and pollen. On the other hand, the larvae which are destined to become queens are fed throughout the whole of their larval period on a concentrated diet of pure royal jelly. Hence the name.

Above him, up in the bedroom, the noise of the footsteps had stopped altogether. The house was quiet. He struck a match and put it to his pipe.

Royal jelly must be a substance of tremendous nourishing power, for on this diet alone, the honey-bee larva increases in weight fifteen hundred times in five days.

That was probably about right, he thought, although for

some reason it had never occured to him to consider larval growth in terms of weight before.

This is as if a seven-and-a-half-pound baby should increase in that time to five tons.

Albert Taylor stopped and read that sentence again. He read it a third time.

This is as if a seven-and-a-half-pound baby . . .

"Mabel!" he cried, jumping up from his chair. "Mabel! Come here!"

He went out into the hall and stood at the foot of the stairs calling for her to come down.

There was no answer.

He ran up the stairs and switched on the light on the landing. The bedroom door was closed. He crossed the landing and opened it and stood in the doorway looking into the dark room. "Mabel," he said. "Come downstairs a moment, will you please? I've just had a bit of an idea. It's about the baby."

The light from the landing behind him cast a faint glow over the bed and he could see her dimly now, lying on her stomach with her face buried in the pillow and her arms up over her head. She was crying again.

"Mabel," he said, going over to her, touching her shoulder. "Please come down a moment. This may be important."

"Go away," she said. "Leave me alone."

"Don't you want to hear about my idea?"

"Oh, Albert, I'm *tired*," she sobbed. "I'm so tired I don't know what I'm doing any more. I don't think I can go on. I don't think I can stand it."

There was a pause. Albert Taylor turned away from her and walked slowly over to the cradle where the baby was lying, and peered in. It was too dark for him to see the child's face, but when he bent down close he could hear the sound of breathing, very faint and quick. "What time is the next feed?" he asked.

"Two o'clock, I suppose."

"And the one after that?"

"Six in the morning."

"I'll do them both," he said. "You go to sleep."

She didn't answer.

"You get properly into bed, Mabel, and go straight to sleep, you understand? And stop worrying. I'm taking over completely for the next twelve hours. You'll give yourself a nervous breakdown going on like this."

"Yes," she said. "I know."

"I'm taking the nipper and myself *and* the alarm clock into the spare room this very moment, so you just lie down and relax and forget all about us. Right?" Already he was pushing the cradle out through the door.

"Oh, Albert," she sobbed.

"Don't you worry about a thing. Leave it to me."

"Albert . . ."

"Yes?"

"I love you, Albert."

"I love you too, Mabel. Now go to sleep."

Albert Taylor didn't see his wife again until nearly eleven o'clock the next morning.

"Good *gracious* me!" she cried, rushing down the stairs in dressing-gown and slippers. "Albert! Just look at the time! I must have slept twelve hours at least! Is everything all right? What happened?"

He was sitting quietly in his armchair, smoking a pipe and reading the morning paper. The baby was in a sort of carrier cot on the floor at his feet, sleeping.

"Hullo, dear," he said, smiling.

She ran over to the cot and looked in. "Did she take anything, Albert? How many times have you fed her? She was due for another one at ten o'clock, did you know that?"

Albert Taylor folded the newspaper neatly into a square and put it away on the side table. "I fed her at two in the morning," he said, "and she took about half an ounce, no more. I fed her again at six and she did a bit better that time, two ounces . . ."

"*Two ounces!* Oh, Albert, that's marvellous!"

"And we just finished the last feed ten minutes ago. There's the bottle on the mantelpiece. Only one ounce left. She drank three. How's that?" He was grinning proudly, delighted with his achievement.

The woman quickly got down on her knees and peered at the baby.

"Don't she look better?" he asked eagerly. "Don't she look fatter in the face?"

"It may sound silly," the wife said, "but I actually think she does. Oh, Albert, you're a marvel! How did you do it?"

"She's turning the corner," he said. "That's all it is. Just like the doctor prophesied, she's turning the corner."

"I pray to God you're right, Albert."

"Of course I'm right. From now on, you watch her go."

The woman was gazing lovingly at the baby.

"You look a lot better yourself too, Mabel."

"I feel wonderful. I'm sorry about last night."

"Let's keep it this way," he said. "I'll do all the night feeds in future. You do the day ones."

She looked up at him across the cot, frowning. "No," she said. "Oh no, I wouldn't allow you to do that."

"I don't want you to have a breakdown, Mabel."

"I won't, not now I've had some sleep."

"Much better we share it."

"No, Albert. This is my job and I intend to do it. Last night won't happen again."

There was a pause. Albert Taylor took the pipe out of his mouth and examined the grain on the bowl. "All right," he said. "In that case I'll just relieve you of the donkey work, I'll do all the sterilizing and the mixing of the food and getting everything ready. That'll help you a bit, anyway."

She looked at him carefully, wondering what could have come over him all of a sudden.

"You see, Mabel, I've been thinking . . ."

"Yes, dear."

"I've been thinking that up until last night I've never even raised a finger to help you with this baby."

"That isn't true."

"Oh yes it is. So I've decided that from now on I'm going to do *my* share of the work. I'm going to be the feed-mixer and the bottle-sterilizer. Right?"

"It's very sweet of you, dear, but I really don't think it's necessary. . . ."

"Come on!" he cried. "Don't change the luck! I done it the last three times and just *look* what happened! When's the next one? Two o'clock, isn't it?"

"Yes."

"It's all mixed," he said. "Everything's all mixed and ready and all you've got to do when the time comes is to go out there to the larder and take it off the shelf and warm it up. That's *some* help, isn't it?"

The woman got up off her knees and went over to him and kissed him on the cheek. "You're such a nice man," she said. "I love you more and more every day I know you."

Later, in the middle of the afternoon, when Albert was outside in the sunshine working among the hives, he heard her calling to him from the house.

"Albert!" she shouted. "Albert, come here!" She was running through the buttercups toward him.

He started forward to meet her, wondering what was wrong.

"Oh, Albert! Guess what!"

"What?"

"I've just finished giving her the two-o'clock feed and she's taken the whole lot!"

"No!"

"Every drop of it! Oh, Albert, I'm so happy! She's going to be all right! She's turned the corner just like you said!" She came up to him and threw her arms around his neck and hugged him, and he clapped her on the back and laughed and said what a marvellous little mother she was.

"Will you come in and watch the next one and see if she does it again, Albert?"

He told her he wouldn't miss it for anything, and she hugged him again, then turned and ran back to the house, skipping over the grass and singing all the way.

Naturally, there was a certain amount of suspense in the air as the time approached for the six-o'clock feed. By five thirty both parents were already seated in the living-room waiting for the moment to arrive. The bottle with the milk formula in it was standing in a saucepan of warm water on the mantelpiece. The baby was asleep in its carrier cot on the sofa.

At twenty minutes to six it woke up and started screaming its head off.

"There you are!" Mrs. Taylor cried. "She's asking for the bottle. Pick her up quick, Albert, and hand her to me here. Give me the bottle first."

He gave her the bottle, then placed the baby on the woman's lap. Cautiously, she touched the baby's lips with the end of the nipple. The baby seized the nipple between its gums and began to suck ravenously with a rapid powerful action.

"Oh, Albert, isn't it wonderful?" she said, laughing.

"It's terrific, Mabel."

In seven or eight minutes, the entire contents of the bottle had disappeared down the baby's throat.

"You clever girl," Mrs. Taylor said. "Four ounces again."

Albert Taylor was leaning forward in his chair, peering intently into the baby's face. "You know what?" he said.

"She even seems as though she's put on a touch of weight already. What do you think?"

The mother looked down at the child.

"Don't she seem bigger and fatter to you, Mabel, than she was yesterday?"

"Maybe she does, Albert. I'm not sure. Although actually there couldn't be any *real* gain in such a short time as this. The important thing is that she's eating normally."

"She's turned the corner," Albert said. "I don't think you need worry about her any more."

"I certainly won't."

"You want me to go up and fetch the cradle back into our own bedroom, Mabel?"

"Yes, please," she said.

Albert went upstairs and moved the cradle. The woman followed with the baby, and after changing its nappy, she laid it gently down on its bed. Then she covered it with sheet and blanket.

"Doesn't she look lovely, Albert?" she whispered. "Isn't that the most beautiful baby you've ever seen in your *entire* life?"

"Leave her be now, Mabel," he said. "Come on downstairs and cook us a bit of supper. We both deserve it."

After they had finished eating, the parents settled themselves in armchairs in the living-room, Albert with his magazine and his pipe, Mrs. Taylor with her knitting. But this was a very different scene from the one of the night before. Suddenly, all tensions had vanished. Mrs. Taylor's handsome oval face was glowing with pleasure, her cheeks were pink, her eyes were sparkling bright, and her mouth was fixed in a little dreamy smile of pure content. Every now and again she would glance up from her knitting and gaze affectionately at her husband. Occasionally, she would stop the clicking of her needles altogether for a few seconds and sit quite still, looking at the ceiling, listening for a cry or a whimper from upstairs. But all was quiet.

"Albert," she said after a while.

"Yes, dear?"

"What was it you were going to tell me last night when you came rushing up to the bedroom? You said you had an idea for the baby."

Albert Taylor lowered the magazine onto his lap and gave her a long sly look.

"Did I?" he said.

"Yes." She waited for him to go on, but he didn't.

"What's the big joke?" she asked. "Why are you grinning like that?"

"It's a joke all right," he said.

"Tell it to me, dear."

"I'm not sure I ought to," he said. "You might call me a liar."

She had seldom seen him looking so pleased with himself as he was now, and she smiled back at him, egging him on.

"I'd just like to see your face when you hear it, Mabel, that's all."

"Albert, what *is* all this?"

He paused, refusing to be hurried.

"You do think the baby's better, don't you?" he asked.

"Of course I do."

"You agree with me that all of a sudden she's feeding

marvellously and looking one-hundred-per-cent different?"

"I do, Albert, yes."

"That's good," he said, the grin widening. "You see, it's me that did it."

"Did what?"

"I cured the baby."

"Yes, dear, I'm sure you did." Mrs. Taylor went right on with her knitting.

"You don't believe me, do you?"

"Of course I believe you, Albert. I give you all the credit, every bit of it."

"Then how did I do it?"

"Well," she said, pausing a moment to think. "I suppose it's simply that you're a brilliant feed-mixer. Ever since you started mixing the feeds she's got better and better."

"You mean there's some sort of an art in mixing the feeds?"

"Apparently there is." She was knitting away and smiling quietly to herself, thinking how funny men were.

"I'll tell you a secret," he said. "You're absolutely right. Although, mind you, it isn't so much *how* you mix it that counts. It's what you put in. You realize that, don't you, Mabel?"

Mrs. Taylor stopped knitting and looked up sharply at her husband. "Albert," she said, "don't tell me you've been putting things into that child's milk?"

He sat there grinning.

"Well, have you or haven't you?"

"It's possible," he said.

"I don't believe it."

He had a strange fierce way of grinning that showed his teeth.

"Albert," she said. "Stop playing with me like this."

"Yes, dear, all right."

"You haven't *really* put anything into her milk, have you? Answer me properly, Albert. This could be serious with such a tiny baby."

"The answer is yes, Mabel."

"*Albert Taylor!* How could you?"

"Now don't get excited," he said. "I'll tell you all about it if you really want me to, but for heaven's sake keep your hair on."

"It was beer!" she cried. "I just know it was beer!"

"Don't be so daft, Mabel, please."

"Then what was it?"

Albert laid his pipe down carefully on the table beside him and leaned back in his chair. "Tell me," he said, "did you ever by any chance happen to hear me mentioning something called royal jelly?"

"I did not."

"It's magic," he said. "Pure magic. And last night I suddenly got the idea that if I was to put some of this into the baby's milk . . ."

"How *dare* you!"

"Now, Mabel, you don't even know what it is yet."

"I don't care what it is," she said. "You can't go putting foreign bodies like that into a tiny baby's milk. You must be mad."

"It's perfectly harmless, Mabel, otherwise I wouldn't have done it. It comes from bees."

"I might have guessed that."

"And it's so precious that practically no one can afford to take it. When they do, it's only one little drop at a time."

"And how much did you give to our baby, might I ask?"

"Ah," he said, "that's the whole point. That's where the difference lies. I reckon that our baby, just in the last four feeds, has already swallowed about fifty times as much royal jelly as anyone else in the world has ever swallowed before. How about that?"

"Albert, stop pulling my leg."

"I swear it," he said proudly.

She sat there staring at him, her brow wrinkled, her mouth slightly open.

"You know what this stuff actually costs, Mabel, if you want to buy it? There's a place in America advertising it for sale this very moment for something like five hundred dollars a pound jar! *Five hundred dollars!* That's more than gold, you know!"

She hadn't the faintest idea what he was talking about.

"I'll prove it," he said, and he jumped up and went across to the large bookcase where he kept all his literature about bees. On the top shelf, the back numbers of *The American Bee Journal* were neatly stacked alongside those of *The British Bee Journal, Beecraft,* and other magazines. He took down the last issue of *The American Bee Journal* and turned to a page of small classified advertisements at the back.

"Here you are," he said. "Exactly as I told you. 'We sell royal jelly—$480 per lb. jar wholesale.'"

He handed her the magazine so she could read it herself.
"Now do you believe me? This is an actual shop in New
York, Mabel. It says so."

"It doesn't say you can go stirring it into the milk of a
practically new-born baby," she said. "I don't know what's
come over you, Albert, I really don't."

"It's curing her, isn't it?"

"I'm not so sure about that, now."

"Don't be so damn silly, Mabel. You know it is."

"Then why haven't other people done it with *their*
babies?"

"I keep telling you," he said. "It's too expensive. Practically nobody in the world can afford to buy royal jelly just
for *eating* except maybe one or two multimillionaries. The
people who buy it are the big companies that make wom-
en's face creams and things like that. They're using it as a
stunt. They mix a tiny pinch of it into a big jar of face
cream and it's selling like hot cakes for absolutely enormous prices. They claim it takes out the wrinkles."

"And does it?"

"Now how on earth would I know that, Mabel? Anyway," he said, returning to his chair, "that's not the point.
The point is this. It's done so much good to our little baby
just in the last few hours that I think we ought to go right
on giving it to her. Now don't interrupt, Mabel. Let me
finish. I've got two hundred and forty hives out there and
if I turn over maybe a hundred of them to making royal
jelly, we ought to be able to supply her with all she wants."

"Albert Taylor," the woman said, stretching her eyes

wide and staring at him. "Have you gone out of your mind?"

"Just hear me through, will you please?"

"I forbid it," she said, "absolutely. You're not to give my baby another drop of that horrid jelly, you understand?"

"Now, Mabel . . ."

"And quite apart from that, we had a shocking honey crop last year, and if you go fooling around with those hives now, there's no telling what might not happen."

"There's nothing wrong with my hives, Mabel."

"You know very well we had only half the normal crop last year."

"Do me a favour, will you?" he said. "Let me explain some of the marvellous things this stuff does."

"You haven't even told me what it is yet."

"All right, Mabel. I'll do that too. Will you listen? Will you give me a chance to explain it?"

She sighed and picked up her knitting once more. "I suppose you might as well get it off your chest, Albert. Go on and tell me."

He paused, a bit uncertain now how to begin. It wasn't going to be easy to explain something like this to a person with no detailed knowledge of apiculture at all.

"You know, don't you," he said, "that each colony has only one queen?"

"Yes."

"And that this queen lays all the eggs?"

"Yes, dear. That much I know."

"All right. Now the queen can actually lay two different kinds of eggs. You didn't know that, but she can. It's what we call one of the miracles of the hive. She can lay eggs that produce drones, and she can lay eggs that produce workers. Now if that isn't a miracle, Mabel, I don't know what is."

"Yes, Albert, all right."

"The drones are the males. We don't have to worry about them. The workers are all females. So is the queen, of course. But the workers are unsexed females, if you see what I mean. Their organs are completely undeveloped, whereas the queen is tremendously sexy. She can actually lay her own weight in eggs in a single day."

He hesitated, marshalling his thoughts.

"Now what happens is this. The queen crawls around on the comb and lays her eggs in what we call cells. You know all those hundreds of little holes you see in a honeycomb? Well, a brood comb is just about the same except the cells don't have honey in them, they have eggs. She lays one egg to each cell, and in three days each of these eggs hatches out into a tiny grub. We call it a larva.

"Now, as soon as this larva appears, the nurse bees—they're young workers—all crowd round and start feeding it like mad. And you know what they feed it on?"

"Royal jelly," Mabel answered patiently.

"Right!" he cried. "That's exactly what they do feed it on. They get this stuff out of a gland in their heads and they start pumping it into the cell to feed the larva. And what happens then?"

He paused dramatically, blinking at her with his small

watery-grey eyes. Then he turned slowly in his chair and reached for the magazine that he had been reading the night before.

"You want to know what happens then?" he asked, wetting his lips.

"I can hardly wait."

" 'Royal jelly,' " he read aloud, " 'must be a substance of tremendous nourishing power, for on this diet alone, the honey-bee larva increases in weight *fifteen hundred times* in five days!' "

"How much?"

"*Fifteen hundred times*, Mabel. And you know what that means if you put it in terms of a human being? It means," he said, lowering his voice, leaning forward, fixing her with those small pale eyes, "it means that in five days a baby weighing seven and a half pounds to start off with would increase in weight to *five tons!*"

For the second time, Mrs. Taylor stopped knitting.

"Now you mustn't take that too literally, Mabel."

"Who says I mustn't?"

"It's just a scientific way of putting it, that's all."

"Very well, Albert. Go on."

"But that's only half the story," he said. "There's more to come. The really amazing thing about royal jelly, I haven't told you yet. I'm going to show you now how it can transform a plain dull-looking little worker bee with practically no sex organs at all into a great big beautiful fertile queen."

"Are you saying our baby is dull-looking and plain?" she asked sharply.

"Now don't go putting words into my mouth, Mabel, please. Just listen to this. Did you know that the queen bee and the worker bee, although they are completely different when they grow up, are both hatched out of exactly the same kind of egg?"

"I don't believe that," she said.

"It's true as I'm sitting here, Mabel, honest it is. Any time the bees want a queen to hatch out of the egg instead of a worker, they can do it."

"How?"

"Ah," he said, shaking a thick forefinger in her direction. "That's just what I'm coming to. That's the secret of the whole thing. Now—what do *you* think it is, Mabel, that makes this miracle happen?"

"Royal jelly," she answered. "You already told me."

"Royal jelly it is!" he cried, clapping his hands and bouncing up on his seat. His big round face was glowing with excitement now, and two vivid patches of scarlet had appeared high up on each cheek.

"Here's how it works. I'll put it very simply for you. The bees want a new queen. So they build an extra-large cell, a queen cell we call it, and they get the old queen to lay one of her eggs in there. The other one thousand nine hundred and ninety-nine eggs she lays in ordinary worker cells. Now. As soon as these eggs hatch out into larvae, the nurse bees rally round and start pumping in the royal jelly. All of them get it, workers as well as queen. But here's the vital thing, Mabel, so listen carefully. Here's where the difference comes. The worker larvae only receive this special marvellous food for the *first three days* of their larval life. After that they have a complete change of diet. What really happens is they get weaned, except that it's not like an ordinary weaning because it's so sudden. After the third day they're put straight away onto more or less routine bees' food—a mixture of honey and pollen—and then about two weeks later they emerge from the cells as workers.

"But not so the larva in the queen cell! This one gets royal jelly *all the way through its larval life.* The nurse bees simply pour it into the cell, so much so in fact that the little larva is literally floating in it. And that's what makes it into a queen!"

"You can't prove it," she said.

"Don't talk so damn silly, Mabel, please. Thousands of people have proved it time and time again, famous scientists in every country in the world. All you have to do is take a larva out of a worker cell and put it in a queen cell— that's what we call grafting—and just so long as the nurse bees keep it well supplied with royal jelly, then presto!— it'll grow up into a queen! And what makes it more marvellous still is the absolutely enormous difference between a queen and a worker when they grow up. The abdomen is a different shape. The sting is different. The legs are different. The . . ."

"In what way are the legs different?" she asked, testing him.

"The legs? Well, the workers have little pollen baskets on their legs for carrying the pollen. The queen has none. Now here's another thing. The queen has fully developed sex organs. The workers don't. And most amazing of all,

Mabel, the queen lives for an average of four to six years. The worker hardly lives that many months. And all this difference simply because one of them got royal jelly and the other didn't!"

"It's pretty hard to believe," she said, "that a food can do all that."

"Of course it's hard to believe. It's another of the miracles of the hive. In fact it's the biggest ruddy miracle of them all. It's such a hell of a big miracle that it's baffled the greatest men of science for hundreds of years. Wait a moment. Stay there. Don't move."

Again he jumped up and went over to the bookcase and started rummaging among the books and magazines.

"I'm going to find you a few of the reports. Here we are. Here's one of them. Listen to this." He started reading aloud from a copy of the *American Bee Journal:*

" 'Living in Toronto at the head of a fine research laboratory given to him by the people of Canada in recognition of his truly great contribution to humanity in the discovery of insulin, Dr. Frederick A. Banting became curious about royal jelly. He requested his staff to do a basic fractional analysis. . . .' "

He paused.

"Well, there's no need to read it all, but here's what happened. Dr. Banting and his people took some royal jelly from queen cells that contained two-day-old larvae, and then they started analyzing it. And what d'you think they found?

"They found," he said, "that royal jelly contained

phenols, sterols, glycerils, dextrose, *and*—now here it comes—and eighty to eighty-five per cent *unidentified acids!*"

He stood beside the bookcase with the magazine in his hand, smiling a funny little furtive smile of triumph, and his wife watched him, bewildered.

He was not a tall man; he had a thick plump pulpy-looking body that was built close to the ground on abbreviated legs. The legs were slightly bowed. The head was huge and round, covered with bristly short-cut hair, and the greater part of the face—now that he had given up shaving altogether—was hidden by a brownish yellow fuzz about an inch long. In one way and another, he was rather grotesque to look at, there was no denying that.

"Eighty to eighty-five per cent," he said, "unidentified acids. Isn't that fantastic?" He turned back to the bookshelf and began hunting through the other magazines.

"What does it mean, unidentified acids?"

"That's the whole point! No one knows! Not even Banting could find out. You've heard of Banting?"

"No."

"He just happens to be about the most famous living doctor in the world today, that's all."

Looking at him now as he buzzed around in front of the bookcase with his bristly head and his hairy face and his plump pulpy body, she couldn't help thinking that somehow, in some curious way, there was a touch of the bee about this man. She had often seen women grow to look like the horses that they rode, and she had noticed that people who bred birds or bull terriers or pomeranians frequently resembled in some small but startling manner the creature of their choice. But up until now it had never occurred to her that her husband might look like a bee. It shocked her a bit.

"And did Banting ever try to eat it," she asked, "this royal jelly?"

"Of course he didn't eat it, Mabel. He didn't have enough for that. It's too precious."

"You know something?" she said, staring at him but smiling a little all the same. "You're getting to look just a teeny bit like a bee yourself, did you know that?"

He turned and looked at her.

"I suppose it's the beard mostly," she said. "I do wish you'd stop wearing it. Even the colour is sort of bee-ish, don't you think?"

"What the hell are you talking about, Mabel?"

"Albert," she said. "Your language."

"Do you want to hear any more of this or don't you?"

"Yes, dear, I'm sorry. I was only joking. Do go on."

He turned away again and pulled another magazine out of the bookcase and began leafing through the pages. "Now just listen to this, Mabel. 'In 1939, Heyl experimented with twenty-one-day-old rats, injecting them with royal jelly in varying amounts. As a result, he found a precocious follicular development of the ovaries directly in proportion to the quantity of royal jelly injected.' "

"There!" she cried. "I knew it!"

"Knew what?"

"I knew something terrible would happen."

"Nonsense. There's nothing wrong with that. Now

here's another, Mabel. 'Still and Burdett found that a male rat which hitherto had been unable to breed, upon receiving a minute daily dose of royal jelly, became a father many times over.' "

"Albert," she cried, "this stuff is *much* too strong to give to a baby! I don't like it at all."

"Nonsense, Mabel."

"Then why do they only try it out on rats, tell me that? Why don't some of these famous scientists take it themselves? They're too clever, that's why. Do you think Dr. Banting is going to risk finishing up with precious ovaries? Not him."

"But they *have* given it to people, Mabel. Here's a whole article about it. Listen." He turned the page and again began reading from the magazine. " 'In Mexico, in 1953, a group of enlightened physicians began prescribing minute doses of royal jelly for such things as cerebral neuritis, arthritis, diabetes, autointoxication from tobacco, impotence in men, asthma, croup, and gout. . . . There are stacks of signed testimonials. . . . A celebrated stockbroker in Mexico City contracted a particularly stubborn case of psoriasis. He became physically unattractive. His clients began to forsake him. His business began to suffer. In desperation he turned to royal jelly—one drop with every meal—and presto!—he was cured in a fortnight. A waiter in the Café Jena, also in Mexico City, reported that his father, after taking minute doses of this wonder substance in capsule form, sired a healthy boy child at the age of ninety. A bullfight promoter in Acapulco, finding himself landed with a rather lethargic-looking bull, injected it with one gram of royal jelly (an excessive dose) just before it entered the arena. Thereupon, the beast became so swift and savage that it promptly dispatched two picadors, three horses, and a matador, and finally . . .' "

"Listen!" Mrs. Taylor said, interrupting him. "I think the baby's crying."

Albert glanced up from his reading. Sure enough, a lusty yelling noise was coming from the bedroom above.

"She must be hungry," he said.

His wife looked at the clock. "Good gracious me!" she cried, jumping up. "It's past her time again already! You mix the feed, Albert, quickly, while I bring her down! But hurry! I don't want to keep her waiting."

In half a minute, Mrs. Taylor was back, carrying the screaming infant in her arms. She was flustered now, still quite unaccustomed to the ghastly nonstop racket that a healthy baby makes when it wants its food. "Do be quick, Albert!" she called, settling herself in the armchair and arranging the child on her lap. "Please hurry!"

Albert entered from the kitchen and handed her the bottle of warm milk. "It's just right," he said. "You don't have to test it."

She hitched the baby's head a little higher in the crook of her arm, then pushed the rubber teat straight into the wide-open yelling mouth. The baby grabbed the teat and began to suck. The yelling stopped. Mrs. Taylor relaxed.

"Oh, Albert, isn't she lovely?"

"She's terrific, Mabel—thanks to royal jelly."

"Now, dear, I don't want to hear another word about that nasty stuff. It frightens me to death."

"You're making a big mistake," he said.

"We'll see about that."

The baby went on sucking the bottle.

"I do believe she's going to finish the whole lot again, Albert."

"I'm sure she is," he said.

And a few minutes later, the milk was all gone.

"Oh, what a good girl you are!" Mrs. Taylor cried, as very gently she started to withdraw the nipple. The baby sensed what she was doing and sucked harder, trying to hold on. The woman gave a quick little tug, and *plop*, out it came.

"Waa! Waa! Waa! Waa! Waa!" the baby yelled.

"Nasty old wind," Mrs. Taylor said, hoisting the child onto her shoulder and patting its back.

It belched twice in quick succession.

"There you are, my darling, you'll be all right now." For a few seconds, the yelling stopped. Then it started again.

"Keep belching her," Albert said. "She's drunk it too quick."

His wife lifted the baby back onto her shoulder. She rubbed its spine. She changed it from one shoulder to the other. She lay it on its stomach on her lap. She sat it up on her knee. But it didn't belch again, and the yelling became louder and more insistent every minute.

"Good for the lungs," Albert Taylor said, grinning. "That's the way they exercise their lungs, Mabel, did you know that?"

"There, there, there," the wife said, kissing it all over the face. "There, there, there."

They waited another five minutes, but not for one moment did the screaming stop.

"Change the nappy," Albert said. "It's got a wet nappy, that's all it is." He fetched a clean one from the kitchen, and Mrs. Taylor took the old one off and put the new one on.

This made no difference at all.

"Waa! Waa! Waa! Waa! Waa!" the baby yelled.

"You didn't stick the safety pin through the skin, did you, Mabel?"

"Of course I didn't," she said, feeling under the nappy with her fingers to make sure.

The parents sat opposite one another in their armchairs, smiling nervously, watching the baby on the mother's lap, waiting for it to tire and stop screaming.

"You know what?" Albert Taylor said at last.

"What?"

"I'll bet she's still hungry. I'll bet all she wants is another swig at that bottle. How about me fetching her an extra lot?"

"I don't think we ought to do that, Albert."

"It'll do her good," he said, getting up from his chair. "I'm going to warm her up a second helping."

He went into the kitchen, and was away several minutes. When he returned he was holding a bottle brimful of milk.

"I made her a double," he announced. "Eight ounces. Just in case."

"Albert! Are you mad! Don't you know it's just as bad to overfeed as it is to underfeed?"

"You don't have to give her the lot, Mabel. You can stop any time you like. Go on," he said, standing over her. "Give her a drink."

Mrs. Taylor began to tease the baby's upper lip with the end of the nipple. The tiny mouth closed like a trap over the rubber teat and suddenly there was silence in the room. The baby's whole body relaxed and a look of absolute bliss came over its face as it started to drink.

"There you are, Mabel! What did I tell you?"

The woman didn't answer.

"She's ravenous, that's what she is. Just look at her suck."

Mrs. Taylor was watching the level of the milk in the bottle. It was dropping fast, and before long three or four ounces out of the eight had disappeared.

"There," she said. "That'll do."

"You can't pull it away now, Mabel."

"Yes, dear. I must."

"Go on, woman. Give her the rest and stop fussing."

"But *Albert* . . ."

"She's famished, can't you see that? Go on, my beauty," he said. "You finish that bottle."

"I don't like it, Albert," the wife said, but she didn't pull the bottle away.

"She's making up for lost time, Mabel, that's all she's doing."

Five minutes later the bottle was empty. Slowly, Mrs. Taylor withdrew the nipple, and this time there was no protest from the baby, no sound at all. It lay peacefully on the mother's lap, the eyes glazed with contentment, the mouth half open, the lips smeared with milk.

"Twelve whole ounces, Mabel!" Albert Taylor said. "Three times the normal amount! Isn't that amazing!"

The woman was staring down at the baby. And now the old anxious tight-lipped look of the frightened mother was slowly returning to her face.

"What's the matter with *you?*" Albert asked. "You're not worried by that, are you? You can't expect her to get back to normal on a lousy four ounces, don't be ridiculous."

"Come here, Albert," she said.

"What?"

"I said come here."

He went over and stood beside her.

"Take a good look and tell me if you see anything different."

He peered closely at the baby. "She seems bigger, Mabel, if that's what you mean. Bigger and fatter."

"Hold her," she ordered. "Go on, pick her up."

He reached out and lifted the baby up off the mother's lap. "Good God!" he cried. "She weighs a ton!"

"Exactly."

"Now isn't that marvellous!" he cried, beaming. "I'll bet she must almost be back to normal already!"

"It frightens me, Albert. It's too quick."

"Nonsense, woman."

"It's that disgusting jelly that's done it," she said. "I hate the stuff."

"There's nothing disgusting about royal jelly," he answered, indignant.

"Don't be a fool, Albert! You think it's *normal* for a child to start putting on weight at this speed?"

"You're never satisfied!" he cried. "You're scared stiff when she's losing and now you're absolutely terrified because she's gaining! What's the matter with you, Mabel?"

The woman got up from her chair with the baby in her arms and started toward the door. "All I can say is," she said, "it's lucky I'm here to see you don't give her any more of it, that's all I can say." She went out, and Albert watched her through the open door as she crossed the hall to the foot of the stairs and started to ascend, and when she reached the third or fourth step she suddenly stopped and stood quite still for several seconds as though remembering something. Then she turned and came down again rather quickly and re-entered the room.

"Albert," she said.

"Yes?"

"I assume there wasn't any royal jelly in this last feed we've just given her?"

"I don't see why you should assume that, Mabel."

"Albert!"

"What's wrong?" he asked, soft and innocent.

"How *dare* you!" she cried.

Albert Taylor's great bearded face took on a pained and puzzled look. "I think you ought to be very glad she's got another big dose of it inside her," he said. "Honest I do. And this *is* a big dose, Mabel, believe you me."

The woman was standing just inside the doorway clasping the sleeping baby in her arms and staring at her husband with huge eyes. She stood very erect, her body absolutely stiff with fury, her face paler, more tight-lipped than ever.

"You mark my words," Albert was saying, "you're going to have a nipper there soon that'll win first prize in any baby show in the *entire* country. Hey, why don't you weigh her now and see what she is? You want me to get the scales, Mabel, so you can weigh her?"

The woman walked straight over to the large table in the centre of the room and laid the baby down and quickly started taking off its clothes. "Yes!" she snapped. "Get the scales!" Off came the little nightgown, then the undervest.

Then she unpinned the nappy and she drew it away and the baby lay naked on the table.

"But Mabel!" Albert cried. "It's a miracle! She's fat as a puppy!"

Indeed, the amount of flesh the child had put on since the day before was astounding. The small sunken chest with the rib-bones showing all over it was now plump and round as a barrel, and the belly was bulging high in the air. Curiously, though, the arms and legs did not seem to have grown in proportion. Still short and skinny, they looked like little sticks protruding from a ball of fat.

"Look!" Albert said. "She's even beginning to get a bit of fuzz on the tummy to keep her warm!" He put out a hand and was about to run the tips of his fingers over the powdering of silky yellowy-brown hairs that had suddenly appeared on the baby's stomach.

"*Don't you touch her!*" the woman cried. She turned and faced him, her eyes blazing, and she looked suddenly like some kind of a little fighting bird with her neck arched over toward him as though she were about to fly at his face and peck his eyes out.

"Now wait a minute," he said, retreating.

"You must be mad!" she cried.

"Now wait just one minute, Mabel, will you please, be- cause if you're still thinking this stuff is dangerous . . . That *is* what you're thinking, isn't it? All right, then. Listen carefully. I shall now proceed to *prove* to you once and for all, Mabel, that royal jelly is absolutely harmless to human beings, even in enormous doses. For example—why do you think we had only half the usual honey crop last summer? Tell me that."

His retreat, walking backwards, had taken him three or four yards away from her, where he seemed to feel more comfortable.

"The reason we had only half the usual crop last sum- mer," he said slowly, lowering his voice, "was because I turned one hundred of my hives over to the production of royal jelly."

"You *what?*"

"Ah," he whispered. "I thought that might surprise you a bit. And I've been making it ever since right under your very nose." His small eyes were glinting at her, and a slow sly smile was creeping around the corners of his mouth.

"You'll never guess the reason, either," he said. "I've been afraid to mention it up to now because I thought it might . . . well . . . sort of embarrass you."

There was a slight pause. He had his hands clasped high in front of him, level with his chest, and he was rubbing one palm against the other, making a soft scraping noise.

"You remember that bit I read you out of the magazine? That bit about the rat? Let me see now, how does it go? 'Still and Burdett found that a male rat which hitherto had been unable to breed . . .' " He hesitated, the grin widening, showing his teeth.

"You get the message, Mabel?"

She stood quite still, facing him.

"The very first time I ever read that sentence, Mabel, I jumped straight out of my chair and I said to myself if it'll work with a lousy rat, I said, then there's no reason on earth why it shouldn't work with Albert Taylor."

He paused again, craning his head forward and turning one ear slightly in his wife's direction, waiting for her to say something. But she didn't.

"And here's another thing," he went on. "It made me feel so absolutely marvellous, Mabel, and so sort of completely different to what I was before that I went right on taking it even after you'd announced the joyful tidings. *Buckets* of it I must have swallowed during the last twelve months."

The big heavy haunted-looking eyes of the woman were moving intently over the man's face and neck. There was no skin showing at all on the neck, not even at the sides below the ears. The whole of it, to a point where it disappeared into the collar of the shirt, was covered all the way around with those shortish silky hairs, yellowy black.

"Mind you," he said, turning away from her, gazing lovingly now at the baby, "it's going to work far better on a tiny infant than on a fully developed man like me. You've only got to look at her to see that, don't you agree?"

The woman's eyes travelled slowly downward and settled on the baby. The baby was lying naked on the table, fat and white and comatose, like some gigantic grub that was approaching the end of its larval life and would soon emerge into the world complete with mandibles and wings.

"Why don't you cover her up, Mabel?" he said. "We don't want our little queen to catch a cold."

GEORGY PORGY

WITHOUT in any way wishing to blow my own trumpet, I think that I can claim to being in most respects a moderately well-matured and rounded individual. I have travelled a good deal. I am adequately read. I speak Greek and Latin. I dabble in science. I can tolerate a mildly liberal attitude in the politics of others. I have compiled a volume of notes upon the evolution of the madrigal in the fifteenth century. I have witnessed the death of a large number of persons in their beds; and in addition, I have influenced, at least I hope I have, the lives of quite a few others by the spoken word delivered from the pulpit.

Yet in spite of all this, I must confess that I have never in my life—well, how shall I put it?—I have never really had anything much to do with women.

To be perfectly honest, up until three weeks ago I had never so much as laid a finger on one of them except perhaps to help her over a stile or something like that when the occasion demanded. And even then I always tried to ensure that I touched only the shoulder or the waist or some other place where the skin was covered, because the one thing I never could stand was actual contact between my skin and theirs. Skin touching skin, my skin, that is, touching the skin of a female, whether it were leg, neck, face, hand, or merely finger, was so repugnant to me that I invariably greeted a lady with my hands clasped firmly behind my back to avoid the inevitable handshake.

I could go further than that and say that any sort of physical contact with them, even when the skin wasn't bare, would disturb me considerably. If a woman stood close to me in a queue so that our bodies touched, or if she squeezed in beside me on a bus seat, hip to hip and thigh to thigh, my cheeks would begin burning like mad and little prickles of sweat would start coming out all over the crown of my head.

This condition is all very well in a schoolboy who has just reached the age of puberty. With him it is simply Dame Nature's way of putting on the brakes and holding the lad back until he is old enough to behave himself like a gentleman. I approve of that.

But there was no reason on God's earth why I, at the ripe old age of thirty-one, should continue to suffer a similar embarrassment. I was well trained to resist temptation, and I was certainly not given to vulgar passions.

Had I been even the slightest bit ashamed of my own personal appearance, then that might possibly have explained the whole thing. But I was not. On the contrary, and though I say it myself, the fates had been rather kind to me in that regard. I stood exactly five and a half feet tall in my stockinged feet, and my shoulders, though they sloped downward a little from the neck, were nicely in balance with my small neat frame. (Personally, I've always thought that a little slope on the shoulder lends a subtle and faintly aesthetic air to a man who is not overly tall, don't you agree?) My features were regular, my teeth were in excellent condition (protruding only a smallish amount from the upper jaw), and my hair, which was an unusually brilliant ginger-red, grew thickly all over my scalp. Good heavens above, I had seen men who were perfect shrimps in comparison with me displaying an astonishing aplomb in their dealings with the fairer sex. And oh, how I envied them! How I longed to do likewise—to be able to share in a few of those pleasant little rituals of contact that I observed continually taking place between men and women—the touching of hands, the peck on the cheek, the linking of arms, the pressure of knee against knee or foot against foot under the dining-table, and most of all, the full-blown violent embrace that comes when two of them join together on the floor—for a dance.

But such things were not for me. Alas, I had to spend my time avoiding them instead. And this, my friends, was easier said than done, even for a humble curate in a small country region far from the fleshpots of the metropolis.

My flock, you understand, contained an inordinate number of ladies. There were scores of them in the parish, and the unfortunate thing about it was that at least sixty per cent of them were spinsters, completely untamed by the benevolent influence of holy matrimony.

I tell you I was jumpy as a squirrel.

One would have thought that with all the careful training my mother had given me as a child, I should have been capable of taking this sort of thing well in my stride; and no doubt I would have done if only she had lived long enough to complete my education. But alas, she was killed when I was still quite young.

She was a wonderful woman, my mother. She used to wear huge bracelets on her wrists, five or six of them at a time, with all sorts of things hanging from them and tinkling against each other as she moved. It didn't matter where she was, you could always find her by listening for the noise of those bracelets. It was better than a cowbell. And in the evenings she used to sit on the sofa in her black trousers with her feet tucked up underneath her, smoking endless cigarettes from a long black holder. And I'd be crouching on the floor, watching her.

"You want to taste my martini, George?" she used to ask.

"Now stop it, Clare," my father would say. "If you're not careful you'll stunt the boy's growth."

"Go on," she said. "Don't be frightened of it. Drink it."

I always did everything my mother told me.

"That's enough," my father said. "He only has to know what it tastes like."

"Please don't interfere, Boris. This is *very* important."

My mother had a theory that nothing in the world should be kept secret from a child. Show him everything. Make him *experience* it.

"I'm not going to have any boy of mine going around whispering dirty secrets with other children and having to guess about this thing and that simply because no one will tell him."

Tell him everything. Make him listen.

"Come over here, George, and I'll tell you what there is to know about God."

She never read stories to me at night before I went to bed; she just "told" me things instead. And every evening it was something different.

"Come over here, George, because now I'm going to tell you about Mohammed."

She would be sitting on the sofa in her black trousers with her legs crossed and her feet tucked up underneath her, and she'd beckon to me in a queer languorous manner with the hand that held the long black cigarette-holder, and the bangles would start jingling all the way up her arm.

"If you must have a religion I suppose Mohammedanism is as good as any of them. It's all based on keeping healthy. You have lots of wives, and you mustn't ever smoke or drink."

"Why mustn't you smoke or drink, Mummy?"

"Because if you've got lots of wives you have to keep healthy and virile."

"What is virile?"

"I'll go into that tomorrow, my pet. Let's deal with one subject at a time. Another thing about the Mohammedan is that he never never gets constipated."

"Now, Clare," my father would say, looking up from his book. "Stick to the facts."

"My dear Boris, you don't know anything about it. Now if only *you* would try bending forward and touching the ground with your forehead morning, noon, and night every day, facing Mecca, you might have a bit less trouble in that direction yourself."

I used to love listening to her, even though I could only understand about half of what she was saying. She really was telling me secrets, and there wasn't anything more exciting than that.

"Come over here, George, and I'll tell you precisely how your father makes his money."

"Now, Clare, that's quite enough."

"Nonsense, darling. Why make a *secret* out of it with the child? He'll only imagine something much much worse."

I was exactly ten years old when she started giving me detailed lectures on the subject of sex. This was the biggest secret of them all, and therefore the most enthralling.

"Come over here, George, because now I'm going to tell you how you came into this world, right from the very beginning."

I saw my father glance up quietly, and open his mouth wide the way he did when he was going to say something vital, but my mother was already fixing him with those brilliant shining eyes of hers, and he went slowly back to his book without uttering a sound.

"Your poor father is embarrassed," she said, and she gave me her private smile, the one that she gave to nobody else, only to me—the one-sided smile where just one corner of her mouth lifted slowly upward until it made a lovely long wrinkle that stretched right up to the eye itself, and became a sort of wink-smile instead.

"Embarrassment, my pet, is the one thing that I want you never to feel. And don't think for a moment that your father is embarrassed only because of *you*."

My father started wriggling about in his chair.

"My God, he's even embarrassed about things like that when he's alone with me, his own wife."

"About things like what?" I asked.

At that point my father got up and quietly left the room.

I think it must have been about a week after this that my mother was killed. It may possibly have been a little later, ten days or a fortnight, I can't be sure. All I know is that we were getting near the end of this particular series of "talks" when it happened; and because I myself was personally involved in the brief chain of events that led up to her death, I can still remember every single detail of that curious night just as clearly as if it were yesterday. I can switch it on in my memory any time I like and run it through in front of my eyes exactly as though it were the reel of a cinema film; and it never varies. It always ends at precisely the same place, no more and no less, and it always begins in the same peculiarly sudden way, with the screen in darkness, and my mother's voice somewhere above me, calling my name:

"George! Wake up, George, wake up!"

And then there is a bright electric light dazzling in my eyes, and right from the very centre of it, but far away, the voice is still calling to me:

"George, wake up and get out of bed and put your dressing-gown on! Quickly! You're coming downstairs. There's something I want you to see. Come on, child,

come on! Hurry up! And put your slippers on. We're going outside."

"Outside?"

"Don't argue with me, George. Just do as you're told."
I am so sleepy I can hardly see to walk, but my mother
takes me firmly by the hand and leads me downstairs and
out through the front door into the night where the cold
air is like a sponge of water in my face, and I open my
eyes wide and see the lawn all sparkling with frost and the
cedar tree with its tremendous arms standing black against
a thin small moon. And overhead a great mass of stars is
wheeling up into the sky.

We hurry across the lawn, my mother and I, her bracelets all jingling like mad and me having to trot to keep
up with her. Each step I take I can feel the crisp frosty
grass crunching softly underfoot.

"Josephine has just started having her babies," my
mother says. "It's a perfect opportunity. You shall watch
the whole process."

There is a light burning in the garage when we get there,
and we go inside. My father isn't there, nor is the car, and
the place seems huge and bare, and the concrete floor is
freezing cold through the soles of my bedroom slippers.
Josephine is reclining on a heap of straw inside the low
wire cage in one corner of the room—a large blue rabbit
with small pink eyes that watch us suspiciously as we go
toward her. The husband, whose name is Napoleon, is now
in a separate cage in the opposite corner, and I notice that
he is standing up on his hind legs scratching impatiently at
the netting.

"Look!" my mother cries. "She's just having the first one! It's almost out!"

We both creep closer to Josephine, and I squat down beside the cage with my face right up against the wire. I am fascinated. Here is one rabbit coming out of another. It is magical and rather splendid. It is also very quick.

"Look how it comes out all neatly wrapped up in its own little cellophane bag!" my mother is saying.

"And just look how she's taking care of it now! The poor darling doesn't have a face-flannel, and even if she did she couldn't hold it in her paws, so she's washing it with her tongue instead."

The mother rabbit rolls her small pink eyes anxiously in our direction, and then I see her shifting position in the straw so that her body is between us and the young one.

"Come round the other side," my mother says. "The silly thing has moved. I do believe she's trying to hide her baby from us."

We go round the other side of the cage. The rabbit follows us with her eyes. A couple of yards away the buck is prancing madly up and down, clawing at the wire.

"Why is Napoleon so excited?" I ask.

"I don't know, dear. Don't you bother about him. Watch Josephine. I expect she'll be having another one soon. Look how carefully she's washing that little baby! She's treating it just like a human mother treats hers! Isn't it funny to think that I did almost exactly the same sort of thing to you once?"

The big blue doe is still watching us, and now, again, she pushes the baby away with her nose and rolls slowly over to face the other way. Then she goes on with her licking and cleaning.

"Isn't it wonderful how a mother knows instinctively just what she has to do?" my mother says. "Now you just imagine, my pet, that that baby is *you*, and Josephine is *me*—wait a minute, come back over here again so you can get a better look."

We creep back around the cage to keep the baby in view.

"See how she's fondling it and kissing it all over! There! She's *really* kissing it now, isn't she! Exactly like me and you!"

I peer closer. It seems a queer way of kissing to me.

"Look!" I scream. "She's eating it!"

And sure enough, the head of the baby rabbit is now disappearing swiftly into the mother's mouth.

"Mummy! Quick!"

But almost before the sound of my scream has died away, the whole of that tiny pink body has vanished down the mother's throat.

I swing quickly around, and the next thing I know I'm looking straight into my own mother's face, not six inches above me, and no doubt she is trying to say something or it may be that she is too astonished to say anything, but all I see is the mouth, the huge red mouth opening wider and wider and wider until it is just a great big round gaping hole with a black black centre, and I scream again, and this time I can't stop. Then suddenly out come her hands, and I can feel her skin touching mine, the long cold fingers closing tightly over my fists, and I jump back and jerk myself free and rush blindly out into the night. I run down the drive and through the front gates, screaming all the way, and then, above the noise of my own voice I can hear the jingle of bracelets coming up behind me in the dark, getting louder and louder as she keeps gaining on me all the way down the long hill to the bottom of the lane and over the bridge onto the main road where the cars are streaming by at sixty miles an hour with headlights blazing.

Then somewhere behind me I hear a screech of tires skidding on the road surface, and then there is silence, and I notice suddenly that the bracelets aren't jingling behind me any more.

Poor Mother.

If only she could have lived a little longer.

I admit that she gave me a nasty fright with those rabbits, but it wasn't her fault, and anyway queer things like that were always happening between her and me. I had come to regard them as a sort of toughening process that did me more good than harm. But if only she could have lived long enough to complete my education, I'm sure I should never have had all that trouble I was telling you about a few minutes ago.

I want to get on with that now. I didn't mean to begin talking about my mother. She doesn't have anything to do with what I originally started out to say. I won't mention her again.

I was telling you about the spinsters in my parish. It's an ugly word, isn't it—spinster? It conjures up the vision either of a stringy old hen with a puckered mouth or of a huge ribald monster shouting around the house in riding-breeches. But these were not like that at all. They were a clean, healthy, well-built group of females, the majority of them highly bred and surprisingly wealthy, and I feel sure that the average unmarried man would have been gratified to have them around.

In the beginning, when I first came to the vicarage, I didn't have too bad a time. I enjoyed a measure of protection, of course, by reason of my calling and my cloth. In addition, I myself adopted a cool dignified attitude that was calculated to discourage familiarity. For a few months, therefore, I was able to move freely among my parishioners, and no one took the liberty of linking her arm in mine at a charity bazaar, or of touching my fingers with hers as she passed me the cruet at suppertime. I was very happy. I was feeling better than I had in years. Even that little nervous habit I had of flicking my earlobe with my fore-finger when I talked began to disappear.

This was what I call my first period, and it extended over approximately six months. Then came trouble.

I suppose I should have known that a healthy male like myself couldn't hope to evade embroilment indefinitely simply by keeping a fair distance between himself and the ladies. It just doesn't work. If anything it has the opposite effect.

I would see them eying me covertly across the room at a whist drive, whispering to one another, nodding, running their tongues over their lips, sucking at their cigarettes, plotting the best approach, but always whispering, and sometimes I overheard snatches of their talk— "What a shy person . . . he's just a trifle nervous, isn't he . . . he's much too tense . . . he needs companionship . . . he wants loosening up . . . we must teach him how to relax." And then slowly, as the weeks went by, they began to stalk me. I knew they were doing it. I could feel it happening although at first they did nothing definite to give themselves away.

That was my second period. It lasted for the best part of a year and was very trying indeed. But it was paradise compared with the third and final phase.

For now, instead of sniping at me sporadically from far away, the attackers suddenly came charging out of the wood with bayonets fixed. It was terrible, frightening. Nothing is more calculated to unnerve a man than the swift unexpected assault. Yet I am not a coward. I will stand my ground against any single individual of my own size under any circumstances. But this onslaught, I am now convinced, was conducted by vast numbers operating as one skilfully co-ordinated unit.

The first offender was Miss Elphinstone, a large woman with moles. I had dropped in on her during the afternoon to solicit a contribution toward a new set of bellows for the organ, and after some pleasant conversation in the library she had graciously handed me a cheque for two guineas. I told her not to bother to see me to the door and I went out into the hall to get my hat. I was about to reach for it when all at once—she must have come tip-toeing up behind me—all at once I felt a bare arm sliding through mine, and one second later her fingers were entwined in my own, and she was squeezing my hand hard, in out, in out, as though it were the bulb of a throat-spray.

"Are you really so Very Reverend as you're always pretending to be?" she whispered.

Well!

All I can tell you is that when that arm of hers came sliding in under mine, it felt exactly as though a cobra was coiling itself around my wrist. I leaped away, pulled open the front door, and fled down the drive without looking back.

The very next day we held a jumble sale in the village hall (again to raise money for the new bellows), and toward the end of it I was standing in a corner quietly drinking a cup of tea and keeping an eye on the villagers crowding round the stalls when all of a sudden I heard a voice beside me saying, "Dear me, what a hungry look you have in those eyes of yours." The next instant a long curvaceous body was leaning up against mine and a hand with red fingernails was trying to push a thick slice of coconut cake into my mouth.

"Miss Prattley," I cried. "Please!"

But she'd got me up against the wall, and with a teacup in one hand and a saucer in the other I was powerless to resist. I felt the sweat breaking out all over me and if my mouth hadn't quickly become full of the cake she was pushing into it, I honestly believe I would have started to scream.

A nasty incident, that one; but there was worse to come. The next day it was Miss Unwin. Now Miss Unwin happened to be a close friend of Miss Elphinstone's *and* of Miss Prattley's, and this of course should have been enough to make me very cautious. Yet who would have thought that she of all people, Miss Unwin, that quiet gentle little mouse who only a few weeks before had presented me with a new hassock exquisitely worked in needlepoint with her own hands, who would have thought that *she* would ever have taken a liberty with anyone? So when she asked me to accompany her down to the crypt to show her the Saxon murals, it never entered my head that there was devilry afoot. But there was.

I don't propose to describe this encounter; it was too painful. And the ones which followed were no less savage. Nearly every day from then on, some new outrageous incident would take place. I became a nervous wreck. At times I hardly knew what I was doing. I started reading the burial service at young Gladys Pitcher's wedding. I dropped Mrs. Harris's new baby into the font during the christening and gave it a nasty ducking. An uncomfortable rash that I hadn't had in over two years reappeared on the side of my neck, and that annoying business with my earlobe came back worse than ever before. Even my hair began coming out in my comb. The faster I retreated, the faster they came after me. Women are like that. Nothing stimulates them quite so much as a display of modesty or shyness in a man. And they became doubly persistent if underneath it all they happen to detect—and here I have a most difficult confession to make—if they happen to detect, as they did in me, a little secret gleam of longing shining in the backs of the eyes.

You see, actually I was mad about women.

Yes, I know. You will find this hard to believe after all that I have said, but it was perfectly true. You must understand that it was only when they touched me with their fingers or pushed up against me with their bodies that I became alarmed. Providing they remained at a safe distance, I could watch them for hours on end with the same peculiar fascination that you yourself might experience in watching a creature you couldn't bear to touch—an octopus, for example, or a long poisonous snake. I loved the smooth white look of a bare arm emerging from a sleeve, curiously naked like a peeled banana. I could get enormously excited just from watching a girl walk across the room in a tight dress; and I particularly enjoyed the back view of a pair of legs when the feet were in rather high heels—the wonderful braced-up look behind the knees, with the legs themselves very taut as though they were made of strong elastic stretched out almost to breaking-point, but not quite. Sometimes, in Lady Birdwell's drawing-room, sitting near the window on a summer's afternoon, I would glance over the rim of my teacup toward the swimming-pool and become agitated beyond measure by the sight of a little patch of sunburned stomach bulging between the top and bottom of a two-piece bathing-suit.

There is nothing wrong in having thoughts like these. All men harbour them from time to time. But they did give me a terrible sense of guilt. Is it me, I kept asking myself, who is unwittingly responsible for the shameless way in which these ladies are now behaving? Is it the gleam in my eye (which I cannot control) that is constantly rousing their passions and egging them on? Am I unconsciously giving them what is sometimes known as the come-hither signal every time I glance their way? Am I?

Or is this brutal conduct of theirs inherent in the very nature of the female?

I had a pretty fair idea of the answer to this question, but that was not good enough for me. I happen to possess a conscience that can never be consoled by guesswork; it has to have proof. I simply had to find out who was really the guilty party in this case—me or them, and with this object in view, I now decided to perform a simple experiment of my own invention, using Snelling's rats.

A year or so previously I had had some trouble with an objectionable choirboy named Billy Snelling. On three consecutive Sundays this youth had brought a pair of white rats into church and had let them loose on the floor during my sermon. In the end I had confiscated the animals and carried them home and placed them in a box in the shed at the bottom of the vicarage garden. Purely for humane reasons I had then proceeded to feed them, and as a result, but without any further encouragement from me, the creatures began to multiply very rapidly. The two became five, and the five became twelve.

It was at this point that I decided to use them for research purposes. There were exactly equal numbers of males and females, six of each, so that conditions were ideal.

I first isolated the sexes, putting them into two separate cages, and I left them like that for three whole weeks. Now a rat is a very lascivious animal, and any zoologist will tell you that for them this is an inordinately long period of separation. At a guess I would say that one week of enforced celibacy for a rat is equal to approximately one year of the same treatment for someone like Miss Elphinstone or Miss Prattley; so you can see that I was doing a pretty fair job in reproducing actual conditions.

When the three weeks were up, I took a large box that was divided across the centre by a little fence, and I placed the females on one side and the males on the other. The fence consisted of nothing more than three single strands of naked wire, one inch apart, but there was a powerful electric current running through the wires.

To add a touch of reality to the proceedings, I gave each female a name. The largest one, who also had the longest whiskers, was Miss Elphinstone. The one with a short thick tail was Miss Prattley. The smallest of them all was Miss Unwin, and so on. The males, all six of them, were *ME*.

I now pulled up a chair and sat back to watch the result.

All rats are suspicious by nature, and when I first put the two sexes together in the box with only the wire between them, neither side made a move. The males stared hard at the females through the fence. The females stared back, waiting for the males to come forward. I could see that both sides were tense with yearning. Whiskers quivered and noses twitched and occasionally a long tail would flick sharply against the wall of the box.

After a while, the first male detached himself from his group and advanced gingerly toward the fence, his belly close to the ground. He touched a wire and was immediately electrocuted. The remaining eleven rats froze, motionless.

There followed a period of nine and a half minutes during which neither side moved; but I noticed that while all the males were now staring at the dead body of their colleague, the females had eyes only for the males.

Then suddenly Miss Prattley with the short tail could stand it no longer. She came bounding forward, hit the wire, and dropped dead.

The males pressed their bodies closer to the ground and gazed thoughtfully at the two corpses by the fence. The females also seemed to be quite shaken, and there was another wait, with neither side moving.

Now it was Miss Unwin who began to show signs of impatience. She snorted audibly and twitched a pink mobile nose-end from side to side, then suddenly she started jerking her body quickly up and down as though she were doing pushups. She glanced round at her remaining four companions, raised her tail high in the air as much as to say "Here I go, girls," and with that she advanced briskly to the wire, pushed her head through it, and was killed.

Sixteen minutes later, Miss Foster made her first move. Miss Foster was a woman in the village who bred cats, and recently she had had the effrontery to put up a large sign outside her house in the High Street, saying FOSTER'S CAT-TERY. Through long association with the creatures she herself seemed to have acquired all their most noxious characteristics, and whenever she came near me in a room I could detect, even through the smoke of her Russian cigarette, a faint but pungent aroma of cat. She had never struck me as having much control over her baser instincts, and it was with some satisfaction, therefore, that I watched her now as she foolishly took her own life in a last desperate plunge toward the masculine sex.

A Miss Montgomery-Smith came next, a small determined woman who had once tried to make me believe that she had been engaged to a bishop. She died trying to creep on her belly under the lowest wire, and I must say I thought this a very fair reflection upon the way in which she lived her life.

And still the five remaining males stayed motionless, waiting.

The fifth female to go was Miss Plumley. She was a devious one who was continually slipping little messages addressed to me into the collection bag. Only the Sunday before, I had been in the vestry counting the money after morning service and had come across one of them tucked inside a folded ten-shilling note. *Your poor throat sounded hoarse today during the sermon*, it said. *Let me bring you a bottle of my own cherry pectoral to soothe it down. Most affectionately, Eunice Plumley.*

Miss Plumley ambled slowly up to the wire, sniffed the centre strand with the tip of her nose, came a fraction too close, and received two hundred and forty volts of alternating current through her body.

The five males stayed where they were, watching the slaughter.

And now only Miss Elphinstone remained on the feminine side.

For a full half-hour neither she nor any of the others

made a move. Finally one of the males stirred himself slightly, took a step forward, hesitated, thought better of it, and slowly sank back into a crouch on the floor.

This must have frustrated Miss Elphinstone beyond measure, for suddenly, with eyes blazing, she rushed forward and took a flying leap at the wire. It was a spectacular jump and she nearly cleared it; but one of her hind legs grazed the top strand, and thus she also perished with the rest of her sex.

I cannot tell you how much good it did me to watch this simple and, though I say it myself, this rather ingenious experiment. In one stroke I had laid open the incredibly lascivious, stop-at-nothing nature of the female. My own sex was vindicated; my own conscience was cleared. In a trice, all those awkward little flashes of guilt from which I had continually been suffering flew out the window. I felt suddenly very strong and serene in the knowledge of my own innocence.

For a few moments I toyed with the absurd idea of electrifying the black iron railings that ran around the vicarage garden; or perhaps just the gate would be enough. Then I would sit back comfortably in a chair in the library and watch through the window as the real Misses Elphinstone and Prattley and Unwin came forward one after the other and paid the final penalty for pestering an innocent male.

Such foolish thoughts!

What I must actually do now, I told myself, was to weave around me a sort of invisible electric fence constructed entirely out of my own personal moral fibre. Behind this I would sit in perfect safety while the enemy, one after another, flung themselves against the wire.

I would begin by cultivating a brusque manner. I would speak crisply to all women, and refrain from smiling at them. I would no longer step back a pace when one of them advanced upon me. I would stand my ground and glare at her, and if she said something that I considered suggestive, I would make a sharp retort.

It was in this mood that I set off the very next day to attend Lady Birdwell's tennis party.

I was not a player myself, but her ladyship had graciously invited me to drop in and mingle with the guests when play was over at six o'clock. I believe she thought that it lent a certain tone to a gathering to have a clergyman present, and she was probably hoping to persuade me to repeat the performance I gave the last time I was there, when I sat at the piano for a full hour and a quarter after supper and entertained the guests with a detailed description of the evolution of the madrigal through the centuries.

I arrived at the gates on my cycle promptly at six o'clock and pedalled up the long drive toward the house. This was the first week of June, and the rhododendrons were massed in great banks of pink and purple all the way along on either side. I was feeling unusually blithe and dauntless. The previous day's experiment with the rats had made it impossible now for anyone to take me by surprise. I knew exactly what to expect and I was armed accordingly. All around me the little fence was up.

"Ah, good evening, Vicar," Lady Birdwell cried, advancing upon me with both arms outstretched.

I stood my ground and looked her straight in the eye. "How's Birdwell?" I said. "Still up in the city?"

I doubt whether she had ever before in her life heard Lord Birdwell referred to thus by someone who had never even met him. It stopped her dead in her tracks. She looked at me queerly and didn't seem to know how to answer.

"I'll take a seat if I may," I said, and walked past her toward the terrace where a group of nine or ten guests were settled comfortably in cane chairs, sipping their drinks. They were mostly women, the usual crowd, all of them dressed in white tennis clothes, and as I strode in among them, my own sober black suiting seemed to give me, I thought, just the right amount of separateness for the occasion.

The ladies greeted me with smiles. I nodded to them and sat down in a vacant chair, but I didn't smile back.

"I think perhaps I'd better finish my story another time," Miss Elphinstone was saying. "I don't believe the vicar would approve." She giggled and gave me an arch look. I knew she was waiting for me to come out with my usual little nervous laugh and to say my usual little sentence about how broad-minded I was; but I did nothing of the sort. I simply raised one side of my upper lip until it shaped itself into a tiny curl of contempt (I had practised in the mirror that morning), and then I said sharply, in a loud voice, "*Mens sano in corpore sana.*"

"What's that?" she cried. "Come again, Vicar."

"A clean mind in a healthy body," I answered. "It's a family motto."

There was an odd kind of silence for quite a long time

after this. I could see the women exchanging glances with one another, frowning, shaking their heads.

"The vicar's in the dumps," Miss Foster announced. She was the one who bred cats. "I think the vicar needs a drink."

"Thank you," I said, "but I never imbibe. You know that."

"Then do let me fetch you a nice cooling glass of fruit cup?"

This last sentence came softly and rather suddenly from someone just behind me, to my right, and there was a note of such genuine concern in the speaker's voice that I turned round.

I saw a lady of singular beauty whom I had met only once before, about a month ago. Her name was Miss Roach, and I remembered that she had struck me then as being a person far out of the usual run. I had been particularly impressed by her gentle and reticent nature; and the fact that I had felt comfortable in her presence proved beyond doubt that she was not the sort of person who would try to impinge herself upon me in any way.

"I'm sure you must be tired after cycling all that distance," she was saying now.

I swivelled right round in my chair and looked at her carefully. She was certainly a striking person—unusually muscular for a woman, with broad shoulders and powerful arms and a huge calf bulging on each leg. The flush of the afternoon's exertions was still upon her, and her face glowed with a healthy red sheen.

"Thank you so much, Miss Roach," I said, "but I never

touch alcohol in any form. Maybe a small glass of lemon squash . . ."

"The fruit cup is only made of fruit, Padre."

How I loved a person who called me "Padre." The word has a military ring about it that conjures up visions of stern discipline and officer rank.

"Fruit cup?" Miss Elphinstone said. "It's harmless."

"My dear man, it's nothing but vitamin C," Miss Foster said.

"Much better for you than fizzy lemonade," Lady Birdwell said. "Carbon dioxide attacks the lining of the stomach."

"I'll get you some," Miss Roach said, smiling at me pleasantly. It was a good open smile, and there wasn't a trace of guile or mischief from one corner of the mouth to the other.

She stood up and walked over to the drink table. I saw her slicing an orange, then an apple, then a cucumber, then a grape, and dropping the pieces into a glass. Then she poured in a large quantity of liquid from a bottle whose label I couldn't quite read without my spectacles, but I fancied that I saw the name JIM on it, or TIM, or PIM, or some such word.

"I hope there's enough left," Lady Birdwell called out. "Those greedy children of mine do love it so."

"Plenty," Miss Roach answered, and she brought the drink to me and set it on the table.

Even without tasting it I could easily understand why children adored it. The liquid itself was dark amber-red and there were great hunks of fruit floating around among the ice cubes; and on top of it all, Miss Roach had placed a sprig of mint. I guessed that the mint had been put there specially for me, to take some of the sweetness away and to lend a touch of grown-upness to a concoction that was otherwise so obviously for youngsters.

"Too sticky for you, Padre?"

"It's delectable," I said, sipping it. "Quite perfect."

It seemed a pity to gulp it down quickly after all the trouble Miss Roach had taken to make it, but it was so refreshing I couldn't resist.

"Do let me make you another?"

I liked the way she waited until I had set the glass on the table, instead of trying to take it out of my hand.

"I wouldn't eat the mint if I were you," Miss Elphinstone said.

"I'd better get another bottle from the house," Lady Birdwell called out. "You're going to need it, Mildred."

"Do that," Miss Roach replied. "I drink gallons of the stuff myself," she went on, speaking to me. "And I don't think you'd say that I'm exactly what you might call emaciated."

"No indeed," I answered fervently. I was watching her again as she mixed me another brew, noticing how the muscles rippled under the skin of the arm that raised the bottle. Her neck also was uncommonly fine when seen from behind; not thin and stringy like the necks of a lot of these so-called modern beauties, but thick and strong with a slight ridge running down either side where the sinews bulged. It wasn't easy to guess the age of a person like this, but I doubted whether she could have been more than forty-eight or -nine.

I had just finished my second big glass of fruit cup when I began to experience a most peculiar sensation. I seemed to be floating up out of my chair, and hundreds of little warm waves came washing in under me, lifting me higher and higher. I felt as buoyant as a bubble, and everything around me seemed to be bobbing up and down and swirling gently from side to side. It was all very pleasant, and I was overcome by an almost irresistible desire to break into song.

"Feeling happy?" Miss Roach's voice sounded miles and miles away, and when I turned to look at her, I was astonished to see how near to me she really was. She, also, was bobbing up and down.

"Terrific," I answered. "I'm feeling absolutely terrific."

Her face was large and pink, and it was so close to me now that I could see the pale carpet of fuzz covering both her cheeks, and the way the sunlight caught each tiny separate hair and made it shine like gold. All of a sudden I found myself wanting to put out a hand and stroke those cheeks of hers with my fingers. To tell the truth, I wouldn't have objected in the least if she had tried to do the same to me.

"Listen," she said softly. "How about the two of us taking a little stroll down the garden to see the lupins?"

"Fine," I answered. "Lovely. Anything you say."

There is a small Georgian summer-house alongside the croquet lawn in Lady Birdwell's garden, and the very next thing I knew, I was sitting inside it on a kind of chaise longue and Miss Roach was beside me. I was still bobbing up and down, and so was she, and so, for that matter, was the summer-house, but I was feeling wonderful. I asked Miss Roach if she would like me to give her a song.

"Not now," she said, encircling me with her arms and squeezing my chest against hers so hard that it hurt.

"Don't," I said, melting.

"That's better," she kept saying. "That's much better, isn't it?"

Had Miss Roach or any other female tried to do this sort of thing to me an hour before, I don't quite know what would have happened. I think I would probably have fainted. I might even have died. But here I was now, the same old me, actually relishing the contact of those enormous bare arms against my body! Also—and this was the most amazing thing of all—I was beginning to feel the urge to reciprocate.

I took the lobe of her left ear between my thumb and forefinger, and tugged it playfully.

"Naughty boy," she said.

I tugged harder and squeezed it a bit at the same time. This roused her to such a pitch that she began to grunt and snort like a hog. Her breathing became loud and stertorous.

"Kiss me," she ordered.

"What?" I said.

"Come on, kiss me."

At that moment, I saw her mouth. I saw this great mouth of hers coming slowly down on top of me, starting to open, and coming closer and closer, and opening wider and wider; and suddenly my whole stomach began to roll right over inside me and I went stiff with terror.

"No!" I shrieked. "Don't!"

I can only tell you that I had never in all my life seen anything more terrifying than that mouth. I simply could not *stand* it coming at me like that. Had it been a red-hot iron someone was pushing into my face I wouldn't have been nearly so petrified, I swear I wouldn't. The strong arms were around me, pinning me down so that I couldn't move, and the mouth kept getting larger and larger, and then all at once it was right on top of me, huge and wet and cavernous, and the next second—I was inside it.

I was right inside this enormous mouth, lying on my stomach along the length of the tongue, with my feet somewhere around the back of the throat; and I knew instinctively that unless I got myself out again at once I was going to be swallowed alive—just like that baby rabbit. I could feel my legs being drawn down the throat by some kind of suction, and quickly I threw up my arms and grabbed hold of the lower front teeth and held on for dear life. My head was near the mouth-entrance, and I could actually look right out between the lips and see a little patch of the world outside—sunlight shining on the polished wooden floor of the summer-house, and on the floor itself a gigantic foot in a white tennis shoe.

I had a good grip with my fingers on the edge of the teeth, and in spite of the suction, I was managing to haul myself up slowly toward the daylight when suddenly the upper teeth came down on my knuckles and started chopping away at them so fiercely I had to let go. I went sliding back down the throat, feet first, clutching madly at this and that as I went, but everything was so smooth and slippery I couldn't get a grip. I glimpsed a bright flash of gold on the left as I slid past the last of the molars, and then three inches farther on I saw what must have been the uvula above me, dangling like a thick red stalactite from the roof of the throat. I grabbed at it with both hands but the thing slithered through my fingers and I went on down.

I remember screaming for help, but I could barely hear the sound of my own voice above the noise of the wind that was caused by the throat-owner's breathing. There seemed to be a gale blowing all the time, a queer erratic gale that blew alternately very cold (as the air came in) and very hot (as it went out again).

I managed to get my elbows hooked over a sharp fleshy ridge—I presume the epiglottis—and for a brief moment I hung there, defying the suction and scrabbling with my feet to find a foothold on the wall of the larynx; but the throat gave a huge heaving swallow that jerked me away, and down I went again.

From then on, there was nothing else for me to catch hold of, and down and down I went until soon my legs were dangling below me in the upper reaches of the stomach, and I could feel the slow powerful pulsing of peristalsis dragging away at my ankles, pulling me down and down and down. . . .

Far above me, outside in the open air, I could hear the distant babble of women's voices:

"It's not true. . . ."

"But my dear Mildred, how awful. . . ."

"The man must be mad. . . ."

"Your poor mouth, just look at it. . . ."

"A sex maniac . . ."

"A sadist . . ."

"Someone ought to write to the bishop. . . ."

And then Miss Roach's voice, louder than the others, swearing and screeching like a parakeet:

"He's damn lucky I didn't kill him, the little bastard! . . . I said to him, listen, I said, if ever I happen to want any of my teeth extracted, I'll go to a dentist, not to a goddam vicar. . . . It isn't as though I'd given him any encouragement either! . . ."

"Where is he now, Mildred?"

"God knows. In the bloody summer-house, I suppose."

"Hey girls, let's go and root him out!"

Oh dear, oh dear. Looking back on it all now, some three weeks later, I don't know how I ever came through the nightmare of that awful afternoon without taking leave of my senses.

A gang of witches like that is a very dangerous thing to fool around with, and had they managed to catch me in the summer-house right then and there when their blood was up, they would likely as not have torn me limb from limb on the spot.

Either that, or I should have been frog-marched down to the police station with Lady Birdwell and Miss Roach leading the procession through the main street of the village.

But of course they didn't catch me.

They didn't catch me then, and they haven't caught me yet, and if my luck continues to hold, I think I've got a fair chance of evading them altogether—or anyway for a few months, until they forget about the whole affair.

As you might guess, I am having to keep entirely to myself and to take no part in public affairs or social life. I find that writing is a most salutary occupation at a time like this, and I spend many hours each day playing with sentences. I regard each sentence as a little wheel, and my ambition lately has been to gather several hundred of them together at once and to fit them all end to end, with the cogs interlocking, like gears, but each wheel a different size, each turning at a different speed. Now and again I try to put a really big one right next to a very small one in such a way that the big one, turning slowly, will make the small one spin so fast that it hums. Very tricky, that.

I also sing madrigals in the evenings, but I miss my own harpsichord terribly.

All the same, this isn't such a bad place, and I have made myself as comfortable as I possibly can. It is a small chamber situated in what is almost certainly the primary section of the duodenal loop, just before it begins to run vertically downward in front of the right kidney. The floor is quite level—indeed it was the first level place I came to during that horrible descent down Miss Roach's throat—and that's the only reason I managed to stop at all. Above me, I can see a pulpy sort of opening that I take to be the pylorus, where the stomach enters the small intestine (I can still remember some of those diagrams my mother used to show me), and below me, there is a funny little hole in the wall where the pancreatic duct enters the lower section of the duodenum.

It is all a trifle bizarre for a man of conservative tastes like myself. Personally I prefer oak furniture and parquet flooring. But there is anyway one thing here that pleases me greatly, and that is the walls. They are lovely and soft, like a sort of padding, and the advantage of this is that I can bounce up against them as much as I wish without hurting myself.

There are several other people about, which is rather surprising, but thank God they are every one of them males. For some reason or other, they all wear white coats, and they bustle around pretending to be very busy and important. In actual fact, they are an uncommonly ignorant bunch of fellows. They don't even seem to realize where they *are*. I try to tell them, but they refuse to listen. Sometimes I get so angry and frustrated with them that I lose my temper and start to shout; and then a sly mistrustful look comes over their faces and they begin backing slowly away, and saying, "Now then. Take it easy. Take it easy, Vicar, there's a good boy. Take it easy."

What sort of talk is that?

But there is one oldish man—he comes in to see me every morning after breakfast—who appears to live slightly closer to reality than the others. He is civil and dignified, and I imagine he is lonely because he likes nothing better than to sit quietly in my room and listen to me talk. The only trouble is that whenever we get onto the subject of our whereabouts, he starts telling me that he's going to help me to escape. He said it again this morning, and we had quite an argument about it.

"But can't you see," I said patiently, "I don't *want* to escape."

"My dear Vicar, why ever not?"

"I keep telling you—because they're all searching for me outside."

"Who?"

"Miss Elphinstone and Miss Roach. and Miss Prattley and all the rest of them."

"What nonsense."

"Oh yes they are! And I imagine they're after *you* as well, but you won't admit it."

"No, my friend, they are not after me."

"Then may I ask precisely what you are doing down here?"

A bit of a stumper for him, that one. I could see he didn't know how to answer it.

"I'll bet you were fooling around with Miss Roach and got yourself swallowed up just the same as I did. I'll bet that's exactly what happened, only you're ashamed to admit it."

He looked suddenly so wan and defeated when I said this that I felt sorry for him.

"Would you like me to sing you a song?" I asked.

But he got up without answering and went quietly out into the corridor.

"Cheer up," I called after him. "Don't be depressed. There is always some balm in Gilead."

GENESIS AND CATASTROPHE
A True Story

"EVERYTHING is normal," the doctor was saying. "Just lie back and relax." His voice was miles away in the distance and he seemed to be shouting at her. "You have a son."

"What?"

"You have a fine son. You understand that, don't you? A fine son. Did you hear him crying?"

"Is he all right, Doctor?"

"Of course he is all right."

"Please let me see him."

"You'll see him in a moment."

"You are certain he is all right?"

"I am quite certain."

"Is he still crying?"

"Try to rest. There is nothing to worry about."

"Why has he stopped crying, Doctor? What happened?"

"Don't excite yourself, please. Everything is normal."

"I want to see him. Please let me see him."

"Dear lady," the doctor said, patting her hand. "You have a fine strong healthy child. Don't you believe me when I tell you that?"

"What is the woman over there doing to him?"

"Your baby is being made to look pretty for you," the doctor said. "We are giving him a little wash, that is all. You must spare us a moment or two for that."

"You swear he is all right?"

"I swear it. Now lie back and relax. Close your eyes. Go on, close your eyes. That's right. That's better. Good girl . . ."

"I have prayed and prayed that he will live, Doctor."

"Of course he will live. What are you talking about?"

"The others didn't."

"What?"

"None of my other ones lived, Doctor."

The doctor stood beside the bed looking down at the pale exhausted face of the young woman. He had never seen her before today. She and her husband were new people in the town. The innkeeper's wife, who had come up to assist in the delivery, had told him that the husband worked at the local customs-house on the border and that the two of them had arrived quite suddenly at the inn with one trunk and one suitcase about three months ago. The husband was a drunkard, the innkeeper's wife had said, an arrogant, overbearing, bullying little drunkard, but the young woman was gentle and religious. And she was very sad. She never smiled. In the few weeks that she had been here, the innkeeper's wife had never once seen her smile. Also there was a rumour that this was the husband's third marriage, that one wife had died and that the other had divorced him for unsavoury reasons. But that was only a rumour.

The doctor bent down and pulled the sheet up a little higher over the patient's chest. "You have nothing to worry about," he said gently. "This is a perfectly normal baby."

"That's exactly what they told me about the others. But I lost them all, Doctor. In the last eighteen months I have lost all three of my children, so you mustn't blame me for being anxious."

"Three?"

"This is my fourth . . . in four years."

The doctor shifted his feet uneasily on the bare floor.

"I don't think you know what it means, Doctor, to lose them all, all three of them, slowly, separately, one by one. I keep seeing them. I can see Gustav's face now as clearly as if he were lying here beside me in the bed. Gustav was a lovely boy, Doctor. But he was always ill. It is terrible when they are always ill and there is nothing you can do to help them."

"I know."

The woman opened her eyes, stared up at the doctor for a few seconds, then closed them again.

"My little girl was called Ida. She died a few days before Christmas. That is only four months ago. I just wish you could have seen Ida, Doctor."

"You have a new one now."

"But Ida was so beautiful."

"Yes," the doctor said. "I know."

"How can you know?" she cried.

"I am sure that she was a lovely child. But this new one is also like that." The doctor turned away from the bed and walked over to the window and stood there looking out. It was a wet grey April afternoon, and across the street he could see the red roofs of the houses and the huge raindrops splashing on the tiles.

"Ida was two years old, Doctor . . . and she was so beautiful I was never able to take my eyes off her from the time I dressed her in the morning until she was safe in bed again at night. I used to live in holy terror of something happening to that child. Gustav had gone and my little Otto had also gone and she was all I had left. Sometimes I used to get up in the night and creep over to the cradle and put my ear close to her mouth just to make sure that she was breathing."

"Try to rest," the doctor said, going back to the bed. "Please try to rest." The woman's face was white and bloodless, and there was a slight bluish-grey tinge around the nostrils and the mouth. A few strands of damp hair hung down over her forehead, sticking to the skin.

"When she died . . . I was already pregnant again when that happened, Doctor. This new one was a good four months on its way when Ida died. 'I don't want it!' I shouted after the funeral. 'I won't have it! I have buried enough children!' And my husband . . . he was strolling among the guests with a big glass of beer in his hand . . . he turned around quickly and said, 'I have news for you, Klara, I have good news.' Can you imagine that, Doctor? We have just buried our third child and he stands there with a glass of beer in his hand and tells me that he has good news. 'Today I have been posted to Braunau,' he says, 'so you can start packing at once. This will be a new start for you, Klara,' he says. 'It will be a new place and you can have a new doctor. . . .' "

"Please don't talk any more."

"You *are* the new doctor, aren't you, Doctor?"

"That's right."

"And here we are in Braunau."

"Yes."

"I am frightened, Doctor."

"Try not to be frightened."

"What chance can the fourth one have now?"

"You must stop thinking like that."

"I can't help it. I am certain there is something inherited that causes my children to die in this way. There must be."

"That is nonsense."

"Do you know what my husband said to me when Otto was born, Doctor? He came into the room and he looked into the cradle where Otto was lying and he said, 'Why do *all* my children have to be so small and weak?' "

"I am sure he didn't say that."

"He put his head right into Otto's cradle as though he were examining a tiny insect and he said, 'All I am saying is why can't they be better *specimens?* That's all I am saying.' And three days after that, Otto was dead. We baptized him quickly on the third day and he died the same evening. And then Gustav died. And then Ida died. All of them died, Doctor . . . and suddenly the whole house was empty. . . ."

"Don't think about it now."

"Is this one so very small?"

"He is a normal child."

"But small?"

"He is a little small, perhaps. But the small ones are often a lot tougher than the big ones. Just imagine, Frau Hitler, this time next year he will be almost learning how to walk. Isn't that a lovely thought?"

She didn't answer this.

"And two years from now he will probably be talking his head off and driving you crazy with his chatter. Have you settled on a name for him yet?"

"A name?"

"Yes."

"I don't know. I'm not sure. I think my husband said that if it was a boy we were going to call him Adolfus."

"That means he would be called Adolf."

"Yes. My husband likes Adolf because it has a certain similarity to Alois. My husband is called Alois."

"Excellent."

"Oh no!" she cried, starting up suddenly from the pillow. "That's the same question they asked me when Otto was born! It means he is going to die! You are going to baptize him at once!"

"Now, now," the doctor said, taking her gently by the shoulders. "You are quite wrong. I promise you you are wrong. I was simply being an inquisitive old man, that is all. I love talking about names. I think Adolfus is a particularly fine name. It is one of my favourites. And look —here he comes now."

The innkeeper's wife, carrying the baby high up on her enormous bosom, came sailing across the room towards the bed. "Here is the little beauty!" she cried, beaming. "Would you like to hold him, my dear? Shall I put him beside you?"

"Is he well wrapped?" the doctor asked. "It is extremely cold in here."

"Certainly he is well wrapped."

The baby was tightly swaddled in a white woollen shawl, and only the tiny pink head protruded. The innkeeper's wife placed him gently on the bed beside the mother. "There you are," she said. "Now you can lie there and look at him to your heart's content."

"I think you will like him," the doctor said, smiling. "He is a fine little baby."

"He has the most lovely hands!" the innkeeper's wife exclaimed. "Such long delicate fingers!"

The mother didn't move. She didn't even turn her head to look.

"Go on!" cried the innkeeper's wife. "He won't bite you!"

"I am frightened to look. I don't dare to believe that I have another baby and that he is all right."

"Don't be so stupid."

Slowly, the mother turned her head and looked at the small, incredibly serene face that lay on the pillow beside her.

"Is this my baby?"

"Of course."

"Oh . . . oh . . . but he is beautiful."

The doctor turned away and went over to the table and began putting his things into his bag. The mother lay on the bed gazing at the child and smiling and touching him and making little noises of pleasure. "Hello, Adolfus," she whispered. "Hello, my little Adolf . . ."

"Ssshh!" said the innkeeper's wife. "Listen! I think your husband is coming."

The doctor walked over to the door and opened it and looked out into the corridor.

"Herr Hitler?"

"Yes."

"Come in, please."

A small man in a dark-green uniform stepped softly into the room and looked around him.

"Congratulations," the doctor said. "You have a son."

The man had a pair of enormous whiskers meticulously groomed after the manner of the Emperor Franz Josef, and he smelled strongly of beer. "A son?"

"Yes."

"How is he?"

"He is fine. So is your wife."

"Good." The father turned and walked with a curious little prancing stride over to the bed where his wife was lying. "Well, Klara," he said, smiling through his whiskers. "How did it go?" He bent down to take a look at the baby. Then he bent lower. In a series of quick jerky movements, he bent lower and lower until his face was only about twelve inches from the baby's head. The wife lay sideways on the pillow, staring up at him with a kind of supplicating look.

"He has the most marvellous pair of lungs," the inn-keeper's wife announced. "You should have heard him screaming just after he came into this world."

"But my God, Klara . . ."

"What is it, dear?"

"This one is even smaller than Otto was!"

The doctor took a couple of quick paces forward. "There is nothing wrong with that child," he said.

Slowly, the husband straightened up and turned away from the bed and looked at the doctor. He seemed bewildered and stricken. "It's no good lying, Doctor," he said. "I know what it means. It's going to be the same all over again."

"Now you listen to me," the doctor said.

"But do you *know* what happened to the others, Doctor?"

"You must forget about the others, Herr Hitler. Give this one a chance."

"But so small and weak!"

"My dear sir, he has only just been born."

"Even so . . ."

"What are you trying to do?" cried the innkeeper's wife. "Talk him into his grave?"

"That's enough!" the doctor said sharply.

The mother was weeping now. Great sobs were shaking her body.

The doctor walked over to the husband and put a hand on his shoulder. "Be good to her," he whispered. "Please. It is very important." Then he squeezed the husband's shoulder hard and began pushing him forward surreptitiously to the edge of the bed. The husband hesitated. The doctor squeezed harder, signalling to him urgently through fingers and thumb. At last, reluctantly, the husband bent down and kissed his wife lightly on the cheek.

"All right, Klara," he said. "Now stop crying."

"I have prayed so hard that he will live, Alois."

"Yes."

"Every day for months I have gone to the church and begged on my knees that this one will be allowed to live."

"Yes, Klara, I know."

"Three dead children is all that I can stand, don't you realize that?"

"Of course."

"He *must* live, Alois. He *must*, he *must* . . Oh God, be merciful unto him now. . . ."

EDWARD THE CONQUEROR

Louisa, holding a dishcloth in her hand, stepped out the kitchen door at the back of the house into the cool October sunshine.

"Edward!" she called. "*Ed-ward!* Lunch is ready!"

She paused a moment, listening; then she strolled out onto the lawn and continued across it—a little shadow attending her—skirting the rose bed and touching the sundial lightly with one finger as she went by. She moved rather gracefully for a woman who was small and plump, with a lilt in her walk and a gentle swinging of the shoulders and the arms. She passed under the mulberry tree onto the brick path, then went all the way along the path until she came to the place where she could look down into the dip at the end of this large garden.

"*Edward!* Lunch!"

She could see him now, about eighty yards away, down in the dip on the edge of the wood—the tallish narrow figure in khaki slacks and dark-green sweater, working be-

side a big bonfire with a fork in his hands, pitching brambles onto the top of the fire. It was blazing fiercely, with
orange flames and clouds of milky smoke, and the smoke
was drifting back over the garden with a wonderful scent
of autumn and burning leaves.

Louisa went down the slope toward her husband. Had
she wanted, she could easily have called again and made
herself heard, but there was something about a first-class
bonfire that impelled her toward it, right up close so she
could feel the heat and listen to it burn.

"Lunch," she said, approaching.

"Oh, hello. All right—yes. I'm coming."

"*What* a good fire."

"I've decided to clear this place right out," her husband
said. "I'm sick and tired of all these brambles." His long
face was wet with perspiration. There were small beads
of it clinging all over his moustache like dew, and two
little rivers were running down his throat onto the turtleneck of the sweater.

"You better be careful you don't overdo it, Edward."

"Louisa, I do wish you'd stop treating me as though I
were eighty. A bit of exercise never did anyone any harm."

"Yes, dear, I know. Oh, Edward! Look! Look!"

The man turned and looked at Louisa, who was pointing
now to the far side of the bonfire.

"Look, Edward! The cat!"

Sitting on the ground, so close to the fire that the flames
sometimes seemed actually to be touching it, was a large
cat of a most unusual colour. It stayed quite still, with

its head on one side and its nose in the air, watching the man and woman with a cool yellow eye.

"It'll get burnt!" Louisa cried, and she dropped the dish-cloth and darted swiftly in and grabbed it with both hands, whisking it away and putting it on the grass well clear of the flames.

"You crazy cat," she said, dusting off her hands. "What's the matter with you?"

"Cats know what they're doing," the husband said. "You'll never find a cat doing something it doesn't want. Not cats."

"Whose is it? You ever seen it before?"

"No, I never have. Damn peculiar colour."

The cat had seated itself on the grass and was regarding them with a sidewise look. There was a veiled inward expression about the eyes, something curiously omniscient and pensive, and around the nose a most delicate air of contempt, as though the sight of these two middle-aged persons—the one small, plump, and rosy, the other lean and extremely sweaty—were a matter of some surprise but very little importance. For a cat, it certainly had an unusual colour—a pure silvery grey with no blue in it at all—and the hair was very long and silky.

Louisa bent down and stroked its head. "You must go home," she said. "Be a good cat now and go on home to where you belong."

The man and wife started to stroll back up the hill toward the house. The cat got up and followed, at a distance first, but edging closer and closer as they went along. Soon it was alongside them, then it was ahead, leading the way across the lawn to the house, and walking as though it owned the whole place, holding its tail straight up in the air, like a mast.

"Go home," the man said. "Go on home. We don't want you."

But when they reached the house, it came in with them, and Louisa gave it some milk in the kitchen. During lunch, it hopped up onto the spare chair between them and sat through the meal with its head just above the level of the table, watching the proceedings with those dark-yellow eyes which kept moving slowly from the woman to the man and back again.

"I don't like this cat," Edward said.

"Oh, I think it's a beautiful cat. I do hope it stays a little while."

"Now, listen to me, Louisa. The creature can't possibly stay here. It belongs to someone else. It's lost. And if it's still trying to hang around this afternoon, you'd better take it to the police. They'll see it gets home."

After lunch, Edward returned to his gardening. Louisa, as usual, went to the piano. She was a competent pianist and a genuine music-lover, and almost every afternoon she spent an hour or so playing for herself. The cat was now lying on the sofa, and she paused to stroke it as she went by. It opened its eyes, looked at her a moment, then closed them again and went back to sleep.

"You're an awfully nice cat," she said. "And such a beautiful colour. I wish I could keep you." Then her fingers, moving over the fur on the cat's head, came into contact with a small lump, a little growth just above the right eye.

"Poor cat," she said. "You've got bumps on your beautiful face. You must be getting old."

She went over and sat down on the long piano bench, but she didn't immediately start to play. One of her special little pleasures was to make every day a kind of concert day, with a carefully arranged programme which she worked out in detail before she began. She never liked to break her enjoyment by having to stop while she wondered what to play next. All she wanted was a brief pause after each piece while the audience clapped enthusiastically and called for more. It was so much nicer to imagine an audience, and now and again while she was playing—on the lucky days, that is—the room would begin to swim and fade and darken, and she would see nothing but row upon row of seats and a sea of white faces upturned toward her, listening with a rapt and adoring concentration.

Sometimes she played from memory, sometimes from music. Today she would play from memory; that was the way she felt. And what should the programme be? She sat before the piano with her small hands clasped on her lap, a plump rosy little person with a round and still quite pretty face, her hair done up in a neat bun at the back of her head. By looking slightly to the right, she could see the cat curled up asleep on the sofa, and its silvery-grey coat was beautiful against the purple of the cushion. How about some Bach to begin with? Or, better still, Vivaldi. The Bach adaptation for organ of the D minor Concerto Grosso. Yes—that first. Then perhaps a little Schumann. *Carnaval?* That would be fun. And after that—well, a touch of Liszt for a change. One of the *Petrarch Sonnets*. The second one—that was the loveliest—the E major. Then another Schumann, another of his gay ones—*Kinderscenen*. And lastly, for the encore, a Brahms waltz, or maybe two of them if she felt like it.

Vivaldi, Schumann, Liszt, Schumann, Brahms. A very nice programme, one that she could play easily without the music. She moved herself a little closer to the piano and paused a moment while someone in the audience—already she could feel that this was one of the lucky days—while someone in the audience had his last cough; then, with the slow grace that accompanied nearly all her movements, she lifted her hands to the keyboard and began to play.

She wasn't, at that particular moment, watching the cat at all—as a matter of fact she had forgotten its presence—but as the first deep notes of the Vivaldi sounded softly in the room, she became aware, out of the corner of one eye, of a sudden flurry, a flash of movement on the sofa to her right. She stopped playing at once. "What is it?" she said, turning to the cat. "What's the matter?"

The animal, who a few seconds before had been sleeping peacefully, was now sitting bolt upright on the sofa, very tense, the whole body aquiver, ears up and eyes wide open, staring at the piano.

"Did I frighten you?" she asked gently. "Perhaps you've never heard music before."

No, she told herself. I don't think that's what it is. On second thought, it seemed to her that the cat's attitude was not one of fear. There was no shrinking or backing away. If anything, there was a leaning forward, a kind of eagerness about the creature, and the face—well, there was rather an odd expression on the face, something of a mixture between surprise and shock. Of course, the face of a cat is a small and fairly expressionless thing, but if you watch carefully the eyes and ears working together, and particularly that little area of mobile skin below the ears and slightly to one side, you can occasionally see the reflection of very powerful emotions. Louisa was watching the face closely now, and because she was curious to see what would happen a second time, she reached out her hands to the keyboard and began again to play the Vivaldi.

This time the cat was ready for it, and all that happened to begin with was a small extra tensing of the body. But as the music swelled and quickened into that first exciting rhythm of the introduction to the fugue, a strange look that amounted almost to ecstasy began to settle upon the creature's face. The ears, which up to then had been pricked up straight, were gradually drawn back, the eyelids drooped, the head went over to one side, and at that moment Louisa could have sworn that the animal was actually *appreciating* the work.

What she saw (or thought she saw) was something she had noticed many times on the faces of people listening very closely to a piece of music. When the sound takes complete hold of them and drowns them in itself, a peculiar, intensely ecstatic look comes over them that you can recognize as easily as a smile. So far as Louisa could see, the cat was now wearing almost exactly this kind of look.

Louisa finished the fugue, then played the siciliana, and all the way through she kept watching the cat on the sofa.

The final proof for her that the animal was listening came at the end, when the music stopped. It blinked, stirred itself a little, stretched a leg, settled into a more comfortable position, took a quick glance round the room, then looked expectantly in her direction. It was precisely the way a concert-goer reacts when the music momentarily releases him in the pause between two movements of a symphony. The behaviour was so thoroughly human it gave her a queer agitated feeling in the chest.

"You like that?" she asked. "You like Vivaldi?"

The moment she'd spoken, she felt ridiculous, but not —and this to her was a trifle sinister—not quite so ridiculous as she knew she should have felt.

Well, there was nothing for it now except to go straight ahead with the next number on the programme, which was *Carnaval.* As soon as she began to play, the cat again stiffened and sat up straighter; then, as it became slowly and blissfully saturated with the sound, it relapsed into that queer melting mood of ecstasy that seemed to have something to do with drowning and with dreaming. It was really an extravagant sight—quite a comical one, too—to see this silvery cat sitting on the sofa and being carried away like this. And what made it more screwy than ever, Louisa thought, was the fact that this music, which the animal seemed to be enjoying so much, was manifestly too *difficult,* too *classical,* to be appreciated by the majority of humans in the world.

Maybe, she thought, the creature's not really enjoying it at all. Maybe it's a sort of hypnotic reaction, like with snakes. After all, if you can charm a snake with music, then why not a cat? Except that millions of cats hear the stuff every day of their lives, on radio and gramophone and piano, and, as far as she knew, there'd never yet been a case of one behaving like this. This one was acting as though it were following every single note. It was certainly a fantastic thing.

But was it not also a wonderful thing? Indeed it was. In fact, unless she was much mistaken, it was a kind of miracle, one of those animal miracles that happen about once every hundred years.

"I could see you *loved* that one," she said when the piece was over. "Although I'm sorry I didn't play it any too well today. Which did you like best—the Vivaldi or the Schumann?"

The cat made no reply, so Louisa, fearing she might lose the attention of her listener, went straight into the next part of the programme—Liszt's second *Petrarch Sonnet*.

And now an extraordinary thing happened. She hadn't played more than three or four bars when the animal's whiskers began perceptibly to twitch. Slowly it drew itself up to an extra height, laid its head on one side, then on the other, and stared into space with a kind of frowning concentrated look that seemed to say, "What's this? Don't tell me. I know it so well, but just for the moment I don't seem to be able to place it." Louisa was fascinated, and with her little mouth half open and half smiling, she continued to play, waiting to see what on earth was going to happen next.

The cat stood up, walked to one end of the sofa, sat down again, listened some more; then all at once it bounded to the floor and leaped up onto the piano bench beside her. There it sat, listening intently to the lovely sonnet, not dreamily this time, but very erect, the large yellow eyes fixed upon Louisa's fingers.

"Well!" she said as she struck the last chord. "So you came up to sit beside me, did you? You like this better than the sofa? All right, I'll let you stay, but you must keep still and not jump about." She put out a hand and stroked the cat softly along the back, from head to tail. "That was Liszt," she went on. "Mind you, he can sometimes be quite horribly vulgar, but in things like this he's really charming."

She was beginning to enjoy this odd animal pantomime, so she went straight on into the next item on the programme, Schumann's *Kinderscenen*.

She hadn't been playing for more than a minute or two when she realized that the cat had again moved, and was now back in its old place on the sofa. She'd been watching her hands at the time, and presumably that was why she hadn't even noticed its going; all the same, it must have been an extremely swift and silent move. The cat was still staring at her, still apparently attending closely to the music, and yet it seemed to Louisa that there was not now the same rapturous enthusiasm there'd been during the previous piece, the Liszt. In addition, the act of leaving the stool and returning to the sofa appeared in itself to be a mild but positive gesture of disappointment.

"What's the matter?" she asked when it was over. "What's wrong with Schumann? What's so marvellous about Liszt?" The cat looked straight back at her with

those yellow eyes that had small jet-black bars lying vertically in their centres.

This, she told herself, is really beginning to get interesting—a trifle spooky, too, when she came to think of it.
But one look at the cat sitting there on the sofa, so bright
and attentive, so obviously waiting for more music, quickly
reassured her.

"All right," she said. "I'll tell you what I'm going to do.
I'm going to alter my programme specially for you. You
seem to like Liszt so much, I'll give you another."

She hesitated, searching her memory for a good Liszt;
then softly she began to play one of the twelve little pieces
from *Der Weihnachtsbaum*. She was now watching the cat
very closely, and the first thing she noticed was that the
whiskers again began to twitch. It jumped down to the
carpet, stood still a moment, inclining its head, quivering
with excitement, and then, with a slow, silky stride, it
walked around the piano, hopped up on the bench, and
sat down beside her.

They were in the middle of all this when Edward came
in from the garden.

"Edward!" Louisa cried, jumping up. "Oh, Edward,
darling! Listen to this! Listen what's happened!"

"What is it now?" he said. "I'd like some tea." He had
one of those narrow, sharp-nosed, faintly magenta faces,
and the sweat was making it shine as though it were a long
wet grape.

"It's the cat!" Louisa cried, pointing to it sitting quietly
on the piano bench. "Just *wait* till you hear what's happened!"

"I thought I told you to take it to the police."

"But, Edward, *listen* to me. This is *terribly* exciting. This is a *musical* cat."

"Oh, yes?"

"This cat can appreciate music, and it can understand it too."

"Now stop this nonsense, Louisa, and let's for God's sake have some tea. I'm hot and tired from cutting brambles and building bonfires." He sat down in an armchair, took a cigarette from a box beside him, and lit it with an immense patent lighter that stood near the box.

"What you don't understand," Louisa said, "is that something extremely exciting has been happening here in our own house while you were out, something that may even be . . . well . . . almost momentous."

"I'm quite sure of that."

"Edward, *please!*"

Louisa was standing by the piano, her little pink face pinker than ever, a scarlet rose high up on each cheek. "If you want to know," she said, "I'll tell you what I think."

"I'm listening, dear."

"I think it might be possible that we are at this moment sitting in the presence of—" She stopped, as though suddenly sensing the absurdity of the thought.

"Yes?"

"You may think it silly, Edward, but it's honestly what I think."

"In the presence of who, for heaven's sake?"

"Of Franz Liszt himself!"

Her husband took a long slow pull at his cigarette and

blew the smoke up at the ceiling. He had the tight-skinned, concave cheeks of a man who has worn a full set of dentures for many years, and every time he sucked at a cigarette, the cheeks went in even more, and the bones of his face stood out like a skeleton's. "I don't get you," he said.

"Edward, listen to me. From what I've seen this afternoon with my own eyes, it really looks as though this might actually be some sort of a reincarnation."

"You mean this lousy cat?"

"Don't talk like that, dear, please."

"You're not ill, are you, Louisa?"

"I'm perfectly all right, thank you very much. I'm a bit confused—I don't mind admitting it, but who wouldn't be after what's just happened? Edward, I swear to you—"

"What *did* happen, if I may ask?"

Louisa told him, and all the while she was speaking, her husband lay sprawled in the chair with his legs stretched out in front of him, sucking at his cigarette and blowing the smoke up at the ceiling. There was a thin cynical smile on his mouth.

"I don't see anything very unusual about that," he said when it was over. "All it is—it's a trick cat. It's been taught tricks, that's all."

"Don't be so silly, Edward. Every time I play Liszt, he gets all excited and comes running over to sit on the stool beside me. But only for Liszt, and nobody can teach a cat the difference between Liszt and Schumann. You don't even know it yourself. But this one can do it every single time. Quite obscure Liszt, too."

"Twice," the husband said. "He's only done it twice."

"Twice is enough."

"Let's see him do it again. Come on."

"No," Louisa said. "Definitely not. Because if this *is* Liszt, as I believe it is, or anyway the soul of Liszt or whatever it is that comes back, then it's certainly not right or even very kind to put him through a lot of silly undignified tests."

"My dear woman! This is a *cat*—a rather stupid grey cat that nearly got its coat singed by the bonfire this morning in the garden. And anyway, what do you know about reincarnation?"

"If his soul is there, that's enough for me," Louisa said firmly. "That's all that counts."

"Come on, then. Let's see him perform. Let's see him tell the difference between his own stuff and someone else's."

"No, Edward. I've told you before, I refuse to put him through any more silly circus tests. He's had quite enough of that for one day. But I'll tell you what I *will* do. I'll play him a little more of his own music."

"A fat lot that'll prove."

"You watch. And one thing is certain—as soon as he recognizes it, he'll refuse to budge off that bench where he's sitting now."

Louisa went to the music shelf, took down a book of Liszt, thumbed through it quickly, and chose another of his finer compositions—the B minor Sonata. She had meant to play only the first part of the work, but once she got started and saw how the cat was sitting there literally quivering with pleasure and watching her hands with that rapturous concentrated look, she didn't have the heart to stop. She played it all the way through. When it was finished, she glanced up at her husband and smiled. "There you are," she said. "You can't tell me he wasn't absolutely *loving* it."

"He just likes the noise, that's all."

"He was *loving* it. Weren't you, darling?" she said, lifting the cat in her arms. "Oh, my goodness, if only he could talk. Just think of it, dear—he met Beethoven in his youth! He knew Schubert and Mendelssohn and Schumann and Berlioz and Grieg and Delacroix and Ingres and Heine and Balzac. And let me see . . . My heavens, he was Wagner's father-in-law! I'm holding Wagner's father-in-law in my arms!"

"Louisa!" her husband said sharply, sitting up straight. "Pull yourself together." There was a new edge to his voice now, and he spoke louder.

Louisa glanced up quickly. "Edward, I do believe you're jealous!"

"Oh, sure, sure I'm jealous—of a lousy grey cat!"

"Then don't be so grumpy and cynical about it all. If you're going to behave like this, the best thing you can do is to go back to your gardening and leave the two of us together in peace. That will be best for all of us, won't it, darling?" she said, addressing the cat, stroking its head. "And later on this evening, we shall have some more music together, you and I, some more of your own work. Oh, yes," she said, kissing the creature several times on the neck, "and we might have a little Chopin, too. You needn't tell me—I happen to know you adore Chopin. You used to be great friends with him, didn't you, darling? As a matter of fact—if I remember rightly—it was in Chopin's apartment that you met the great love of your life, Madame Something-or-Other. Had three illegitimate children by her, too, didn't you? Yes, you did, you naughty thing, and don't go trying to deny it. So you shall have some Chopin," she said, kissing the cat again, "and that'll probably bring back all sorts of lovely memories to you, won't it?"

"Louisa, stop this at once!"

"Oh, don't be so stuffy, Edward."

"You're behaving like a perfect idiot, woman. And anyway, you forget we're going out this evening, to Bill and Betty's for canasta."

"Oh, but I couldn't *possibly* go out now. There's no question of that."

Edward got up slowly from his chair, then bent down and stubbed his cigarette hard into the ashtray. "Tell me something," he said quietly. "You don't really believe this —this twaddle you're talking, do you?"

"But of *course* I do. I don't think there's any question about it now. And, what's more, I consider that it puts a tremendous responsibility upon us, Edward—upon both of us. You as well."

"You know what I think," he said. "I think you ought to see a doctor. And damn quick, too."

With that, he turned and stalked out of the room, through the French windows, back into the garden.

Louisa watched him striding across the lawn toward his bonfire and his brambles, and she waited until he was out of sight before she turned and ran to the front door, still carrying the cat.

Soon she was in the car, driving to town.

She parked in front of the library, locked the cat in the car, hurried up the steps into the building, and headed straight for the reference room. There she began searching the cards for books on two subjects—REINCARNATION and LISZT.

Under REINCARNATION she found something called *Recurring Earth-Lives—How and Why*, by a man called F. Milton Willis, published in 1921. Under LISZT she found two biographical volumes. She took out all three books, returned to the car, and drove home.

Back in the house, she placed the cat on the sofa, sat herself down beside it with her three books, and prepared to do some serious reading. She would begin, she decided, with Mr. F. Milton Willis's work. The volume was thin and a trifle soiled, but it had a good heavy feel to it, and the author's name had an authoritative ring.

The doctrine of reincarnation, she read, states that spiritual souls pass from higher to higher forms of animals. "A man can, for instance, no more be reborn as an animal than an adult can re-become a child."

She read this again. But how did he know? How could he be so sure? He couldn't. No one could possibly be certain about a thing like that. At the same time, the statement took a good deal of the wind out of her sails.

"Around the centre of consciousness of each of us, there are, besides the dense outer body, four other bodies, invisible to the eye of flesh, but perfectly visible to people whose faculties of perception of superphysical things have undergone the requisite development. . . ."

She didn't understand that one at all, but she read on, and soon she came to an interesting passage that told how long a soul usually stayed away from the earth before returning in someone else's body. The time varied according to type, and Mr. Willis gave the following breakdown:

Drunkards and the unemployable	40/50	YEARS
Unskilled labourers	60/100	"
Skilled workers	100/200	"
The bourgeoisie	200/300	"
The upper-middle classes	500	"
The highest class of gentleman farmers	600/1000	"
Those in the Path of Initiation	1500/2000	"

Quickly she referred to one of the other books, to find out how long Liszt had been dead. It said he died in Bayreuth in 1886. That was sixty-seven years ago. Therefore, according to Mr. Willis, he'd have to have been an unskilled labourer to come back so soon. That didn't seem to fit at all. On the other hand, she didn't think much of the author's methods of grading. According to him, "the highest class of gentleman farmer" was just about the most superior being on the earth. Red jackets and stirrup cups and the bloody, sadistic murder of the fox. No, she thought, that isn't right. It was a pleasure to find herself beginning to doubt Mr. Willis.

Later in the book, she came upon a list of some of the more famous reincarnations. Epictetus, she was told, returned to earth as Ralph Waldo Emerson. Cicero came back as Gladstone, Alfred the Great as Queen Victoria, William the Conqueror as Lord Kitchener. Ashoka Vardhana, King of India in 272 B.C., came back as Colonel Henry Steel Olcott, an esteemed American lawyer. Pythagoras returned as Master Koot Hoomi, the gentleman who founded the Theosophical Society with Mme Blavatsky and Colonel H. S. Olcott (the esteemed American lawyer, alias Ashoka Vardhana, King of India). It didn't say who Mme Blavatsky had been. But "Theodore Roosevelt," it said, "has for numbers of incarnations played great parts as a leader of men. . . . From him descended the royal line of ancient Chaldea, he having been, about 30,000 B.C., appointed Governor of Chaldea by the Ego we know as Caesar who was then ruler of Persia. . . . Roosevelt and Caesar have been together time after time as military and administrative leaders; at one time, many thousands of years ago, they were husband and wife. . . ."

That was enough for Louisa. Mr. F. Milton Willis was clearly nothing but a guesser. She was not impressed by his dogmatic assertions. The fellow was probably on the right track, but his pronouncements were extravagant, especially the first one of all, about animals. Soon she hoped to be able to confound the whole Theosophical Society with her proof that man could indeed reappear as a lower animal. Also that he did not have to be an unskilled labourer to come back within a hundred years.

She now turned to one of the Liszt biographies, and she was glancing through it casually when her husband came in again from the garden.

"What are you doing now?" he asked.

"Oh—just checking up a little here and there. Listen, my dear, did you know that Theodore Roosevelt once was Caesar's wife?"

"Louisa," he said, "look—why don't we stop this nonsense? I don't like to see you making a fool of yourself like this. Just give me that goddamn cat and I'll take it to the police station myself."

Louisa didn't seem to hear him. She was staring openmouthed at a picture of Liszt in the book that lay on her lap. "My God!" she cried. "Edward, look!"

"What?"

"Look! The warts on his face! I forgot all about them! He had these great warts on his face and it was a famous thing. Even his students used to cultivate little tufts of hair on their own faces in the same spots, just to be like him."

"What's that got to do with it?"

"Nothing. I mean not the students. But the warts have."

"Oh, Christ," the man said. "Oh, Christ God Almighty."

"The cat has them, too! Look, I'll show you."

She took the animal onto her lap and began examining its face. "There! There's one! And there's another! Wait a minute! I do believe they're in the same places! Where's that picture?"

It was a famous portrait of the musician in his old age, showing the fine powerful face framed in a mass of long grey hair that covered his ears and came halfway down his neck. On the face itself, each large wart had been faithfully reproduced, and there were five of them in all.

"Now, in the picture there's *one* above the right eyebrow." She looked above the right eyebrow of the cat. "Yes! It's there! In exactly the same place! And another on the left, at the top of the nose. That one's there, too! And one just below it on the cheek. And two fairly close together under the chin on the right side. Edward! Edward! Come and look! They're exactly the same."

"It doesn't prove a thing."

She looked up at her husband who was standing in the centre of the room in his green sweater and khaki slacks, still perspiring freely. "You're scared, aren't you, Edward? Scared of losing your precious dignity and having people think you might be making a fool of yourself just for once."

"I refuse to get hysterical about it, that's all."

Louisa turned back to the book and began reading some more. "This is interesting," she said. "It says here that Liszt loved all of Chopin's works except one—the Scherzo in B flat minor. Apparently he hated that. He called it the 'Governess Scherzo,' and said that it ought to be reserved solely for people in that profession."

"So what?"

"Edward, listen. As you insist on being so horrid about all this, I'll tell you what I'm going to do. I'm going to play this scherzo right now and you can stay here and see what happens."

"And then maybe you will deign to get us some supper."

Louisa got up and took from the shelf a large green volume containing all of Chopin's works. "Here it is. Oh yes, I remember it. It *is* rather awful. Now, listen—or, rather, watch. Watch to see what he does."

She placed the music on the piano and sat down. Her husband remained standing. He had his hands in his pockets and a cigarette in his mouth, and in spite of himself he was watching the cat, which was now dozing on the sofa. When Louisa began to play, the first effect was as dramatic as ever. The animal jumped up as though it had been stung, and it stood motionless for at least a minute, the ears pricked up, the whole body quivering. Then it became restless and began to walk back and forth along the length of the sofa. Finally, it hopped down onto the floor, and with its nose and tail held high in the air, it marched slowly, majestically, from the room.

"There!" Louisa cried, jumping up and running after it. "That does it! That really proves it!" She came back carrying the cat which she put down again on the sofa. Her whole face was shining with excitement now, her fists were clenched white, and the little bun on top of her head was loosening and going over to one side. "What about it, Edward? What d'you think?" She was laughing nervously as she spoke.

"I must say it was quite amusing."

"*Amusing!* My dear Edward, it's the most wonderful thing that's ever happened! Oh, goodness me!" she cried, picking up the cat again and hugging it to her bosom. "isn't it marvellous to think we've got Franz Liszt staying in the house?"

"Now, Louisa. Don't let's get hysterical."

"I can't help it, I simply can't. And to *imagine* that he's actually going to live with us for always!"

"I beg your pardon?"

"Oh, Edward! I can hardly talk from excitement. And d'you know what I'm going to do next? Every musician in the whole world is going to want to meet him, that's a fact, and ask him about the people he knew—about Beethoven and Chopin and Schubert—"

"He can't talk," her husband said.

"Well—all right. But they're going to want to meet him anyway, just to see him and touch him and to play their own music to him, modern music he's never heard before."

"He wasn't that great. Now, if it had been Bach or Beethoven . . ."

"Don't interrupt, Edward, please. So what I'm going to do is to notify all the important living composers everywhere. It's my duty. I'll tell them Liszt is here, and invite them to visit him. And you know what? They'll come flying in from every corner of the earth!"

"To see a grey cat?"

"Darling, it's the same thing. It's *him*. No one cares what he *looks* like. Oh, Edward, it'll be the most exciting thing there ever was!"

"They'll think you're mad."

"You wait and see." She was holding the cat in her arms and petting it tenderly but looking across at her husband, who now walked over to the French windows and stood there staring out into the garden. The evening was beginning, and the lawn was turning slowly from green to black, and in the distance he could see the smoke from his bonfire rising straight up in a white column.

"No," he said, without turning round, "I'm not having

it. Not in this house. It'll make us both look perfect fools."

"Edward, what do you mean?"

"Just what I say. I absolutely refuse to have you stirring up a lot of publicity about a foolish thing like this. You happen to have found a trick cat. O.K.—that's fine. Keep it, if it pleases you. I don't mind. But I don't wish you to go any further than that. Do you understand me, Louisa?"

"Further than what?"

"I don't want to hear any more of this crazy talk. You're acting like a lunatic."

Louisa put the cat slowly down on the sofa. Then slowly she raised herself to her full small height and took one pace forward. "*Damn* you, Edward!" she shouted, stamping her foot. "For the first time in our lives something really exciting comes along and you're scared to death of having anything to do with it because someone may laugh at you! That's right, isn't it? You can't deny it, can you?"

"Louisa," her husband said. "That's quite enough of that. Pull yourself together now and stop this at once." He walked over and took a cigarette from the box on the table, then lit it with the enormous patent lighter. His wife stood watching him, and now the tears were beginning to trickle out of the inside corners of her eyes, making two little shiny rivers where they ran through the powder on her cheeks.

"We've been having too many of these scenes just lately, Louisa," he was saying. "No no, don't interrupt. Listen to me. I make full allowance for the fact that this may be an awkward time of life for you, and that—"

"Oh, my God! You idiot! You pompous idiot! Can't you

see that this is different, this is—this is something miraculous? Can't you see *that?*"

At that point, he came across the room and took her firmly by the shoulders. He had the freshly lit cigarette between his lips, and she could see faint contours on his skin where the heavy perspiration had dried in patches. "Listen," he said. "I'm hungry. I've given up my golf and I've been working all day in the garden, and I'm tired and hungry and I want some supper. So do you. Off you go now to the kitchen and get us both something good to eat."

Louisa stepped back and put both hands to her mouth. "My heavens!" she cried. "I forgot all about it. He must be absolutely famished. Except for some milk, I haven't given him a thing to eat since he arrived."

"Who?"

"Why, *him*, of course. I must go at once and cook something really special. I wish I knew what his favourite dishes used to be. What do you think he would like best, Edward?"

"*Goddamn* it, Louisa!"

"Now, Edward, please. I'm going to handle this *my* way just for once. You stay here," she said, bending down and touching the cat gently with her fingers. "I won't be long."

Louisa went into the kitchen and stood for a moment, wondering what special dish she might prepare. How about a soufflé? A nice cheese soufflé? Yes, that would be rather special. Of course, Edward didn't much care for them, but that couldn't be helped.

She was only a fair cook, and she couldn't be sure of al-

ways having a soufflé come out well, but she took extra
trouble this time and waited a long while to make certain
the oven had heated fully to the correct temperature.
While the soufflé was baking and she was searching around
for something to go with it, it occurred to her that Liszt
had probably never in his life tasted either avocado pears or
grapefruit, so she decided to give him both of them at once
in a salad. It would be fun to watch his reaction. It really
would.

When it was all ready, she put it on a tray and carried
it into the living-room. At the exact moment she entered,
she saw her husband coming in through the French windows from the garden.

"Here's his supper," she said, putting it on the table and
turning toward the sofa. "Where is he?"

Her husband closed the garden door behind him and
walked across the room to get himself a cigarette.

"Edward, where is he?"

"Who?"

"You know who."

"Ah, yes. Yes, that's right. Well—I'll tell you." He was
bending forward to light the cigarette, and his hands were
cupped around the enormous patent lighter. He glanced
up and saw Louisa looking at him—at his shoes and the
bottoms of his khaki slacks, which were damp from walking in long grass.

"I just went out to see how the bonfire was going," he
said.

Her eyes travelled slowly upward and rested on his
hands.

"It's still burning fine," he went on. "I think it'll keep going all night."

But the way she was staring made him uncomfortable.

"What is it?" he said, lowering the lighter. Then he looked down and noticed for the first time the long thin scratch that ran diagonally clear across the back of one hand, from the knuckle to the wrist.

"*Edward!*"

"Yes," he said, "I know. Those brambles are terrible. They tear you to pieces. Now, just a minute, Louisa. What's the matter?"

"*Edward!*"

"Oh, for God's sake, woman, sit down and keep calm. There's nothing to get worked up about. Louisa! Louisa, *sit down!*"

PIG

ONCE upon a time, in the City of New York, a beautiful baby boy was born into this world, and the joyful parents named him Lexington.

No sooner had the mother returned home from the hospital carrying Lexington in her arms than she said to her husband, "Darling, now you must take me out to a most marvellous restaurant for dinner so that we can celebrate the arrival of our son and heir."

Her husband embraced her tenderly and told her that any woman who could produce such a beautiful child as Lexington deserved to go absolutely any place she wanted. But was she strong enough yet, he enquired, to start running around the city late at night?

"No, she said, she wasn't. But what the hell.

So that evening they both dressed themselves up in fancy clothes, and leaving little Lexington in care of a trained infant's nurse who was costing them twenty dollars a day and was Scottish into the bargain, they went out to the finest and most expensive restaurant in town. There they each ate a giant lobster and drank a bottle of champagne between them, and after that, they went on to a nightclub, where they drank another bottle of champagne and then sat holding hands for several hours while they recalled and discussed and admired each individual physical feature of their lovely newborn son.

They arrived back at their house on the East Side of Manhattan at around two o'clock in the morning and the husband paid off the taxi-driver and then began feeling in his pockets for the key to the front door. After a while, he announced that he must have left it in the pocket of his other suit, and he suggested they ring the bell and get the nurse to come down and let them in. An infant's nurse at twenty dollars a day must expect to be hauled out of bed occasionally in the night, the husband said.

So he rang the bell. They waited. Nothing happened. He rang it again, long and loud. They waited another minute. Then they both stepped back onto the street and shouted the nurse's name (McPottle) up at the nursery windows on the third floor, but there was still no response. The house was dark and silent. The wife began to grow apprehensive. Her baby was imprisoned in this place, she told herself. Alone with McPottle. And who was McPottle? They had known her for two days, that was all, and she had a thin mouth, a small disapproving eye, and a starchy bosom, and quite clearly she was in the habit of sleeping much too soundly for safety. If she couldn't hear the front-door bell, then how on earth did she expect to hear a baby crying? Why, this very second the poor thing might be swallowing its tongue or suffocating on its pillow.

"He doesn't use a pillow," the husband said. "You are not to worry. But I'll get you in if that's what you want." He was feeling rather superb after all the champagne, and now he bent down and undid the laces of one of his black patent-leather shoes, and took it off. Then, holding it by the toe, he flung it hard and straight right through the dining-room window on the ground floor.

"There you are," he said, grinning. "We'll deduct it from McPottle's wages."

He stepped forward and very carefully put a hand through the hole in the glass and released the catch. Then he raised the window.

"I shall lift you in first, little mother," he said, and he took his wife around the waist and lifted her off the ground. This brought her big red mouth up level with his own, and very close, so he started kissing her. He knew from experience that women like very much to be kissed in this position, with their bodies held tight and their legs dangling in the air, so he went on doing it for quite a long time, and she wiggled her feet, and made loud gulping noises down in her throat. Finally, the husband turned her round and began easing her gently through the open window into the dining-room. At this point, a police patrol car came nosing silently along the street toward them. It stopped about thirty yards away, and three cops of Irish extraction leaped out of the car and started running in the direction of the husband and wife, brandishing revolvers.

"Stick 'em up!" the cops shouted. "Stick 'em up!" But it was impossible for the husband to obey this order without letting go of his wife, and had he done this she would either have fallen to the ground or would have been left dangling half in and half out of the house, which is a terribly uncomfortable position for a woman; so he continued gallantly to push her upward and inward through the window. The cops, all of whom had received medals before for killing robbers, opened fire immediately, and although they were still running, and although the wife in particular was presenting them with a very small target indeed, they succeeded in scoring several direct hits on each body—sufficient anyway to prove fatal in both cases.

Thus, when he was no more than twelve days old, little Lexington became an orphan.

II

The news of this killing, for which the three policemen subsequently received citations, was eagerly conveyed to all relatives of the deceased couple by newspaper reporters, and the next morning, the closest of these relatives, as well as a couple of undertakers, three lawyers, and a priest, climbed into taxis and set out for the house with the broken window. They assembled in the living-room, men and women both, and they sat around in a circle on the sofas and armchairs, smoking cigarettes and sipping sherry and debating what on earth should be done now with the oaby upstairs, the orphan Lexington.

It soon became apparent that none of the relatives was

particularly keen to assume responsibility for the child, and the discussions and arguments continued all through the day. Everybody declared an enormous, almost an irresistible desire to look after him, and would have done so with the greatest of pleasure were it not for the fact that their apartment was too small, or that they already had one baby and couldn't possibly afford another, or that they wouldn't know what to do with the poor little thing when they went abroad in the summer, or that they were getting on in years, which surely would be most unfair to the boy when he grew up, and so on and so forth. They all knew, of course, that the father had been heavily in debt for a long time and that the house was mortgaged and that consequently there would be no money at all to go with the child.

They were still arguing like mad at six in the evening when suddenly, in the middle of it all, an old aunt of the deceased father (her name was Glosspan) swept in from Virginia, and without even removing her hat and coat, not even pausing to sit down, ignoring all offers of a martini, a whisky, a sherry, she announced firmly to the assembled relatives that she herself intended to take sole charge of the infant boy from then on. What was more, she said, she would assume full financial responsibility on all counts, including education, and everyone else could go on back home where they belonged and give their consciences a rest. So saying, she trotted upstairs to the nursery and snatched Lexington from his cradle and swept out of the house with the baby clutched tightly in her arms, while the relatives simply sat and stared and smiled and looked relieved, and McPottle the nurse stood stiff with disapproval at the head of the stairs, her lips compressed, her arms folded across her starchy bosom.

And thus it was that the infant Lexington, when he was thirteen days old, left the City of New York and travelled southward to live with his Great Aunt Glosspan in the State of Virginia.

III

Aunt Glosspan was nearly seventy when she became guardian to Lexington, but to look at her you would never have guessed it for one minute. She was as sprightly as a woman half her age, with a small, wrinkled, but still quite beautiful face and two lovely brown eyes that sparkled at you in the nicest way. She was also a spinster, though you would never have guessed that either, for there was nothing spinsterish about Aunt Glosspan. She was never bitter or gloomy or irritable; she didn't have a moustache; and she wasn't in the least bit jealous of other people, which in itself is something you can seldom say about either a spinster or a virgin lady, although of course it is not known for certain whether Aunt Glosspan qualified on both counts.

But she was an eccentric old woman, there was no doubt about that. For the past thirty years she had lived a strange isolated life all by herself in a tiny cottage high up on the slopes of the Blue Ridge Mountains, several miles from the nearest village. She had five acres of pasture, a plot for growing vegetables, a flower garden, three cows, a dozen hens, and a fine cockerel.

And now she had little Lexington as well.

She was a strict vegetarian and regarded the consumption of animal flesh as not only unhealthy and disgusting, but horribly cruel. She lived upon lovely clean foods like milk, butter, eggs, cheese, vegetables, nuts, herbs, and fruit, and she rejoiced in the conviction that no living creature would be slaughtered on her account, not even a shrimp. Once, when a brown hen of hers passed away in the prime of life from being eggbound, Aunt Glosspan was so distressed that she nearly gave up egg-eating altogether.

She knew not the first thing about babies, but that didn't worry her in the least. At the railway station in New York, while waiting for the train that would take her and Lexington back to Virginia, she bought six feeding-bottles, two dozen diapers, a box of safety pins, a carton of milk for the journey, and a small paper-covered book called *The Care of Infants*. What more could anyone want? And when the train got going, she fed the baby some milk, changed its nappies after a fashion, and laid it down on the seat to sleep. Then she read *The Care of Infants* from cover to cover.

"There is no problem here," she said, throwing the book out the window. "No problem at all."

And curiously enough there wasn't. Back home in the cottage everything went just as smoothly as could be. Little Lexington drank his milk and belched and yelled and slept exactly as a good baby should, and Aunt Glosspan glowed with joy whenever she looked at him, and showered him with kisses all day long.

IV

By the time he was six years old, young Lexington had grown into a most beautiful boy with long golden hair and deep blue eyes the colour of cornflowers. He was bright and cheerful, and already he was learning to help his old aunt in all sorts of different ways around the property, collecting the eggs from the chicken house, turning the handle of the butter churn, digging up potatoes in the vegetable garden, and searching for wild herbs on the side of the mountain. Soon, Aunt Glosspan told herself, she would have to start thinking about his education.

But she couldn't bear the thought of sending him away to school. She loved him so much now that it would kill her to be parted from him for any length of time. There was, of course, that village school down in the valley, but it was a dreadful-looking place, and if she sent him there she just knew they would start forcing him to eat meat the very first day he arrived.

"You know what, my darling?" she said to him one day when he was sitting on a stool in the kitchen watching her make cheese. "I don't really see why I shouldn't give you your lessons myself."

The boy looked up at her with his large blue eyes, and gave her a lovely trusting smile. "That would be nice," he said.

"And the very first thing I should do would be to teach you how to cook."

"I think I would like that, Aunt Glosspan."

"Whether you like it or not, you're going to have to learn some time," she said. "Vegetarians like us don't have nearly so many foods to choose from as ordinary people, and therefore they must learn to be doubly expert with what they have."

"Aunt Glosspan," the boy said, "what *do* ordinary people eat that we don't?"

"Animals," she answered, tossing her head in disgust.

"You mean *live* animals?"

"No," she said. "Dead ones."

The boy considered this for a moment.

"You mean when they die they *eat* them instead of *burying* them?"

"They don't wait for them to die, my pet. They kill them."

"How do they kill them, Aunt Glosspan?"

"They usually slit their throats with a knife."

"But what *kind* of animals?"

"Cows and pigs mostly, and sheep."

"Cows!" the boy cried. "You mean like Daisy and Snowdrop and Lily?"

"Exactly, my dear."

"But *how* do they eat them, Aunt Glosspan?"

"They cut them up into bits and they cook the bits. They like it best when it's all red and bloody and sticking to the bones. They love to eat lumps of cow's flesh with the blood oozing out of it."

"Pigs too?"

"They adore pigs."

"Lumps of bloody pig's meat," the boy said. "Imagine that. What else do they eat, Aunt Glosspan?"

"Chickens."

"Chickens!"

"Millions of them."

"Feathers and all?"

"No, dear, not the feathers. Now run along outside and get Aunt Glosspan a bunch of chives, will you, my darling?"

Shortly after that, the lessons began. They covered five subjects, reading, writing, geography, arithmetic, and cooking, but the latter was by far the most popular with both teacher and pupil. In fact, it very soon became apparent that young Lexington possessed a truly remarkable talent in this direction. He was a born cook. He was dextrous and quick. He could handle his pans like a juggler. He could slice a single potato into twenty paper-thin slivers in less time than it took his aunt to peel it. His palate was exquisitely sensitive, and he could taste a pot of strong onion soup and immediately detect the presence of a single tiny leaf of sage. In so young a boy, all this was a bit bewildering to Aunt Glosspan, and to tell the truth she didn't quite know what to make of it. But she was proud as proud could be, all the same, and predicted a brilliant future for the child.

"What a mercy it is," she said, "that I have such a wonderful little fellow to look after me in my dotage." And a couple of years later, she retired from the kitchen for good, leaving Lexington in sole charge of all household cooking. The boy was now ten years old, and Aunt Glosspan was nearly eighty.

V

With the kitchen to himself, Lexington straight away began experimenting with dishes of his own invention. The old favourites no longer interested him. He had a violent urge to create. There were hundreds of fresh ideas in his head. "I will begin," he said, "by devising a chestnut soufflé." He made it and served it up for supper that very night. It was terrific. "You are a genius!" Aunt Glosspan cried, leaping up from her chair and kissing him on both cheeks. "You will make history!"

From then on, hardly a day went by without some new delectable creation being set upon the table. There was Brazil-nut soup, hominy cutlets, vegetable ragout, dandelion omelette, cream-cheese fritters, stuffed-cabbage surprise, stewed foggage, shallots *à la bonne femme*, beetroot mousse piquant, prunes Stroganoff, Dutch rarebit, turnips on horseback, flaming spruce-needle tarts, and many many other beautiful compositions. Never before in her life, Aunt Glosspan declared, had she tasted such food as this; and in the mornings, long before lunch was due, she would go out onto the porch and sit there in her rocking-chair, speculating about the coming meal, licking her chops, sniffing the aromas that came wafting out through the kitchen window.

"What's that you're making in there today, boy?" she would call out.

"Try to guess, Aunt Glosspan."

"Smells like a bit of salsify fritters to me," she would say, sniffing vigorously.

Then out he would come, this ten-year-old child, a little grin of triumph on his face, and in his hands a big steaming pot of the most heavenly stew made entirely of parsnips and lovage.

"You know what you ought to do," his aunt said to him, gobbling the stew. "You ought to set yourself down this very minute with paper and pencil and write a cooking-book."

He looked at her across the table, chewing his parsnips slowly.

"Why not?" she cried. "I've taught you how to write and I've taught you how to cook and now all you've got to do is put the two things together. You write a cooking-book, my darling, and it'll make you famous the whole world over."

"All right," he said. "I will."

And that very day, Lexington began writing the first page of that monumental work which was to occupy him for the rest of his life. He called it *Eat Good and Healthy*.

VI

Seven years later, by the time he was seventeen, he had recorded over nine thousand different recipes, all of them original, all of them delicious.

But now, suddenly, his labors were interrupted by the tragic death of Aunt Glosspan. She was afflicted in the night by a violent seizure, and Lexington, who had rushed into her bedroom to see what all the noise was about, found her lying on her bed yelling and cussing and twisting herself up into all manner of complicated knots. Indeed, she was a terrible sight to behold, and the agitated youth danced around her in his pyjamas, wringing his hands, and wondering what on earth he should do. Finally, in an effort to cool her down, he fetched a bucket of water from the pond in the cow field and tipped it over her head, but this only intensified the paroxysms, and the old lady expired within the hour.

"This is really too bad," the poor boy said, pinching her several times to make sure that she was dead. "And how sudden! How quick and sudden! Why only a few hours ago she seemed in the very best of spirits. She even took three large helpings of my most recent creation, devilled mushroomburgers, and told me how succulent it was."

After weeping bitterly for several minutes, for he had loved his aunt very much, he pulled himself together and carried her outside and buried her behind the cowshed.

The next day, while tidying up her belongings, he came across an envelope that was addressed to him in Aunt Glosspan's handwriting. He opened it and drew out two fifty-dollar bills and a letter. *Darling boy*, the letter said. *I know that you have never yet been down the mountain since you were thirteen days old, but as soon as I die you must put on a pair of shoes and a clean shirt and walk down to the village and find the doctor. Ask the doctor to give you a death certificate to prove that I am dead. Then take this certificate to my lawyer, a man called Mr. Samuel Zuckermann, who lives in New York City and who has a*

copy of my will. Mr. Zuckermann will arrange everything.
The cash in this envelope is to pay the doctor for the
certificate and to cover the cost of your journey to New
York. Mr. Zuckermann will give you more money when
you get there, and it is my earnest wish that you use it to
further your researches into culinary and vegetarian mat-
ters, and that you continue to work upon that great book
of yours until you are satisfied that it is complete in every
way. Your loving aunt—Glosspan.

Lexington, who had always done everything his aunt
told him, pocketed the money, put on a pair of shoes and a
clean shirt, and went down the mountain to the village
where the doctor lived.

"Old Glosspan?" the doctor said. "My God, is *she*
dead?"

"Certainly she's dead," the youth answered. "If you will
come back home with me now I'll dig her up and you can
see for yourself."

"How deep did you bury her?" the doctor asked.

"Six or seven feet down, I should think."

"And how long ago?"

"Oh, about eight hours."

"Then she's dead," the doctor announced. "Here's the
certificate."

VII

Our hero now set out for the City of New York to find
Mr. Samuel Zuckermann. He travelled on foot, and he
slept under hedges, and he lived on berries and wild
herbs, and it took him sixteen days to reach the metropolis.

"What a fabulous place this is!" he cried as he stood at the corner of Fifty-seventh Street and Fifth Avenue, staring around him. "There are no cows or chickens anywhere, and none of the women looks in the least like Aunt Glosspan."

As for Mr. Samuel Zuckermann, he looked like nothing that Lexington had ever seen before.

He was a small spongy man with livid jowls and a huge magenta nose, and when he smiled, bits of gold flashed at you marvellously from lots of different places inside his mouth. In his luxurious office, he shook Lexington warmly by the hand and congratulated him upon his aunt's death.

"I suppose you knew that your dearly beloved guardian was a woman of considerable wealth?" he said.

"You mean the cows and the chickens?"

"I mean half a million bucks," Mr. Zuckermann said.

"How much?"

"Half a million dollars, my boy. And she's left it all to you." Mr. Zuckermann leaned back in his chair and clasped his hands over his spongy paunch. At the same time, he began secretly working his right forefinger in through his waistcoat and under his shirt so as to scratch the skin around the circumference of his navel—a favourite exercise of his, and one that gave him a peculiar pleasure. "Of course, I shall have to deduct fifty per cent for my services," he said, "but that still leaves you with two hundred and fifty grand."

"I am rich!" Lexington cried. "This is wonderful! How soon can I have the money?"

"Well," Mr. Zuckermann said, "luckily for you, I happen to be on rather cordial terms with the tax authorities around here, and I am confident that I shall be able to persuade them to waive all death duties and back taxes."

"How kind you are," murmured Lexington.

"I should naturally have to give somebody a small honorarium."

"Whatever you say, Mr. Zuckermann."

"I think a hundred thousand would be sufficient."

"Good gracious, isn't that rather excessive?"

"Never undertip a tax-inspector or a policeman," Mr. Zuckermann said. "Remember that."

"But how much does it leave for me?" the youth asked meekly.

"One hundred and fifty thousand. But then you've got the funeral expenses to pay out of that."

"*Funeral* expenses?"

"You've got to pay the funeral parlour. Surely you know that?"

"But I buried her myself, Mr. Zuckermann, behind the cowshed."

"I don't doubt it," the lawyer said. "So what?"

"I never used a funeral parlour."

"Listen," Mr. Zuckermann said patiently. "You may not know it, but there is a law in this State which says that no beneficiary under a will may receive a single penny of his inheritance until the funeral parlour has been paid in full."

"You mean that's a *law?*"

"Certainly it's a law, and a very good one it is, too. The

funeral parlour is one of our great national institutions. It
must be protected at all cost."

Mr. Zuckermann himself, together with a group of
public-spirited doctors, controlled a corporation that
owned a chain of nine lavish funeral parlours in the city,
not to mention a casket factory in Brooklyn and a post-
graduate school for embalmers in Washington Heights.
The celebration of death was therefore a deeply religious
affair in Mr. Zuckermann's eyes. In fact, the whole business affected him profoundly, almost as profoundly, one
might say, as the birth of Christ affected the shopkeeper.

"You had no right to go out and bury your aunt like
that," he said. "None at all."

"I'm very sorry, Mr. Zuckermann."

"Why, it's downright subversive."

"I'll do whatever you say, Mr. Zuckermann. All I want
to know is how much I'm going to get in the end, when
everything's paid."

There was a pause. Mr. Zuckermann sighed and frowned
and continued secretly to run the tip of his finger around
the rim of his navel.

"Shall we say fifteen thousand?" he suggested, flashing a
big gold smile. "That's a nice round figure."

"Can I take it with me this afternoon?"

"I don't see why not."

So Mr. Zuckermann summoned his chief cashier and
told him to give Lexington fifteen thousand dollars out of
the petty cash, and to obtain a receipt. The youth, who by
this time was delighted to be getting anything at all, accepted the money gratefully and stowed it away in his

knapsack. Then he shook Mr. Zuckermann warmly by the hand, thanked him for all his help, and went out of the office.

"The whole world is before me!" our hero cried as he emerged into the street. "I now have fifteen thousand dollars to see me through until my book is published. And after that, of course, I shall have a great deal more." He stood on the pavement, wondering which way to go. He turned left and began strolling slowly down the street, staring at the sights of the city.

"What a revolting smell," he said, sniffing the air. "I can't stand this." His delicate olfactory nerves, tuned to receive only the most delicious kitchen aromas, were being tortured by the stench of the diesel-oil fumes pouring out of the backs of the buses.

"I must get out of this place before my nose is ruined altogether," he said. "But first, I've simply got to have something to eat. I'm starving." The poor boy had had nothing but berries and wild herbs for the past two weeks, and now his stomach was yearning for solid food. I'd like a nice hominy cutlet, he told himself. Or maybe a few juicy salsify fritters.

He crossed the street and entered a small restaurant. The place was hot inside, and dark and silent. There was a strong smell of cooking-fat and cabbage water. The only other customer was a man with a brown hat on his head, crouching intently over his food, who did not look up as Lexington came in.

Our hero seated himself at a corner table and hung his knapsack on the back of his chair. This, he told himself, is going to be most interesting. In all my seventeen years I have tasted only the cooking of two people, Aunt Glosspan and myself—unless one counts Nurse McPottle, who must have heated my bottle a few times when I was an infant. But I am now about to sample the art of a new chef altogether, and perhaps, if I am lucky, I may pick up a couple of useful ideas for my book.

A waiter approached out of the shadows at the back, and stood beside the table.

"How do you do," Lexington said. "I should like a large hominy cutlet please. Do it twenty-five seconds each side, in a very hot skillet with sour cream, and sprinkle a pinch of lovage on it before serving—unless of course your chef knows of a more original method, in which case I should be delighted to try it."

The waiter laid his head over to one side and looked carefully at his customer. "You want the roast pork and cabbage?" he asked. "That's all we got left."

"Roast what and cabbage?"

The waiter took a soiled handkerchief from his trouser pocket and shook it open with a violent flourish, as though he were cracking a whip. Then he blew his nose loud and wet.

"You want it or don't you?" he said, wiping his nostrils.

"I haven't the foggiest idea what it is," Lexington replied, "but I should love to try it. You see, I am writing a cooking-book and . . ."

"One pork and cabbage!" the waiter shouted, and somewhere in the back of the restaurant, far away in the darkness, a voice answered him.

The waiter disappeared. Lexington reached into his knapsack for his personal knife and fork. These were a present from Aunt Glosspan, given him when he was six years old, made of solid silver, and he had never eaten with any other instruments since. While waiting for the food to arrive, he polished them lovingly with a piece of soft muslin.

Soon the waiter returned carrying a plate on which there lay a thick greyish-white slab of something hot. Lexington leaned forward anxiously to smell it as it was put down before him. His nostrils were wide open now to receive the scent, quivering and sniffing.

"But this is absolute heaven!" he exclaimed. "What an aroma! It's tremendous!"

The waiter stepped back a pace, watching his customer carefully.

"Never in my life have I smelled anything as rich and wonderful as this!" our hero cried, seizing his knife and fork. "What on earth is it made of?"

The man in the brown hat looked around and stared, then returned to his eating. The waiter was backing away toward the kitchen.

Lexington cut off a small piece of the meat, impaled it on his silver fork, and carried it up to his nose so as to smell it again. Then he popped it into his mouth and began to chew it slowly, his eyes half closed, his body tense.

"This is fantastic!" he cried. "It is a brand-new flavour! Oh, Glosspan, my beloved Aunt, how I wish you were with me now so you could taste this remarkable dish! Waiter! Come here at once! I want you!"

The astonished waiter was now watching from the other end of the room, and he seemed reluctant to move any closer.

"If you will come and talk to me I will give you a present," Lexington said, waving a hundred-dollar bill. "Please come over here and talk to me."

The waiter sidled cautiously back to the table, snatched away the money, and held it up close to his face, peering at it from all angles. Then he slipped it quickly into his pocket.

"What can I do for you, my friend?" he asked.

"Look," Lexington said. "If you will tell me what this delicious dish is made of, and exactly how it is prepared, I will give you another hundred."

"I already told you," the man said. "It's pork."

"And what exactly is pork?"

"You never had roast pork before?" the waiter asked, staring.

"For heaven's sake, man, tell me what it is and stop keeping me in suspense like this."

"It's pig," the waiter said. "You just bung it in the oven."

"*Pig!*"

"All pork is pig. Didn't you know that?"

"You mean *this* is *pig's meat?*"

"I guarantee it."

"But . . . but . . . that's impossible," the youth stammered. "Aunt Glosspan, who knew more about food than anyone else in the world, said that meat of any kind was disgusting, revolting, horrible, foul, nauseating, and beastly. And yet this piece that I have here on my plate is without a doubt the most delicious thing that I have ever tasted. Now how on earth do you explain that? Aunt Glosspan certainly wouldn't have told me it was revolting if it wasn't."

"Maybe your aunt didn't know how to cook it," the waiter said.

"Is that possible?"

"You're damn right it is. Especially with pork. Pork has to be very well done or you can't eat it."

"Eureka!" Lexington cried. "I'll bet that's exactly what happened! She did it wrong!" He handed the man another hundred-dollar bill. "Lead me to the kitchen," he said. "Introduce me to the genius who prepared this meat."

Lexington was at once taken into the kitchen, and there he met the cook who was an elderly man with a rash on one side of his neck.

"This will cost you another hundred," the waiter said.

Lexington was only too glad to oblige, but this time he gave the money to the cook. "Now listen to me," he said, "I have to admit that I am really rather confused by what the waiter has just been telling me. Are you quite positive that the delectable dish which I have just been eating was prepared from pig's flesh?"

The cook raised his right hand and began scratching the rash on his neck.

"Well," he said, looking at the waiter and giving him a sly wink, "all I can tell you is that I *think* it was pig's meat."

"You mean you're not sure?"

"One can't ever be sure."

"Then what else could it have been?"

"Well," the cook said, speaking very slowly and still staring at the waiter. "There's just a chance, you see, that it might have been a piece of human stuff."

"You mean a man?"

"Yes."

"Good heavens."

"Or a woman. It could have been either. They both taste the same."

"Well—now you really do surprise me," the youth declared.

"One lives and learns."

"Indeed one does."

"As a matter of fact, we've been getting an awful lot of it just lately from the butcher's in place of pork," the cook declared.

"Have you really?"

"The trouble is, it's almost impossible to tell which is which. They're both very good."

"The piece I had just now was simply superb."

"I'm glad you liked it," the cook said. "But to be quite honest, I think that was a bit of pig. In fact, I'm almost sure it was."

"You are?"

"Yes, I am."

"In that case, we shall have to assume that you are right," Lexington said. "So now will you please tell me— and here is another hundred dollars for your trouble—will you please tell me precisely how you prepared it?"

The cook, after pocketing the money, launched out

upon a colourful description of how to roast a loin of pork, while the youth, not wanting to miss a single word of so great a recipe, sat down at the kitchen table and recorded every detail in his notebook.

"Is that all?" he asked when the cook had finished.

"That's all."

"But there must be more to it than that, surely?"

"You got to get a good piece of meat to start off with," the cook said. "That's half the battle. It's got to be a good hog and it's got to be butchered right, otherwise it'll turn out lousy whichever way you cook it."

"Show me how," Lexington said. "Butcher me one now so I can learn."

"We don't butcher pigs in the kitchen," the cook said. "That lot you just ate came from a packing-house over in the Bronx."

"Then give me the address!"

The cook gave him the address, and our hero, after thanking them both many times for all their kindnesses, rushed outside and leapt into a taxi and headed for the Bronx.

VIII

The packing-house was a big four-storey brick building, and the air around it smelled sweet and heavy, like musk. At the main entrance gates, there was a large notice which said VISITORS WELCOME AT ANY TIME, and thus encouraged, Lexington walked through the gates and entered a cobbled yard which surrounded the building itself. He then followed a series of signposts (THIS WAY FOR THE

GUIDED TOURS), and came eventually to a small corrugated-iron shed set well apart from the main building (VISITORS WAITING-ROOM). After knocking politely on the door, he went in.

There were six other people ahead of him in the waiting-room. There was a fat mother with her two little boys aged about nine and eleven. There was a bright-eyed young couple who looked as though they might be on their honeymoon. And there was a pale woman with long white gloves, who sat very upright, looking straight ahead, with her hands folded on her lap. Nobody spoke. Lexington wondered whether they were all writing cooking-books, like himself, but when he put this question to them aloud, he got no answer. The grown-ups merely smiled mysteriously to themselves and shook their heads, and the two children stared at him as though they were seeing a lunatic.

Soon, the door opened and a man with a merry pink face popped his head into the room and said, "Next, please." The mother and the two boys got up and went out.

About ten minutes later, the same man returned. "Next, please," he said again, and the honeymoon couple jumped up and followed him outside.

Two new visitors came in and sat down—a middle-aged husband and a middle-aged wife, the wife carrying a wicker shopping-basket containing groceries.

"Next, please," said the guide, and the woman with the long white gloves got up and left.

Several more people came in and took their places on the stiff-backed wooden chairs.

Soon the guide returned for the third time, and now it was Lexington's turn to go outside.

"Follow me, please," the guide said, leading the youth across the yard toward the main building.

"How exciting this is!" Lexington cried, hopping from one foot to the other. "I only wish that my dear Aunt Glosspan could be with me now to see what I am going to see."

"I myself only do the preliminaries," the guide said. "Then I shall hand you over to someone else."

"Anything you say," cried the ecstatic youth.

First they visited a large penned-in area at the back of the building where several hundred pigs were wandering around. "Here's where they start," the guide said. "And over there's where they go in."

"Where?"

"Right there." The guide pointed to a long wooden shed that stood against the outside wall of the factory. "We call it the shackling-pen. This way, please."

Three men wearing long rubber boots were driving a dozen pigs into the shackling-pen just as Lexington and the guide approached, so they all went in together.

"Now," the guide said, "watch how they shackle them."

Inside, the shed was simply a bare wooden room with no roof, but there was a steel cable with hooks on it that kept moving slowly along the length of one wall, parallel with the ground, about three feet up. When it reached the end of the shed, this cable suddenly changed direction and climbed vertically upward through the open roof toward the top floor of the main building.

The twelve pigs were huddled together at the far end of the pen, standing quietly, looking apprehensive. One of the men in rubber boots pulled a length of metal chain down from the wall and advanced upon the nearest animal, approaching it from the rear. Then he bent down and quickly looped one end of the chain around one of the animal's hind legs. The other end he attached to a hook on the moving cable as it went by. The cable kept moving. The chain tightened. The pig's leg was pulled up and back, and then the pig itself began to be dragged backwards. But it didn't fall down. It was rather a nimble pig, and somehow it managed to keep its balance on three legs, hopping from foot to foot and struggling against the pull of the chain, but going back and back all the time until at the end of the pen where the cable changed direction and went vertically upward, the creature was suddenly jerked off its feet and borne aloft. Shrill protests filled the air.

"Truly a fascinating process," Lexington said. "But what was that funny cracking noise it made as it went up?"

"Probably the leg," the guide answered. "Either that or the pelvis."

"But doesn't that matter?"

"Why should it matter?" the guide asked. "You don't eat the bones."

The rubber-booted men were busy shackling the rest of the pigs, and one after another they were hooked to the moving cable and hoisted up through the roof, protesting loudly as they went.

"There's a good deal more to this recipe than just picking herbs," Lexington said. "Aunt Glosspan would never have made it."

At this point, while Lexington was gazing skyward at the last pig to go up, a man in rubber boots approached him quietly from behind and looped one end of a chain around the youth's own left ankle, hooking the other end to the moving belt. The next moment, before he had time to realize what was happening, our hero was jerked off his feet and dragged backwards along the concrete floor of the shackling-pen.

"Stop!" he cried. "Hold everything! My leg is caught!"

But nobody seemed to hear him, and five seconds later, the unhappy young man was jerked off the floor and hoisted vertically upward through the open roof of the pen, dangling upside down by one ankle, and wriggling like a fish.

"Help!" he shouted. "Help! There's been a frightful mistake! Stop the engines! Let me down!"

The guide removed a cigar from his mouth and looked up serenely at the rapidly ascending youth, but he said nothing. The men in rubber boots were already on their way out to collect the next batch of pigs.

"Oh save me!" our hero cried. "Let me down! Please let me down!" But he was now approaching the top floor of the building where the moving belt curled over like a snake and entered a large hole in the wall, a kind of doorway without a door; and there, on the threshold, waiting to greet him, clothed in a dark-stained yellow rubber apron, and looking for all the world like Saint Peter at the Gates of Heaven, the sticker stood.

Lexington saw him only from upside down, and very briefly at that, but even so he noticed at once the expression of absolute peace and benevolence on the man's face, the cheerful twinkle in the eyes, the little wistful smile, the dimples in his cheeks—and all this gave him hope.

"Hi there," the sticker said, smiling.

"Quick! Save me!" our hero cried.

"With pleasure," the sticker said, and taking Lexington gently by one ear with his left hand, he raised his right hand and deftly slit open the boy's jugular vein with a knife.

The belt moved on. Lexington went with it. Everything was still upside down and the blood was pouring out of his throat and getting into his eyes, but he could still see after a fashion, and he had a blurred impression of being in an enormously long room, and at the far end of the room there was a great smoking cauldron of water, and there were dark figures, half hidden in the steam, dancing around the edge of it, brandishing long poles. The conveyor-belt seemed to be travelling right over the top of the cauldron, and the pigs seemed to be dropping down one by one into the boiling water, and one of the pigs seemed to be wearing long white gloves on its front feet.

Suddenly our hero started to feel very sleepy, but it wasn't until his good strong heart had pumped the last drop of blood from his body that he passed on out of this, the best of all possible worlds, into the next.

THE CHAMPION OF THE WORLD

ALL day, in between serving customers, we had been crouching over the table in the office of the filling-station, preparing the raisins. They were plump and soft and swollen from being soaked in water, and when you nicked them with a razor-blade the skin sprang open and the jelly stuff inside squeezed out as easily as you could wish.

But we had a hundred and ninety-six of them to do altogether and the evening was nearly upon us before we had finished.

"Don't they look marvellous!" Claud cried, rubbing his hands together hard. "What time is it, Gordon?"

"Just after five."

Through the window we could see a station-waggon pulling up at the pumps with a woman at the wheel and about eight children in the back eating ice-creams.

"We ought to be moving soon," Claud said. "The whole thing'll be a washout if we don't arrive before sunset, you realize that." He was getting twitchy now. His

face had the same flushed and pop-eyed look it got before a dog-race or when there was a date with Clarice in
the evening.

We both went outside and Claud gave the woman the
number of gallons she wanted. When she had gone, he remained standing in the middle of the driveway squinting
anxiously up at the sun which was now only the width of
a man's hand above the line of trees along the crest of the
ridge on the far side of the valley.

"All right," I said. "Lock up."

He went quickly from pump to pump, securing each
nozzle in its holder with a small padlock.

"You'd better take off that yellow pullover," he said.

"Why should I?"

"You'll be shining like a bloody beacon out there in the
moonlight."

"I'll be all right."

"You will not," he said. "Take it off, Gordon, please.
I'll see you in three minutes." He disappeared into his
caravan behind the filling-station, and I went indoors and
changed my yellow pullover for a blue one.

When we met again outside, Claude was dressed in a
pair of black trousers and a dark-green turtleneck sweater.
On his head he wore a brown cloth cap with the peak
pulled down low over his eyes, and he looked like an
apache actor out of a nightclub.

"What's under there?" I asked, seeing the bulge at his
waistline.

He pulled up his sweater and showed me two thin but
very large white cotton sacks which were bound neat and

tight around his belly. "To carry the stuff," he said darkly.

"I see."

"Let's go," he said,

"I still think we ought to take the car."

"It's too risky. They'll see it parked."

"But it's over three miles up to that wood."

"Yes," he said. "And I suppose you realize we can get six months in the clink if they catch us."

"You never told me that."

"Didn't I?"

"I'm not coming," I said. "It's not worth it."

"The walk will do you good, Gordon. Come on."

It was a calm sunny evening with little wisps of brilliant white cloud hanging motionless in the sky, and the valley was cool and very quiet as the two of us began walking together along the grass verge on the side of the road that ran between the hills toward Oxford.

"You got the raisins?" Claud asked.

"They're in my pocket."

"Good," he said. "Marvellous."

Ten minutes later we turned left off the main road into a narrow lane with high hedges on either side and from now on it was all uphill.

"How many keepers are there?" I asked.

"Three."

Claud threw away a half-finished cigarette. A minute later he lit another.

"I don't usually approve of new methods," he said. "Not on this sort of a job."

"Of course."

"But by God, Gordon, I think we're onto a hot one this time."

"You do?"

"There's no question about it."

"I hope you're right."

"It'll be a milestone in the history of poaching," he said. "But don't you go telling a single soul how we've done it, you understand. Because if this ever leaked out we'd have every bloody fool in the district doing the same thing and there wouldn't be a pheasant left."

"I won't say a word."

"You ought to be very proud of yourself," he went on. "There's been men with brains studying this problem for hundreds of years and not one of them's ever come up with anything even a quarter as artful as you have. Why didn't you tell me about it before?"

"You never invited my opinion," I said.

And that was the truth. In fact, up until the day before, Claud had never even offered to discuss with me the sacred subject of poaching. Often enough, on a summer's evening when work was finished, I had seen him with cap on head sliding quietly out of his caravan and disappearing up the road toward the woods; and sometimes, watching him through the window of the filling-station, I would find myself wondering exactly what he was going to do, what wily tricks he was going to practise all alone up there under the trees in the dead of night. He seldom came back until very late, and never, absolutely never did he bring any of the spoils with him personally on his return. But the following afternoon—and I couldn't imagine how he did it—there would always be a pheasant or a hare or a brace of partridges hanging up in the shed behind the filling-station for us to eat.

This summer he had been particularly active, and during the last couple of months he had stepped up the tempo to a point where he was going out four and sometimes five nights a week. But that was not all. It seemed to me that recently his whole attitude toward poaching had undergone a subtle and mysterious change. He was more purposeful about it now, more tight-lipped and intense than before, and I had the impression that this was not so much a game any longer as a crusade, a sort of private war that Claud was waging single-handed against an invisible and hated enemy.

But who?

I wasn't sure about this, but I had a suspicion that it was none other than the famous Mr. Victor Hazel himself, the owner of the land and the pheasants. Mr. Hazel was a pie and sausage manufacturer with an unbelievably arrogant manner. He was rich beyond words, and his property stretched for miles along either side of the valley. He was a self-made man with no charm at all and precious few virtues. He loathed all persons of humble station, having once been one of them himself, and he strove desperately to mingle with what he believed were the right kind of folk. He hunted with the hounds and gave shooting-parties and wore fancy waistcoats, and every weekday he drove an enormous black Rolls-Royce past the filling-station on his way to the factory. As he flashed by, we would sometimes catch a glimpse of the great glistening butcher's face above the wheel, pink as a ham, all soft and inflamed from eating too much meat.

Anyway, yesterday afternoon, right out of the blue, Claud had suddenly said to me, "I'll be going on up to Hazel's woods again tonight. Why don't you come along?"

"Who, me?"

"It's about the last chance this year for pheasants," he had said. "The shooting-season opens Saturday and the birds'll be scattered all over the place after that—if there's any left."

"Why the sudden invitation?" I had asked, greatly suspicious.

"No special reason, Gordon. No reason at all."

"Is it risky?"

He hadn't answered this.

"I suppose you keep a gun or something hidden away up there?"

"A gun!" he cried, disgusted. "Nobody ever *shoots* pheasants, didn't you know that? You've only got to fire a *cap-pistol* in Hazel's woods and the keepers'll be on you."

"Then how do you do it?"

"Ah," he said, and the eyelids drooped over the eyes, veiled and secretive.

There was a long pause. Then he said, "Do you think you could keep your mouth shut if I was to tell you a thing or two?"

"Definitely."

"I've never told this to anyone else in my whole life, Gordon."

"I am greatly honoured," I said. "You can trust me completely."

He turned his head, fixing me with pale eyes. The eyes were large and wet and ox-like, and they were so near to me that I could see my own face reflected upside down in the centre of each.

"I am now about to let you in on the three best ways in the world of poaching a pheasant," he said. "And seeing that you're the guest on this little trip, I am going to give you the choice of which one you'd like us to use tonight. How's that?"

"There's a catch in this."

"There's no catch, Gordon. I swear it."

"All right, go on."

"Now, here's the thing," he said. "Here's the first big secret." He paused and took a long suck at his cigarette. "Pheasants," he whispered softly, "is *crazy* about raisins."

"Raisins?"

"Just ordinary raisins. It's like a mania with them. My dad discovered that more than forty years ago just like he discovered all three of these methods I'm about to describe to you now."

"I thought you said your dad was a drunk."

"Maybe he was. But he was also a great poacher, Gordon. Possibly the greatest there's ever been in the history of England. My dad studied poaching like a scientist."

"Is that so?"

"I mean it. I really mean it."

"I believe you."

"Do you know," he said, "my dad used to keep a whole

flock of prime cockerels in the back yard purely for ex-
perimental purposes."

"Cockerels?"

"That's right. And whenever he thought up some new
stunt for catching a pheasant, he'd try it out on a cockerel
first to see how it worked. That's how he discovered
about raisins. It's also how he invented the horsehair
method."

Claud paused and glanced over his shoulder as though to
make sure that there was nobody listening. "Here's how
it's done," he said. "First you take a few raisins and you
soak them overnight in water to make them nice and
plump and juicy. Then you get a bit of good stiff horse-
hair and you cut it up into half-inch lengths. Then you
push one of these lengths of horsehair through the middle
of each raisin so that there's about an eighth of an inch of
it sticking out on either side. You follow?"

"Yes."

"Now—the old pheasant comes along and eats one of
these raisins. Right? And you're watching him from behind a tree. So what then?"

"I imagine it sticks in his throat."

"That's obvious, Gordon. But here's the amazing thing.
Here's what my dad discovered. The moment this happens, the bird *never moves his feet again!* He becomes
absolutely rooted to the spot, and there he stands pumping
his silly neck up and down just like it was a piston, and all
you've got to do is walk calmly out from the place where
you're hiding and pick him up in your hands."

"I don't believe that."

"I swear it," he said. "Once a pheasant's had the horse-hair you can fire a rifle in his ear and he won't even jump. It's just one of those unexplainable little things. But it takes a genius to discover it."

He paused, and there was a gleam of pride in his eye now as he dwelt for a moment or two upon the memory of his father, the great inventor.

"So that's Method Number One," he said. "Method Number Two is even more simple still. All you do is you have a fishing-line. Then you bait the hook with a raisin and you fish for the pheasant just like you fish for a fish. You pay out the line about fifty yards and you lie there on your stomach in the bushes waiting till you get a bite. Then you haul him in."

"I don't think your father invented that one."

"It's very popular with fishermen," he said, choosing not to hear me. "Keen fishermen who can't get down to the seaside as often as they want. It gives them a bit of the old thrill. The only trouble is it's rather noisy. The pheasant squawks like hell as you haul him in, and then every keeper in the wood comes running."

"What is Method Number Three?" I asked.

"Ah," he said. "Number Three's a real beauty. It was the last one my dad ever invented before he passed away."

"His final great work?"

"Exactly, Gordon. And I can even remember the very day it happened, a Sunday morning it was, and suddenly my dad comes into the kitchen holding a huge white cockerel in his hands and he says, 'I think I've got it.' There's a little smile on his face and a shine of glory in his eyes and he comes in very soft and quiet and he puts the bird down right in the middle of the kitchen table and he says, 'By God, I think I've got a good one this time.' 'A good what?' Mum says, looking up from the sink. 'Horace, take that filthy bird off my table.' The cockerel has a funny little paper hat over its head, like an ice-cream cone upside down, and my dad is pointing to it proudly. 'Stroke him,' he says. 'He won't move an inch.' The cockerel starts scratching away at the paper hat with one of its feet, but the hat seems to be stuck on with glue and it won't come off. 'No bird in the world is going to run away once you cover up his eyes,' my dad says, and he starts poking the cockerel with his finger and pushing it around on the table, but it doesn't take the slightest bit of notice. 'You can have this one,' he says, talking to Mum. 'You can kill it and dish it up for dinner as a celebration of what I have just invented.' And then straight away he takes me by the arm and marches me quickly out the door and off we go over the fields and up into the big forest the other side of Haddenham which used to belong to the Duke of Buckingham, and in less than two hours we get five lovely fat pheasants with no more trouble than it takes to go out and buy them in a shop."

Claud paused for breath. His eyes were huge and moist and dreamy as they gazed back into the wonderful world of his youth.

"I don't quite follow this," I said. "How did he get the paper hats over the pheasants' heads up in the woods?"

"You'd never guess it."

"I'm sure I wouldn't."

"Then here it is. First of all you dig a little hole in the ground. Then you twist a piece of paper into the shape of a cone and you fit this into the hole, hollow end upward, like a cup. Then you smear the paper cup all around the inside with bird-lime and drop in a few raisins. At the same time you lay a trail of raisins along the ground leading up to it. Now—the old pheasant comes pecking along the trail, and when he gets to the hole he pops his head inside to gobble the raisins and the next thing he knows he's got a paper hat stuck over his eyes and he can't see a thing. Isn't it marvellous what some people think of, Gordon? Don't you agree?"

"Your dad was a genius," I said.

"Then take your pick. Choose whichever one of the three methods you fancy and we'll use it tonight."

"You don't think they're all just a trifle on the crude side, do you?"

"Crude!" he cried, aghast. "Oh my God! And who's been having roasted pheasant in the house nearly every single day for the last six months and not a penny to pay?"

He turned and walked away toward the door of the workshop. I could see that he was deeply pained by my remark.

"Wait a minute," I said. "Don't go."

"You want to come or don't you?"

"Yes, but let me ask you something first. I've just had a bit of an idea."

"Keep it," he said. "You are talking about a subject you don't know the first thing about."

"Do you remember that bottle of sleeping-pills the doc gave me last month when I had a bad back?"

"What about them?"

"Is there any reason why those wouldn't work on a pheasant?"

Claud closed his eyes and shook his head pityingly from side to side.

"Wait," I said.

"It's not worth discussing," he said. "No pheasant in the world is going to swallow those lousy red capsules. Don't you know any better than that?"

"You are forgetting the raisins," I said. "Now listen to this. We take a raisin. Then we soak it till it swells. Then we make a tiny slit in one side of it with a razor-blade. Then we hollow it out a little. Then we open up one of my red capsules and pour all the powder into the raisin. Then we get a needle and cotton and very carefully we sew up the slit. Now . . ."

Out of the corner of my eye, I saw Claud's mouth slowly beginning to open.

"Now," I said. "We have a nice clean-looking raisin with two and a half grains of seconal inside it, and let me tell *you* something now. That's enough dope to knock the average *man* unconscious, never mind about *birds!*"

I paused for ten seconds to allow the full impact of this to strike home.

"What's more, with this method we could operate on a really grand scale. We could prepare *twenty* raisins if we felt like it, and all we'd have to do is scatter them around the feeding-grounds at sunset and then walk away. Half an hour later we'd come back, and the pills would be beginning to work, and the pheasants would be up in the trees by then, roosting, and they'd be starting to feel groggy, and they'd be wobbling and trying to keep their balance, and soon every pheasant that had eaten *one single raisin* would keel over unconscious and fall to the ground. My dear boy, they'd be dropping out of the trees like apples, and all we'd have to do is walk around picking them up!"

Claud was staring at me, rapt.

"Oh Christ," he said softly.

"And they'd never catch us either. We'd simply stroll through the woods dropping a few raisins here and there as we went, and even if they were *watching* us they wouldn't notice anything."

"Gordon," he said, laying a hand on my knee and gazing at me with eyes large and bright as two stars. "If this thing works, it will *revolutionize* poaching."

"I'm glad to hear it."

"How many pills have you got left?" he asked.

"Forty-nine. There were fifty in the bottle and I've only used one."

"Forty-nine's not enough. We want at least two hundred."

"Are you mad!" I cried.

He walked slowly away and stood by the door with his back to me, gazing at the sky.

"Two hundred's the bare minimum," he said quietly. "There's really not much point in doing it unless we have two hundred."

What is it now, I wondered. What the hell's he trying to do?

"This is the last chance we'll have before the season opens," he said.

"I couldn't possibly get any more."

"You wouldn't want us to come back empty-handed, would you?"

"But why so *many?*"

Claude turned his head and looked at me with large innocent eyes. "Why not?" he said gently. "Do you have any objection?"

My God, I thought suddenly. The crazy bastard is out to wreck Mr. Victor Hazel's opening-day shooting-party.

"You get us two hundred of those pills," he said, "and then it'll be worth doing."

"I can't."

"You could try, couldn't you?"

Mr. Hazel's party took place on the first of October every year and it was a very famous event. Debilitated gentlemen in tweed suits, some with titles and some who were merely rich, motored in from miles around with their gun-bearers and dogs and wives, and all day long the noise of shooting rolled across the valley. There were always enough pheasants to go around, for each summer the woods were methodically restocked with dozens and dozens of young birds at incredible expense. I had heard it said that the cost of rearing and keeping each pheasant up to the time when it was ready to be shot was well over five pounds (which is approximately the price of two hundred loaves of bread). But to Mr. Hazel it was worth every penny of it. He became, if only for a few hours, a big cheese in a little world and even the Lord Lieutenant of the County slapped him on the back and tried to remember his first name when he said goodbye.

"How would it be if we just reduced the dose?" Claud asked. "Why couldn't we divide the contents of one capsule among four raisins?"

"I suppose you could if you wanted to."

"But would a quarter of a capsule be strong enough for each bird?"

One simply had to admire the man's nerve. It was dangerous enough to poach a single pheasant up in those woods at this time of year and here he was planning to knock off the bloody lot.

"A quarter would be plenty," I said.

"You're sure of that?"

"Work it out for yourself. It's all done by body-weight. You'd still be giving about twenty times more than is necessary."

"Then we'll quarter the dose," he said, rubbing his hands. He paused and calculated for a moment. "We'll have one hundred and ninety-six raisins!"

"Do you realize what that involves?" I said. "They'll take hours to prepare."

"What of it!" he cried. "We'll go tomorrow instead. We'll soak the raisins overnight and then we'll have all morning and afternoon to get them ready."

And that was precisely what we did.

Now, twenty-four hours later, we were on our way. We had been walking steadily for about forty minutes and

we were nearing the point where the lane curved around
to the right and ran along the crest of the hill toward the
big wood where the pheasants lived. There was about a
mile to go.

"I don't suppose by any chance these keepers might be
carrying guns?" I asked.

"All keepers carry guns," Claud said.

I had been afraid of that.

"It's for the vermin mostly."

"Ah."

"Of course there's no guarantee they won't take a pot
at a poacher now and again."

"You're joking."

"Not at all. But they only do it from behind. Only when
you're running away. They like to pepper you in the
legs at about fifty yards."

"They can't do that!" I cried. "It's a criminal offence!"

"So is poaching," Claud said.

We walked on awhile in silence. The sun was below the
high hedge on our right now and the lane was in shadow.

"You can consider yourself lucky this isn't thirty years
ago," he went on. "They used to shoot you on sight in
those days."

"Do you believe that?"

"I know it," he said. "Many's the night when I was a
nipper I've gone into the kitchen and seen my old dad lying face downward on the table and Mum standing over
him digging the grapeshot out of his buttocks with a
potato knife."

"Stop," I said. "It makes me nervous."

"You believe me, don't you?"

"Yes, I believe you."

"Toward the end he was so covered in tiny little white scars he looked exactly like it was snowing."

"Yes," I said. "All right."

"Poacher's arse, they used to call it," Claud said. "And there wasn't a man in the whole village who didn't have a bit of it one way or another. But my dad was the champion."

"Good luck to him," I said.

"I wish to hell he was here now," Claud said, wistful. "He'd have given anything in the world to be coming with us on this job tonight."

"He could take my place," I said. "Gladly."

We had reached the crest of the hill and now we could see the wood ahead of us, huge and dark with the sun going down behind the trees and little sparks of gold shining through.

"You'd better let me have those raisins," Claud said.

I gave him the bag and he slid it gently into his trouser pocket.

"No talking once we're inside," he said. "Just follow me and try not to go snapping any branches."

Five minutes later we were there. The lane ran right up to the wood itself and then skirted the edge of it for about three hundred yards with only a little hedge between. Claud slipped through the hedge on all fours and I followed.

It was cool and dark inside the wood. No sunlight came in at all.

"This is spooky," I said.

"Ssshh!"

Claud was very tense. He was walking just ahead of me, picking his feet up high and putting them down gently on the moist ground. He kept his head moving all the time, the eyes sweeping slowly from side to side, searching for danger. I tried doing the same, but soon I began to see a keeper behind every tree, so I gave it up.

Then a large patch of sky appeared ahead of us in the roof of the forest and I knew that this must be the clearing. Claud had told me that the clearing was the place where the young birds were introduced into the woods in early July, where they were fed and watered and guarded by the keepers, and where many of them stayed from force of habit until the shooting began.

"There's always plenty of pheasants in the clearing," he had said.

"Keepers too, I suppose."

"Yes, but there's thick bushes all around and that helps."

We were now advancing in a series of quick crouching spurts, running from tree to tree and stopping and waiting and listening and running on again, and then at last we were kneeling safely behind a big clump of alder right on the edge of the clearing and Claud was grinning and nudging me in the ribs and pointing through the branches at the pheasants.

The place was absolutely stiff with birds. There must have been two hundred of them at least strutting around among the tree-stumps.

"You see what I mean?" Claud whispered.

It was an astonishing sight, a sort of poacher's dream come true. And how close they were! Some of them were not more than ten paces from where we knelt. The hens were plump and creamy-brown and they were so fat their breast-feathers almost brushed the ground as they walked. The cocks were slim and beautiful, with long tails and brilliant red patches around the eyes, like scarlet spectacles. I glanced at Claud. His big ox-like face was transfixed in ecstasy. The mouth was slightly open and the eyes had a kind of glazy look about them as they stared at the pheasants.

I believe that all poachers react in roughly the same way as this on sighting game. They are like women who sight large emeralds in a jeweller's window, the only difference being that the women are less dignified in the methods they employ later on to acquire the loot. Poacher's arse is nothing to the punishment that a female is willing to endure.

"Ah-ha," Claud said softly. "You see the keeper?"

"Where?"

"Over the other side, by that big tree. Look carefully."

"My God!"

"It's all right. He can't see *us*."

We crouched close to the ground, watching the keeper. He was a smallish man with a cap on his head and a gun under his arm. He never moved. He was like a little post standing there.

"Let's go," I whispered.

The keeper's face was shadowed by the peak of his cap, but it seemed to me that he was looking directly at us.

"I'm not staying here," I said.

"Hush," Claud said.

Slowly, never taking his eyes from the keeper, he reached into his pocket and brought out a single raisin. He placed it in the palm of his right hand, and then quickly, with a little flick of the wrist, he threw the raisin high into the air. I watched it as it went sailing over the bushes and I saw it land within a yard or so of two henbirds standing together beside an old tree-stump. Both birds turned their heads sharply at the drop of the raisin. Then one of them hopped over and made a quick peck at the ground and that must have been it.

I glanced up at the keeper. He hadn't moved.

Claud threw a second raisin into the clearing; then a third, and a fourth, and a fifth.

At this point, I saw the keeper turn away his head in order to survey the wood behind him.

Quick as a flash, Claud pulled the paper bag out of his pocket and tipped a huge pile of raisins into the cup of his right hand.

"Stop," I said.

But with a great sweep of the arm he flung the whole handful high over the bushes into the clearing.

They fell with a soft little patter, like raindrops on dry leaves, and every single pheasant in the place must either have seen them coming or heard them fall. There was a flurry of wings and a rush to find the treasure.

The keeper's head flicked round as though there were a spring inside his neck. The birds were all pecking away madly at the raisins. The keeper took two quick paces forward and for a moment I thought he was going in to investigate. But then he stopped, and his face came up and his eyes began travelling slowly around the perimeter of the clearing.

"Follow me," Claud whispered. "And *keep down.*" He started crawling away swiftly on all fours, like some kind of a monkey.

I went after him. He had his nose close to the ground and his huge tight buttocks were winking at the sky and it was easy to see now how poacher's arse had come to be an occupational disease among the fraternity.

We went along like this for about a hundred yards.

"Now run," Claud said.

We got to our feet and ran, and a few minutes later we emerged through the hedge into the lovely open safety of the lane.

"It went marvellous," Claud said, breathing heavily. "Didn't it go absolutely marvellous?" The big face was scarlet and glowing with triumph.

"It was a mess," I said.

"What!" he cried.

"Of course it was. We can't possibly go back now. That keeper knows there was someone there."

"He knows nothing," Claud said. "In another five minutes it'll be pitch dark inside the wood and he'll be sloping off home to his supper."

"I think I'll join him."

"You're a great poacher," Claud said. He sat down on the grassy bank under the hedge and lit a cigarette.

The sun had set now and the sky was a pale smoke blue,

faintly glazed with yellow. In the wood behind us the shadows and the spaces in between the trees were turning from
grey to black.

"How long does a sleeping-pill take to work?" Claud
asked.

"Look out," I said. "There's someone coming."

The man had appeared suddenly and silently out of the
dusk and he was only thirty yards away when I saw him.

"Another bloody keeper," Claud said.

We both looked at the keeper as he came down the lane
toward us. He had a shotgun under his arm and there was
a black Labrador walking at his heels. He stopped when he
was a few paces away and the dog stopped with him and
stayed behind him, watching us through the keeper's
legs.

"Good evening," Claud said, nice and friendly.

This one was a tall bony man about forty with a swift
eye and a hard cheek and hard dangerous hands.

"I know you," he said softly, coming closer. "I know the
both of you."

Claud didn't answer this.

"You're from the fillin'-station. Right?"

His lips were thin and dry, with some sort of a brownish crust over them.

"You're Cubbage and Hawes and you're from the fillin'-
station on the main road. Right?"

"What are we playing?" Claud said. "Twenty Questions?"

The keeper spat out a big gob of spit and I saw it go
floating through the air and land with a plop on a patch of

dry dust six inches from Claud's feet. It looked like a little baby oyster lying there.

"Beat it," the man said. "Go on. Get out."

Claud sat on the bank smoking his cigarette and looking at the gob of spit.

"Go on," the man said. "Get out."

When he spoke, the upper lip lifted above the gum and I could see a row of small discoloured teeth, one of them black, the others quince and ochre.

"This happens to be a public highway," Claud said. "Kindly do not molest us."

The keeper shifted the gun from his left arm to his right.

"You're loiterin'," he said, "with intent to commit a felony. I could run you in for that."

"No you couldn't," Claud said.

All this made me rather nervous.

"I've had my eye on you for some time," the keeper said, looking at Claud.

"It's getting late," I said. "Shall we stroll on?"

Claud flipped away his cigarette and got slowly to his feet. "All right," he said. "Let's go."

We wandered off down the lane the way we had come, leaving the keeper standing there, and soon the man was out of sight in the half-darkness behind us.

"That's the head keeper," Claud said. "His name is Rabbetts."

"Let's get the hell out," I said.

"Come in here," Claud said.

There was a gate on our left leading into a field and we climbed over it and sat down behind the hedge.

"Mr. Rabbetts is also due for his supper," Claud said. "You mustn't worry about him."

We sat quietly behind the hedge waiting for the keeper to walk past us on his way home. A few stars were showing and a bright three-quarter moon was coming up over the hills behind us in the east.

"Here he is," Claud whispered. "Don't move."

The keeper came loping softly up the lane with the dog padding quick and soft-footed at his heels, and we watched them through the hedge as they went by.

"He won't be coming back tonight," Claud said.

"How do you know that?"

"A keeper never waits for you in the wood if he knows where you live. He goes to your house and hides outside and watches for you to come back."

"That's worse."

"No, it isn't, not if you dump the loot somewhere else before you go home. He can't touch you then."

"What about the other one, the one in the clearing?"

"He's gone too."

"You can't be sure of that."

"I've been studying these bastards for months, Gordon, honest I have. I know all their habits. There's no danger."

Reluctantly I followed him back into the wood. It was pitch dark in there now and very silent, and as we moved cautiously forward the noise of our footsteps seemed to go echoing around the walls of the forest as though we were walking in a cathedral.

"Here's where we threw the raisins," Claud said.

I peered through the bushes.

The clearing lay dim and milky in the moonlight.

"You're quite sure the keeper's gone?"

"I *know* he's gone."

I could just see Claud's face under the peak of his cap, the pale lips, the soft pale cheeks, and the large eyes with a little spark of excitement dancing slowly in each.

"Are they roosting?"

"Yes."

"Whereabouts?"

"All around. They don't go far."

"What do we do next?"

"We stay here and wait. I brought you a light," he added, and he handed me one of those small pocket flashlights shaped like a fountain-pen. "You may need it."

I was beginning to feel better. "Shall we see if we can spot some of them sitting in the trees?" I said.

"No."

"I should like to see how they look when they're roosting."

"This isn't a nature-study," Claud said. "Please be quiet."

We stood there for a long time waiting for something to happen.

"I've just had a nasty thought," I said. "If a bird can keep its balance on a branch when it's asleep, then surely there isn't any reason why the pills should make it fall down."

Claud looked at me quick.

"After all," I said, "it's not dead. It's still only sleeping."

"It's doped," Claud said.

"But that's just a *deeper* sort of sleep. Why should we

expect it to fall down just because it's in a *deeper* sleep?"

There was a gloomy silence.

"We should've tried it with chickens," Claud said. "My dad would've done that."

"Your dad was a genius," I said.

At that moment there came a soft thump from the wood behind us.

"Hey!"

"Ssshh!"

We stood listening.

Thump.

"There's another!"

It was a deep muffled sound as though a bag of sand had been dropped from about shoulder height.

Thump!

"They're pheasants!" I cried.

"Wait!"

"I'm sure they're pheasants!"

Thump! Thump!

"You're right!"

We ran back into the wood.

"Where were they?"

"Over here! Two of them were over here!"

"I thought they were this way."

"Keep looking!" Claud shouted. "They can't be far."

We searched for about a minute.

"Here's one!" he called.

When I got to him he was holding a magnificent cock-bird in both hands. We examined it closely with out flash-lights.

"It's doped to the gills," Claud said. "It's still alive, I can feel its heart, but it's doped to the bloody gills."

Thump!

"There's another!"

Thump! Thump!

"Two more!"

Thump!

Thump! Thump! Thump!

"Jesus Christ!"

Thump! Thump! Thump! Thump!

Thump! Thump!

All around us the pheasants were starting to rain down out of the trees. We began rushing around madly in the dark, sweeping the ground with our flashlights.

Thump! Thump! Thump! This lot fell almost on top of me. I was right under the tree as they came down and I found all three of them immediately—two cocks and a hen. They were limp and warm, the feathers wonderfully soft in the hand.

"Where shall I put them?" I called out. I was holding them by the legs.

"Lay them here, Gordon! Just pile them up here where it's light!"

Claud was standing on the edge of the clearing with the moonlight streaming down all over him and a great bunch of pheasants in each hand. His face was bright, his eyes big and bright and wonderful, and he was staring around him like a child who has just discovered that the whole world is made of chocolate.

Thump!

Thump! Thump!

"I don't like it," I said. "It's too many."

"It's beautiful!" he cried and he dumped the birds he was carrying and ran off to look for more.

Thump! Thump! Thump! Thump! Thump!

It was easy to find them now. There were one or two lying under every tree. I quickly collected six more, three in each hand, and ran back and dumped them with the others. Then six more. Then six more after that.

And still they kept falling.

Claud was in a whirl of ecstasy now, dashing about like a mad ghost under the trees. I could see the beam of his flashlight waving around in the dark and each time he found a bird he gave a little yelp of triumph.

Thump! Thump! Thump!

"That bugger Hazel ought to hear this!" he called out.

"Don't shout," I said. "It frightens me."

"What's that?"

"Don't *shout*. There might be keepers."

"Screw the keepers!" he cried. "They're all eating!"

For three or four minutes, the pheasants kept on falling. Then suddenly they stopped.

"Keep searching!" Claud shouted. "There's plenty more on the ground!"

"Don't you think we ought to get out while the going's good?"

"No," he said.

We went on searching. Between us we looked under every tree within a hundred yards of the clearing, north, south, east, and west, and I think we found most of them in the end. At the collecting-point there was a pile of pheasants as big as a bonfire.

"It's a miracle," Claud was saying. "It's a bloody miracle." He was staring at them in a kind of trance.

"We'd better just take half a dozen each and get out quick," I said.

"I would like to count them, Gordon."

"There's no time for that."

"I must count them."

"No," I said. "Come on."

"One . . .

"Two . . .

"Three . . .

"Four . . ."

He began counting them very carefully, picking up each bird in turn and laying it carefully to one side. The moon was directly overhead now and the whole clearing was brilliantly illuminated.

"I'm not standing around here like this," I said. I walked back a few paces and hid myself in the shadows, waiting for him to finish.

"A hundred and seventeen . . . a hundred and eighteen . . . a hundred and nineteen . . . *a hundred and twenty!*" he cried. "*One hundred and twenty birds!* It's an all-time record!"

I didn't doubt it for a moment.

"The most my dad ever got in one night was fifteen and he was drunk for a week afterwards!"

"You're the champion of the world," I said. "Are you ready now?"

"One minute," he answered and he pulled up his sweater

and proceeded to unwind the two big white cotton sacks from around his belly. "Here's yours," he said, handing one of them to me. "Fill it up quick."

The light of the moon was so strong I could read the small print along the base of the sack. J. W. CRUMP, it said. KESTON FLOUR MILLS, LONDON S.W. 17.

"You don't think that bastard with the brown teeth is watching us this very moment from behind a tree?"

"There's no chance of that," Claud said. "He's down at the filling-station like I told you, waiting for us to come home."

We started loading the pheasants into the sacks. They were soft and floppy-necked and the skin underneath the feathers was still warm.

"There'll be a taxi waiting for us in the lane," Claud said.

"What?"

"I always go back in a taxi, Gordon, didn't you know that?"

I told him I didn't.

"A taxi is anonymous," Claud said. "Nobody knows who's inside a taxi except the driver. My dad taught me that."

"Which driver?"

"Charlie Kinch. He's only too glad to oblige."

We finished loading the pheasants and then we humped the sacks onto our shoulders and started staggering through the pitch-black wood toward the lane.

"I'm not walking all the way back to the village with this," I said. My sack had sixty birds inside it and it must have weighed a hundredweight and a half at least.

"Charlie's never let me down yet," Claud said.

We came to the margin of the wood and peered through the hedge into the lane. Claud said, "Charlie boy" very softly and the old man behind the wheel of the taxi not five yards away poked his head out into the moonlight and gave us a sly toothless grin. We slid through the hedge, dragging the sacks after us along the ground.

"Hullo!" Charlie said. "What's this?"

"It's cabbages," Claud told him. "Open the door."

Two minutes later we were safely inside the taxi, cruising slowly down the hill toward the village.

It was all over now bar the shouting. Claud was triumphant, bursting with pride and excitement, and he kept leaning forward and tapping Charlie Kinch on the shoulder and saying, "How about it, Charlie? How about this for a haul?" and Charlie kept glancing back popeyed at the huge bulging sacks lying on the floor between us and saying, "Jesus Christ, man, how did you do it?"

"There's six brace of them for you, Charlie," Claud said. And Charlie said, "I reckon pheasants is going to be a bit scarce up at Mr. Victor Hazel's opening-day shoot this year," and Claud said, "I imagine they are, Charlie, I imagine they are."

"What in God's name are you going to do with a hundred and twenty pheasants?" I asked.

"Put them in cold storage for the winter," Claud said. "Put them in with the dogmeat in the deep-freeze at the filling-station."

"Not tonight, I trust?"

"No, Gordon, not tonight. We leave them at Bessie's house tonight."

"Bessie who?"

"Bessie Organ."

"Bessie *Organ!*"

"Bessie always delivers my game, didn't you know that?"

"I don't know anything," I said. I was completely stunned. Mrs. Organ was the wife of the Reverend Jack Organ, the local vicar.

"Always choose a respectable woman to deliver your game," Claud announced. "That's correct, Charlie, isn't it?"

"Bessie's a right smart girl," Charlie said.

We were driving through the village now and the street-lamps were still on and the men were wandering home from the pubs. I saw Will Prattley letting himself in quietly by the side door of his fishmonger's shop and Mrs. Prattley's head was sticking out the window just above him, but he didn't know it.

"The vicar is very partial to roasted pheasant," Claud said.

"He hangs it eighteen days," Charlie said, "then he gives it a couple of good shakes and all the feathers drop off."

The taxi turned left and swung in through the gates of the vicarage. There were no lights on in the house and no-body met us. Claud and I dumped the pheasants in the coalshed at the rear, and then we said goodbye to Charlie Kinch and walked back in the moonlight to the filling-station, empty-handed. Whether or not Mr. Rabbetts was watching us as we went in, I do not know. We saw no sign of him.

"Here she comes," Claud said to me the next morning.

"Who?"

"Bessie—Bessie Organ." He spoke the name proudly and with a slight proprietary air, as though he were a general referring to his bravest officer.

I followed him outside.

"Down there," he said, pointing.

Far away down the road I could see a small female figure advancing toward us.

"What's she pushing?" I asked.

Claud gave me a sly look.

"There's only one safe way of delivering game," he announced, "and that's under a baby."

"Yes," I murmured, "yes, of course."

"That'll be young Christopher Organ in there, aged one and a half. He's a lovely child, Gordon."

I could just make out the small dot of a baby sitting high up in the pram, which had its hood folded down.

"There's sixty or seventy pheasants at least under that little nipper," Claud said happily. "You jus' imagine that."

"You can't put sixty or seventy pheasants in a pram."

"You can if it's got a good deep well underneath it, and if you take out the mattress and pack them in tight, right up to the top. All you need then is a sheet. You'll be surprised how little room a pheasant takes up when it's limp."

We stood beside the pumps waiting for Bessie Organ to

arrive. It was one of those warm windless September mornings with a darkening sky and a smell of thunder in the air.

"Right through the village bold as brass," Claud said. "Good old Bessie."

"She seems in rather a hurry to me."

Claud lit a new cigarette from the stub of the old one. "Bessie is never in a hurry," he said.

"She certainly isn't walking normal," I told him. "You look."

He squinted at her through the smoke of his cigarette. Then he took the cigarette out of his mouth and looked again.

"Well?" I said.

"She does seem to be going a tiny bit quick, doesn't she?" he said carefully.

"She's going damn quick."

There was a pause. Claud was beginning to stare very hard at the approaching woman.

"Perhaps she doesn't want to be caught in the rain, Gordon. I'll bet that's exactly what it is, she thinks it's going to rain and she don't want the baby to get wet."

"Why doesn't she put the hood up?"

He didn't answer this.

"She's *running!*" I cried. "Look!" Bessie had suddenly broken into a full sprint.

Claud stood very still, watching the woman; and in the silence that followed I fancied I could hear a baby screaming.

"What's up?"

He didn't answer.

"There's something wrong with that baby," I said. "Listen."

At this point, Bessie was about two hundred yards away from us but closing fast.

"Can you hear him now?" I said.

"Yes."

"He's yelling his head off."

The small shrill voice in the distance was growing louder every second, frantic, piercing, nonstop, almost hysterical.

"He's having a fit," Claud announced.

"I think he must be."

"That's why she's running, Gordon. She wants to get him in here quick and put him under a cold tap."

"I'm sure you're right," I said. "In fact I know you're right. Just listen to that noise."

"If it isn't a fit, you can bet your life it's something like it."

"I quite agree."

Claud shifted his feet uneasily on the gravel of the driveway. "There's a thousand and one different things keep happening every day to little babies like that," he said.

"Of course."

"I knew a baby once who caught his fingers in the spokes of the pram wheel. He lost the lot. It cut them clean off."

"Yes."

"Whatever it is," Claud said, "I wish to Christ she'd stop running."

A long truck loaded with bricks came up behind Bessie

and the driver slowed down and poked his head out the window to stare. Bessie ignored him and flew on, and she was so close now I could see her big red face with the mouth wide open, panting for breath. I noticed she was wearing white golves on her hands, very prim and dainty, and there was a funny little white hat to match perched right on the top of her head, like a mushroom.

Suddenly, out of the pram, straight up into the air, flew an enormous pheasant!

Claud let out a cry of horror.

The fool in the truck going along beside Bessie started roaring with laughter.

The pheasant flapped around drunkenly for a few seconds, then it lost height and landed in the grass by the side of the road.

A grocer's van came up behind the truck and began hooting to get by. Bessie kept on running.

Then—*whoosh!*—a second pheasant flew up out of the pram.

Then a third, and a fourth. Then a fifth.

"My God!" I said. "It's the pills! They're wearing off!"

Claud didn't say anything.

Bessie covered the last fifty yards at a tremendous pace, and she came swinging into the driveway of the filling-station with birds flying up out of the pram in all directions.

"What the hell's going on?" she cried.

"Go round the back!" I shouted. "Go round the back!"

But she pulled up sharp against the first pump in the line

and before we could reach her she had seized the screaming infant in her arms and dragged him clear.

"No! No!" Claud cried, racing toward her. "Don't lift
the baby! Put him back! Hold down the sheet!" But she
wasn't even listening, and with the weight of the child suddenly lifted away, a great cloud of pheasants rose up out of
the pram, fifty or sixty of them, at least, and the whole sky
above us was filled with huge brown birds clapping their
wings furiously to gain height.

Claud and I started running up and down the driveway
waving our arms to frighten them off the premises. "Go
away!" we shouted. "Shoo! Go away!" But they were too
dopey still to take any notice of us and within half a minute down they came again and settled themselves like a
swarm of locusts all over the front of my filling-station. The
place was covered with them. They sat wing to wing along
the edges of the roof and on the concrete canopy that came
out over the pumps, and a dozen at least were clinging to
the sill of the office window. Some had flown down onto
the rack that held the bottles of lubricating-oil, and others
were sliding about on the bonnets of my second-hand cars.
One cockbird with a fine tail was perched superbly on top
of a petrol pump, and quite a number, those that were too
drunk to stay aloft, simply squatted in the driveway at our
feet, fluffing their feathers and blinking their small eyes.

Across the road, a line of cars had already started forming behind the brick-lorry and the grocery-van, and
people were opening their doors and getting out and beginning to cross over to have a closer look. I glanced at my

watch. It was twenty to nine. Any moment now, I thought, a large black car is going to come streaking along the road from the direction of the village, and the car will be a Rolls, and the face behind the wheel will be the great glistening butcher's face of Mr. Victor Hazel, maker of sausages and pies.

"They near pecked him to pieces!" Bessie was shouting, clasping the screaming baby to her bosom.

"You go on home, Bessie," Claud said, white in the face.

"Lock up," I said. "Put out the sign. We've gone for the day."

THE GREAT SWITCHEROO

THERE were about forty people at Jerry and Samantha's cocktail-party that evening. It was the usual crowd, the usual discomfort, the usual appalling noise. People had to stand very close to one another and shout to make themselves heard. Many were grinning, showing capped white teeth. Most of them had a cigarette in the left hand, a drink in the right.

I moved away from my wife, Mary, and her group. I headed for the small bar in the far corner, and when I got there, I sat down on a bar-stool and faced the room. I did this so that I could look at the women. I settled back with my shoulders against the bar-rail, sipping my Scotch and examining the women one by one over the rim of my glass.

I was studying not their figures but their faces, and what interested me there was not so much the face itself but the big red mouth in the middle of it all. And even then, it wasn't the whole mouth but only the lower lip.

The lower lip, I had recently decided, was the great re-
vealer. It gave away more than the eyes. The eyes hid
their secrets. The lower lip hid very little. Take, for example, the lower lip of Jacinth Winkleman, who was
standing nearest to me. Notice the wrinkles on that lip,
how some were parallel and some radiated outward. No
two people have the same pattern of lip-wrinkles, and
come to think of it, you could catch a criminal that way
if you had his lip-print on file and he had taken a drink
at the scene of the crime. The lower lip is what you suck
and nibble when you're ruffled, and Martha Sullivan was
doing that right now as she watched from a distance her
fatuous husband slobbering over Judy Martinson. You
lick it when lecherous. I could see Ginny Lomax licking
hers with the tip of her tongue as she stood beside Ted
Dorling and gazed up into his face. It was a deliberate
lick, the tongue coming out slowly and making a slow
wet wipe along the entire length of the lower lip. I saw
Ted Dorling looking at Ginny's tongue, which was what
she wanted him to do.

It really does seem to be a fact, I told myself, as my
eyes wandered from lower lip to lower lip across the
room, that all the less attractive traits of the human animal, arrogance, rapacity, gluttony, lasciviousness, and the
rest of them, are clearly signalled in that little carapace
of scarlet skin. But you have to know the code. The
protuberant or bulging lower lip is supposed to signify
sensuality. But this is only half true in men and wholly
untrue in women. In women, it is the thin line you should
look for, the narrow blade with the sharply delineated

bottom edge. And in the nymphomaniac there is a tiny just visible crest of skin at the top centre of the lower lip.

Samantha, my hostess, had that.

Where was she now, Samantha?

Ah, there she was, taking an empty glass out of a guest's hand. Now she was heading my way to refill it.

"Hello, Vic," she said. "You all alone?"

She's a nympho-bird all right, I told myself. But a very rare example of the species, because she is entirely and utterly monogamous. She is a married monogamous nympho-bird who stays forever in her own nest.

She is also the fruitiest female I have ever set eyes upon in my whole life.

"Let me help you," I said, standing up and taking the glass from her hand. "What's wanted in here?"

"Vodka on the rocks," she said. "Thanks, Vic." She laid a lovely long white arm upon the top of the bar and she leaned forward so that her bosom rested on the bar-rail, squashing upward. "Oops," I said, pouring vodka outside the glass.

Samantha looked at me with huge brown eyes but said nothing.

"I'll wipe it up," I said.

She took the refilled glass from me and walked away. I watched her go. She was wearing black pants. They were so tight around the buttocks that the smallest mole or pimple would have shown through the cloth. But Samantha Rainbow had not a blemish on her bottom. I caught myself licking my own lower lip. That's right, I thought. I want her. I lust after that woman. But it's too risky to try. It would be suicide to make a pass at a girl like that. First of all, she lives next door, which is too close. Secondly, as I have already said, she is monogamous. Thirdly, she is thick as a thief with Mary, my own wife. They exchange dark female secrets. Fourthly, her husband, Jerry, is my very old and good friend, and not even I, Victor Hammond, though I am churning with lust, would dream of trying to seduce the wife of a man who is my very old and trusty friend.

Unless . . .

It was at this point, as I sat on the bar-stool letching over Samantha Rainbow, that an interesting idea began to filter quietly into the centre of my brain. I remained still, allowing the idea to expand. I watched Samantha across the room, and began fitting her into the framework of the idea. Oh, Samantha, my gorgeous and juicy little jewel, I shall have you yet.

But could anybody seriously hope to get away with a crazy lark like that?

No, not in a million nights.

One couldn't even *try* it unless Jerry agreed. So why think about it?

Samantha was standing about six yards away, talking to Gilbert Mackesy. The fingers of her right hand were curled around a tall glass. The fingers were long and almost certainly dexterous.

Assuming, just for the fun of it, that Jerry did agree, then even so, there would still be gigantic snags along the way. There was, for example, the little matter of physical characteristics. I had seen Jerry many times at the club having a shower after tennis, but right now I couldn't for the life of me recall the necessary details. It wasn't the sort of thing one noticed very much. Usually, one didn't even look.

Anyway, it would be madness to put the suggestion to Jerry point-blank. I didn't know him *that* well. He might be horrified. He might even turn nasty. There could be an ugly scene. I must test him out, therefore, in some subtle fashion.

"You know something?" I said to Jerry about an hour later when we were sitting together on the sofa having a last drink. The guests were drifting away and Samantha was by the door saying goodbye to them. My own wife, Mary, was out on the terrace talking to Bob Swain. I could see her through the open french windows. "You know something funny?" I said to Jerry as we sat together on the sofa.

"What's funny?" Jerry asked me.

"A fellow I had lunch with today told me a fantastic story. Quite unbelievable."

"What story?" Jerry said. The whisky had begun to make him sleepy.

"This man, the one I had lunch with, had a terrific letch after the wife of his friend who lived nearby. And his friend had an equally big letch after the wife of the man I had lunch with. Do you see what I mean?"

"You mean two fellers who lived close to each other both fancied each other's wives."

"Precisely," I said.

"Then there was no problem," Jerry said.

"There was a very big problem," I said. "The wives were both very faithful and honourable women."

"Samantha's the same," Jerry said. "She wouldn't look at another man."

"Nor would Mary," I said. "She's a fine girl."

Jerry emptied his glass and set it down carefully on the sofa-table. "So what happened in your story?" he said. "It sounds dirty."

"What happened," I said, "was that these two randy sods cooked up a plan which made it possible for each of them to ravish the other's wife without the wives ever knowing it. If you can believe such a thing."

"With chloroform?" Jerry said.

"Not at all. They were fully conscious."

"Impossible," Jerry said. "Someone's been pulling your leg."

"I don't think so," I said. "From the way this man told it to me, with all the little details and everything, I don't think he was making it up. In fact, I'm sure he wasn't. And listen, they didn't do it just once, either. They've been doing it every two or three weeks for months!"

"And the wives don't know?"

"They haven't a clue."

"I've got to hear this," Jerry said. "Let's get another drink first."

We crossed to the bar and refilled our glasses, then returned to the sofa.

"You must remember," I said, "that there had to be a tremendous lot of preparation and rehearsal beforehand. And many intimate details had to be exchanged to give the plan a chance of working. But the essential part of the scheme was simple:

"They fixed a night, call it Saturday. On that night the husbands and wives were to go up to bed as usual, at say eleven or eleven thirty.

"From then on, normal routine would be preserved. A little reading, perhaps, a little talking, then out with the lights.

"After lights out, the husbands would at once roll over and pretend to go to sleep. This was to discourage their wives from getting fresh, which at this stage must on no account be permitted. So the wives went to sleep. But the husbands stayed awake. So far so good.

"Then at precisely one a.m., by which time the wives would be in a good deep sleep, each husband would slide quietly out of bed, put on a pair of bedroom slippers and creep downstairs in his pyjamas. He would open the front door and go out into the night, taking care not to close the door behind him.

"They lived," I went on, "more or less across the street from one another. It was a quiet suburban neighbourhood and there was seldom anyone about at that hour. So these two furtive pyjama-clad figures would pass each other as they crossed the street, each one heading for another house, another bed, another woman."

Jerry was listening to me carefully. His eyes were a little glazed from drink, but he was listening to every word.

"The next part," I said, "had been prepared very thoroughly by both men. Each knew the inside of his friend's house almost as well as he knew his own. He knew how to find his way in the dark both downstairs and up without knocking over the furniture. He knew his way to the stairs and exactly how many steps there were to the top and which of them creaked and which didn't. He knew on which side of the bed the woman upstairs was sleeping.

"Each took off his slippers and left them in the hall, then up the stairs he crept in his bare feet and pyjamas. This part of it, according to my friend, was rather exciting. He was in a dark silent house that wasn't his own, and on his way to the main bedroom he had to pass no less than three children's bedrooms where the doors were always left slightly open."

"Children!" Jerry cried. "My God, what if one of them had woken up and said, 'Daddy, is that you?' "

"That was all taken care of," I said. "Emergency procedure would then come into effect immediately. Also if the wife, just as he was creeping into her room, woke up and said, 'Darling, what's wrong? Why are you wandering about?'; then again, emergency procedure."

"What emergency procedure?" Jerry said.

"Simple," I answered. "The man would immediately dash downstairs and out the front door and across to his own house and ring the bell. This was a signal for the other character, no matter what he was doing at the time, also to rush downstairs at full speed and open the door and let the other fellow in while he went out. This would get them both back quickly to their proper houses."

"With egg all over their faces," Jerry said.

"Not at all," I said.

"That doorbell would have woken the whole house," Jerry said.

"Of course," I said. "And the husband, returning upstairs in his pyjamas, would merely say, 'I went to see who the hell was ringing the bell at this ungodly hour. Couldn't find anyone. It must have been a drunk.' "

"What about the other guy?" Jerry asked. "How does he explain why he rushed downstairs when his wife or child spoke to him?"

"He would say, 'I heard someone prowling about outside, so I rushed down to get him, but he escaped.' 'Did you actually see him?' his wife would ask anxiously. 'Of course I saw him,' the husband would answer. 'He ran off down the street. He was too damn fast for me.' Whereupon the husband would be warmly congratulated for his bravery."

"Okay," Jerry said. "That's the easy part. Everything so far is just a matter of good planning and good timing. But what happens when these two horny characters actually climb into bed with each other's wives?"

"They go right to it," I said.

"The wives are sleeping," Jerry said.

"I know," I said. "So they proceed immediately with some very gentle but very skilful love-play, and by the time these dames are fully awake, they're as randy as rattlesnakes."

"No talking, I presume," Jerry said.

"Not a word."

"Okay, so the wives are awake," Jerry said. "And their hands get to work. So just for a start, what about the

574 The Roald Dahl Omnibus

simple question of body size? What about the difference between the new man and the husband? What about tallness and shortness and fatness and thinness? You're not telling me these men were physically identical?"

"Not identical, obviously," I said. "But they were more or less similar in build and height. That was essential. They were both clean-shaven and had roughly the same amount of hair on their heads. That sort of similarity is commonplace. Look at you and me, for instance. We're roughly the same height and build, aren't we?"

"Are we?" Jerry said.

"How tall are you?" I said.

"Six foot exactly."

"I'm five eleven," I said. "One inch difference. What do you weigh?"

"One hundred and eighty-seven."

"I'm a hundred and eighty-four," I said. "What's three pounds among friends?"

There was a pause. Jerry was looking out through the french windows onto the terrace where my wife, Mary, was standing. Mary was still talking to Bob Swain and the evening sun was shining in her hair. She was a dark pretty girl with a bosom. I watched Jerry. I saw his tongue come out and go sliding along the surface of his lower lip.

"I guess you're right," Jerry said, still looking at Mary. "I guess we are about the same size, you and me." When he turned back and faced me again, there was a little red rose high up on each cheek. "Go on about these two men," he said. "What about some of the other differences?"

"You mean faces?" I said. "No one's going to see faces in the dark."

"I'm not talking about faces," Jerry said.

"What are you talking about, then?"

"I'm talking about their cocks," Jerry said. "That's what it's all about, isn't it? And you're not going to tell me . . ."

"Oh yes, I am," I said. "Just so long as both men were either circumcised or uncircumcised, then there was really no problem."

"Are you seriously suggesting that all men have the same size in cocks?" Jerry said. "Because they don't."

"I know they don't," I said.

"Some are enormous," Jerry said. "And some are titchy."

"There are always exceptions," I told him. "But you'd be surprised at the number of men whose measurements are virtually the same, give or take a centimetre. According to my friend, ninety percent are normal. Only ten percent are notably large or small."

"I don't believe that," Jerry said.

"Check on it sometime," I said. "Ask some well-travelled girl."

Jerry took a long slow sip of his whisky, and his eyes over the top of his glass were looking again at Mary on the terrace. "What about the rest of it?" he said.

"No problem," I said.

"No problem, my arse," he said. "Shall I tell you why this is a phony story?"

"Go ahead."

"Everybody knows that a wife and husband who have been married for some years develop a kind of routine. It's inevitable. My God, a new operator would be spotted instantly. You know damn well he would. You can't suddenly wade in with a totally different style and expect the woman not to notice it, and I don't care how randy she was. She'd smell a rat in the first minute!"

"A routine can be duplicated," I said. "Just so long as every detail of that routine is described beforehand."

"A bit personal, that," Jerry said.

"The whole thing's personal," I said. "So each man tells his story. He tells precisely what he usually does. He tells everything. The lot. The works. The whole routine from beginning to end."

"Jesus," Jerry said.

"Each of these men," I said, "had to learn a new part. He had, in effect, to become an actor. He was impersonating another character."

"Not so easy, that," Jerry said.

"No problem at all, according to my friend. The only thing one had to watch out for was not to get carried away and start improvising. One had to follow the stage directions very carefully and stick to them."

Jerry took another pull at his drink. He also took another look at Mary on the terrace. Then he leaned back against the sofa, glass in hand.

"These two characters," he said. "You mean they actually pulled it off?"

"I'm damn sure they did," I said. "They're still doing it. About once every three weeks."

"Fantastic story," Jerry said. "And a damn crazy dangerous thing to do. Just imagine the sort of hell that would break loose if you were caught. Instant divorce. Two divorces, in fact. One on each side of the street. Not worth it."

"Takes a lot of guts," I said.

"The party's breaking up," Jerry said. "They're all going home with their goddamn wives."

I didn't say any more after that. We sat there for a couple of minutes sipping our drinks while the guests began drifting toward the hall.

"Did he say it was fun, this friend of yours?" Jerry asked suddenly.

"He said it was a gas," I answered. "He said all the normal pleasures got intensified one hundred percent because of the risk. He swore it was the greatest way of doing it in the world, impersonating the husband and the wife not knowing it."

At that point, Mary came in through the french windows with Bob Swain. She had an empty glass in one hand and a flame-coloured azalea in the other. She had picked the azalea on the terrace.

"I've been watching you," she said, pointing the flower at me like a pistol. "You've hardly stopped talking for the last ten minutes. What's he been telling you, Jerry?"

"A dirty story," Jerry said, grinning.

"He does that when he drinks," Mary said.

"Good story," Jerry said. "But totally impossible. Get him to tell it to you sometime."

"I don't like dirty stories," Mary said. "Come along, Vic. It's time we went."

"Don't go yet," Jerry said, fixing his eyes upon her splendid bosom. "Have another drink."

"No thanks," she said. "The children'll be screaming for their supper. I've had a lovely time."

"Aren't you going to kiss me goodnight?" Jerry said, getting up from the sofa. He went for her mouth, but she turned her head quickly and he caught only the edge of her cheek.

"Go away, Jerry," she said. "You're drunk."

"Not drunk," Jerry said. "Just lecherous."

"Don't you get lecherous with me, my boy," Mary said sharply. "I hate that sort of talk." She marched away across the room, carrying her bosom before her like a battering-ram.

"So long, Jerry," I said. "Fine party."

Mary, full of dark looks, was waiting for me in the hall. Samantha was there, too, saying goodbye to the last guests —Samantha with her dexterous fingers and her smooth skin and her smooth, dangerous thighs. "Cheer up, Vic," she said to me, her white teeth showing. She looked like the creation, the beginning of the world, the first morning. "Goodnight, Vic darling," she said, stirring her fingers in my vitals.

I followed Mary out of the house. "You feeling all right?" she asked.

"Yes," I said. "Why not?"

"The amount you drink is enough to make anyone feel ill," she said.

There was a scrubby old hedge dividing our place from Jerry's and there was a gap in it we always used. Mary and I walked through the gap in silence. We went into the house and she cooked up a big pile of scrambled eggs and bacon, and we ate it with the children.

After the meal, I wandered outside. The summer evening was clear and cool and because I had nothing else to do I decided to mow the grass in the front garden. I got the mower out of the shed and started it up. Then I began the old routine of marching back and forth behind it. I like mowing grass. It is a soothing operation, and on our front lawn I could always look at Samantha's house going one way and think about her going the other.

I had been at it for about ten minutes when Jerry came strolling through the gap in the hedge. He was smoking a pipe and had his hands in his pockets and he stood on the edge of the grass, watching me. I pulled up in front of him, but left the motor ticking over.

"Hi, sport," he said. "How's everything?"

"I'm in the doghouse," I said. "So are you."

"Your little wife," he said, "is just too goddamn prim and prissy to be true."

"Oh, I know that."

"She rebuked me in my own house," Jerry said.

"Not very much."

"It was enough," he said, smiling slightly.

"Enough for what?"

"Enough to make me want to get a little bit of my own back on her. So what would you think if I suggested you and I have a go at that thing your friend told you about at lunch?"

When he said this, I felt such a surge of excitement my stomach nearly jumped out of my mouth. I gripped the handles of the mower and started revving the engine.

"Have I said the wrong thing?" Jerry asked.

I didn't answer.

"Listen," he said. "If you think it's a lousy idea, let's just forget I ever mentioned it. You're not mad at me, are you?"

"I'm not mad at you, Jerry," I said. "It's just that it never entered my head that *we* should do it."

"It entered mine," he said. "The set-up is perfect. We wouldn't even have to cross the street." His face had gone suddenly bright and his eyes were shining like two stars. "So what do you say, Vic?"

"I'm thinking," I said.

"May be you don't fancy Samantha."

"I don't honestly know," I said.

"She's lots of fun," Jerry said. "I guarantee that."

At this point, I saw Mary come out onto the front porch. "There's Mary," I said. "She's looking for the children. We'll talk some more tomorrow."

"Then it's a deal?"

"It could be, Jerry. But only on condition we don't

rush it. I want to be dead sure everything is right before we start. Damn it all, this is a whole brand-new can of beans!"

"No, it's not!" he said. "Your friend said it was a gas. He said it was easy."

"Ah, yes," I said. "My friend. Of course. But each case is different." I opened the throttle on the mower and went whirring away across the lawn. When I got to the far side and turned around, Jerry was already through the gap in the hedge and walking up to his front door.

The next couple of weeks was a period of high conspiracy for Jerry and me. We held secret meetings in bars and restaurants to discuss strategy, and sometimes he dropped into my office after work and we had a planning session behind the closed door. Whenever a doubtful point arose, Jerry would always say, "How did your friend do it?" And I would play for time and say, "I'll call him up and ask him about that one."

After many conferences and much talk, we agreed upon the following main points:

1. That D-Day should be a Saturday.

2. That on D-Day evening we should take our wives out to a good dinner, the four of us together.

3. That Jerry and I should leave our houses and cross over through the gap in the hedge at precisely one a.m. Sunday morning.

4. That instead of lying in bed in the dark until one a.m. came along, we should both, as soon as our wives were asleep, go quietly downstairs to the kitchen and drink coffee.

5. That we should use the front doorbell idea if an emergency arose.

6. That the return cross-over time was fixed for two a.m.

7. That while in the wrong bed, questions (if any) from the woman must be answered by an "Uh-uh" sounded with the lips closed tight.

8. That I myself must immediately give up cigarettes and take to a pipe so that I would "smell" the same as Jerry.

9. That we should at once start using the same brand of hair oil and after-shave lotion.

10. That as both of us normally wore our wrist-watches in bed, and they were much the same shape, it was decided not to exchange. Neither of us wore rings.

11. That each man must have something unusual about him that the woman would identify positively with her own husband. We therefore invented what became known as "The Sticking-Plaster Ploy." It worked like this: On D-Day evening, when the couples arrived back in their own homes immediately after the dinner, each husband would make a point of going to the kitchen to cut himself a piece of cheese. At the same time, he would carefully stick a large bit of plaster over the tip of the fore-finger of his right hand. Having done this, he would hold up the finger and say to his wife, "I cut myself. It's nothing, but it was bleeding a bit." Thus, later on, when the men have switched beds, each woman will be made very much aware of the plaster-covered finger (the man would

see to that), and will associate it directly with her own husband. An important psychological ploy, this, calculated to dissipate any tiny suspicion that might enter the mind of either female.

So much for the basic plans. Next came what we referred to in our notes as "Familiarisation with the Layout." Jerry schooled me first. He gave me three hours' training in his own house one Sunday afternoon when his wife and children were out. I had never been into their bedroom before. On the dressing table were Samantha's perfumes, her brushes, and all her other little things. A pair of her stockings was draped over the back of a chair. Her nightdress, white and blue, was hanging behind the door leading to the bathroom.

"Okay," Jerry said. "It'll be pitch dark when you come in. Samantha sleeps on this side, so you must tiptoe around the end of the bed and slide in on the other side, over there. I'm going to blindfold you and let you practise."

At first, with the blindfold on, I wandered all over the room like a drunk. But after about an hour's work, I was able to negotiate the course pretty well. But before Jerry would finally pass me out, I had to go blindfolded all the way from the front door through the hall, up the stairs, past the children's rooms, into Samantha's room and finish up in exactly the right place. And I had to do it silently, like a thief. All this took three hours of hard work, but I got it in the end.

The following Sunday morning when Mary had taken

our children to church, I was able to give Jerry the same sort of work-out in my house. He learned the ropes faster than me, and within an hour he had passed the blindfold test without placing a foot wrong.

It was during this session that we decided to disconnect each woman's bedside lamp as we entered the bedroom. So Jerry practised finding the plug and pulling it out with his blindfold on, and the following weekend, I was able to do the same in Jerry's house.

Now came by far the most important part of our training. We called it "Spilling the Beans," and it was here that both of us had to describe in every detail the procedure we adopted when making love to our own wives. We agreed not to worry ourselves with any exotic variations that either of us might or might not occasionally practice. We were concerned only with teaching one another the most commonly used routine, the one least likely to arouse suspicion.

The session took place in my office at six o'clock on a Wednesday evening, after the staff had gone home. At first, we were both slightly embarrassed, and neither of us wanted to begin. So I got out the bottle of whisky, and after a couple of stiff drinks, we loosened up and the teach-in started. While Jerry talked I took notes, and vice versa. At the end of it all, it turned out that the only real difference between Jerry's routine and my own was one of tempo. But what a difference it was! He took things (if what he said was to be believed) in such a leisurely fashion and he prolonged the moments to such an extravagant degree that I wondered privately to myself whether his partner did not sometimes go to sleep in the middle of it all. My job, however, was not to criticise but to copy, and I said nothing.

Jerry was not so discreet. At the end of my personal description, he had the temerity to say, "Is that really what you do?"

"What do you mean?" I asked.

"I mean is it all over and done with as quickly as that?"

"Look," I said. "We aren't here to give each other lessons. We're here to learn the facts."

"I know that," he said. "But I'm going to feel a bit of an ass if I copy your style exactly. My God, you go through it like an express train whizzing through a country station!"

I stared at him, mouth open.

"Don't look so surprised," he said. "The way you told it to me, anyone would think . . ."

"Think what?" I said.

"Oh, forget it," he said.

"Thank you," I said. I was furious. There are two things in this world at which I happen to know I excel. One is driving an automobile and the other is you-know-what. So to have him sit there and tell me I didn't know how to behave with my own wife was a monstrous piece of effrontery. It was he who didn't know, not me. Poor Samantha. What she must have had to put up with over the years.

"I'm sorry I spoke," Jerry said. He poured more whisky into our glasses. "Here's to the great switcheroo!" he said. "When do we go?"

"Today is Wednesday," I said. "How about this coming Saturday?"

"Christ," Jerry said.

"We ought to do it while everything's still fresh in our minds," I said. "There's an awful lot to remember."

Jerry walked to the window and looked down at the traffic in the street below. "Okay," he said, turning around. "Saturday it shall be!" Then we drove home in our separate cars.

"Jerry and I thought we'd take you and Samantha out to dinner Saturday night," I said to Mary. We were in the kitchen and she was cooking hamburgers for the children.

She turned around and faced me, frying-pan in one hand, spoon in the other. Her blue eyes looked straight into mine. "My Lord, Vic," she said. "How nice. But what are we celebrating?"

I looked straight back at her and said, "I thought it would be a change to see some new faces. We're always meeting the same old bunch of people in the same old houses."

She took a step forward and kissed me on the cheek. "What a good man you are," she said. "I love you."

"Don't forget to phone the baby-sitter."

"No, I'll do it tonight," she said.

Thursday and Friday passed by very quickly, and suddenly it was Saturday. It was D-Day. I woke up feeling madly excited. After breakfast, I couldn't sit still, so I decided to go out and wash the car. I was in the middle of this when Jerry came strolling through the gap in the hedge, pipe in mouth.

"Hi, sport," he said. "This is the day."

"I know that," I said. I also had a pipe in my mouth. I was forcing myself to smoke it, but I had trouble keeping it alight, and the smoke burned my tongue.

"How're you feeling?" Jerry asked.

"Terrific," I said. "How about you?"

"I'm nervous," he said.

"Don't be nervous, Jerry."

"This is one hell of a thing we're trying to do," he said. "I hope we pull it off."

I went on polishing the windshield. I had never known Jerry to be nervous of anything before. It worried me a bit.

"I'm damn glad we're not the first people ever to try it," he said. "If no one had ever done it before, I don't think I'd risk it."

"I agree," I said.

"What stops me being too nervous," he said, "is the fact that your friend found it so fantastically easy."

"My friend said it was a cinch," I said. "But for Chrissake, Jerry, don't be nervous when the time comes. That would be disastrous."

"Don't worry," he said. "But Jesus, it's exciting, isn't it?"

"It's exciting all right," I said.

"Listen," he said. "We'd better go easy on the booze tonight."

"Good idea," I said. "See you at eight thirty."

At half past eight, Samantha, Jerry, Mary, and I drove in Jerry's car to Billy's Steak House. The restaurant, despite its name, was high-class and expensive, and the girls had put on long dresses for the occasion. Samantha was wearing something green that didn't start until it was halfway down her front, and I had never seen her looking lovelier. There were candles on our table. Samantha was seated opposite me and whenever she leaned forward with her face close to the flame, I could see that tiny crest of skin at the top centre of her lower lip. "Now," she said as she accepted a menu from the waiter, "I wonder what I'm going to have tonight."

Ho-ho-ho, I thought, that's a good question.

Everything went fine in the restaurant and the girls enjoyed themselves. When we arrived back at Jerry's house, it was eleven forty-five, and Samantha said, "Come in and have a nightcap."

"Thanks," I said, "but it's a bit late. And the baby-sitter has to be driven home." So Mary and I walked across to our house, and *now*, I told myself as I entered the front door, *from now on* the count-down begins. I must keep a clear head and forget nothing.

While Mary was paying the baby-sitter, I went to the fridge and found a piece of Canadian cheddar. I took a knife from the drawer and a strip of plaster from the cupboard. I stuck the plaster around the tip of the forefinger of my right hand and waited for Mary to turn around.

"I cut myself," I said holding up the finger for her to see. "It's nothing, but it was bleeding a bit."

"I'd have thought you'd had enough to eat for the evening," was all she said. But the plaster registered on her mind and my first little job had been done.

I drove the baby-sitter home and by the time I got back up to the bedroom it was round about midnight and Mary was already half asleep with her light out. I switched out the light on my side of the bed and went into the bathroom to undress. I pottered about in there for ten minutes or so and when I came out, Mary, as I had hoped, was well and truly sleeping. There seemed no point in getting into bed beside her. So I simply pulled back the covers a bit on my side to make it easier for Jerry, then with my slippers on, I went downstairs to the kitchen and switched on the electric kettle. It was now twelve seventeen. Forty-three minutes to go.

At twelve thirty-five, I went upstairs to check on Mary and the kids. Everyone was sound asleep.

At twelve fifty-five, five minutes before zero hour, I went up again for a final check. I went right up close to Mary's bed and whispered her name. There was no answer. Good. *That's it! Let's go!*

I put a brown raincoat over my pyjamas. I switched off the kitchen light so that the whole house was in darkness. I put the front door lock on the latch. And then, feeling an enormous sense of exhilaration. I stepped silently out into the night.

There were no lamps on our street to lighten the dark-

590   *The Roald Dahl Omnibus*

ness. There was no moon or even a star to be seen. It was a black black night, but the air was warm and there was a little breeze blowing from somewhere.

I headed for the gap in the hedge. When I got very close, I was able to make out the hedge itself and find the gap. I stopped there, waiting. Then I heard Jerry's footsteps coming toward me.

"Hi, sport," he whispered. "Everything okay?"

"All ready for you," I whispered back.

He moved on. I heard his slippered feet padding softly over the grass as he went toward my house. I went toward his.

I opened Jerry's front door. It was even darker inside than out. I closed the door carefully. I took off my raincoat and hung it on the door knob. I removed my slippers and placed them against the wall by the door. I literally could not see my hands before my face. Everything had to be done by touch.

My goodness, I was glad Jerry had made me practise blindfolded for so long. It wasn't my feet that guided me now but my fingers. The fingers of one hand or another were never for a moment out of contact with something, a wall, the banister, a piece of furniture, a window-curtain. And I knew or thought I knew exactly where I was all the time. But it was an awesome eerie feeling trespassing on tiptoe through someone else's house in the middle of the night. As I fingered my way up the stairs, I found myself thinking of the burglars who had broken into our front room last winter and stolen the television set. When the police came next morning, I pointed out to them an enormous turd lying in the snow outside the garage. "They nearly always do that," one of the cops told me. "They can't help it. They're scared."

I reached the top of the stairs. I crossed the landing with my right fingertips touching the wall all the time. I started down the corridor, but paused when my hand found the door of the first children's-room. The door was slightly open. I listened. I could hear young Robert Rainbow, aged eight, breathing evenly inside. I moved on. I found the door to the second children's-bedroom. This one belonged to Billy, aged six, and Amanda, three. I stood listening. All was well.

The main bedroom was at the end of the corridor, about four yards on. I reached the door. Jerry had left it open, as planned. I went in. I stood absolutely still just inside the door, listening for any sign that Samantha might be awake. All was quiet. I felt my way around the wall until I reached Samantha's side of the bed. Immediately, I knelt on the floor and found the plug connecting her bedside lamp. I drew it from its socket and laid it on the carpet. Good. Much safer now. I stood up. I couldn't see Samantha, and at first I couldn't hear anything either. I bent low over the bed. Ah yes, I could hear her breathing. Suddenly I caught a whiff of the heavy musky perfume she had been using that evening, and I felt the blood rushing to my groin. Quickly I tiptoed around the big bed, keeping two fingers in gentle contact with the edge of the bed the whole way.

All I had to do now was get in. I did so, but as I put my weight upon the mattress, the creaking of the springs underneath sounded as though someone was firing a rifle in the room. I lay motionless, holding my breath. I could hear my heart thumping away like an engine in my throat. Samantha was facing away from me. She didn't move. I pulled the covers up over my chest and turned toward her. A female glow came out of her to me. Here we go, then! *Now!*

I slid a hand over and touched her body. Her nightdress was warm and silky. I rested the hand gently on her hip. Still she didn't move. I waited a minute or so, then I allowed the hand that lay upon the hip to steal onward and go exploring. Slowly, deliberately, and very accurately, my fingers began the process of setting her on fire.

She stirred. She turned onto her back. Then she murmured sleepily, "Oh, dear . . . Oh, my goodness me . . . Good heavens, darling?"

I, of course, said nothing. I just kept on with the job.

A couple of minutes went by.

She was lying quite still.

Another minute passed. Then another. She didn't move a muscle.

I began to wonder how much longer it would be before she caught alight.

I persevered.

But why the silence? Why this absolute and total immobility, this frozen posture?

Suddenly it came to me. I had forgotten completely about Jerry! I was so hotted up, I had forgotten all about his own personal routine! I was doing it my way, not his! His way was far more complex than mine. It was ridiculously elaborate. It was quite unnecessary. But it was what she was used to. And now she was noticing the difference and trying to figure out what on earth was going on.

But it was too late to change direction now. I must keep going.

I kept going. The woman beside me was like a coiled spring lying there. I could feel the tension under her skin. I began to sweat.

Suddenly, she uttered a queer little groan.

More ghastly thoughts rushed through my mind. Could she be ill? Was she having a heart attack? Ought I to get the hell out quick?

She groaned again, louder this time. Then all at once, she cried out, "Yes-yes-yes-yes-yes!" and like a bomb whose slow fuse has finally reached the dynamite, she exploded into life. She grabbed me in her arms and went for me with such incredible ferocity, I felt I was being set upon by a tiger.

Or should I say a tigress?

I never dreamed a woman could do the things Samantha did to me then. She was a whirlwind, a dazzling frenzied whirlwind that tore me up by the roots and spun me around and carried me high into the heavens, to places I did not know existed.

I myself did not contribute. How could I? I was helpless. I was the palm-tree spinning in the heavens, the lamb in the claws of the tiger. It was as much as I could do to keep breathing.

Thrilling it was, all the same, to surrender to the hands

of a violent woman, and for the next ten, twenty, thirty minutes—how would I know?—the storm raged on. But I have no intention here of regaling the reader with bizarre details. I do not approve of washing juicy linen in public. I am sorry, but there it is. I only hope that my reticence will not create too strong a sense of anticlimax. Certainly, there was nothing "anti" about my own climax, and in the final searing paroxysm I gave a shout which should have awakened the entire neighbourhood. Then I collapsed. I crumpled up like a drained wineskin.

Samantha, as though she had done no more than drink a glass of water, simply turned away from me and went right back to sleep.

Phew!

I lay still, recuperating slowly.

I had been right, you see, about that little thing on her lower lip, had I not?

Come to think of it, I had been right about more or less everything that had to do with this incredible escapade. What a triumph! I felt wonderfully relaxed and well-spent.

I wondered what time it was. My watch was not a luminous one. I'd better go. I crept out of bed. I felt my way, a trifle less cautiously this time, around the bed, out of the bedroom, along the corridor, down the stairs and into the hall of the house. I found my raincoat and slippers. I put them on. I had a lighter in the pocket of my raincoat. I used it and read the time. It was eight minutes before two. Later than I thought, I opened the front door and stepped out into the black night.

My thoughts now began to concentrate upon Jerry. Was he all right? Had he gotten away with it? I moved through the darkness toward the gap in the hedge.

"Hi, sport," a voice whispered beside me.

"Jerry!"

"Everything okay?" Jerry asked.

"Fantastic," I said. "Amazing. What about you?"

"Same with me," he said. I caught the flash of his white teeth grinning at me in the dark. "We made it, Vic!" he whispered, touching my arm. "You were right! It worked! It was sensational!"

"See you tomorrow," I whispered. "Go home."

We moved apart. I went through the hedge and entered my house. Three minutes later, I was safely back in my own bed, and my own wife was sleeping soundly alongside me.

The next morning was Sunday. I was up at eight thirty and went downstairs in pyjamas and dressing-gown, as I always do on a Sunday, to make breakfast for the family. I had left Mary sleeping. The two boys, Victor, aged nine, and Wally, seven, were already down.

"Hi, Daddy," Wally said.

"I've got a great new breakfast," I announced.

"What?" both boys said together. They had been into town and fetched the Sunday paper and were now reading the comics.

"We make some buttered toast and we spread orange marmalade on it," I said. "Then we put strips of crisp bacon on top of the marmalade."

"Bacon!" Victor said. "With *orange marmalade?*"

"I know. But you wait till you try it. It's wonderful."

I poured out the grapefruit juice and drank two glasses of it myself. I set another on the table for Mary when she came down. I switched on the electric kettle, put bread in the toaster, and started to fry the bacon. At this point, Mary came into the kitchen. She had a flimsy peach-coloured chiffon thing over her nightdress.

"Good morning," I said, watching her over my shoulder as I manipulated the frying-pan.

She did not answer. She went to her chair at the kitchen table and sat down. She started to sip her juice. She looked neither at me nor at the boys. I went on frying the bacon.

"Hi, Mummy," Wally said.

She didn't answer this either.

The smell of the bacon fat was beginning to turn my stomach.

"I'd like some coffee," Mary said, not looking around. Her voice was very odd.

"Coming right up," I said. I pushed the frying-pan away from the heat and quickly made a cup of black instant coffee. I placed it before her.

"Boys," she said, addressing the children, "would you please do your reading in the other room till breakfast is ready."

"Us?" Victor said. "Why?"

"Because I say so."

"Are we going something wrong?" Wally asked.

"No, honey, you're not. I just want to be left alone for a moment with Daddy."

I felt myself shrink inside my skin. I wanted to run. I wanted to rush out the front door and go running down the street and hide.

"Get yourself a coffee, Vic," she said, "and sit down." Her voice was quite flat. There was no anger in it. There was just nothing. And she still wouldn't look at me. The boys went out, taking the comics section with them.

"Shut the door," Mary said to them.

I put a spoonful of powdered coffee into my cup and poured boiling water over it. I added milk and sugar. The silence was shattering. I crossed over and sat down in my chair opposite her. It might just as well have been an electric chair, the way I was feeling.

"Listen, Vic," she said, looking into her coffee cup. "I want to get this said before I lose my nerve and then I won't be able to say it."

"For heaven's sake, what's all the drama about?" I asked. "Has something happened?"

"Yes, Vic, it has."

"What?"

Her face was pale and still and distant, unconscious of the kitchen around her.

"Come on, then, out with it," I said bravely.

"You're not going to like this very much," she said, and her big blue haunted-looking eyes rested a moment on my face, then travelled away.

"What am I not going to like very much?" I said. The sheer terror of it all was beginning to stir my bowels. I felt the same way as those burglars the cops had told me about.

"You know I hate talking about love-making and all that sort of thing," she said. "I've never once talked to you about it all the time we've been married."

"That's true," I said.

She took a sip of her coffee, but she wasn't tasting it. "The point is this," she said. "I've never liked it. If you really want to know, I've hated it."

"Hated what?" I asked.

"Sex," she said. "Doing it."

"Good Lord!" I said.

"It's never given me even the slightest little bit of pleasure."

This was shattering enough in itself, but the real cruncher was still to come, I felt sure of that.

"I'm sorry if that surprises you," she added.

I couldn't think of anything to say, so I kept quiet.

Her eyes rose again from the coffee cup and looked into mine, watchful, as if calculating something, then fell again. "I wasn't ever going to tell you," she said. "And I never would have if it hadn't been for last night."

I said very slowly, "What about last night?"

"Last night," she said, "I suddenly found out what the whole crazy thing is all about."

"You did?"

She looked full at me now, and her face was as open as a flower. "Yes," she said. "I surely did."

I didn't move.

"Oh, darling!" she cried, jumping up and rushing over and giving me an enormous kiss. "Thank you so much for last night! You were marvellous! And I was marvellous! We were both marvellous! Don't look so embarrassed, my darling! You ought to be proud of yourself! You were fantastic! I love you! I do! I do!"

I just sat there.

She leaned close to me and put an arm around my shoulders. "And now," she said softly, "now that you have . . . I don't quite know how to say this . . . now that you have sort of discovered what it is I *need*, everything is going to be so marvellous from now on!"

I still sat there. She went slowly back to her chair. A big tear was running down one of her cheeks. I couldn't think why.

"I was right to tell you, wasn't I?" she said, smiling through her tears.

"Yes," I said. "Oh, yes." I stood up and went over to the cooker so that I wouldn't be facing her. Through the kitchen window, I caught sight of Jerry crossing his garden with the Sunday paper under his arm. There was a lilt in his walk, a little prance of triumph in each pace he took, and when he reached the steps of his front porch, he ran up them two at a time.

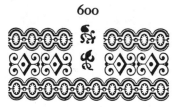

THE LAST ACT

ANNA was in the kitchen washing a head of Boston lettuce for the family supper when the doorbell rang. The bell itself was on the wall directly above the sink, and it never failed to make her jump if it rang when she happened to be near. For this reason, neither her husband nor any of the children ever used it. It seemed to ring extra loud this time, and Anna jumped extra high.

When she opened the door, two policemen were standing outside. They looked at her out of pale waxen faces, and she looked back at them, waiting for them to say something.

She kept looking at them, but they didn't speak or move. They stood so still and so rigid that they were like two wax figures somebody had put on her doorstep as a joke. Each of them was holding his helmet in front of him in his two hands.

"What is it?" Anna asked.

They were both young, and they were wearing leather

gauntlets up to their elbows. She could see their enormous motorcycles propped up along the edge of the sidewalk behind them, and dead leaves were falling around the motorcycles and blowing along the sidewalk and the whole of the street was brilliant in the yellow light of a clear, gusty September evening. The taller of the two policemen shifted uneasily on his feet. Then he said quietly, "Are you Mrs. Cooper, ma'am?"

"Yes, I am."

The other said, "Mrs. Edmund J. Cooper?"

"Yes." And then slowly it began to dawn upon her that these men, neither of whom seemed anxious to explain his presence, would not be behaving as they were unless they had some distasteful duty to perform.

"Mrs. Cooper," she heard one of them saying, and from the way he said it, as gently and softly as if he were comforting a sick child, she knew at once that he was going to tell her something terrible. A great wave of panic came over her, and she said, "What's happened?"

"We have to inform you, Mrs. Cooper . . ."

The policeman paused, and the woman, watching him, felt as though her whole body were shrinking and shrinking and shrinking inside its skin.

". . . that your husband was involved in an accident on the Hudson River Parkway at approximately five forty-five this evening, and died in the ambulance . . ."

The policeman who was speaking produced the crocodile wallet she had given Ed on their twentieth wedding anniversary, two years back, and as she reached out to take it, she found herself wondering whether it might not still be warm from having been close to her husband's chest only a short while ago.

"If there's anything we can do," the policeman was saying, "like calling up somebody to come over . . . some friend or relative maybe . . ."

Anna heard his voice drifting away, then fading out altogether, and it must have been about then that she began to scream. Soon she became hysterical, and the two policemen had their hands full trying to control her until the doctor arrived some forty minutes later and injected something into her arm.

She was no better, though, when she woke up the following morning. Neither her doctor nor her children were able to reason with her in any way at all, and had she not been kept under almost constant sedation for the next few days, she would undoubtedly have taken her own life. In the brief lucid periods between drug-takings, she acted as though she were demented, calling out her husband's name and telling him that she was coming to join him as soon as she possibly could. It was terrible to listen to her. But in defence of her behaviour, it should be said at once that this was no ordinary husband she had lost.

Anna Greenwood had married Ed Cooper when they were both eighteen, and over the time they were together, they grew to be closer and more dependent upon each other than it is possible to describe in words. Every year that went by, their love became more intense and overwhelming, and toward the end, it had reached such a ridiculous peak that it was almost impossible for them to endure the daily separation caused by Ed's departure for the office in the mornings. When he returned at night he would rush through the house to seek her out, and she, who had heard the noise of the front door slamming, would drop everything and rush simultaneously in his direction, meeting him head on, recklessly, at full speed, perhaps halfway up the stairs, or on the landing, or between the kitchen and the hall; and as they came together, he would take her in his arms and hug her and kiss her for minutes on end as though she were yesterday's bride. It was wonderful. It was so utterly unbelievably wonderful that one is very nearly able to understand why she should have had no desire and no heart to continue living in a world where her husband did not exist anymore.

Her three children, Angela (twenty), Mary (nineteen), and Billy (seventeen and a half), stayed around her constantly right from the start of the catastrophe. They adored their mother, and they certainly had no intention of letting her commit suicide if they could help it. They worked hard and with loving desperation to convince her that life could still be worth living, and it was due entirely to them that she managed in the end to come out of the nightmare and climb back slowly into the ordinary world.

Four months after the disaster, she was pronounced "moderately safe" by the doctors, and she was able to return, albeit rather listlessly, to the old routine of running the house and doing the shopping and cooking the meals for her grown-up children.

Before the snows of that winter had melted away, Angela married a young man from Rhode Island and went off to live in the suburbs of Providence.

A few months later, Mary married a fair-haired giant from a town called Slayton, in Minnesota, and away she flew for ever and ever and ever. And although Anna's heart was now beginning to break all over again into tiny pieces, she was proud to think that neither of the two girls had the slightest inkling of what was happeningg to her. ("Oh, Mummy, isn't it wonderful!" "Yes, my darling, I think it's the most beautiful wedding there's ever been! I'm even more excited than you are!" etc., etc.)

And then, to put the lid on everything, her beloved Billy, who had just turned eighteen, went off to begin his first year at Yale.

So all at once, Anna found herself living in a completely empty house.

It is an awful feeling, after twenty-three years of boisterous, busy, magical family life, to come down alone to breakfast in the mornings, to sit there in silence with a cup of coffee and a piece of toast, and to wonder what you are going to do with the day that lies ahead. The room you are sitting in, which has heard so much laughter, and seen so many birthdays, so many Christmas trees, so many presents being opened, is quiet now and feels curiously cold. The air is heated and the temperature itself is normal, but the place still makes you shiver. The clock has stopped because you were never the one who wound it in the first place. A chair stands crooked on its legs, and you sit staring at it, wondering why you hadn't noticed it before. And when you glance up again, you have a sudden panicky feeling that all the four walls of the room have begun creeping in upon you very very slowly when you weren't looking.

In the beginning, she would carry her coffee cup over to the telephone and start calling up friends. But all her friends had husbands and children, and although they were always as nice and warm and cheerful as they could possibly be, they simply could not spare the time to sit and chat with a desolate lady from across the way first thing in the morning. So then she started calling up her married daughters instead.

They, also, were sweet and kind to her at all times, but Anna detected, very soon, a subtle change in their attitudes toward her. She was no longer number one in their lives. They had husbands now, and were concentrating everything upon them. Gently but firmly, they were moving their mother into the background. It was quite a shock. But she knew they were right. They were absolutely right. She was no longer entitled to impinge upon their lives or to make them feel guilty for neglecting her.

She saw Dr. Jacobs regularly, but he wasn't really any help. He tried to get her to talk and she did her best, and sometimes he made little speeches to her full of oblique remarks about sex and sublimation. Anna never properly understood what he was driving at, but the burden of his song appeared to be that she should get herself another man.

She took to wandering around the house and fingering things that used to belong to Ed. She would pick up one of his shoes and put her hand into it and feel the little dents that the ball of his foot and his toes had made upon the sole. She found a sock with a hole in it, and the pleasure it gave her to darn that sock was indescribable. Occasionally, she took out a shirt, a tie, and a suit, and laid them on the bed, all ready for him to wear, and once, one rainy Sunday morning, she made an Irish stew . . .

It was hopeless to go on.

So how many pills would she need to make absolutely sure of it this time? She went upstairs to her secret store and counted them. There were only nine. Was that enough? She doubted that it was. Oh, hell. The one thing she was not prepared to face all over again was failure—the rush to the hospital, the stomach-pump, the seventh floor of the Payne Whitney Pavilion, the psychiatrists, the humiliation, the misery of it all . . .

In that case, it would have to be a razor-blade. But the trouble with the razor-blade was that it had to be done properly. Many people failed miserably when they tried to use the razor-blade on the wrist. In fact, nearly all of them failed. They didn't cut deep enough. There was a big artery down there somewhere that simply had to be reached. Veins were no good. Veins made plenty of mess, but they never quite managed to do the trick. Then again, the razor-blade was not an easy thing to hold, not if one had to make a firm incision, pressing it right home all the way, deep deep down. But *she* wouldn't fail. The ones who failed were the ones who actually *wanted* to fail. She wanted to succeed.

She went to the cupboard in the bathroom, searching for blades. There weren't any. Ed's razor was still there, and so was hers. But there was no blade in either of them, and no little packet lying alongside. That was understandable. Such things had been removed from the house on an earlier occasion. But there was no problem. Anyone could buy a packet of razor-blades.

She returned to the kitchen and took the calender down from the wall. She chose September 23rd, which was Ed's birthday, and wrote "r-b" (for razor-blades) against the date. She did this on September 9th, which gave her exactly two weeks' grace to put her affairs in order. There was much to be done—old bills to be paid, a new will to be written, the house to be tidied up, Billy's college fees to be taken care of for the next four years, letters to the children, to her own parents, to Ed's mother, and so on and so forth.

Yet, busy as she was, she found that those two weeks, those fourteen long days, were going far too slowly for her liking. She wanted to use the blade, and eagerly every morning she counted the days that were left. She was like a child counting the days before Christmas. For wherever it was that Ed Cooper had gone when he died, even if it were only to the grave, she was impatient to join him.

It was in the middle of this two-week period that her friend Elizabeth Paoletti came calling on her at eight thirty one morning. Anna was making coffee in the kitchen at the time, and she jumped when the bell rang and jumped again when it gave a second long blast.

Liz came sweeping in through the front door, talking nonstop as usual. "Anna, my darling woman, I need your help! Everyone's down with the flu at the office. You've *got* to come! Don't argue with me! I know you can type and I know you haven't got a damn thing in the world to do all day except mope. Just grab your hat and purse and let's get going. Hurry up, girl, hurry up! I'm late as it is!"

Anna said, "Go away, Liz. Leave me alone."

"The cab is waiting," Liz said.

"Please," Anna said, "don't try to bully me now. I'm not coming."

"You are coming," Liz said. "Pull yourself together. Your days of glorious martyrdom are over."

Anna continued to resist, but Liz wore her down, and in the end she agreed to go along just for a few hours.

Elizabeth Paoletti was in charge of an adoption society, one of the best in the city. Nine of the staff were down with the flu. Only two were left, excluding herself. "You don't know a thing about the work," she said in the cab, "but you're just going to have to help us all you can . . ."

The office was bedlam. The telephones alone nearly drove Anna mad. She kept running from one cubicle to the next, taking messages that she did not understand. And there were girls in the waiting room, young girls with ashen stony faces, and it became part of her duty to type their answers on an official form.

"The father's name?"

"Don't know."

"You've no idea?"

"What's the father's name got to do with it?"

"My dear, if the father is known, then his consent has to be obtained as well as yours before the child can be offered for adoption."

"The father isn't known, don't worry."

"You're quite sure about that?"

"Jesus, I told you, didn't I?"

At lunchtime, somebody brought her a sandwich, but there was no time to eat it. At nine o'clock that night, exhausted and famished and considerably shaken by some of the knowledge she had acquired, Anna staggered home, took a stiff drink, fried up some eggs and bacon, and went to bed.

"I'll call for you at eight o'clock tomorrow morning," Liz had said. "And for God's sake be ready." Anna was ready. And from then on she was hooked.

It was as simple as that.

All she'd needed right from the beginning was a good hard job of work to do, and plenty of problems to solve —other people's problems instead of her own.

The work was arduous and often quite shattering emotionally, but Anna was absorbed by every moment of it, and within about—we are skipping right forward now— within about a year and a half, she began to feel moderately happy once again. She was finding it more and more difficult to picture her husband vividly, to see him precisely as he was when he ran up the stairs to meet her, or when he sat across from her at supper in the evenings. The exact sound of his voice was becoming less easy to recall, and even the face itself, unless she glanced at a photograph, was no longer sharply etched in the memory. She still thought about him constantly, but she discovered that she could do so now without bursting into tears, and when she looked back on the way she had behaved a while ago, she felt slightly embarrassed. She started taking a mild interest in her clothes and in her hair, she returned to using lipstick and to shaving the hair from her legs. She enjoyed her food, and when people smiled at her, she smiled right back at them and meant it. In other words, she was back in the swim once again. She was pleased to be alive.

It was at this point that Anna had to go down to Dallas on office business.

Liz's office did not normally operate beyond state lines, but in this instance, a couple who had adopted a baby through the agency had subsequently moved away from New York and gone to live in Texas. Now, five months after the move, the wife had written to say that she no longer wanted to keep the child. Her husband, she announced, had died of a heart attack soon after they'd arrived in Texas. She herself had remarried almost at once, and her new husband "found it impossible to adjust to an adopted baby . . ."

Now this was a serious situation, and quite apart from the welfare of the child itself, there were all manner of legal obligations involved.

Anna flew down to Dallas in a plane that left New York very early, and she arrived before breakfast. After checking in at her hotel, she spent the next eight hours with the persons concerned in the affair, and by the time she had done all that could be done that day, it was around four thirty in the afternoon and she was utterly exhausted. She took a cab back to the hotel, and went up to her room. She called Liz on the phone to report the situation, then she undressed and soaked herself for a long time in a warm bath. Afterward, she wrapped up in a towel and lay on the bed, smoking a cigarette.

Her efforts on behalf of the child had so far come to nothing. There had been two lawyers there who had treated her with absolute contempt. How she hated them. She detested their arrogance and their softly spoken hints that nothing she might do would make the slightest difference to their client. One of them kept his feet up on the table all the way through the discussion, and both of them had rolls of fat on their bellies, and the fat spilled out into their shirts like liquid and hung in huge folds over their belted trouser-tops.

Anna had visited Texas many times before in her life, but until now she had never gone there alone. Her visits had always been with Ed, keeping him company on business trips; and during those trips, he and she had often spoken about the Texans in general and about how difficult it was to like them. One could ignore their coarseness and their vulgarity. It wasn't that. But there was, it seemed, a quality of ruthlessness still surviving among these people, something quite brutal, harsh, inexorable, that it was impossible to forgive. They had no bowels of compassion, no pity, no tenderness. The only so-called virtue they possessed—and this they paraded ostentatiously and endlessly to strangers—was a kind of professional benevolence. It was plastered all over them. Their voices, their smiles, were rich and syrupy with it. But it left Anna cold. It left her quite, quite cold inside.

"Why do they love acting so tough?" she used to ask.

"Because they're children," Ed would answer. "They're dangerous children who go about trying to imitate their grandfathers. Their grandfathers *were* pioneers. These people aren't."

It seemed that they lived, these present-day Texans, by a sort of egotistic will, push and be pushed. Everybody was pushing. Everybody was being pushed. And it was all very fine for a stranger in their midst to step aside and announce firmly, "I will *not* push, and I will *not* be pushed." That was impossible. It was especially impossible in Dallas. Of all the cities in the state, Dallas was the one that had always disturbed Anna the most. It was such a godless city, she thought, such a rapacious, gripped, iron, godless city. It was a place that had run amok with its money, and no amount of gloss and phony culture and syrupy talk could hide the fact that the great golden fruit was rotten inside.

Anna lay on the bed with her bath towel around her. She was alone in Dallas this time. There was no Ed with her now to envelop her in his incredible strength and love; and perhaps it was because of this that she began, all of a sudden, to feel slightly uneasy. She lit a second cigarette and waited for the uneasiness to pass. It didn't pass; it got worse. A hard little knot of fear was gathering itself in the top of her stomach, and there it stayed, growing bigger every minute. It was an unpleasant feeling, the kind one might experience if one were alone in the house at night and heard, or thought one heard, a footstep in the next room.

In this place there were a million footsteps, and she could hear them all.

She got off the bed and went over to the window, still wrapped in her towel. Her room was on the twenty-second floor, and the window was open. The great city lay pale and milky-yellow in the evening sunshine. The street below was solid with automobiles. The sidewalk was filled with people. Everybody was hustling home from work, pushing and being pushed. She felt the need of a friend. She wanted very badly to have someone to talk to at this moment. She would have liked a house to go to, a house with a family—a wife and husband and children and rooms full of toys, and the husband and wife would fling their arms around her at the front door and cry out, "Anna! How marvellous to see you! How long can you stay? A week, a month, a year?"

All of a sudden, as so often happens in situations like this, her memory went *click*, and she said aloud, "Conrad Kreuger! Good heavens above! *He* lives in Dallas . . . at least he used to . . ."

She hadn't seen Conrad since they were classmates in high school, in New York. They were both about seventeen then, and Conrad had been her beau, her love, her everything. For over a year they had gone around together, and each of them had sworn eternal loyalty to the other, with marriage in the near future. Then suddenly Ed Cooper had flashed into her life, and that, of course, had been the end of the romance with Conrad. But Conrad did not seem to have taken the break too badly. It cer-

tainly couldn't have *shattered* him, because not more than
a month or two later he had started going strong with
another girl in the class . . .

Now what was *her* name?

A big handsome bosomy girl she was, with flaming
red hair and a peculiar name, a very old-fashioned name.
What was it? Arabella? No, not Arabella. Ara-something,
though. Araminty? Yes! Araminty it was! And what is
more, within a year or so, Conrad Kreuger had married
Araminty and had carried her back with him to Dallas,
the place of his birth.

Anna went over to the bedside table and picked up the
telephone directory.

Kreuger, Conrad P., M.D.

That was Conrad all right. He had always said he was
going to be a doctor. The book gave an office number and
a residence number.

Should she phone him?

Why not?

She glanced at her watch. It was five twenty. She lifted
the receiver and gave the number of his office.

"Doctor Kreuger's surgery," a girl's voice answered.

"Hello," Anna said. "Is Doctor Kreuger there?"

"The doctor is busy right now. May I ask who's calling?"

"Will you please tell him that Anna Greenwood telephoned him."

"Who?"

"Anna Greenwood."

"Yes, Miss Greenwood. Did you wish for an appointment?"

"No, thank you."

"Is there something I can do for you?"

Anna gave the name of her hotel, and asked the girl to pass it on to Dr. Kreuger.

"I'll be very glad to," the secretary said. "Goodbye, Miss Greenwood."

"Goodbye," Anna said. She wondered whether Dr. Conrad P. Kreuger would remember her name after all these years. She believed he would. She lay back again on the bed and began trying to recall what Conrad himself used to look like. Extraordinarily handsome, that he was. Tall . . . lean . . . big-shouldered . . . with almost pure-black hair . . . and a marvellous face . . . a strong carved face like one of those Greek heroes, Perseus or Ulysses. Above all, though, he had been a very gentle boy, a serious, decent, quiet, gentle boy. He had never kissed her much—only when he said goodbye in the evenings. And he'd never gone in for necking, as all the others had. When he took her home from the movies on Saturday nights, he used to park his old Buick outside her house and sit there in the car beside her, just talking and talking about the future, his future and hers, and how he was going to go back to Dallas to become a famous doctor. His refusal to indulge in necking and all the nonsense that went with it had impressed her no end. He respects me, she used to say. He loves me. And she was probably right. In any event, he had been a nice man, a nice good man.

And had it not been for the fact that Ed Cooper was a super-nice, super-good man, she was sure she would have married Conrad Kreuger.

The telephone rang. Anna lifted the receiver. "Yes," she said. "Hello."

"Anna Greenwood?"

"Conrad Kreuger!"

"My dear Anna! What a fantastic surprise. Good gracious me. After all these years."

"It's a long time, isn't it?"

"It's a lifetime. Your voice sounds just the same."

"So does yours."

"What brings you to our fair city? Are you staying long?"

"No, I have to go back tomorrow. I hope you didn't mind my calling you."

"Hell no, Anna. I'm delighed. Are you all right?"

"Yes, I'm fine. I'm fine now. I had a bad time of it for a bit after Ed died . . ."

"What!"

"He was killed in an automobile two and a half years ago."

"Oh gee, Anna, I *am* sorry. How terrible. I . . . I don't know what to say. . . ."

"Don't say anything."

"You're okay now?"

"I'm fine. Working like a slave."

"That's the girl . . ."

"How's . . . how's Araminty?"

"Oh, she's fine."

"Any children?"

"One," he said. "A boy. How about you?"

"I have three, two girls and a boy."

"Well, well, what d'you know! Now listen, Anna . . ."

"I'm listening."

"Why don't I run over to the hotel and buy you a drink? I'd like to do that. I'll bet you haven't changed one iota."

"I look old, Conrad."

"You're lying."

"I feel old, too."

"You want a good doctor?"

"Yes. I mean no. Of course I don't. I don't want any more doctors. All I need is . . . well . . ."

"Yes?"

"This place worries me, Conrad I guess I need a friend. That's all I need."

"You've got one. I have just one more patient to see, and then I'm free. I'll meet you down in the bar, the something room, I've forgotten what it's called, at six, in about half an hour. Will that suit you?"

"Yes," she said. "Of course. And . . . thank you, Conrad." She replaced the receiver, then got up from the bed, and began to dress.

She felt mildly flustered. Not since Ed's death had she been out and had a drink alone with a man. Dr. Jacobs would be pleased when she told him about it on her return. He wouldn't congratulate her madly, but he would certainly be pleased. He'd say it was a step in the right direction, a beginning. She still went to him regularly, and now that she had gotten so much better, his oblique references had become far less oblique and he had more than once told her that her depressions and suicidal tendencies would never completely disappear until she had actually and physically "replaced" Ed with another man.

"But it is impossible to replace a person one has loved to distraction," Anna had said to him the last time he had brought up the subject. "Heavens above, doctor, when Mrs. Crummlin-Brown's parakeet died last month, her *parakeet*, mind you, not her husband, she was so shook up about it, she swore she'd never have another bird again!"

"Mrs. Cooper," Dr. Jacobs had said, "one doesn't normally have sexual intercourse with a parakeet."

"Well . . . no . . ."

"That's why it doesn't have to be replaced. But when a husband dies, and the surviving wife is still an active and a healthy woman, she will invariably get a replacement within three years if she possibly can. And vice versa."

Sex. It was about the only thing that sort of doctor ever thought about. He had sex on the brain.

By the time Anna had dressed and taken the elevator downstairs, it was ten minutes after six. The moment she walked into the bar, a man stood up from one of the tables. It was Conrad. He must have been watching the door. He came across the floor to meet her. He was smiling nervously. Anna was smiling, too. One always does.

"Well, well," he said. "Well well well," and she, expecting the usual peck on the cheek, inclined her face upward toward his own, still smiling. But she had forgotten how formal Conrad was. He simply took her hand in his and shook it—once. "This *is* a surprise," he said. "Come and sit down."

The room was the same as any other hotel drinking-room. It was lit by dim lights, and filled with many small tables. There was a saucer of peanuts on each table, and there were leather bench-seats all around the walls. The waiters were rigged out in white jackets and maroon pants. Conrad led her to a corner table, and they sat down facing each other. A waiter was standing over them at once.

"What will you have?" Conrad asked.

"Could I have a martini?"

"Of course. Vodka?"

"No, gin, please."

"One gin martini," he said to the waiter. "No. Make it two. I've never been much of a drinker, Anna, as you probably remember, but I think this calls for a celebration."

The waiter went away. Conrad leaned back in his chair and studied her carefully. "You look pretty good," he said.

"You look pretty good yourself, Conrad," she told him. And so he did. It was astonishing how little he had aged in twenty-five years. He was just as lean and handsome as he'd ever been—in fact, more so. His black hair was still black, his eyes were clear, and he looked altogether like a man who was no more than thirty years old.

"You *are* older than me, aren't you?" he said.

"What sort of a question is that?" she said, laughing. "Yes Conrad, I am exactly one year older than you. I'm forty-two."

"I thought you were." He was still studying her with the utmost care, his eyes travelling all over her face and neck and shoulders. Anna felt herself blushing.

"Are you an enormously successful doctor?" she asked. "Are you the best in town?"

He cocked his head over to one side, right over, so that the ear almost touched the top of the shoulder. It was a mannerism that Anna had always liked. "Successful?" he said. "Any doctor can be successful these days in a big city—financially, I mean. But whether or not I am absolutely first rate at my job is another matter. I only hope and pray that I am."

The drinks arrived and Conrad raised his glass and said, "Welcome to Dallas, Anna. I'm so pleased you called me up. It's good to see you again."

"It's good to see you, too, Conrad," she said, speaking the truth.

He looked at her glass. She had taken a huge first gulp, and the glass was now half empty. "You prefer gin to vodka?" he asked.

"I do," she said, "yes."

"You ought to change over."

"Why?"

"Gin is not good for females."

"It's not?"

"It's very bad for them."

"I'm sure it's just as bad for males," she said.

"Actually, no. It isn't nearly so bad for males as it is for females."

"Why is it bad for females?"

"It just is," he said. "It's the way they're built. What kind of work are you engaged in, Anna? And what brought you all the way down to Dallas? Tell me about you."

"Why is gin bad for females?" she said, smiling at him. He smiled back at her and shook his head, but he didn't answer.

"Go on," she said.

"No, let's drop it."

"You can't leave me up in the air like this," she said. "It's not fair."

After a pause, he said, "Well, if you really want to know, gin contains a certain amount of the oil which is squeezed out of juniper berries. They use it for flavouring."

"What does it do?"

"Plenty."

"Yes, but what?"

"Horrible things."

"Conrad, don't be shy. I'm a big girl now."

He was still the same old Conrad, she thought, still as diffident, as scrupulous, as shy as ever. For that she liked him. "If this drink is really doing horrible things to me," she said, "then it is unkind of you not to tell me what those things are."

Gently, he pinched the lobe of his left ear with the thumb and forefinger of his right hand. Then he said,

"Well, the truth of the matter is, Anna, oil of juniper has a direct inflammatory effect upon the uterus."

"Now come on!"

"I'm not joking."

"Mother's ruin," Anna said. "It's an old wives' tale."

"I'm afraid not."

"But you're talking about women who are pregnant."

"I'm talking about all women, Anna." He had stopped smiling now, and he was speaking quite seriously. He seemed concerned about her welfare.

"What do you specialise in?" she asked him. "What kind of medicine? You haven't told me that."

"Gynecology and obstetrics."

"Ah-ha!"

"Have you been drinking gin for many years?" he asked.

"Oh, about twenty," Anna said.

"Heavily?"

"For heaven's sake, Conrad, stop worrying about my insides. I'd like another martini, please."

"Of course."

He called the waiter and said, "One vodka martini."

"No," Anna said, "gin."

He sighed and shook his head and said, "Nobody listens to her doctor these days."

"You're not my doctor."

"No," he said. "I'm your friend."

"Let's talk about your wife," Anna said. "Is she still as beautiful as ever?"

He waited a few moments, then he said, "Actually, we're divorced."

"Oh, no!"

"Our marriage lasted for the grand total of two years. It was hard work to keep it going even that long."

For some reason, Anna was profoundly shocked. "But she was such a beautiful girl," she said. "What happened?"

"Everything happened, everything you could possibly think of that was bad."

"And the child?"

"She got him. They always do." He sounded very bitter. "She took him back to New York. He comes to see me once a year, in the summer. He's twenty years old now. He's at Princeton."

"Is he a fine boy?"

"He's a wonderful boy," Conrad said. "But I hardly know him. It isn't much fun."

"And you never married again?"

"No, never. But that's enough about me. Let's talk about you."

Slowly, gently, he began to draw her out on the subject of her health and the bad times she had gone through after Ed's death. She found she didn't mind talking to him about it, and she told him more or less the whole story.

"But what makes your doctor think you're not completely cured?" he said. "You don't look very suicidal to me."

"I don't think I am. Except that sometimes, not often, mind you, but just occasionally, when I get depressed, I have the feeling that it wouldn't take such a hell of a big push to send me over the edge."

"In what way?"

"I kind of start edging toward the bathroom cupboard."

"What do you have in the bathroom cupboard?"

"Nothing very much. Just the ordinary equipment a girl has for shaving her legs."

"I see." Conrad studied her face for a few moments, then he said, "Is that how you were feeling just now when you called me?"

"Not quite. But I'd been thinking about Ed. And that's always a bit dangerous."

"I'm glad you called."

"So am I," she said.

Anna was getting to the end of her second martini. Conrad changed the subject and began talking about his practise. She was watching him rather than listening to him. He was so damned handsome it was impossible not to watch him. She put a cigarette between her lips, then offered the pack to Conrad.

"No, thanks," he said, "I don't." He picked up a book of matches from the table and gave her a light, then he blew out the match and said, "Are those cigarettes mentholated?"

"Yes, they are."

She took a deep drag, and blew the smoke slowly up into the air. "Now go ahead and tell me that they're going to shrivel up my entire reproductive system," she said.

He laughed and shook his head.

"Then why did you ask?"

"Just curious, that's all."

"You're lying. I can tell it from your face. You were about to give me the figures for the incidence of lung cancer in heavy smokers."

"Lung cancer has nothing to do with menthol, Anna," he said, and he smiled and took a tiny sip of his original martini, which he had so far hardly touched. He set the glass back carefully on the table. "You still haven't told me what work you are doing," he went on, "or why you came to Dallas."

"Tell me about menthol first. If it's even half as bad as the juice of the juniper berry, I think I ought to know about it quick."

He laughed and shook his head.

"Please!"

"No, ma'am."

"Conrad, you simply cannot start things up like this and then drop them. It's the second time in five minutes."

"I don't want to be a medical bore," he said.

"You're not being a bore. These things are fascinating. Come on! Tell! Don't be mean."

It was pleasant to be sitting there feeling moderately high on two big martinis, and making easy talk with this graceful man, this quiet, comfortable, graceful person. He was not being coy. Far from it. He was simply being his normal scrupulous self.

"Is it something shocking?" she asked.

"No. You couldn't call it that."

He picked up the packet of cigarettes still lying in front of her, and studied the label. "The point is this," he said. "If you inhale menthol, you absorb it into the blood-stream. And that isn't good, Anna. It does things to you. It has certain very definite effects upon the central nerv-ous system. Doctors still prescribe it occasionally."

"I know that," she said. "Nose-drops and inhalations."

"That's one of its minor uses. Do you know the other?"

"You rub it on the chest when you have a cold."

"You can if you like, but it wouldn't help."

"You put it in ointment and it heals cracked lips."

"That's camphor."

"So it is."

He waited for her to have another guess.

"Go ahead and tell me," she said.

"It may surprise you a bit."

"I'm ready to be surprised."

"Menthol," Conrad said, "is a well-known anti-aphrodisiac."

"A what?"

"It suppresses sexual desire."

"Conrad, you're making these things up."

"I swear to you I'm not."

"Who uses it?"

"Very few people nowadays. It has too strong a flavour. Saltpetre is much better."

"Ah yes. I know about saltpetre."

"What do you know about saltpetre?"

"They give it to prisoners," Anna said. "They sprinkle

it on their cornflakes every morning to keep them quiet."

"They also use it in cigarettes," Conrad said.

"You mean prisoners' cigarettes?"

"I mean *all* cigarettes."

"That's nonsense."

"Is it?"

"Of course it is."

"Why do you say that?"

"Nobody would stand for it," she said.

"They stand for cancer."

"That's quite different, Conrad. How do you know that they put saltpetre in cigarettes?"

"Have you never wondered," he said, "what makes a cigarette go on burning when you lay it in the ashtray? Tobacco doesn't burn of its own accord. Any pipe smoker will tell you that."

"They use special chemicals," she said.

"Exactly; they use saltpetre."

"Does saltpetre burn?"

"Sure it burns. It used to be one of the prime ingredients of old-fashioned gunpowder. Fuses, too. It makes very good fuses. That cigarette of yours is a first-rate slow-burning fuse, is it not?"

Anna looked at her cigarette. Though she hadn't drawn on it for a couple of minutes, it was still smouldering away and the smoke was curling upward from the tip in a slim blue-grey spiral.

"So this has menthol in it *and* saltpetre?" she said.

"Absolutely."

"And they're *both* anti-aphrodisiacs?"

"Yes. You're getting a double dose."

"It's ridiculous, Conrad. It's too little to make any difference."

He smiled but didn't answer this.

"There's not enough there to inhibit a cockroach," she said.

"That's what you think, Anna. How many do you smoke a day?"

"About thirty."

"Well," he said, "I guess it's none of my business." He paused, and then he added, "But you and I would be a lot better off today if it was."

"Was what?"

"My business."

"Conrad, what *do* you mean?"

"I'm simply saying that if you, once upon a time, hadn't suddenly decided to drop me, none of this misery would have happened to either of us. We'd still be happily married to each other."

His face had suddenly taken on a queer sharp look.

"Drop you?"

"It was quite a shock, Anna."

"Oh dear," she said, "but everybody drops everybody else at that age, don't they?"

"I wouldn't know," Conrad said.

"You're not cross with me still, are you, for doing that?"

"Cross!" he said. "Good God, Anna! Cross is what children get when they lose a toy! I lost a wife!"

She stared at him, speechless.

"Tell me," he went on, "didn't you have any idea how I felt at the time?"

"But Conrad, we were so *young*."

"It destroyed me, Anna. It just about destroyed me."

"But how . . ."

"How what?"

"How, if it meant so much, could you turn right around and get engaged to somebody else a few weeks later?"

"Have you never heard of the rebound?" he asked.

She nodded, gazing at him in dismay.

"I was wildly in love with you, Anna."

She didn't answer.

"I'm sorry," he said. "That was a silly outburst. Please forgive me."

There was a long silence.

Conrad was leaning back in his chair, studying her from a distance. She took another cigarette from the pack, and lit it. Then she blew out the match and placed it carefully in the ashtray. When she glanced up again, he was still watching her. There was an intent, far look in his eyes.

"What are you thinking about?" she asked.

He didn't answer.

"Conrad," she said, "do you still hate me for doing what I did?"

"Hate you?"

"Yes, hate me. I have a queer feeling that you do. I'm sure you do, even after all these years."

"Anna," he said.

"Yes, Conrad?"

He hitched his chair closer to the table, and leaned forward. "Did it ever cross your mind . . ."

He stopped.

She waited.

He was looking so intensely earnest all of a sudden that she leaned forward herself.

"Did what cross my mind?" she asked.

"The fact that you and I . . . that both of us . . . have a bit of unfinished business."

She stared at him.

He looked back at her. "Don't be shocked," he said, "please."

"Shocked?"

"You look as though I'd just asked you to jump out of the window with me."

The room was full of people now, and it was very noisy. It was like being at a cocktail-party. You had to shout to be heard.

Conrad's eyes waited on her, impatient, eager.

"I'd like another martini," she said.

"Must you?"

"Yes," she said, "I must."

In her whole life, she had been made love to by only one man—her husband, Ed.

And it had always been wonderful.

Three thousand times?

She thought more. Probably a good deal more. Who counts?

Assuming, though, for the sake of argument, that the

exact figure (for there has to be an exact figure) was three thousand, six hundred and eighty . . .

. . . and knowing that every single time it happened it was an act of pure, passionate, authentic love-making between the same man and the same woman . . .

. . . then how in heaven's name could an entirely new man, an unloved stranger, hope to come in suddenly on the three thousand, six hundred and eighty-*first* time and be even halfway acceptable?

He'd be a trespasser.

All the memories would come rushing back. She would be lying there suffocated by memories.

She had raised this very point with Dr. Jacobs during one of her sessions a few months back, and old Jacobs had said, "There will be no nonsense about memories, my dear Mrs. Cooper. I wish you would forget that. Only the present will exist."

"But how do I get there?" she had said. "How can I summon up enough nerve suddenly to go upstairs to a bedroom and take off my clothes in front of a new man, a stranger, in cold blood? . . ."

"Cold blood!" he had cried. "Good God, woman, it'll be boiling hot!" And later he had said, "Do at any rate try to believe me, Mrs. Cooper, when I tell you that any woman who has been deprived of sexual congress after more than twenty years of practise—of uncommonly frequent practise in your case, if I understand you correctly—any woman in those circumstances is going to suffer continually from severe psychological disturbances until the routine is re-established. You are feeling a lot better, I know that, but it is my duty to inform you that you are by no means back to normal . . ."

To Conrad, Anna said, "This isn't by any chance a therapeutic suggestion, is it?"

"*A what?*"

"A therapeutic suggestion."

"What in the world do you mean?"

"It sounds exactly like a plot hatched up by my Dr. Jacobs."

"Look," he said, and now he leaned right across the table and touched her left hand with the tip of one finger. "When I knew you before, I was too damn young and nervous to make that sort of a proposition, much as I wanted to. I didn't think there was any particular hurry then, anyway. I figured we had a whole lifetime before us. I wasn't to know you were going to drop me."

Her martini arrived. Anna picked it up and began to drink it fast. She knew exactly what it was going to do to her. It was going to make her float. A third martini always did that. Give her a third martini and within seconds her body would become completely weightless and she would go floating around the room like a whisp of hydrogen gas.

She sat there holding the glass with both hands as though it were a sacrament. She took another gulp. There was not much of it left now. Over the rim of her glass she could see Conrad watching her with disapproval as she drank. She smiled at him radiantly.

"You're not against the use of anaesthetics when you operate, are you?" she asked.

"Please, Anna, don't talk like that."

"I am beginning to float," she said.

"So I see," he answered. "Why don't you stop there?"

"What did you say?"

"I said, why don't you stop?"

"Do you want me to tell you why?"

"No," he said. He made a little forward movement with his hands as though he were going to take her glass away from her, so she quickly put it to her lips and tipped it high, holding it there for a few seconds to allow the last drop to run out. When she looked at Conrad again, he was placing a ten-dollar bill on the waiter's tray, and the waiter was saying, "Thank *you*, sir. Thank you indeed," and the next thing she knew she was floating out of the room and across the lobby of the hotel with Conrad's hand cupped lightly under one of her elbows, steering her toward the elevators. They floated up to the twenty-second floor, and then along the corridor to the door of her bedroom. She fished the key out of her purse and unlocked the door and floated inside. Conrad followed, closing the door behind him. Then very suddenly, he grabbed hold of her and folded her up in his enormous arms and started kissing her with great gusto.

She let him do it.

He kissed her all over her mouth and cheeks and neck, taking deep breaths in between the kisses. She kept her eyes open, watching him in a queer detached sort of way, and the view she got reminded her vaguely of the blurry close-up view of a dentist's face when he is working on an upper back tooth.

Then all of a sudden, Conrad put his tongue into one of
her ears. The effect of this upon her was electric. It was
as though a live two-hundred-volt plug had been pushed
into an empty socket, and all the lights came on and the
bones began to melt and the hot molten sap went running down into her limbs and she exploded into a frenzy.
It was the kind of marvellous, wanton, reckless, flaming
frenzy that Ed used to provoke in her so very often in
the olden days by just a touch of the hand here and
there. She flung her arms around Conrad's neck and
started kissing him back with far more gusto than he had
ever kissed her, and although he looked at first as though
he thought she were going to swallow him alive, he soon
recovered his balance.

Anna hadn't the faintest idea how long they stood
there embracing and kissing with such violence, but it
must have been for quite a while. She felt such happiness,
such . . . such *confidence* again at last, such sudden
overwhelming confidence in herself that she wanted to
tear off her clothes and do a wild dance for Conrad in
the middle of the room. But she did no such foolish thing.
Instead, she simply floated away to the edge of the bed
and sat down to catch her breath. Conrad quickly sat
down beside her. She leaned her head against his chest
and sat there glowing all over while he gently stroked her
hair. Then she undid one button of his shirt and slid her
hand inside and laid it against his chest. Through the ribs,
she could feel the beating of his heart.

"What do I see here?" Conrad said.

"What do you see where, my darling?"

"On your scalp. You want to watch this, Anna."

"You watch it for me, dearest."

"Seriously," he said, "you know what this looks like? It looks like a tiny touch of androgenic alopecia."

"Good."

"No, it is not good. It's actually an inflammation of the hair follicles, and it causes baldness. It's quite common on women in their later years."

"Oh, shut up, Conrad," she said, kissing him on the side of the neck. "I have the most gorgeous hair."

She sat up and pulled off his jacket. Then she undid his tie and threw it across the room.

"There's a little hook on the back of my dress," she said. "Undo it, please."

Conrad unhooked the hook, then unzipped the zipper and helped her to get out of the dress. She had on a rather nice pale-blue slip. Conrad was wearing an ordinary white shirt, as doctors do, but it was now open at the neck, and this suited him. His neck had a little ridge of sinewy muscle running up vertically on either side, and when he turned his head the muscle moved under the skin. It was the most beautiful neck Anna had ever seen.

"Let's do this very very slowly," she said. "Let's drive ourselves crazy with anticipation."

His eyes rested a moment on her face, then travelled away, all the way down the length of her body, and she saw him smile.

"Shall we be very stylish and dissipated, Conrad, and order a bottle of champagne? I can ask room service to bring it up, and you can hide in the bathroom when they come in."

"No," he said. "You've had enough to drink already. Stand up, please."

The tone of his voice caused her to stand up at once.

"Come here," he said.

She went close to him. He was still sitting on the bed, and now, without getting up, he reached forward and began to take off the rest of her clothes. He did this slowly and deliberately. His face had become suddenly rather pale.

"Oh, darling," she said, "how marvellous! You've got that famous thing! A real thick clump of hair growing out of each of your ears! You know what that means, don't you? It's *the* absolutely positive sign of enormous virility!" She bent down and kissed him on the ear. He went on taking off her clothes—the bra, the shoes, the girdle, the pants, and finally the stockings, all of which he dropped in a heap on the floor. The moment he had peeled off her last stocking and dropped it, he turned away. He turned right away from her as though she didn't exist, and now he began to undress himself.

It was rather odd to be standing so close to him in nothing but her own skin and him not even giving a second look. But perhaps men did these things. Ed might have been an exception. How could *she* know? Conrad took off his white shirt first, and after folding it very carefully, he stood up and carried it to a chair and laid it on one of the arms. He did the same with his undershirt.

Then he sat down again on the edge of the bed and started removing his shoes. Anna remained quite still, watching him. His sudden change of mood, his silence, his curious intensity, were making her a bit afraid. But they were also exciting her. There was a stealth, although a menace in his movements, as though he were some splendid animal treading softly toward the kill. A leopard.

She became hypnotised watching him. She was watching his fingers, the surgeon's fingers, as they untied and loosened the laces of the left shoe, easing it off the foot, and placing it neatly half under the bed. The right shoe came next. Then the left sock and the right sock, both of them being folded together and laid with the utmost precision across the toes of the shoes. Finally the fingers moved up to the top of the trousers, where they undid one button and then began to manipulate the zipper. The trousers, when taken off, were folded along the creases, then carried over to the chair. The underpants followed.

Conrad, now naked, walked slowly back to the edge of the bed, and sat. Then at last, he turned his head and noticed her. She stood waiting . . . and trembling. He looked her slowly up and down. Then abruptly, he shot out a hand and took her by the wrist, and with a sharp pull he had her sprawled across the bed.

The relief was enormous. Anna flung her arms around him and held onto him tightly, oh so tightly, for fear that he might go away. She was in mortal fear that he might go away and not come back. And there they lay, she holding onto him as though he were the only thing left in the world to hold onto, and he, strangely quiet, watchful, intent, slowly disentangling himself and beginning to touch her now in a number of different places with those fingers of his, those expert surgeon's fingers. And once again she flew into a frenzy.

The things he did to her during the next few moments were terrible and exquisite. He was, she knew, merely getting her ready, preparing her, or as they say in the hospital, prepping her for the operation itself, but oh God, she had never known or experienced anything even remotely like this. And it was all exceedingly quick, for in what seemed to her no more than a few seconds, she had reached that excruciating point of no return where the whole room becomes compressed into a single tiny blinding speck of light that is going to explode and tear one to pieces at the slightest extra touch. At this stage, in a swift rapacious parabola, Conrad swung his body on top of hers for the final act.

And now Anna felt her passion being drawn out of her as if a long live nerve were being drawn slowly out of her body, a long live thread of electric fire, and she cried out to Conrad to go on and on and on, and as she did so, in the middle of it all, somewhere above her, she heard another voice, and this other voice grew louder and louder, more and more insistent, demanding to be heard:

"I said are you *wearing* something?" the voice wanted to know.

"Oh darling, what is it?"

"I keep asking you, are you *wearing* something?"

"Who, me?"

"There's an obstruction here. You must be wearing a sheath or some other appliance."

"Of course not, darling. Everything's wonderful. Oh, do be quiet."

"Everything is *not* wonderful, Anna."

Like a picture on a screen, the room swam back into focus. In the foreground was Conrad's face. It was suspended above her, on naked shoulders. The eyes were looking directly into hers. The mouth was still talking.

"If you're going to use a device, then for heaven's sake learn to introduce it in the proper manner. There is nothing so aggravating as careless positioning. The sheath has to be placed right back against the cervix."

"But I'm not using anything!"

"You're not? Well, there's still an obstruction."

Not only the room but the whole world as well seemed slowly to be sliding away from under her now.

"I feel sick," she said.

"You what?"

"I feel sick."

"Don't be childish, Anna."

"Conrad, I'd like you to go, please. Go now."

"What on earth are you talking about?"

"Go away from me, Conrad!"

"That's ridiculous, Anna. Okay, I'm sorry I spoke. Forget it."

"*Go away!*" she cried. "*Go away! Go away! Go away!*"

She tried to push him away from her, but he was huge and strong and he had her pinned.

"Calm yourself," he said. "Relax. You can't suddenly change your mind like this, in the middle of everything. And for heaven's sake, don't start weeping."

"Leave me alone, Conrad, I beg you."

He seemed to be gripping her with everything he had, arms and elbows, hands and fingers, thighs and knees, ankles and feet. He was like a toad the way he gripped her. He was exactly like an enormous clinging toad, gripping and grasping and refusing to let go. She had seen a toad once doing precisely this. It was copulating with a frog on a stone beside a stream, and there it sat, motionless, repulsive, with an evil yellow gleam in its eye, gripping the frog with its two powerful front paws and refusing to let go . . .

"Now stop struggling, Anna. You're acting like a hysterical child. For God's sake, woman, what's eating you?"

"You're hurting me!" she cried.

"*Hurting* you?"

"It's hurting me terribly!"

She told him this only to get him away.

"You know why it's hurting?" he said.

"Conrad! Please!"

"Now wait a minute, Anna. Allow me to explain . . ."

"No!" she cried. "I've had enough explaining!"

"My dear woman . . ."

"No!" She was struggling desperately to free herself, but he still had her pinned.

"The reason it hurts," he went on, "is that you are not manufacturing any fluid. The mucosa is virtually dry . . ."

"Stop!"

"The actual name is senile atrophic vaginitis. It comes with age, Anna. That's why it's called *senile* vaginitis. There's not much one can do . . ."

At that point, she started to scream. The screams were not very loud, but they were screams nevertheless, terrible, agonised, stricken screams, and after listening to them for a few seconds, Conrad, in a single graceful movement, suddenly rolled away from her and pushed her to one side with both hands. He pushed her with such force that she fell onto the floor.

She climbed slowly to her feet, and as she staggered into the bathroom, she was crying "Ed! . . . Ed! . . . Ed! . . ." in a queer supplicating voice. The door shut.

Conrad lay very still listening to the sounds that came from behind the door. As first, he heard only the sobbing of the woman, but a few seconds later, above the sobbing, he heard the sharp metallic click of a cupboard being opened. Instantly, he sat up and vaulted off the bed and began to dress himself with great speed. His clothes so neatly folded, lay ready at hand, and it took him no more than a couple of minutes to put them on. When that was done, he crossed to the mirror and wiped the lipstick off his face with a handkerchief. He took a comb from his

pocket and ran it through his fine black hair. He walked
once around the bed to see if he had forgotten anything,
and then, carefully, like a man who is tiptoeing from a
room where a child is sleeping, he moved out into the
corridor, closing the door softly behind him.

BITCH

I HAVE so far released for publication only one episode from Uncle Oswald's diaries. It concerned, as some of you may remember, a carnal encounter between my uncle and a Syrian female leper in the Sinai Desert. Six years have gone by since its publication and nobody has yet come forward to make trouble. I am therefore encouraged to release a second episode from these curious pages. My lawyer has advised against it. He points out that some of the people concerned are still living and are easily recognisable. He says I will be sued mercilessly. Well, let them sue. I am proud of my uncle. He knew how life should be lived. In a preface to the first episode I said that Casanova's *Memoirs* read like a parish magazine beside Uncle Oswald's diaries, and that the great lover himself, when compared with my uncle, appears positively undersexed. I stand by that, and given time I shall prove it to the world. Here then is a little episode from Vol. XXIII, precisely as Uncle Oswald wrote it:

Paris
Wednesday.

Breakfast at ten. I tried the new honey. It was delivered yesterday in an early Sèvres *sucrier* which had that lovely canary-coloured ground known as *jonquille*. "From Suzie," the note said, "and thank you." It is nice to be appreciated. And the honey was interesting. Suzie Jolibois had, among other things, a small farm south of Casablanca, and was fond of bees. Her hives were set in the midst of a plantation of *cannabis indica*, and the bees drew their nectar exclusively from this source. They lived, those bees, in a state of perpetual euphoria and were disinclined to work. The honey was therefore very scarce. I spread a third piece of toast. The stuff was almost black. It had a pungent aroma. The telephone rang. I put the receiver to my ear and waited. I never speak first when called. After all, I'm not phoning them. They're phoning me.

"Oswald! Are you there?"

I knew the voice. "Yes, Henri," I said. "Good morning."

"Listen!" he said, speaking fast and sounding excited. "I think I've got it! I'm almost certain I've got it! Forgive me if I'm out of breath, but I've just had a rather fantastic experience. It's all right now. Everything's fine. Will you come over?"

"Yes," I said. "I'll come over." I replaced the receiver and poured myself another cup of coffee. Had Henri really done it at last? If he had, then I wanted to be around to share the fun.

I must pause here to tell you how I met Henri Biotte.

Some three years ago I drove down to Provence to spend a summer weekend with a lady who was interesting to me simply because she possessed an extraordinarily powerful muscle in a region where other women have no muscles at all. An hour after my arrival, I was strolling alone on the lawn beside the river when a small dark man approached me. He had black hairs on the backs of his hands and he made me a little bow and said, "Henri Biotte, a fellow guest."

"Oswald Cornelius," I said.

Henri Biotte was as hairy as a goat. His chin and cheeks were covered with bristly black hair and thick tufts of it were sprouting from his nostrils. "May I join you?" he said, falling into step beside me and starting immediately to talk. And what a talker he was! How Gallic, how excitable. He walked with a mad little hop, and his fingers flew as if he wanted to scatter them to the four winds of heaven, and his words went off like firecrackers, with terrific speed. He was a Belgian chemist, he said, working in Paris. He was an olfactory chemist. He had devoted his life to the study of olfaction.

"You mean smell?" I said.

"Yes, yes!" he cried. "Exactly! I am an expert on smells. I know more about smells than anyone else in the world!"

"Good smells or bad?" I asked, trying to slow him down.

"Good smells, lovely smells, glorious smells!" he said. "I make them! I can make any smell you want!"

He went on to tell me he was the chief perfume blender to one of the great couturiers in the city. And his

nose, he said, placing a hairy finger on the tip of his hairy
proboscis, probably looked just like any other nose, did
it not? I wanted to tell him it had more hairs sprouting
from the noseholes than wheat from the prairies and why
didn't he get his barber to snip them out, but instead I
confessed politely that I could see nothing unusual about
it.

"Quite so," he said. "But in actual fact it is a smelling
organ of phenomenal sensitivity. With two sniffs it can
detect the presence of a single drop of macrocyclic musk
in a gallon of geranium oil."

"Extraordinary," I said.

"On the Champs-Elysées," he went on, "which is a
wide thoroughfare, my nose can identify the precise perfume being used by a woman walking on the other side
of the street."

"With the traffic in between?"

"With heavy traffic in between," he said.

He went on to name two of the most famous perfumes
in the world, both of them made by the fashion house he
worked for. "Those are my personal creations," he said
modestly. "I blended them myself. They have made a
fortune for the celebrated old bitch who runs the business."

"But not for you?"

"Me! I am but a poor miserable employee on a salary,"
he said, spreading his palms and hunching his shoulders
so high they touched his earlobes. "One day, though, I
shall break away and pursue my dream."

"You have a dream?"

"I have a glorious, tremendous, exciting dream, my dear sir!"

"Then why don't you pursue it?"

"Because first I must find a man farsighted enough and wealthy enough to back me."

Ah-ha, I thought, so that's what it's all about. "With a reputation like yours, that shouldn't be too difficult," I said.

"The sort of rich man I seek is hard to find," he said. "He must be a sporty gambler with a very keen appetite for the bizarre."

That's me, you clever little bugger, I thought. "What is this dream you wish to pursue?" I asked him. "Is it making perfumes?"

"My dear fellow!" he cried. "Anyone can make *perfumes!* I'm talking about *the* perfume! The *only* one that counts!"

"Which would that be?"

"Why, the *dangerous* one, of course! And when I have made it, I shall rule of world!"

"Good for you," I said.

"I am not joking, Monsieur Cornelius. Would you permit me to explain what I am driving at?"

"Go ahead."

"Forgive me if I sit down," he said, moving toward a bench. "I had a heart-attack last April and I have to be careful."

"I'm sorry to hear that."

"Oh, don't be sorry. All will be well so long as I don't overdo things."

It was a lovely afternoon and the bench was on the lawn near the riverbank and we sat down on it. Beside us, the river flowed slow and smooth and deep, and there were little clouds of waterflies hovering over the surface. Across the river there were willows along the bank and beyond the willows an emerald-green meadow, yellow with buttercups, and a single cow grazing. The cow was brown and white.

"I will tell you what kind of perfume I wish to make," he said. "But it is essential I explain a few other things to you on the way or you will not fully understand. So please bear with me a while." One hand lay limp upon his lap, the hairy part upward. It looked like a black rat. He was stroking it gently with the fingers of the other hand.

"Let us consider first," he said, "the phenomenon that occurs when a dog meets a bitch in heat. The dog's sexual drive is tremendous. All self-control disappears. He has only one thought in his head, which is to fornicate on the spot, and unless he is prevented by force, he will do so. But do you know what it is that causes this tremendous sex-drive in a dog?"

"Smell," I said.

"Precisely, Monsieur Cornelius. Odorous molecules of a special conformation enter the dog's nostrils and stimulate his olfactory nerve-endings. This causes urgent signals to be sent to the olfactory bulb and thence to the higher brain centres. It is *all* done by smell. If you sever a dog's olfactory nerve, he will lose interest in sex. This is also true of many other mammals, but it is not true of man. Smell has nothing to do with the sexual appetite of the human male. He is stimulated in this respect by sight, by tactility, and by his lively imagination. Never by smell."

"What about perfume?" I said.

"It's all rubbish!" he answered. "All those expensive scents in small bottles, the ones I make, they have no aphrodisiac effect at all upon a man. Perfume was never intended for that purpose. In the old days, women used it to conceal the fact that they stank. Today, when they no longer stink, they use it purely for narcissistic reasons. They enjoy putting it on and smelling their own good smells. Men hardly notice the stuff. I promise you that."

"I do," I said.

"Does it stir you physically?"

"No, not physically. Aesthetically, yes."

"You enjoy the smell. So do I. But there are plenty of other smells. I enjoy more—the bouquet of a good Lafite, the scent of a fresh Comice pear, or the smell of the air blowing in from the sea on the Brittany coast."

A trout jumped high in midstream and the sunlight flashed on its body. "You must forget," said Monsieur Biotte, "all the nonsense about musk and ambergris and the testicular secretions of the civet cat. We make our perfumes from chemicals these days. If I want a musky odour I use ethylene sebacate. Penylacetic acid will give me civet and benzaldehyde will provide the smell of almonds. No sir, I am no longer interested in mixing up chemicals to make pretty smells."

For some minutes his nose had been running slightly,

wetting the black hairs in his nostrils. He noticed it and produced a handkerchief and gave it a blow and a wipe. "What I intend to do," he said, "is to produce a perfume which will have the same electrifying effect upon a man as the scent of a bitch in heat has upon a dog! One whiff and that'll be it! The man will lose all control. He'll rip off his pants and ravish the lady on the spot!"

"We could have some fun with that," I said.

"We could rule the world!" he cried.

"Yes, but you told me just now that smell has nothing to do with the sexual appetite of the human male."

"It doesn't," he said. "But it used to. I have evidence that in the period of the post-glacial drift, when primitive man was far more closely related to the ape than he is now, he still retained the ape-like characteristic of jumping on any right-smelling female he ran across. And later, in the Palaeolithic and Neolithic periods, he continued to become sexually animated by smell, but to a lesser and lesser degree. By the time the higher civilisations had come along in Egypt and China around 2000 B.C., evolution had played its part and had completely suppressed man's ability to be stimulated sexually by smell. Am I boring you?"

"Not at all. But tell me, does that mean an actual physical change had taken place in man's smelling apparatus?"

"Absolutely not," he said. "Otherwise there'd be nothing we could do about it. The little mechanism that enabled our ancestors to smell these subtle odours is still there. I happen to know it is. Listen, you've seen how some people can make their ears move a tiny bit?"

"I can do it myself," I said, doing it.

"You see," he said, "the ear-moving muscle is still there. It's a leftover from the time when man used to be able to cock his ears forward for better hearing, like a dog. He lost that ability over a hundred thousand years ago, but the muscle remains. And the same applies to our smelling apparatus. The mechanism for smelling those secret smells is still there, but we have lost the ability to use it."

"How can you be so certain it's still there?" I asked.

"Do you know how our smelling system works?" he said.

"Not really."

"Then I shall tell you, otherwise I cannot answer your question. Attend closely, please. Air is sucked in through the nostrils and passes the three baffle-shaped turbinate bones in the upper part of the nose. There it gets warmed and filtered. This warm air now travels up and over two clefts that contain the smelling organs. These organs are patches of yellowish tissue, each about an inch square. In this tissue are embedded the nerve-fibers and nerve-endings of the olfactory nerve. Every nerve-ending consists of an olfactory cell bearing a cluster of tiny hair-like filaments. These filaments act as receivers. 'Receptors' is a better word. And when the receptors are tickled or stimulated by odorous molecules, they send signals to the brain. If, as you come downstairs in the morning, you sniff into your nostrils the odorous molecules of frying bacon, these will stimulate your receptors, the receptors will flash a signal along the olfactory nerve to the brain, and the brain will interpret it in terms of the character and intensity of the odour. And that is when you cry out, "Ah-ha, bacon for breakfast!"

"I never eat bacon for breakfast," I said.

He ignored this.

"These receptors," he went on, "these tiny hair-like filaments are what concern us. And now you are going to ask me how on earth they can tell the difference between one odorous molecule and another, between, say, peppermint and camphor?"

"How can they?" I said. I was interested in this.

"Attend more closely than ever now, please," he said. "At the end of each receptor is an indentation, a sort of cup, except that it isn't round. This is the 'receptor site.' Imagine now thousands of these little hair-like filaments with tiny cups at their extremities, all waving about like the tendrils of sea anemones and waiting to catch in their cups any odorous molecules that pass by. That, you see, is what actually happens. When you sniff a certain smell, the odorous molecules of the substance which made that smell go rushing around inside your nostrils and get caught by the little cups, the receptor sites. Now the important thing to remember is this. Molecules come in all shapes and sizes, and the little cups or receptor sites are also differently shaped. Thus, the molecules lodge only in the receptor sites which fit them. Pepperminty molecules go only into special pepperminty receptor sites. Camphor molecules, which have a quite different shape, will fit only into the special camphor receptor sites, and so on. It's rather like those toys for small children where they have to fit variously shaped pieces into the right holes."

"Let me see if I understand you," I said. "Are you saying that my brain will know it is a pepperminty smell simply because the molecule has lodged in a pepperminty receptor site?"

"Precisely."

"But you are surely not suggesting there are differently shaped receptor sites for every smell in the world?"

"No," he said. "As a matter of fact, man has only seven differently shaped sites."

"Why only seven?"

"Because our sense of smell recognizes only seven 'pure primary odours.' All the rest are 'complex odours' made up by mixing the primaries."

"Are you sure of that?"

"Positive. Our sense of taste has even less. It recognises only four primaries—sweet, sour, salt, and bitter! All other tastes are mixtures of these."

"What are the seven pure primary odours?" I asked him.

"Their names are of no importance to us," he said. "Why confuse the issue?"

"I'd like to hear them."

"All right," he said. "They are camphoraceous, pungent, musky, ethereal, floral, pepperminty, and putrid. Don't look so sceptical, please. This isn't *my* discovery. Very learned scientists have worked on it for years. And their conclusions are quite accurate, *except in one respect.*"

"What's that?"

"*There is an eighth pure primary odour which they don't know about, and an eighth receptor site to receive the curiously shaped molecules of that odour!*"

"Ah-ha-ha!" I said. "I see what you're driving at."

"Yes," he said, "the eighth pure primary odour is the sexual stimulant that caused primitive man to behave like a dog thousands of years ago. It has a very peculiar molecular structure."

"Then you know what it is?"

"Of course I know what it is."

"And you say we still retain the receptor sites for these peculiar molecules to fit into?"

"Absolutely."

"This mysterious smell," I said, "does it ever reach our own nostrils nowadays?"

"Frequently."

"Do we smell it? I mean, are we aware of it?"

"No."

"You mean the molecules don't get caught in the receptor sites?"

"They do, my dear fellow, they do. But nothing happens. No signal is sent off to the brain. The telephone line is out of action. It's like that ear muscle. The mechanism is still there, but we've lost the ability to use it properly."

"And what do you propose to do about that?" I asked.

"I shall reactivate it," he said. "We are dealing with nerves here, not muscles. And these nerves are not dead or injured, they're merely dormant. I shall probably in-

crease the intensity of the smell a thousandfold and add
a catalyst."

"Go on," I said.

"That's enough."

"I should like to hear more," I said.

"Forgive me for saying so, Monsieur Cornelius, but I
don't think you know enough about organoleptic quality
to follow me any further. The lecture is over."

Henri Biotte sat smug and quiet on the bench beside
the river stroking the back of one hand with the fingers
of the other. The tufts of hair sprouting from his nostrils
gave him a pixie look, but that was camouflage. He struck
me rather as a dangerous and dainty little creature, someone who lurked behind stones with a sharp eye and a
sting in his tail, waiting for the lone traveller to come by.
Surreptitiously I searched his face. The mouth interested
me. The lips had a magenta tinge, possibly something to
do with his heart trouble. The lower lip was caruncular
and pendulous. It bulged out in the middle like a purse,
and could easily have served as a receptacle for small
coins. The skin of the lip seemed to be blown up very
tight, as though by air, and it was constantly wet, not
from licking but from an excess of saliva in the mouth.

And there he sat, this Monsieur Henri Biotte, smiling
a wicked little smile and waiting patiently for me to react.
He was a totally unmoral man, that much was clear, but
then so was I. He was also a wicked man, and although I
cannot in all honesty claim wickedness as one of my own
virtues, I find it irresistible in others. A wicked man has
a lustre all his own. Then again, there was something

diabolically splendid about a person who wished to set back the sex habits of civilised man half a million years.

Yes, he had me hooked. So there and then, sitting beside the river in the garden of the lady from Provence, I made an offer to Henri. I suggested he should leave his present employment forthwith and set himself up in a small laboratory. I would pay all the bills for this little venture as well as making good his salary. It would be a five-year contract, and we would go fifty-fifty on anything that came out of it.

Henri was ecstatic. "You mean it?" he cried. "You are serious?"

I held out my hand. He grasped it in both of his and shook it vigorously. It was like shaking hands with a yak. "We shall control mankind!" he said. "We'll be the gods of the earth!" He flung his arms around me and embraced me and kissed me first on one cheek, then on the other. Oh, this awful Gallic kissing. Henri's lower lip felt like the wet underbelly of a toad against my skin. "Let's keep the celebrations until later," I said, wiping myself dry with a linen handkerchief.

Henri Biotte made apologies and excuses to his hostess and rushed back to Paris that night. Within a week he had given up his old job and had rented three rooms to serve as a laboratory. These were on the third floor of a house on the Left Bank, on the Rue de Cassette, just off the Boulevard Raspaille. He spent a great deal of my money equipping the place with complicated apparatus, and he even installed a large cage into which he put two apes, a male and a female. He also took on an assistant, a clever and moderately presentable young lady called Jeanette. And with all that, he set to work.

You should understand that for me this little venture was of no great importance. I had plenty of other things to amuse me. I used to drop in on Henri maybe a couple of times a month to see how things were going, but otherwise I left him entirely to himself. My mind wasn't on his job. I hadn't the patience for that kind of research. And when results failed to come quickly, I began to lose all interest. Even the pair of oversexed apes ceased to amuse me after a while.

Only once did I derive any pleasure from my visits to his laboratory. As you must know by now, I can seldom resist even a moderately presentable woman. And so, on a certain rainy Thursday afternoon, while Henri was busy applying electrodes to the olfactory organs of a frog in one room, I found myself applying something infinitely more agreeable to Jeanette in the other room. I had not, of course, expected anything out of the ordinary from this little frolic. I was acting more out of habit than anything else. But my goodness, what a surprise I got! Beneath her white overall, this rather austere research chemist turned out to be a sinewy and flexible female of immense dexterity. The experiments she performed, first with the oscillator, then with the high-speed centrifuge, were absolutely breathtaking. In fact, not since that Turkish tightrope walker in Ankara (see Vol. XXI) had I experienced anything quite like it. Which all goes to show for the thousandth time that women are as inscrutable as the ocean. You never know what you have under your keel, deep water or shallow, until you have heaved the lead.

I did not bother to visit the laboratory again after that. You know my rule. I never return to a female a second time. With me at any rate, women invariably pull out all the stops during the first encounter, and a second meeting can therefore be nothing more than the same old tune on the same old fiddle. Who wants that? Not me. So when I suddenly heard Henri's voice calling urgently to me over the telephone that morning at breakfast, I had almost forgotten his existence.

I drove through the fiendish Paris traffic to the Rue de Cassette. I parked the car and took the tiny elevator to the third floor. Henri opened the door of the laboratory. "Don't move!" he cried. "Stay right where you are!" He scuttled away and returned in a few seconds holding a little tray upon which lay two greasy-looking red rubber objects. "Noseplugs," he said. "Put them in, please. Like me. Keep out the molecules. Go on, ram them in tight. You'll have to breathe through your mouth, but who cares?"

Each noseplug had a short length of blue string attached to its blunt lower end, presumably for pulling it back out of the nostril. I could see the two bits of blue string dangling from Henri's nostrils. I inserted my own noseplugs. Henri inspected them. He rammed them in tighter with his thumb. Then he went dancing back into the lab, waving his hairy hands and crying out, "Come in now, my dear Oswald! Come in, come in! Forgive my excitement, but this is a great day for me!" The plugs in his nose made him speak as though he had a bad cold. He hopped over to a cupboard and reached inside. He brought out one of those small square bottles made of very thick glass that hold about an ounce of perfume. He carried it over to where I stood, cupping his hands around it as though it were a tiny bird. "Look! Here it is! The most precious fluid in the entire world!"

This is the sort of rubbishy overstatement I dislike intensely. "So you think you've done it?" I said.

"I know I've done it, Oswald! I am certain I've done it!"

"Tell me what happened."

"That's not so easy," he said. "But I can try."

He placed the little bottle carefully on the bench. "I had left this particular blend, Number 1076, to distill overnight," he went on. "That was because only one drop of distillate is produced every half hour. I had it dripping into a sealed beaker to prevent evaporation. All these fluids are extremely volatile. And so, soon after I arrived at eight thirty this morning, I went over to Number 1076 and lifted the seal from the beaker. I took a tiny sniff. Just one tiny sniff. Then I replaced the seal."

"And then?"

"Oh, my God, Oswald, it was fantastic! I completely lost control of myself! I did things I would never in a million years have dreamed of doing!"

"Such as what?"

"My dear fellow, I went completely wild! I was like a wild beast, an animal! I was not human! The civilising influences of centuries simply dropped away! I was Neolithic!"

"What did you do?"

"I can't remember the next bit very clearly. It was all so quick and violent. But I became overwhelmed by the most terrifying sensation of lust it is possible to imagine. Everything else was blotted out of my mind. All I wanted was a woman. I felt that if I didn't get hold of a woman immediately, I would explode."

"Lucky Jeanette," I said, glancing toward the next room. "How is she now?"

"Jeanette left me over a year ago," he said. "I replaced her with a brilliant young chemist called Simone Gautier."

"Lucky Simone, then."

"No, no!" Henri cried. "That was the awful thing! She hadn't arrived! Today of all days, she was late for work! I began to go mad. I dashed out into the corridor and down the stairs. I was like a dangerous animal. I was hunting for a woman, any woman, and heaven help her when I found her!"

"And who did you find?"

"Nobody, thank God. Because suddenly, I regained my senses. The effect had worn off. It was very quick, and I was standing alone on the second-floor landing. I felt cold. But I knew at once exactly what had happened. I ran back upstairs and re-entered this room with my nostrils pinched tightly between finger and thumb. I went straight to the drawer where I stored the noseplugs. Ever since I started working on this project, I have kept a supply of noseplugs ready for just such an occasion. I rammed in the plugs. Now I was safe."

"Can't the molecules get up into the nose through the mouth?" I asked him.

"They can't reach the receptor sites," he said. "That's why you can't smell through your mouth. So I went over to the apparatus and switched off the heat. I then transferred the tiny quantity of precious fluid from the beaker to this very solid airtight bottle you see here. In it there are precisely eleven cubic centimetres of Number 1076."

"Then you telephoned me."

"Not immediately, no. Because at that point, Simone arrived. She took one look at me and ran into the next room, screaming."

"Why did she do that?"

"My God, Oswald, I was standing there stark naked and I hadn't realised it. I must have ripped off all my clothes!"

"Then what?"

"I got dressed again. After that, I went and told Simone exactly what had happened. When she heard the truth, she became as excited as me. Don't forget, we've been working on this together for over a year now."

"Is she still here?"

"Yes. She's next door in the other lab."

It was quite a story Henri had told me. I picked up the little square bottle and held it against the light. Through the thick glass I could see about half an inch of fluid, pale and pinkish-grey, like the juice of a ripe quince.

"Don't drop it," Henri said. "Better put it down." I put it down. "The next step," he went on, "will be to make an accurate test under scientific conditions. For that I shall have to spray a measured quantity onto a woman and then let a man approach her. It will be necessary for me to observe the operation at close range."

"You are a dirty old man," I said.

"I am an olfactory chemist," he said primly.

"Why don't I go out into the street with my noseplugs in," I said, "and spray some onto the first woman who comes along. You can watch from the window here. It ought to be fun."

"It would be fun all right," Henri said. "But not very scientific. I must make the test indoors under controlled conditions."

"And I will play the male part," I said.

"No, Oswald."

"What do you mean, no? I insist."

"Now listen to me," Henri said. "We have not yet found out what will happen when a woman is present. This stuff is very powerful, I am certain of that. And you, my dear sir, are not exactly young. It could be extremely dangerous. It could drive you beyond the limit of your endurance."

I was stung. "There are no limits to my endurance," I said.

"Rubbish," Henri said. "I refuse to take chances. That is why I have engaged the fittest and strongest young man I could find."

"You mean you've already done this?"

"Certainly I have," Henri said. "I am excited and impatient. I want to get on. The boy will be here any minute."

"Who is he?"

"A professional boxer."

"Good God."

"His name is Pierre Lacaille. I am paying him one thousand francs for the job."

"How did you find him?"

"I know a lot more people than you think, Oswald. I am not a hermit."

"Does the man know what he's in for?"

"I have told him only that he is to participate in a scientific experiment that has to do with the psychology of sex. The less he knows the better."

"And the woman? Who will you use there?"

"Simone, of course," Henri said. "She is a scientist in her own right. She will be able to observe the reactions of the male even more closely than me."

"That she will," I said. "Does she realise what might happen to her?"

"Very much so. And I had one hell of a job persuading her to do it. I had to point out that she would be participating in a demonstration that will go down in history. It will be talked about for hundreds of years."

"Nonsense," I said.

"My dear sir, through the centuries there are certain great epic moments of scientific discovery that are never forgotten. Like the time when Dr. Horace Wells of Hartford, Connecticut, had a tooth pulled out in 1844."

"What was so historic about that?"

"Dr. Wells was a dentist who had been playing about with nitrous oxide gas. One day, he got a terrible toothache. He knew the tooth would have to come out, and he called in another dentist to do the job. But first he persuaded his colleague to put a mask over his face and turn on the nitrous oxide. He became unconscious and the tooth was extracted and he woke up again as fit as a flea. Now *that*, Oswald, was the first operation ever performed in the world under general anaesthesia. It started something big. We shall do the same."

At this point, the doorbell rang. Henri grabbed a pair of noseplugs and carried them with him to the door. And there stood Pierre, the boxer. But Henri would not allow him to enter until the plugs were rammed firmly up his nostrils. I believe the fellow came thinking he was going to act in a blue film, but the business with the plugs must have quickly disillusioned him. Pierre Lacaille was a bantamweight, small, muscular, and wiry. He had a flat face and a bent nose. He was about twenty-two and not very bright.

Henri introduced me, then ushered us straight into the adjoining laboratory where Simone was working. She was standing by the lab bench in a white overall, writing something in a notebook. She looked up at us through thick glasses as we came in. The glasses had a white plastic frame.

"Simone," Henri said, "this is Pierre Lacaille." Simone looked at the boxer but said nothing. Henri didn't bother to introduce me.

Simone was a slim thirtyish woman with a pleasant scrubbed face. Her hair was brushed back and plaited into a bun. This, together with the white spectacles, the white overall, and the white skin of her face, gave her a quaint antiseptic air. She looked as though she had been sterilised for thirty minutes in an autoclave and should be handled with rubber gloves. She gazed at the boxer with large brown eyes.

"Let's get going," Henri said. "Are you ready?"

"I don't know what's going to happen," the boxer said. "But I'm ready." He did a little dance on his toes.

Henri was also ready. He had obviously worked the whole thing out before I arrived. "Simone will sit in that chair," he said, pointing to a plain wooden chair set in the middle of the laboratory. "And you, Pierre, will stand on the six-metre mark with your noseplugs still in."

There were chalk lines on the floor indicating various distances from the chair, from half a metre up to six metres.

"I shall begin by spraying a small quantity of liquid onto the lady's neck," Henri went on addressing the boxer. "You will then remove your noseplugs and start walking slowly toward her." To me he said, "I wish first of all to discover the effective range, the exact distance he is from the subject when the molecules hit."

"Does he start with his clothes on?" I asked.

"Exactly as he is now."

"And is the lady expected to cooperate or to resist?"

"Neither. She must be a purely passive instrument in his hands."

Simone was still looking at the boxer. I saw her slide the end of her tongue slowly over her lips.

"This perfume," I said to Henri, "does it have any effect upon a woman?"

"None whatsoever," he said. "That is why I am sending Simone out now to prepare the spray." The girl went into the main laboratory, closing the door behind her.

"So you spray something on the girl and I walk toward her," the boxer said. "What happens then?"

"We shall have to wait and see," Henri said. "You are not worried, are you?"

"Me, worried?" the boxer said. "About a woman?"

"Good boy," Henri said. Henri was becoming very excited. He went hopping from one end of the room to the other, checking and rechecking the position of the chair on its chalk mark and moving all breakables such as glass beakers and bottles and test-tubes off the bench onto a high shelf. "This isn't the ideal place," he said, "but we must make the best of it." He tied a surgeon's mask over the lower part of his face, then handed one to me.

"Don't you trust the noseplugs?"

"It's just an extra precaution," he said. "Put it on."

The girl returned carrying a tiny stainless-steel spray-gun. She gave the gun to Henri. Henri took a stop watch from his pocket. "Get ready, please," he said. "You, Pierre, stand over there on the six-metre mark." Pierre did so. The girl seated herself in the chair. It was a chair without arms. She sat very prim and upright in her spot-less white overall with her hands folded on her lap, her knees together. Henri stationed himself behind the girl. I stood to one side. "Are we ready?" Henri cried.

"Wait," said the girl. It was the first word she had spoken. She stood up, removed her spectacles, placed them on a high shelf, then returned to her seat. She smoothed the white overall along her thighs, then clasped her hands together and laid them again on her lap.

"Are we ready now?" Henri said.

"Let her have it," I said. "Shoot."

Henri aimed the little spray-gun at an area of bare skin just below Simone's ear. He pulled the trigger. The gun made a soft hiss and a fine misty spray came out of its nozzle.

"Pull your noseplugs out!" Henri called to the boxer as he skipped quickly away from the girl and took up a position next to me. The boxer caught hold of the strings dangling from his nostrils and pulled. The Vaselined rubber plugs slid out smoothly.

"Come on, come on!" Henri shouted. "Start moving! Drop the plugs on the floor and come forward slowly!" The boxer took a pace forward. "Not so fast!" Henri cried. "Slowly does it! That's better! Keep going! Keep going! Don't stop!" He was crazy with excitement, and I must admit I was getting a bit worked up myself. I glanced at the girl. She was crouching in the chair, just a few yards away from the boxer, tense, motionless, watching his every move, and I found myself thinking about a white female rat I had once seen in a cage with a huge python. The python was going to swallow the rat and the rat knew it, and the rat was crouching very low and still, hypnotised, transfixed, utterly fascinated by the slow advancing movements of the snake.

The boxer edged forward.

As he passed the five-metre mark, the girl unclasped her hands. She laid them palms downward on her thighs. Then she changed her mind and placed them more or less underneath her buttocks, gripping the seat of the chair on either side, bracing herself, as it were, against the coming onslaught.

The boxer had just passed the two-metre mark when the smell hit him. He stopped dead. His eyes glazed and he swayed on his legs as though he had been tapped on the head with a mallet. I thought he was going to keel over, but he didn't He stood there swaying gently from side to side like a drunk. Suddenly he started making noises through his nostrils, queer little snorts and grunts that reminded me of a pig sniffing around its trough. Then without any warning at all, he sprang at the girl. He ripped off her white overall, her dress, and her underclothes. After that, all hell broke loose.

There is little point in describing exactly what went on during the next few minutes. You can guess most of it anyway. I do have to admit, though, that Henri had probably been right in choosing an exceptionally fit and healthy young man. I hate to say it, but I doubt my middle-aged body could have stood up to the incredibly violent gymnastics the boxer seemed driven to perform. I am not a voyeur. I hate that sort of thing. But in this case, I stood there absolutely transfixed. The sheer animal ferocity of the man was frightening. He was like a wild beast. And right in the middle of it all, Henri did an interesting thing. He produced a revolver and rushed up to the boxer and shouted, "Get away from that girl! Leave her alone or I'll shoot you!" The boxer ignored him, so Henri fired a shot just over the top of his head and yelled, "I mean it, Pierre! I shall kill you if you don't stop!" The boxer didn't even look up.

Henri was hopping and dancing about the room and shouting, "It's fantastic! It's magnificent! Unbelievable! It works! It works! We've done it, my dear Oswald! We've done it!"

The action stopped as quickly as it had begun. The boxer suddenly let go of the girl, stood up, blinked a few times, and then said, "Where the hell am I? What happened?"

Simone, who seemed to have come through it all with no bones broken, jumped up, grabbed her clothes, and ran into the next room. "Thank you, mademoiselle," said Henri as she flew past him.

The interesting thing was that the bemused boxer hadn't the faintest idea what he had been doing. He stood there naked and covered with sweat, gazing around the room and trying to figure out how in the world he came to be in that condition.

"What did I do?" he asked. "Where's the girl?"

"You were terrific!" Henri shouted, throwing him a towel. "Don't worry about a thing! The thousand francs is all yours!"

Just then the door flew open and Simone, still naked,

ran back into the lab. "Spray me again!" she cried. "Oh, Monsieur Henri, spray me just one more time!" Her face was alight, her eyes shining brilliantly.

"The experiment is over," Henri said. "Go away and dress yourself." He took her firmly by the shoulders and pushed her back into the other room. Then he locked the door.

Half an hour later, Henri and I sat celebrating our success in a small café down the street. We were drinking coffee and brandy. "How long did it go on?" I asked.

Six minutes and thirty-two seconds," Henri said.

I sipped my brandy and watched the people strolling by on the sidewalk. "What's the next move?"

"First, I must write up my notes," Henri said. "Then we shall talk about the future."

"Does anyone else know the formula?"

"Nobody."

"What about Simone?"

"She doesn't know it."

"Have you written it down?"

"Not so anyone else could understand it. I shall do that tomorrow."

"Do it first thing," I said. "I'll want a copy. What shall we call the stuff? We need a name."

"What do you suggest?"

"*Bitch*," I said. "Let's call it *Bitch*." Henri smiled and nodded his head slowly. I ordered more brandy. "It would be great stuff for stopping a riot," I said. "Much better than tear-gas. Imagine the scene if you sprayed it on an angry mob."

"Nice," Henri said. "Very nice."

"Another thing we could do, we could sell it to very fat, very rich women at fantastic prices."

"We could do that," Henri answered.

"Do you think it would cure loss of virility in men?" I asked him.

"Of course," Henri said. "Impotence would go out the window."

"What about octogenarians?"

"Them, too," he said, "though it would kill them at the same time."

"And marriages on the rocks?"

"My dear fellow," Henri said. "The possibilities are legion."

At that precise moment, the seed of an idea came sneaking slowly into my mind. As you know, I have a passion for politics. And my strongest passion, although I am English, is for the politics of the United States of America. I have always thought it is over there, in that mighty and mixed-up nation, that the destinies of mankind must surely lie. And right now, there was a President in office whom I could not stand. He was an evil man who pursued evil policies. Worse than that, he was a humourless and unattractive creature. So why didn't I, Oswald Cornelius, remove him from office?

The idea appealed to me.

"How much *Bitch* have you got in the lab at the moment?" I asked.

"Exactly ten cubic centimetres," Henri said.

"And how much is one dose?"

"We used one cc for our test."

"That's all I want," I said. "One cc. I'll take it home with me today, and a set of noseplugs."

"No," Henri said. "Let's not play around with it at this stage. It's too dangerous."

"It is my property," I said. "Half of it is mine. Don't forget our agreement."

In the end, he had to give in. But he hated doing it. We went back to the lab, inserted our noseplugs, and Henri measured out precisely one cc of *Bitch* into a small scent-bottle. He sealed the stopper with wax and gave me the bottle. "I implore you to be discreet," he said. "This is probably the most important scientific discovery of the century, and it must not be treated as a joke."

From Henri's place, I drove directly to the workshop of an old friend, Marcel Brossollet. Marcel was an inventor and manufacturer of tiny precise scientific gadgets. He did a lot of work for surgeons, devising new types of heart-valves and pacemakers and those little one-way valves that reduce intracranial pressure in hydrocephalics.

"I want you to make me," I said to Marcel, "a capsule that will hold exactly one cc of liquid. To this little capsule, there must be attached a timing device that will split open the capsule and release the liquid at a predetermined moment. The entire thing must not be more than half an inch thick. The smaller the better. Can you manage that?"

"Very easily," Marcel said. "A thin plastic capsule, a tiny section of razor-blade to split the capsule, a spring to flip the razor-blade, and the usual pre-set alarm system on a very small ladies watch. Should the capsule be fillable?"

"Yes. Make it so I myself can fill it and seal it up. Can I have it in a week?"

"Why not?" Marcel said. "It is very simple."

The next morning brought dismal news. That lecherous little slut Simone had apparently sprayed herself with the entire remaining stock of *Bitch*, nine cubic centimetres of it, the moment she arrived at the lab! She had then sneaked up behind Henri, who was just settling himself at his desk to write up his notes.

I don't have to tell you what happened next. And worst of all, the silly girl had forgotten that Henri had a serious heart condition. Damn it, he wasn't even allowed to climb a flight of stairs. So when the molecules hit him the poor fellow didn't stand a chance. He was dead within a minute, killed in action as they say, and that was that.

The infernal woman might at least have waited until he had written down the formula. As it was, Henri left not a single note. I searched the lab after they had taken away his body, but I found nothing. So now more than ever, I was determined to make good use of the only remaining cubic centimetre of *Bitch* in the world.

A week later, I collected from Marcel Brossollet a beautiful little gadget. The timing device consisted of the smallest watch I had ever seen, and this, together with the capsule and all the other parts, had been secured to a tiny aluminum plate three eighths of an inch square. Marcel showed me how to fill and seal the capsule and set the timer. I thanked him and paid the bill.

As soon as possible, I travelled to New York. In Manhattan, I put up at the Plaza Hotel. I arrived there at about three in the afternoon. I took a bath, had a shave, and asked room service to send me up a bottle of Glen-livet and some ice. Feeling clean and comfortable in my dressing-gown, I poured myself a good strong drink of the delicious malt whisky, then settled down in a deep chair with the morning's *New York Times*. My suite overlooked Central Park, and through the open window I could hear the hum of traffic and the blaring of cab-drivers' horns on Central Park South. Suddenly, one of the smaller headlines on the front page of the paper caught my eye. It said, PRESIDENT ON T.V. TONIGHT. I read on. *The President is expected to make an important foreign policy statement when he speaks tonight at the dinner to be given in his honor by the Daughters of the American Revolution in the ballroom of the Waldorf Astoria . . .*

My God, what a piece of luck!

I had been prepared to wait in New York for many weeks before I got a chance like this. The President of the United States does not often appear with a bunch of women on television. And that was exactly how I had to have him. He was an extraordinarily slippery customer. He had fallen into many a sewer and had always come out smelling of shit. Yet he managed every time to convince the nation that the smell was coming from someone else, not him. So the way I figured it was this. A man who rapes a woman in full sight of twenty million viewers across the country would have a pretty hard time denying he ever did it.

I read on. *The President will speak for approximately twenty minutes, commencing at nine p.m., and all major T.V. networks will carry the speech. He will be introduced by Mrs. Elvira Ponsonby, the incumbent President of the Daughters of the American Revolution. When interviewed in her suite at the Waldorf Towers, Mrs. Ponsonby said . . .*

It was perfect! Mrs. Ponsonby would be seated on the President's right. At ten past nine precisely, with the President well into his speech and half the population of the United States watching, a little capsule nestling seretly in the region of Mrs. Ponsonby's bosom would be punctured and half a centimetre of *Bitch* would come oozing out onto her gilt lamé ball-gown. The President's head would come up, he would sniff and sniff again, his eyes would bulge, his nostrils would flare, and he would start snorting like a stallion. Then suddenly he would turn and grab hold of Mrs. Ponsonby. She would be flung across the dining-table and the President would leap on top of her, with the pie à la mode and strawberry short-cake flying in all directions.

I leaned back and closed my eyes, savouring the delicious scene. I saw the headlines in the papers the next morning:

PRESIDENT'S BEST PERFORMANCE TO DATE

PRESIDENTIAL SECRETS REVEALED TO NATION

PRESIDENT INAUGURATES BLUE T.V.

and so on.

He would be impeached the next day and I would slip quietly out of New York and head back to Paris. Come to think of it, I would be leaving tomorrow!

I checked the time. It was nearly four o'clock. I dressed myself without hurrying. I took the elevator down to the main lobby and strolled across to Madison Avenue. Somewhere around Sixty-second Street, I found a good florist's shop. There I bought a corsage of three massive orchid blooms all fastened together. The orchids were cattleyas, white with mauve splotches on them. They were particularly vulgar. So, undoubtedly, was Mrs. Elvira Ponsonby. I had the shop pack them in a handsome box tied up with gold string. Then I strolled back to the Plaza, carrying the box, and went up to my suite.

I locked all doors leading to the corridor in case the maid should come in to turn back the bed. I got out the noseplugs and Vaselined them carefully. I inserted them in my nostrils, ramming them home very hard. I tied a surgeon's mask over my lower face as an extra precaution, just as Henri had done. I was ready now for the next step.

With an ordinary nose-dropper, I transferred my precious cubic centimetre of *Bitch* from the scent-bottle to the tiny capsule. The hand holding the dropper shook a little as I did this, but all went well. I sealed the capsule. After that, I wound up the tiny watch and set it to the correct time. It was three minutes after five o'clock. Lastly, I set the timer to go off and break the capsule at ten minutes past nine.

The stems of the three huge orchid blooms had been tied together by the florist with a broad one-inch wide ribbon and it was a simple matter for me to remove the ribbon and secure my little capsule and timer to the orchid stems with cotton thread. When that was done, I wound the ribbon back around the stems and over my gadget. Then I retied the bow. It was a nice job.

Next, I telephoned the Waldorf and learned that the dinner was to begin at eight o'clock, but that the guests must be assembled in the ball-room by seven thirty, before the President arrived.

At ten minutes to seven, I paid off my cab outside the Waldorf Towers entrance and walked into the building. I crossed the small lobby and placed my orchid box on the reception desk. I leaned over the desk, getting as close as possible to the clerk. "I have to deliver this package to Mrs. Elvira Ponsonby," I whispered, using a slight American accent. "It is a gift from the President."

The clerk looked at me suspiciously.

"Mrs. Ponsonby is introducing the President before he speaks tonight in the ball-room," I added. "The President wishes her to have this corsage right away."

"Leave it here and I'll have it sent up to her suite," the clerk said.

"No, you won't," I told him. "My orders are to deliver it in person. What's the number of her suite?"

The man was impressed. "Mrs. Ponsonby is in five-o-one," he said.

I thanked him and went into the elevator. When I got out at the fifth floor and walked along the corridor, the elevator operator stayed and watched me. I rang the bell to five-o-one.

The door was opened by the most enormous female I had ever seen in my life. I have seen giant women in circuses. I have seen lady wrestlers and weight-lifters. I have seen the huge Masai women in the plains below Kilimanjaro. But never had I seen a female so tall and broad and thick as this one. Nor so thoroughly repugnant. She was groomed and dressed for the greatest occasion of her life, and in the two seconds that elapsed before either of us spoke, I was able to take most of it in—the metallic silver-blue hair with every strand glued into place, the brown pig-eyes, the long sharp nose sniffing for trouble, the curled lips, the prognathous jaw, the powder, the mascara, the scarlet lipstick and, most shattering of all, the massive shored-up bosom that projected like a balcony in front of her. It suck out so far it was a miracle she didn't topple forward with the weight of it all. And there she stood, this pneumatic giant, swathed from neck to ankles in the stars and stripes of the American flag.

"Mrs. Elvira Ponsonby?" I murmured.

"I am Mrs. Ponsonby," she boomed. "What do you want? I am extremely busy."

"Mrs. Ponsonby," I said. "The President has ordered me to deliver this to you in person."

She melted immediately. "The dear man!" she shouted. "How perfectly gorgeous of him!" Two massive hands reached out to grab the box. I let her have it.

"My instructions are to make sure you open it before you go to the banquet," I said.

"Sure I'll open it," she said. "Do I have to do it in front of you?"

"If you wouldn't mind."

"Okay, come on in. But I don't have much time."

I followed her into the living-room of the suite. "I am to tell you," I said, "that it comes with all good wishes from one President to another."

"Ha!" she roared. "I like that! What a gorgeous man he is!" She untied the gold string of the box and lifted the lid. "I guessed it!" she shouted. "Orchids! How splendid! They're far grander than this poor little thing I'm wearing!"

I had been so dazzled by the galaxy of stars across her bosom that I hadn't noticed the single orchid pinned to the lefthand side.

"I must change over at once," she said. "The President will be expecting me to wear his gift."

"He certainly will," I said.

Now to give you an idea of how far her chest stuck out in front of her, I must tell you that when she reached forward to unpin the flower, she was only just able to touch it even with her arms fully extended. She fiddled around with the pin for quite a while, but she couldn't really see what she was doing and it wouldn't come undone. "I'm terrified of tearing this gorgeous gown," she said. "Here, you do it." She swung around and thrust her mammoth bust in my face. I hesitated. "Go on!" she boomed. "I don't have all night!" I went to it, and in the end I managed to get the pin unhooked from her dress.

I put aside the single orchid and lifted my own flowers carefully from the box.

"Have they got a pin?" she asked.

"I don't believe they have," I said. That was something I'd forgotten.

"No matter," she said. "We'll use the old one." She removed the safety-pin from the first orchid, and then, before I could stop her, she seized the three orchids I was holding and jabbed the pin hard into the white ribbon around the stems. She jabbed it almost exactly into the spot where my little capsule of *Bitch* was lying hidden. The pin struck something hard and wouldn't go through. She jabbed it again. Again it struck metal. "What the hell's under here?" she snorted.

"Let me do it!" I cried, but it was too late, because the wet stain of *Bitch* from the punctured capsule was already spreading over the white ribbon and one hundredth of a second later the smell hit me. It caught me smack under the nose and it wasn't actually like a smell at all because a smell is something intangible. You cannot feel a smell. But this stuff was palpable. It was solid. It felt as though some kind of fiery liquid were being squirted up my nostrils under high pressure. It was exceedingly uncomfortable. I could feel it pushing higher and higher, penetrating far beyond the nasal passages, forcing its way up behind the forehead and reaching for the brain. Suddenly the stars and stripes on Mrs. Ponsonby's dress began to wobble and bobble about and the whole room started wobbling and I could hear my heart thumping in my head. It felt as though I were going under an anaesthetic.

At that point, I must have blacked out completely, if only for a couple of seconds.

When I came around again, I was standing naked in a rosy room and there was a funny feeling in my groin. I looked down and saw that my beloved sexual organ was three feet long and thick to match. It was still growing. It was lengthening and swelling at a tremendous rate. At the same time, my body was shrinking. Smaller and smaller shrank my body. Bigger and bigger grew my astonishing organ, and it went on growing, by God, until it had enveloped my entire body and absorbed it within itself. I was now a gigantic perpendicular penis, seven feet tall and as handsome as they come.

I did a little dance around the room to celebrate my splendid new condition. On the way I met a maiden in a star-spangled dress. She was very big as maidens go. I drew myself up to my full height and declaimed in a loud voice:

"The summer's flower is to the summer sweet,
It flourishes despite the summer's heat.
But tell me truly, did you ever see
A sexual organ quite so grand as me?"

The maiden leapt up and flung her arms as far around me as she could. Then she cried out:

"Shall I compare thee to a summer's day?
Shall I . . . Oh dear, I know not what to say.
But all my life I've had an itch to kiss
A man who could erect himself like this."

A moment later, the two of us were millions of miles up in outer space, flying through the universe in a shower of meteorites all red and gold. I was riding her bareback, crouching forward and gripping her tightly between my thighs. "Faster!" I shouted, jabbing long spurs into her flanks. "Go faster!" Faster and still faster she flew, spurting and spinning around the rim of the sky, her mane streaming with sun, and snow waving out of her tail. The sense of power I had was overwhelming. I was unassailable, supreme. I was the Lord of the Universe, scattering the planets and catching the stars in the palm of my hand and tossing them away as though they were Ping-Pong balls.

Oh, ecstasy and ravishment! Oh, Jericho and Tyre and Sidon! The walls came tumbling down and the firmament disintegrated, and out of the smoke and fire of the explosion, the sitting-room in the Waldorf Towers came swimming slowly back into my consciousness like a rainy day. The place was a shambles. A tornado would have done less damage. My clothes were on the floor. I started dressing myself very quickly. I did it in about thirty seconds flat. And as I ran toward the door, I heard a voice that seemed to be coming from somewhere behind an upturned table in the far corner of the room. "I don't know who you are, young man," it said. "But you've certainly done me a power of good."